ABOUT THE BLOOD

Also by Keith C. Blackmore

Mountain Man

Mountain Man
Safari
Hellifax
Well Fed
Make Me King
Mindless
Skull Road
Mountain Man Prequel
Mountain Man 2nd Prequel: Them Early Days
The Hospital: A Mountain Man Story
Mountain Man Omnibus: Books 1–3

131 Days

131 Days
House of Pain
Spikes and Edges
About the Blood
To Thunderous Applause
131 Days Omnibus: Books 1–3

Breeds

Breeds
Breeds 2
Breeds 3
Breeds: The Complete Trilogy

Isosceles Moon

Isosceles Moon
Isosceles Moon 2

The Bear That Fell from the Stars
Bones and Needles
Cauldron Gristle
Flight of the Cookie Dough Mansion
The Majestic 311
The Missing Boatman
Private Property
The Troll Hunter
White Sands, Red Steel

131 DAYS

BOOK 4

ABOUT THE BLOOD

KEITH C. BLACKMORE

*Thanks very much to Kelly, Kristina, and Sheri
for going over the manuscript.
If you see any mistakes, they're undoubtedly mine.*

All rights reserved. No part of this publication may be reproduced, stored in a retrieval system, or transmitted in any form or by any means electronic, mechanical, photocopying, recording, or otherwise without prior written permission from Podium Publishing.

This is a work of fiction. Names, characters, places, and incidents are either products of the author's imagination or used fictitiously. Any resemblance to actual events, locales, or persons, living, dead, or undead, is entirely coincidental.

Copyright © 2018 by Keith C. Blackmore

Cover design by Karri Klawiter

ISBN: 978-1-0394-8353-8

Published in 2024 by Podium Publishing
www.podiumaudio.com

ABOUT THE BLOOD

1

Underneath Sunja's Pit, the door to the House of Ten's private chamber opened.

The afterglow waning from his third and final victory of the day, a fragrant and sweat-shining Junger entered. He rubbed a hand over his bristly hair, wiped a palm on his leggings, and looked ahead. His dark eyes narrowed, and his smile faded.

Waiting with his back against a stone arch of brown brick was Goll, the house master. His dusky eyes were simmering slits of annoyance. The cuts he'd sustained weeks before had healed into pink lines while the bruises had faded away nearly completely. The arena sands shimmering behind him, Goll wasn't in the best of spirits despite Junger's three successive victories. Two of those had avenged the deaths of the Ten's fallen while the last had been over a house gladiator, all decisively won.

"You miserable bastard," Goll said, barely containing his anger.

Junger eased inside the chamber and glanced around. "Where are the others?"

"I've sent them away," Goll said, "so I could speak with you. In private."

Ah, Junger mouthed, noticing the short sword the house master was wearing for this conversation. Despite the weapon, he closed the door.

"Who are you?" Goll asked pointedly. "Truly. And why are you here?"

Junger smiled gently. "It's the fighting season. I'm fighting."

"You're not fighting. You're *playing*."

The Perician shrugged.

"Where exactly did you train again?" Goll demanded.

"I believe I've already had this conversation," Junger replied.

"The names, you unfit he-bitch."

"Too many to mention, Master Goll."

"Your trainers?"

"Too many to remember."

Being in a particularly venomous state, Goll's fingers curled around his short sword's hilt. "Seddon above, I'll strike you down if you don't give me an answer this instant."

Junger cocked an eyebrow. "Master Goll. My history is my own. I think I've shown I'm committed to the House of Ten. That's all that matters. I've avenged the Ten's name twice over and defeated a gladiator belonging to a rival house, one fight after the other, but you know all that. You wanted the people to remember me? As of this day, they'll remember. You wanted the other houses to fear us? From here on, they will. So, forgive me. I don't understand why you're angry. Didn't you wager upon my match?"

"The house's finances are not your concern."

"Fine," Junger allowed, holding out his hands. "Then I'd like to have my winnings for the day."

"Oh, you'll get your coin, have no worries about that."

Junger sighed. "Truth be known, I don't have any worries, Master Goll. And you're as much a mystery to me as I am to you. A mystery and . . . a marvel. You're a fine warrior. Anyone can see that. And you're the master of this house. I daresay if it wasn't for you, there wouldn't be a house."

Goll's eyes narrowed.

ABOUT THE BLOOD

"I didn't know what you were about," Junger continued, "that day when you addressed the Free Trained, looking for prospects. Didn't know what to expect. I did know I'd had enough of breathing in the foul air of the Pit's underbelly. Anything else, I could manage. I didn't expect the villa. Or the taskmaster. Or the trainers. Say what you will of me. Think what you like. But I'll tell you now, for nothing, I believe you alone are the House of Ten. No insult intended to the others, but you are its hub, its heart. And for that, I thank you. For allowing me to fight under the Ten's banner."

Goll's expression remained the same, if a touch guarded.

"So, Master Goll," Junger went on, "be satisfied that even though I didn't kill my opponents, I did defeat them. Soundly. All in the Ten's name. That should count for something, if not a little trust on your part. I trusted you, after all."

The tension slowly dissipated in the room, punctuated by a few odd yells outside the window. The voices distracted the Kree, and he peered out into the arena, seeing attendants combing the sands. Goll sighed and shook his head. Relaxing just a little, he regarded Junger once again.

He walked toward the door, passing the Perician. "You come with me," he said.

"Are we done?"

"For now," Goll replied. "Be mysterious if that suits you. I don't care. I have a house to manage."

"Master Goll."

The Kree stopped outside the door, framed in dull white.

"Why are *you* doing all this?" Junger asked.

The question stopped Goll, who didn't answer right away. He gazed off at some unknown point farther on down the tunnel. "I was trained by the Weapon Masters of Kree to fight in these games. Despite what some might think, I believe the taskmasters and trainers who prepared me for these games to be the best. I was sent here to fight. Win. And win everything. Be this year's champion. For them. And for me. Especially for me."

Junger waited. "And what happened?"

Goll huffed with contained frustration. "Baylus the Butcher happened. Returned for one final season. And I was the unlucky bastard who drew him. Facing a legend in my first match. Why he returned . . ." He shrugged. "I'm still ashamed of taking his life when he spared mine. He cut me. Enough to ruin my chances of anything. So instead of fighting in the arena itself, I adapted. Shifted my goals. I came here to win, and I still intend to win, but a different way. I'll hoist the Ten above all the rest. I'll lead these men to heights no one's ever imagined. Because if I can't become champion myself, I'll raise another to the title and slap the cheeks of those unfit maggots who seek to keep them down. There's an air of arrogance about these games, Perician, and you're hearing that from a man guilty of arrogance himself. There's a stink of pride here, of self-importance, amongst the ruling houses, especially if they discover you're from outside Sunja's borders. I don't care for it. These Sunjan overlords need to be taught a lesson, and I thought of myself as the ass slapper to do it. I still am, but sadly, not as a gladiator, but as a house master."

Goll's eyes returned to Junger. "And though I changed my goal at these games, despite my saying otherwise, it's taking me time to . . . accept the role. However, I see what you can do. I suspect you're capable of so much more. Seddon take me, you just might be the one to win these games."

Junger studied the Kree in a new and admiring light. "Well. There's nothing I can do about your condition, Master Goll, but if you're looking to . . . outshine the other houses, then perhaps I can help. While I can, anyway."

Goll scowled. "Leaving, are you?"

"At the end." Junger shrugged indifference.

"Even if you win?"

"Who would want to return to competition after winning it all?"

"Baylus did."

"Yes," Junger said. "I wonder about that. About his decision. The competition gets into the blood, I'll grant you that, but to return to this one last time?" His expression suggested he thought it unfit.

Outside, voices drifted closer to the chamber's window, socializing after the day's fights. The sound dispelled the serious atmosphere in the room. Goll frowned and stared black spite at the other man, but his annoyance was fading. Despite all that had been said, staying angry at the man was hard. The Perician was right. He'd won a great deal for both the Ten and himself that day. If he wanted to be a mystery, Goll would let him.

"Come on then, you unfit bastard," the Kree house master said. "Just as well you fight for us than against."

"It is, Master Goll. It truly is. I'm glad you see it that way."

Their confrontation over, the pair left Sunja's Pit.

Outside the arena walls constructed of red brick and massive oak timbers, spectators lingered and talked amongst themselves about the day's events. Some kept to the growing shadows, staying out of the sun. Others crowded the food and drink stalls, spending a few coins. When Goll and Junger cleared the Vathian columns of black-veined marble, heads turned in their direction. Faces lit with recognition. Conversations ceased. People pointed fingers and whispered at the departing pair.

Goll barely noticed any of that. His thoughts were elsewhere, rejoining Clavellus and the others and preparing for the days to come. He would have kept right on thinking those thoughts . . . until the voices started.

"Well fought this day, Perician!" someone yelled.

"You're a hellion, man!" cried another.

"Keep fighting!"

"Perician, when do you fight again?"

"Are you married?"

Some even waved.

Taking the attention in stride, Junger smiled and even waved back.

"Friendly lot," he said.

Goll increased his pace as his sour mood returned.

In short time, they returned to Shan's house. The healer's wife greeted Goll with an icy air, none too pleased about her husband spending his days at a faraway villa while she minded their home alone. Only two of the Ten were inside. Torello lay stretched out upon an examination table, his swollen ankle somewhere in a hornet's nest of bandages. Brozz sat upon a cot, stripped to the waist, his cheeks and jaw swollen to thrice their size. Red stitches lined a long gash in the gladiator's chest. A shorter cut had split his left cheek. Ointment glistened darkly, jammed deep into the wounds, and the air stank of sour onions. Metal gleamed and the smell rankled Goll.

Shan nodded at the pair of newcomers as he stepped in front of his patient.

Goll thought the healer appeared a little disheveled.

Shan flexed his shoulders, inhaled, and took hold of Brozz's nose. "Now," he whispered. "This might—"

Crick!

Brozz's eyes clenched shut, but he made not a sound as the healer straightened him out.

Shan released the Sarlander.

"All done," the healer announced in a tired tone. He bent at the waist and extracted a pair of dark rods from the pit fighter's face. "Just a couple of wooden strips here. One on each side of your beak. Keep everything in place, to ensure nothing happens, and then a bundling around your head."

"The cut?" Brozz whispered and pointed to his face.

"That's next. Apologies."

"None required."

Shan went for a spool of thread.

"Enjoying the grease, I see," Junger observed brightly and received a dour look from the Sarlander.

"Where are the others?" Goll asked.

Dark eyes studied the house master. "Gone," Brozz reported slowly, a nasal twang to his words. "To the alehouses. Left the coin upstairs and charged Pratos and Valka to watch it."

Goll's face slackened. "What?"

"They're gone," Torello said, one arm folded behind his head. "Wish I was with them, truth be known."

"And Muluk followed?"

Torello grunted that was so.

"Of course Muluk followed," Goll fumed, feeling stupid for even asking.

Shan returned to Brozz, who grimaced, clearly not enjoying the next bit of work. Needle and thread at the ready, the healer flexed his elbows, leaned in close, and got sewing.

"Clades, too," Torello added.

Heat rose to Goll's cheeks. "Which one?"

"Alehouse?" the Sunjan asked. "I don't know. They didn't say."

"Shan?" Goll asked.

The healer paused in his stitching and shook his head.

Goll's anger rose unchecked. *Of course they didn't say.* That would be too easy.

"Come with me," he ordered Junger and headed back outside, returning to the evening heat.

The Perician followed.

2

"Lads, *that* is a roast," Clavellus exclaimed, a fierce glow to his sun-browned cheeks. He stopped and jabbed a finger at the food one table over, drawing bothered looks from the eaters.

"We'll bring something back for the lads," the taskmaster said, his white beard flexing. "We *have* to bring something back for the lads."

"We're going back after we eat?" Clades asked.

"Saimon's bells, no, we're not going back after we eat. I intend to have a sizeable glow on by the time we finish eating. I'm talking about being pickled, good Clades. Substantially pickled. This is a celebration feast, young man." Clavellus gripped the once Sujin's shoulder. "The House of Ten *won*. Won *convincingly*. *Decisively*. Right and proper."

"I was merely thinking of Pratos and—"

"The lads will be fine." Clavellus dismissed the suggestion with a hand. "*More* than fine. They'll have the others with them."

Clades smiled weakly. Though the taskmaster had asked him to accompany them to an alehouse, the soldier wasn't entirely comfortable leaving the Ten's winnings—Four small sacks of gold—with just Pratos and Valka. He'd heard about the unknown forces attempting to rob the Ten's coin weeks earlier and thought the security a little lacking. The question wasn't one of skill, for he knew Pratos and Valka to be more than capable—the question was one of numbers.

That was only one concern, though, and not even the main worry.

The old taskmaster was enjoying himself a touch *too* much, in Clades's opinion. The man was *loud*. He had been loud all the way to that particular establishment, and he was becoming even louder with every passing moment.

"Sit, lads, sit," Clavellus commanded and did so himself, having selected a table in the very middle of a crowded floor, where smoke hung around the edges like a dream.

The sun hadn't just dropped yet, but the lamps were already lit and burning, and the smell of beer wafted across the nose. A stoic Machlann sat while Muluk appeared only too happy to plop down upon a thick bench.

Clades decided to stand, watching for threats and noting the potential for several. Men and women were observing them from darkened alcoves, their eyes glittering, wondering what to make of the new arrivals.

"Sit, lad, sit!" Clavellus insisted, his voice carrying.

Clades hesitated before lowering himself next to Muluk.

"We're the House of Ten, dammit. *Ten*," Clavellus declared and slapped the table's surface, startling the younger men. "And we've cause to celebrate, if only just this evening. So let us drink and eat and enjoy each other's company while we can, for we may never again. And by drink I mean *drink*. Until our eyes cross."

Muluk smiled, warming to the prospect. Machlann remained silent and unreadable.

Clades, however, was very much aware of a rising interest from the alehouse's patrons. A few men drinking at the bar's counter paused in their conversations and half cocked their heads, leaning in the Ten's direction.

"We'll have a pitcher," Clavellus continued. "Maybe even three. You look like you're able to take a pitcher at least, Muluk."

"I could," Muluk answered brightly. "It's thirsty work walking here. And a warm evening."

"It is thirsty work," Clavellus agreed and briefly studied the man. "I haven't talked with you much, Muluk. We'll remedy that tonight. And no titles while drinking. Just our names, understood?"

That was indeed fine with the Kree, who nodded.

"Excellent, excellent." Clavellus stood. "Four pitchers here. Bring us the Black!"

Clades attempted to rise, but the taskmaster waved him down.

Across the floor, the barkeep, a pudgy, bearded soul, lifted a finger to show he'd heard.

"Now, what will you men have?" Clavellus chuckled and dropped into his seat. "Daresay you could probably finish off those yourself, Muluk. Am I correct?"

"Daresay I could," he answered, flashing a smile.

Clades felt his unease rise another notch at the eager-looking Kree.

"Daresay you could," Clavellus repeated fondly before glancing around the interior.

Clades scanned the floor as well. Bare timbers and posts held up an impressive ceiling. Dust puffed through cracks as unseen people walked overhead. Several patrons had gone back to their food and drink while a few more thoughtful types eyed the Ten's table. Smoke rose from pipes, masking that lingering but not unpleasant whiff of beer.

Still uneasy, Clades made to rise again.

"Sit down and stay," Clavellus insisted, pulling the man back. "Seddon above, lad, is the bench that hard?"

Clades shook his head.

"Then stay right there. Appreciate the alehouse for what it is. Take it all in. The sights and smells. The sounds. Ah, I've missed it."

The craftsmanship of the premises drew the taskmaster's eye, and he studied the layout with greater interest. Then, the inspection completed, he scrutinised the people. "I don't see anyone I know, Machlann. Not a damned soul."

"Be surprised if we did," the trainer remarked.

"Suppose so." Clavellus thought for a moment. "The faces might change, but it's still Sunja. Been away too long—far too long. But this is a new beginning. Start of history. This day, with the House of Ten."

The old man slapped the table's surface once again. Muluk chuckled, basking in the taskmaster's enthusiasm. Clades became even more aware of the alehouse shadows.

"Did you already drink something before we got here?" Muluk asked the taskmaster.

"Why do you ask?" Clavellus asked in return.

"You seem . . . pickled already."

The taskmaster laughed. "Only on life. *This* life. I cannot tell you how good it is to return to Sunja. To the games. And as a *victor*. That alone is making my heart damn near burst. The lads have made me proud. You've all made me proud."

Clavellus grabbed Machlann's shoulder and shook the trainer, who glared but otherwise didn't seem to mind.

"And you seem strangely quiet," Muluk put to the trainer.

"*Pah*," Clavellus scoffed. "Don't mind him. He's all knobs and fire on the training grounds but get him in around pretty alehouse wenches? Simmers down like he's been doused with ice water. Even on a day as grand as this. Think of it. Today the Ten defeated a pair of house gladiators," the taskmaster continued. "A pair of absolute brutes, and we *defeated* them. Two of *ours* defeated two of *theirs*! You understand the significance of that?"

Muluk let it be known that he did not.

"Let me tell you, then," Clavellus explained. "To them, we're shite. Cow kisses in the road, waiting to be split by a wagon's wheel. That's us. We're unfit for these games. Unfit to grace the sands of the Pit. And for our lads to put down *house-trained* men, well, that's"—the old man's eyes lit up, and the cords in his neck protruded to the breaking point—"that's right and proper *inspiring*. It's grand to be alive, Muluk. Very grand."

Very much so, Clades had to agree, still eyeing the crowd.

"What we did today demands *this*," Clavellus declared with two sweeping hands. "A little celebration. A right and proper celebration. Not even the great dark one will stop me from enjoying the night. Seddon above. *Two* house gladiators and we're *still* in the games. We should be all dead. All dead. The houses have aligned against us, and we threw fistfuls of gurry back in their faces. *In their faces!*"

"In their faces!" an eager Muluk repeated, becoming infected with the old man's energy.

"And even better?" Clavellus asked. "That hellion Perician is a right and proper *hellpup*." He held his face to contain the laughter.

Clades thought the old taskmaster looked a touch unfit.

A serving maid arrived, carrying a platter full of pitchers and mugs. Clavellus leaned back and watched her unload the drinks upon the table. When she finished, the taskmaster paid her and kept her hand, placing an extra gold coin there.

"That's for you," he said, meaning it. "And all I ask is you keep watch over us. Keep the Black flowing when I wave. Many thanks."

The gesture warmed Clades, but the pitchers containing Sunjan Black—exceptionally strong beer—worried him. No sooner had she departed than Clavellus attacked the drinks.

"Here you are, good Clades"—the taskmaster pushed a mug over and warned him with a finger—"and don't you dare say no. Not this first one. You'll drink with us, or I'll . . . I don't know what I'll do, but you won't be happy about it."

Clavellus didn't wait for an answer. He snatched up his drink and jabbed it into the air. "For the Ten." Then with a solemnness that was striking, he said, "For our fallen. For *their* fallen. And for the future."

Mugs clacked together, and the black beer was downed.

Clavellus gasped a third of the way along before resuming. He finished and thumped his mug down.

"More," he whispered and reached for a refill.

"More!" an enthusiastic Muluk agreed, enjoying himself far too much for Clades's liking.

Machlann nursed his own beer, and the once Sujin wondered if the man had drunk anything at all.

"Tip that thing back, good Clades," Clavellus ordered with a cheerful vengeance. "You tip that thing back. You'll not have another chance. Well, you might . . ."

"Ah, I'd rather take this one slowly."

"You don't like the Black?"

Clades became aware of both Machlann and Muluk watching him, so he took care with his reply. "Truth be known, Master Clavellus—"

"You call me Clavellus this night."

"Ah, Clavellus. Truth be known, I intended to see my wife later this evening, Master—ah, Clavellus. I haven't seen her for a while now. No doubt she fears me dead."

"You have a missus?" Machlann asked, puzzled, his bushy beard flexing.

"He has a missus," said Muluk.

"When did you see her last?" Clavellus asked with concern.

Again the three of them waited for an answer.

Clades had to think about it. "Not since I took up employment with you, I believe."

"All this time?" Clavellus whispered in shock. "*Unfit*. If I hadn't seen my Nala . . ."

"It's not unusual. Not for the wives of Sujins."

"Does Goll know this?" Machlann asked.

At the mention of the Kree, Clavellus's merriment noticeably dimmed.

"No, he doesn't," Clades answered.

"Well then, perhaps we'll finish this and be on our way." Muluk nodded at the others, saving his most sympathetic expression for the soldier.

"Hold on, hold on," groaned Clavellus. "Look. Clades. You're a fine lad. And you're in the Ten's employ. If she doesn't mind leaving your home here, then by all means, you bring your wife and family to my villa. We have rooms. Plenty of rooms. We have extra rooms for my staff and household guard. More rooms than people, truth be known, but we've had to mind our expenses through the years. And if those rooms aren't to her liking, we'll make a room she does like. I've meant to build some small hovels outside of my walls but well within distance of the villa if danger ever threatened. If you both wish it so, I'd welcome you into my home. Until you decide if you're staying with the Ten, that is."

"I'm staying," Clades said, well pleased with the offer. "I'll ask her. And Master Goll."

Clavellus frowned and stuck his chin out at Muluk. "Look there. We have a house master amongst us."

"So we do." The Kree grinned through his collected cuts and bruises. "Aye that. Bring her to the villa. If Clavellus doesn't mind, then why should I?"

"There you have it," Clavellus shouted and pounded the table hard enough to turn heads. "When you're able, speak with her. Just allow us to finish these drinks, and we'll be off. In fact, why wait? We'll be fine, you head on home now."

Head on home? That didn't settle well on Clades's mind. "I don't think that's wise, Master—ah . . . Clavellus."

The taskmaster was chugging from his mug once again. He wiped his beard when finished. "Why?"

"It's best I remain here. Until you're ready to leave. After these pitchers."

The words soured Clavellus's mood. "We have a nursemaid, Machlann."

The trainer didn't reply, choosing to indulge in a well-timed sip.

Clavellus joined him. When he finished, he aimed a finger at the once Sujin. "Lords above, that's sweet. That's some fine piss right there, let me tell you. Now then, *you*. You speak wisdom beyond your years, good Clades. We'll do just that. Finish these and then move on. Move on, I say. To some other place where the fish are biting. I caught the scent of roasting chickens before we entered here. Bit of hunting is good. Let's see if we can find where that tempting smell was coming from."

"They were quite tempting," Muluk said, finishing his own drink.

"For our wives," Clavellus said and thrust his mug into the air once again. "Seddon take me . . ." The older man suddenly faltered, looking sad. Then he drowned the feeling with beer.

"You have children?" Machlann asked the soldier.

"No."

Clavellus reached for more of the Black. "Machlann isn't one for beer, good Muluk, if you can believe that. So it's up to you and me to finish these pitchers before we go hunting. And before Goll comes looking."

"And he will," Machlann said.

"Guaranteed he will," Clavellus repeated. "So let's get at it. I know you have potential, Muluk, but I'll tell you now, I earned this shaking hand of mine for a reason."

I wager I know why, Clades thought, and when the taskmaster drank again, the Kree matched him, more than ready for a challenge.

Drink for drink.

Pitcher for pitcher.

All the while faces watched them from the shadows.

And when Goll finally did visit that particular alehouse . . .

They were long gone.

3

A gold tooth bounced and rattled to a stop upon a table, shattering the meditative splendor of burning snow orchids. Brejo frowned at the interruption. The evening meal had been overly filling—a meaty roast of pork complemented by well-cooked vegetables, all covered in a satisfying juice—and both Brejo and Calagu decided that an after-supper fog of the Osgarman bud would complement the food perfectly.

Then Jaro arrived, disturbing the streamers of smoke, causing them to coil and twist in death throes.

Brejo rose unsteadily from his couch. He glared, eyes red rimmed, demanding an explanation. From the hazy corners of the brothers' private court, Calagu struggled to escape his own comfortable nest. His pallid face contorted with unfit intoxication.

"What is it?" Brejo croaked, his voice sounding even more parched than usual.

Jaro pointed at the table. "Recognize it?"

Brejo turned his attention to the fragment of gold before him.

Calagu entered the scene from the other side, unpleasant curiosity dawning on his ashen face.

"A tooth?" Brejo asked. "Is that what that is?" He picked up the shaped metal, dropped it into a palm, and chased it with a finger.

"Lords above," Calagu whispered. "That belongs to Strach."

Brejo froze, horrified.

"Where did you find it?" Calagu asked.

"A pair of the lads discovered it near a sewer grate," Jaro said, waving at the smoke. "The deep one, where we rid ourselves of a corpse or two when needed. There was blood as well."

"Could he have slipped?" Calagu asked.

Jaro frowned. "Slipped and fell down a sewer? *That* sewer?"

"The hole's much too small for that," Brejo muttered. "That's why our lads actually use it. A topper has to be properly cut to fit through. No one can fall."

"Have you sent anyone down to search for him?" Calagu demanded, becoming more animated. "We need to be certain. It might be someone else."

"Sewer's too deep," Jaro said grimly. "And the rats would've gotten to him by now. Chewed his face off. We wondered where he was. That's him. He's there."

"Dead?" Brejo exclaimed hoarsely and handed the tooth to Calagu. The gang leader returned to his couch, held his head, and attempted to squeeze sense into his skull.

"Our brother is truly dead?" Calagu asked, holding the tooth up for better inspection.

Jaro nodded with an executioner's solemnness.

"I keep expecting him to wander into the room at any time," Brejo whispered, staring into space.

"No more," Calagu muttered.

"Are you sure?" Brejo asked of Jaro.

Any other time, the big man would've frowned at being questioned so. This time, however, he made an exception and nodded.

"Well." Brejo exhaled, and his face became hard. "Someone's *murdered* him."

"One of us," Calagu hissed, rage building.

"Our brother," Brejo added, anger creeping into his voice.

"We need to find them," Calagu said, eyes widening to the size of bucklers. "Find them and end them in the slowest way possible. This is Strach! Our blood! Perhaps someone thinks they can kill him and escape our attention? Someone is *wrong*."

"Oh, they won't escape," Brejo vowed, the snow-orchid bliss all but gone. "Jaro, spread the word to the streets. I don't care what you do, who you smash, or who you kill. Find out who did this. A name, a face, a gurry shape, even. *Any*thing. Uncover a scent, and find where it leads. Offer coin to the one who brings us word of Strach's killer."

"Could this be an attack?" Calagu asked. "A rival trying to weaken our hold on the city?"

Brejo glared at him. "No more orchid for you. Of course this was an attack. Why else would they push Strach down the very hole we fill with corpses? Someone knows what that sewer is used for. Some hellpup sent us a message. Some unfit crust of maggot shite who believes themselves to be our equal or thinks they can simply kill us at leisure. We'll find him, whoever it is, and cut our thoughts into their hide. Someone has forgotten the Sons' reputation. We'll make them remember. Dying Seddon, we'll make *Sunja* remember."

Brejo met Jaro's dark and luminous eyes. "Go!"

The gang's chief enforcer exited. News of Strach's death had upset his brothers. They'd be even more upset once the snow orchid's effects fully left them. He didn't want to be in Brejo's company when that happened. The oldest brother was capable of horrible acts of violence. Jaro was the appointed enforcer for the family, but truth be known, Brejo could very well have filled that position and with greater enthusiasm.

The warehouse's dark corridors barely contained Jaro's shadowy form as he strode along with purpose. He couldn't rightly say he'd miss Strach even though the man was blood. Strach believed himself royalty on the streets, a dangerous notion when he should have been staying to the shadows. The man's arrogance had killed him. Jaro had long suspected it was only a matter of time before his brother crossed the wrong person. Even Brejo and Calagu had openly mused about killing Strach, partly in jest, but at times furious enough to make Jaro wonder.

ABOUT THE BLOOD

Business would return to usual when Brejo and Calagu regained their senses. Jaro knew that, but he also knew the city's rats and street snakes would be very active in the days to come.

A fresh wind battered his face as he opened a door. A wooden walkway linked two buildings by way of a single, thick slab of wood suspended three levels above an alley. The Iron Games were held in the lower levels of the next structure, but Jaro had no intention of heading down into those depraved depths. The plank flexed under his considerable weight as he crossed. He opened another door and entered a room lit by a single candle. A few scant pieces of furniture lay scattered about, filling the place. Bardal and Sunjack waited in the flickering gloom. The two killers reeked of restrained violence. Physically, they were powerfully built, wearing white shirts with black vests. Long sleeves hid the inked chains, worms, and dragons decorating their arms. Bardal was the shorter of the pair and possessed the look of a butcher who'd long since grown bored with the profession. Sunjack was several fingers taller and could look Jaro straight in the eye. Sunjack reveled in dispensing pain. Both men would gut a passerby without warning if the notion took them.

The men waited, two well-trained dogs listening for a word.

"Get word to the rats and the snakes," Jaro said. "Search for whoever killed Strach. And while they're at it, find the one called Borchus. Do both. The coin will be doubled for the effort."

The pair of men exchanged looks.

Jaro's eyes shifted from one to the other. "Start wringing necks and squeezing bells."

4

Led by Clavellus, the small group walked through back alleys. They passed closing shop fronts and the shut doors of private homes before entering a maze of white stone walls and wooden balconies. Small public wells went by, and children with wet faces glanced up as the men passed. The taskmaster waved and stopped, dug out a gold coin, and charged the oldest to buy something sweet for the entire pack and split the goods equally. The children ran off. Men and women peeked out from half-opened shutters, wondering what was happening outside their homes.

Cheeks glowing and eyes glassy, Clavellus navigated those puzzling back-way turns as though he'd visited them just the day before. Clades stopped and looked back several times, committing landmarks and structures to memory. Somewhere along the way, the beer he'd drunk made him feel better about the evening, and therein he recognized danger. Gripping his sword's hilt like a talisman, he followed the others.

"Keep up," Clavellus called out to him. "If you get lost, you'll never find your way back."

"The lad's *from* this way," Machlann said, the beer loosening his tongue.

"Daresay he's not from back here." Clavellus looked back at the soldier. "Are you, lad?"

"I recognize some places."

"*Eeee* see?" a victorious Machlann growled.

"Yes, yes, you were right." Clavellus waved dismissively. "This way. I remember it well enough. As long as . . . ah *yes*!"

They connected with another alley, walked past a collection of puddles, garbage, and broken planks, and emerged in a wider street, one that brimmed with all manner of alehouses, eating establishments, and food stalls. None of the garish ribbons and streamers decorating other parts of the city were there, but other sights to behold were. Huge wooden decks with benches and tables glistened darkly in both directions until people cluttered the line of view. More people sat and lounged in the shade. Drinks were being lifted and consumed. Meals were in the process of being eaten. A blend of cooking meat, chicken and roasts alike, along with mystery spices, enhanced the air, leaving it even more of a pleasure to breathe. The grinning head of a pig rested on a table just next to an alehouse's main entrance. Stag horns adorned other open doorways. Pipe smoke wafted by. Women called out to passing groups of men, attempting to lure them inside their businesses. Men called out to women and their escorts, trying to do the same. String music flowed underneath it all, tugging Clades's ears as he attempted to locate the source.

Clavellus and Machlann stood at the alley mouth and marveled at it all.

"You feel that, Clades?" the taskmaster asked.

The once Sujin blinked. "No, what?"

"The energy, lad, the energy."

"I feel it," an eager Muluk announced.

"No doubt you do," Clavellus said. "And no doubt of what you might do to a keg of wine or beer if left alone with it, but I'm not sure of this one."

The taskmaster indicated Clades.

"I know this quarter," the once Sujin said in a wary tone, having visited the place back when he wasn't a married man.

"What is it, then?" Muluk asked.

"Arbin's Row."

"Row?" Machlann cocked an eyebrow. "It was called 'alley' when I saw it last."

"And how long ago was that?" Clavellus asked.

"You were there."

"So thirty years ago, at least. Maybe even thirty-one. Far too long. We were . . . well . . ." The taskmaster caught himself. "We were working with others then."

"Arbin's Alley?" Muluk asked the older men.

"*Row* now," Clavellus said brightly. "Arbin's *Row*. The name's changed, but the feeling hasn't. Nor the purpose. This way."

With that, Clavellus dove into the meandering stream of street walkers. The others followed while the taskmaster split the masses with smiles and slaps on the shoulders. Clades was surprised to see the people greeting the old man in return. And Muluk. Even Machlann, too, but to a lesser degree. The trainer projected a sternness that dampened smiles. His mouth was all but hidden underneath his thick moustache and gray beard, and like the taskmaster, his sun-blasted skin resembled scratched leather rather than actual flesh.

Muluk was damn near looking everywhere at once. Clades didn't share the Kree's enthusiasm for the area, but he had his own distant memories. The Row was a realm for drinkers, eaters, and those filled with debauched intent. It was a long secluded strip run by old businesses and managed by older families, much in the same way as the gladiatorial houses and stables. Many a Sujin had frequented that pleasure seekers' paradise, which was quietly observed and patrolled by the Street Watch. The city guard stationed themselves at either end of the area, containing the street. Arbin had been an old Sunjan merchant who'd perished long before Clades had come of age. He'd heard the stories of the man whose love for food and drink had inspired the street's name. Clades recalled too much drink being the cause of the man's death, but not before he transformed the family properties once lining the streets into well-known locales of revelry.

The Row had been, and remained, the largest, most concentrated area of alehouses, taverns, and other entertainment in the entire city.

The old taskmaster, clearly once well acquainted with the street, gazed upon those aging establishments like a forgotten treasure trove being rediscovered. Clades saw that wistful expression and didn't like the look of it. He remembered the sayings about the place, which dampened his hope for an early end to the evening. There was no such thing as an early end in Arbin's Row, only late nights and later mornings.

Even worse, the Row was away from the main streets, markets, and public spots, hidden amongst a tangle of narrow lanes and back alleys. The chances of Master Goll finding them were very slim, indeed.

Clavellus had chosen well.

He led them to the front of a tavern wedged between a pair of much larger alehouses. Clavellus and the others disappeared inside, but Clades lingered. Above the door and on a sign was the painting of two angry boars locking tusks. A name was there, but a sleepy-looking enforcer guarding the entrance blocked Clades from reading it.

"You got a blade there," the bald enforcer rumbled and pointed. "You keep it there for the time inside. Understood?"

Clades nodded that he would do just that.

The enforcer, with a long spike of a beard hanging off his chin, waved the soldier inside.

Most of the lamps weren't yet lit, but a few flickering baubles illuminated a tavern clean and polished and pleasing to the eye. Patrons lounged at a small bar area to one side. Others gathered around a collection of tables arranged throughout the place. Serving women and men whisked through the tables, some carrying platters of food. Others carried mugs and pitchers.

Into this, Clavellus waded, straight to the back, where he found a table situated under a pair of lit lamps. "Here," he announced and directed the others to sit.

He waved to a young woman, who quickly arrived at their table. She picked at her green apron before inquiring about his needs with a look.

"Sunjan Black," he said happily. "If you have it. Three pitchers, and was that roast chicken that pulled me off the street?"

"Most likely was," she answered.

"Three of those as well. With whatever bread you have back there."

The woman took the order and disappeared through a kitchen door.

"Now then," Clavellus said. "I do believe we're set. This is my plan. We eat, finish our drinks, and continue on to the next place. Have another round and move on again, repeating everything until dawn. Make our way along until we reach the Street Watch. How does that sound to you?"

Muluk nodded, his dark, disheveled, wild-man expression lighting up at the prospect of some serious drinking. Yellow teeth shone wickedly out of that mass of facial hair.

Machlann held his tongue and didn't object in the least.

Clavellus looked at Clades.

"Well—" the once Sujin started.

"Excellent!" the older man exclaimed. "But not so much drinking for you, good Clades. I won't insist on that. You are . . . our enforcer. For the evening. Though I don't expect any tangles needing your attention."

Clades wasn't sure about that, so he kept his mouth shut.

"Do you remember this place?" Muluk asked the taskmaster.

"Here?" Clavellus touched the table. "Sweet Lords, no. I hardly remember any of these places. The buildings all look the same after a pitcher, and I drank more than just one, truth be known. But I don't remember eating bad food in any of these places. Or heard tell of such."

Their server left the kitchen and went directly to the bar area.

"Prepare yourself, Muluk," the taskmaster warned. "My wagers were exceptionally rewarding today."

The words struck an uneasy chord within Clades.

They ate—roasted chicken, assorted vegetables, and a delectable gravy that very much agreed with Clades. And they drank. Heavily. Often. The bitter Sunjan Black, mostly. The beer was brutally strong, cool, and thick enough to be a second meal. Clades nursed a mug of that hair-curling juice along with his food and wondered if he should ask for water.

He did not, however.

Plates were emptied and pitchers drained. More people piled into the tavern, a trickle of torsos and smiling faces. More lamps were lit. The banter increased in volume. Clavellus presided at the table, his back to a wall. Clades sat beside him, amazed at the amount of fluid the old man was taking in and keeping down. The taskmaster fidgeted in his chair at times, as if his guts were shifting things around to make room for more beer. He spoke fondly of history and games gone by. He spoke of old champions and the weapons they'd used, the tactics they'd employed. Muluk listened while his movements slowed and his eyes crossed. When the serving woman returned, Clavellus informed her the food was excellent and asked her to convey that thought to whoever had prepared it.

He placed a single coin onto her hand just before she cleared the table.

They consumed more beer and continued talking, the subject being Muluk and his days as a young boy in distant Kree. Clades, perhaps the only man whose senses weren't spinning, noticed the taskmaster squirming with each swallow. The older man twisted and rocked while listening, his hand trembling until he removed it from the table.

Clades knew the man wanted to be away, out there in the day's dying light, walking to the next establishment.

So when Muluk spoke the words, "So I decided to come here," Clavellus slapped the table and stood.

"Well told, good Muluk, well told." The taskmaster pointed toward the door. "Now, we go."

"All right," the Kree said without taking offense.

A pair of enforcers eyed the foursome as they exited. A pink-and-gold skyline shone overhead and through rooftops. More people walked Arbin's Row, preoccupied with their own drinking adventures. Some strolled, some staggered, and some ducked inside an entrance just as others were exiting.

Clavellus held up a hand, stopping his little gang, and looked right as if catching a whiff of something. He then looked left and, deciding all was well, waved the pack onward. They crossed the street while string instruments carried a spirited tune deeper down the Row, providing even more color to the evening.

Clades was certain he'd only had two drinks, but his senses had clouded. He could feel it in his step as well. *Damnation.* He would make it a point not to drink anything else if it wasn't water.

Clavellus, however, was skipping along as if splashing through rain puddles.

The taskmaster halted three doors down from the previous tavern and studied the swinging doors of an alehouse. A pair of towering Sunjans guarded the entrance. The two men were perhaps too large and cumbersome for the Pit, but in their current position, they were deathly intimidating with their numerous facial scars and steady gazes. One of the men—an unshaven brute who appeared to have no teeth—cocked an irritated eyebrow at the blade Clades carried.

"Don't worry about him, lad," Clavellus hurried to explain. "He's with me. They're all with me. He's merely protection. That's all. Protection. Not that I need it *here*, with the likes of you two watching the place, but out *there*. Out *there*, I say. In the Row. But if you disagree, Seddon please, say your mind, and he'll surrender his weapon. We don't wish to cause any trouble or offense."

Clades didn't rightly appreciate the taskmaster surrendering his sword for him, but he had to admit, the man spoke well.

The enforcer seemingly agreed as well as he swung his attention from Clavellus to Clades, frowned with a touch of sleepiness, and nodded that entering was fine—with the blade.

"My thanks," Clavellus said and disappeared inside.

The others followed, and Clades held onto his sword sheath, not meeting the enforcer's eyes.

Pipe smoke accosted them, amazingly strong despite the ventilation in the place. The alehouse had two levels, the upper one open with a thick timber for patrons to lean upon and gaze at those beneath. Smoke rose above their heads. Men and women were drinking and talking and enjoying themselves. Near the back, two men were playing fiddles on a low stage while a third was pounding a crude drum.

"The bar," Clavellus growled and pointed, his bald crown gleaming with sweat.

"The bar," Muluk repeated, his mouth falling open with a note of worship in his tone. The keenness again worried Clades.

Machlann made no move at all. The old trainer leered with all the intensity of someone soon to be right and proper unfit. Clades wasn't the only one who noticed the squished glare emanating from the trainer. Patrons peeked at him over raised mugs, wondering what to make of the old boy, probably wondering if he was about to fall over.

Clades wondered himself.

"Might a table—" the once Sujin started to say, pointing to a spot far and away from everyone else.

Clavellus and the others left him for the bar.

Unimpressed, Clades went after them.

More beer appeared. Clavellus handed a mug to the once Sujin and smiled at Clades's uneasy frown. Once the drinks were in place, Clavellus raised his into the air.

"For the Ten, lads," he said, a touch loudly. "The Ten!"

"The Ten!" repeated the others, though Clades didn't raise his voice.

They drank—pulls long enough to make eyes water and guts bulge. Saimon take him, Clades drank as well, not wishing to offend his companions. The beer wasn't the Black that time but a much more pleasant brew. Clades downed several mouthfuls before inspecting the contents with approval.

"What do you think of that?" Clavellus asked, wiping his great white beard.

"Quite good," Clades answered.

"He says it's quite good, Machlann," Clavellus reported with evil glee. "He's says it's quite good."

"P'raps you should try the Gold?" the trainer asked.

Clades screwed up his face at that. "Wine? After the beer?"

"Just a taste, my son, just a taste," Machlann assured him.

Clavellus had already ordered mugs for all and kept a place for him near the bar.

"No pitchers?" Clades asked.

"Not here," the taskmaster replied. "No need to overdo it. Now then"—he lifted the wine—"for that hellion called Junger. May he flourish right to the end."

"Junger," Muluk and Machlann repeated.

"Junger," Clades said a beat later and sipped.

Seddon above. That wasn't the first time he'd drunk Sunjan Gold, but that particular mug of wine was practically slipping down his throat. Smooth. Better than smooth.

"Eh?" Clavellus asked.

"It's good," Clades replied.

"You lot with the games?" the barkeep asked. He was a younger sort, perhaps in his thirties, and a bit hard looking. Inked swords and daggers covered his forearms.

"We are," Clavellus said. "Belong to the House of Ten."

"Ohhh," the barkeep said, marginally impressed. "A house, eh?"

"You follow the games?"

"Nah. Not at all. Too violent for me. All that blood," he said with an exaggerated shiver. "Not for me. The missus likes it, though. She loves all that. Young men hackin' away at each other. Bare-chested brutes all sweaty and in armor, just swingin' at each other's heads, tryin' to take 'em off. She loves it. *Loves* it."

Clades had nothing to say to any of that.

"Your missus like to wager?" Clavellus asked the barkeep.

That put the man on edge. "Every now and then."

"Tell her these names. Junger. Of Pericia. And Goll of Kree."

"What? They dangerous or something?"

"Very dangerous."

"Have a chance, do they?"

Clavellus blinked as if clearing his head. "They have a *very* good chance. And that's the word of a taskmaster. And his trainer. That handsome bastard right there."

On cue, Machlann nodded with drunken wisdom and bared whatever teeth he had remaining.

The barkeep was becoming increasingly interested. "Well, I'll do that then. See what comes of it. My thanks."

"You didn't mention Brozz," Muluk said when the barkeep turned away to other customers.

"Brozz is a good man," Clavellus admitted. "But he's hurt. Badly. Between you and the ... the rest of us, I don't expect him to continue. For much longer. I'll be happy to be wrong, however. Machlann?"

"Aye that. Happy to be wrong."

"Finish that wine, and we'll be off," Clavellus said to his bodyguard.

Clades did as he was told.

5

They drank *more*, emptying pitchers with alarming speed.

Every mug they downed, Clades watched and readied himself to jump back, very much aware of the deep breaths Muluk was taking and the hitches in Machlann's chest. Clavellus clenched his shaking hand into a fist at times, not that it stopped the trembling. That knobby, knuckly bauble of flesh and bone reminded the once Sujin of poisonous snakes with tails that rattled just before they struck. In the taskmaster's case, Clades believed the shaking fist was an indicator of a thirst and stomach not quite satisfied.

They walked—from tavern to alehouse, from alehouse to tavern. How they did such a thing became more and more remarkable to the Ten's designated enforcer for the evening. They staggered and lurched but managed to avoid other people entirely. There was an art there. And more than just a bit of drunken sorcery.

The passing faces of strangers became forgettable blurs.

The alleyways became deep, mysterious pits of night where forms coupled.

The doorways became open maws of firelight stuffed with people. Clades didn't drink at every place, but he drank enough to challenge his tolerance. The others were damn near pickled to near epic proportions. Their steps became sloppy. Their speech slurred into a new and interesting language where flying spittle was socially acceptable. Clavellus no longer talked of honorable houses anymore but of the dirtiest, most underhanded characters that ever plagued the games.

"That kog wassa . . . kog. Wassa a kog, I say. A right and proper *kog*. A punce. A truly *dewy* punce. Sweaty, dewy punce. The worst. And no bells. Nothing there at all. None. The worst kind, y'see. The worst kind. Worse than . . . *bald* ones. Truly. Not a bell on him. No. Nooooo. Evil. Evil. *Kog!*"

Muluk bumped into a post and apologized profusely before realizing he was reaching for a nonexistent shoulder. Machlann walked straight into the paths of oncoming people, warding them out of his way with a murderous glare, his tuft of gray hair wild in the night, like a miniature man waving a frosty lantern back and forth, warning all of certain doom.

Clades kept closest to him.

"Foul bastard, to the core," Clavellus rambled. "To the core, I say. Foul. Foul. A shite trough has more . . . more honor, has a greater purpose than . . . that one." The taskmaster, red-eyed and staring, led them to a lamplit cavern of wood and merriment and song, where figures lounged behind open shutters.

"Who're you talking about, again?" Muluk asked, having missed the name at some point. The words didn't leave the Kree like that, though. They came out more like "WhuuuRUH, mmmyuuu . . . talkinto—ah—atalkinto, aguh. Again." The last syllable tumbled out as if his brain very much disapproved of the slurring and was stomping a foot in hopes of knocking something back into place.

"Pay attention," Clavellus warned, somehow having understood that frightening mash of grunts and squeaks. "Next time. Can't repeat anything right now. Can't spare the time. And you don't know who's listening."

"*Eeeee* pay attention," Machlann repeated and belched loudly enough to startle a couple walking nearby.

Two enforcers stopped them from entering the enormous alehouse. One of the guards, one-eyed and with his hair tied into a long tail at the back, studied Clades and his sheathed sword.

"You're a right and proper savage, aren't you?" Clavellus asked slyly, examining the single-eyed enforcer. Miraculously, the taskmaster sounded perfectly lucid despite the alcoholic might flooding his brain. He looked at the other guard. "You're not bad, but he's a . . . right . . . frightening pisser. Daresay not too many challenge you, am I right? You're monstrous. Monstrous, I say. Luh—look. *Look!* Have nuh—*no* fear. That one? He's with me, and I'm friend to . . . to all. But . . . if you want his blade . . . take it."

"Take it," Muluk echoed, but it came out sounding like a child getting his bells caught between two pieces of lumber.

"He doesn't need it," Clavellus added without missing a beat, but his words were becoming increasingly slurred, and in the oddest places. "Not with yu . . . you two hellions at the door. Saimon below, lad. The owner know you're out here? Does he luh . . . does he luh . . . does he *lose* business because of you? You'd make the Visigar ride their horses. To death. Trying to . . . escape into the sunset." He managed a near theatrical flourish of a hand at the word *sunset*. "Muh . . . make Paw Savages run for open water. Turn the Nordish around and make them run for the muh. Their *muh* . . . their hills. You ever fight in the Pit?"

The smaller of the pair looked at his much larger companion.

"No," the big man said, his one eye crunched in thought, attempting to detect a joke at his expense.

"Swuh . . . swing a blade, can you?"

The big one half shrugged.

"Take orders?"

A nod.

"You get tired of this—this business—you seek out the House. Of Ten," Clavellus said, fingers flickering, as if practicing spellcraft. "You find us, and we'll get started on yuh . . .

you right away. Provided you're younger than twenty-*suh* . . . twenty-*suh* . . . than him."

He indicated Muluk, who immediately smiled. The picture was frightening.

"We prefer," the taskmaster resumed with stubborn determination, "to start training no later than that. You understand."

"Aye that," the big man said. "Carry on, then."

Clavellus slapped the enforcer's shoulder, gripped it, and gave it a friendly squeeze. The enforcer shook his head at the effort, but he was smiling when he did so. Machlann and Muluk followed the taskmaster inside. The doorframe caught Muluk's shoulder with a solid clap, distracting the enforcers. The Kree said nothing and proceeded inside.

The larger one stopped Clades, planting a hand squarely on his chest. "You pull that steel in there, and I'll run the whole length of it through your pisser."

Despite being partially armored by the alcohol, Clades nodded as if underwater. "Understood."

"Right then. Carry on."

Clades carried on.

More people. More smoke. Laughter brayed, pleasant yet disturbing. The music was louder, played by a four-man band, assaulting their ears like a storm of hornets. More women, some of which eyed the once Sujin upon entering. More cleavage, which widened Muluk's eyes. Clades didn't bother with the ladies and moved quickly to the bar, passing crowded tables.

Clavellus was there, at the counter, and he was talking.

No, the old man was *shouting*, and not only the barkeep but the drinkers lounging in the general area were listening.

"Ten!" Clavellus said and hoisted a mug. "To the Ten! Free Trained all. Remember that at the end of the season. Remember! Here, Clades, I kept this one for you." He held out a drink.

Clades took it, not minding in the least, but eyed Muluk magically appearing at his side. He glanced over his shoulder, back toward where he thought he'd lost the Kree to the women, and decided it didn't really matter.

They drank again.

Clades sputtered and choked on the first gulp, much to the amusement of those around him.

"*Eeee*," Machlann chuckled, sounding like some distant fire giant basking in a volcano.

"What was that?" Clades gasped, wiping at his face.

"Sunjan firewater," Clavellus growled, smacking his lips.

"Firewater?"

"Don't care for firewater?"

Muluk said something then, but damned if Clades could understand what it was. *Firewater*, he thought and felt his guts rumble with annoyance. He'd only taken a mouthful, but that fearsome concoction equaled at least five mugs of beer. Men had died drinking too much of the overpowering brew. The drink didn't just kick one in the face, it stomped on one's skull.

"Is there anything you're not going to drink tonight?" Clades asked.

The taskmaster chuckled and took another shot.

"I wasn't lying about that lad outside the door," he said to Machlann when he finished. "Frightful man. He had . . . he had the look . . . of a butcher. Enjoying his work. I tell you."

"Who was the most frightful man you'd ever encountered during the games?" Muluk asked, getting the question out without slurring or spitting.

What scared Clades the most, however, was that he suddenly, quite clearly, understood every last syllable.

"Roshdon," Clavellus said while Machlann said, "Bivek the Six," in the same sloppy breath.

That got the two men arguing. Machlann became the steadiest, growling his reasons, spittle flying, while Clavellus sought to talk over the trainer, spraying even more.

In the end, they agreed to disagree.

Then they grabbed rags from the barkeep to clean their faces.

"Who was the worst killer you've ever known in the games?" Muluk asked when the froth had stopped flying and the whiskers were wiped clean.

"Luttros," the trainer said.

"Mendil the Axe," Clavellus said more loudly and shook his head at Machlann. "Luttros was a right and proper daisy."

"Nothing wrong with daisies."

"Never *said* there was anything wrong with daisies. There's not."

"Daisies can be vicious."

"Daisies can be vicious," the taskmaster repeated with scorn. "Listen to yourself."

"Jundal the Vathian," Machlann immediately countered.

That sobered the taskmaster. "Forgot about that monster. He *was* a right vicious one. Point taken. Pleasant enough sort to talk with. But once . . . in the Pit . . . vicious. Vicious."

"And he's still alive," Machlann said, his speech steadying with practice.

"He is?"

"Returned to Vathia. Works the ground now. Grows vegetables of some sort. With some blade work on the side."

"Jundal," Clavellus said fondly, remembering times gone by. "Truly vicious bastard. All the same."

"All right," Muluk said, his brow knotting up with effort. "Who was the most frightful, most deadliest killer in the games?"

"Tardus Tan," both men said in unison.

"Right and proper killer," Machlann said.

"Hellion born," Clavellus added and had to steady himself by the bar. "Used a pair of hand axes."

"Spiked," Machlann said.

"Spiked," the other agreed.

"Used them well. Guaranteed."

"Until he came up against that one, Vinndar the Vice."

Muluk's drunken face lit up. "Who was he?"

Clavellus shook his head. "The man who . . . who killed Tardus Tan. That's who."

"All he needs to be," Machlann added. "And all he'll be remembered for."

"A lesson learned from that fight," the taskmaster said.

"What was that?" Muluk asked.

Clavellus laughed. "Never fight Vinndar the Vice."

And on it went.

Until the firewater hit.

Hit them all.

Hard.

"A toash," Clavellus said and swung his mug left and right, spilling beer—he'd switched back after two shots of firewater. The spillage annoyed the barkeeps. "Apolo . . . a*polo* . . . sorry about that. Now then. Lads. A toash, I said. All of you."

He fixed his three companions with a wet look that warned they'd better listen. "I have . . . a toash. To you. Three of you. Lads. Thank you. For coming with me. This night. I appreciate. The gesture. You've made . . . you've made an old man happy. And me as well."

Machlann muttered a sentence positively soaked in firewater.

Clavellus chuckled and shook the man's shoulder, and all seemed well because of it. "Apologies, always, old friend. Haveta make a jab. Every now and then. Keep you alive, you know."

Machlann nodded weakly and flopped a hand, meaning Clavellus should think nothing of it.

"So, thank you for entertaining," Clavellus said. "On such a happy night. I feel better than years. Than I *have* in years. The Ten will prevail. The Perician will avail. And I say here. Now. The Perician will *win* the games."

He drank, and the others joined him, even Clades because, after the firewater, nothing really mattered anymore.

"Who are you?" asked the barkeep, an older, heavyset man wiping out a mug.

"The House of Ten." Clavellus drew himself up. "And I'm Clavellus of Sunja. Taskmaster. Of the lot. That man there"—he pointed at Machlann—"is the most gifted. And unfit trainer. You'll ever have the pleasure of meeting."

Machlann frowned at the introduction, but Clades could see the man was pleased.

Clavellus pointed again. "That one. Is the noble house master."

Muluk glared, on the verge of toppling to the floor.

"And that one . . ." Clavellus stopped at Clades. "I forget."

Muluk abruptly laughed and sprayed beer, catching half in his hands.

Clavellus looped an arm around Clades's neck. "I joke, of course. This one. Is our enforcer. An honorable man. Who's putting up with us. When he could be . . . with his missus. I'll remember that."

Clades sighed, somewhat touched himself.

"Where's the one called Junger, then?" the barkeep asked.

"He's not here," Clavellus said.

"Heard that name twice this night," the barkeep admitted. "And not from you. Different folk."

Machlann and Clavellus exchanged looks, both pleased, but the taskmaster more so. Then his smile wilted under that white beard of his, and his muddy brown eyes widened in surprise then narrowed in disappointment. He looked past Clades, who turned around to see Goll standing there behind him.

Clavellus lowered his mug with drunken guilt.

"Master Goll," he said. "You're . . . late."

The Kree stood glaring, seething, with the Perician at his side. Men and women whispered and turned at the pair's appearance, especially Junger. More than a few patrons quieted in respect for the warrior standing in their midst. Clades saw the stares fasten onto Junger.

The Perician, dressed in a common shirt and breeches, with his sword sheathed and hanging from his waist scabbard, appeared unconcerned with the sudden attention.

"Enjoying the city's delights I see," Goll observed, jawline twitching.

"Yesh," the taskmaster said, drawing himself up. "I am."

"A good thing I found you."

"For one of us," Clavellus muttered and blinked slowly, as if the collective power of everything he'd downed finally hammered him all at once. He pursed his lips, exhaled as if winded, and swayed ever so slightly. "Probably you."

Goll studied the others. An unfit Muluk fluttered fingers at his fellow countryman in weak greeting.

"Couldn't resist, could you?" Goll asked.

Muluk shrugged innocently and pointed at Clades. "Thadasmisseses."

"What?"

Muluk frowned and went over the line again in his head. "The lad . . . has . . . a missus. The lad. Him. Clades. Has a wife. Hasn't seen the woman since . . ." Muluk blinked very slowly. "Since he joined us. That's wrong, Goll. Very wrong. We talked. About that. Clavellus offered them a room. At the villa. If she wants it. If he wants it. I said it was fine. *Phsst.*" He fizzled, wetting his lips and surrounding facial hair.

"Very generous," Goll remarked and considered Clades. "I don't remember you saying you had a wife."

"I don't remember telling you," an apologetic Clades said.

"Seddon above." Goll glanced around the alehouse then told Junger, "Help me get them back."

Machlann frowned but kept his tongue. Clades liked the old man for that.

"*We're leaving*, now," Clavellus announced in a drunken blast that startled the crowd. "We're leaving. Take one last look. Before we leave. This place. This fine establishment. I mean that. When next you see *this* man, he will be champion of this year's games."

Clavellus presented Junger, startling him that time.

Goll's face puckered up tighter than a dog's blossom.

"A champion!" Clavellus shouted, daring anyone to challenge him. "Most of you don't know who I am, but some of you do. Some of you know me very well. I've overseen the training . . . of . . . a thousand war hounds. Bred for the arena. And I tell you. Now. In all honesty. The House of Ten . . . will achieve greatness this season. Greatness! Because of this hellion standing before you all. Mark my words!"

He finished with a drunken smile. "And remember to wager."

His speech subdued the alehouse's festive mood. Someone coughed. A woman blinked as if kicked in the head. A man slurred some nonsense before his face struck his table's surface.

Message delivered, Clavellus gestured for Goll to lead the way.

Gathering themselves up, the group left the alehouse. Junger led the way, his hands loose and swinging. A swaying Clades guarded the rear though he sensed no ill will from the gathered people. All the same, he watched the shadows, scanning recesses where indistinct shapes lingered.

Along the walk back to the healer's house, Goll's unimpressed words rang clear on the summer night air. "Satisfied, Master Clavellus?"

The taskmaster walked with his head held high, a smile on his face. "Without question, you brazen. Dew-sack. Of a Kree."

No sooner had the group of men departed the drinking establishment than one man straightened in his chair. He'd been sitting at a round table with a few other men, drinking, talking—but also watching. When the men from the House of Ten departed, the watcher finished his drink, slapped his nearest companion on the shoulder, and left the alehouse.

He filled his lungs with night air, warm and inviting, and watched the little group stagger away at best speed.

Taking his time, the watcher wandered out into the street, evading passersby and drifting toward wherever the shadows seemed thickest.

When the Ten had reached a comfortable distance, he sniffed and followed at leisure, so as to not draw attention.

He wasn't supposed to be working, but with his job, he supposed he was working all the time.

Clavellus. The entire alehouse knew the old topper's name by the time he'd finsihed his first pitcher. The House of Ten.

The watcher knew them. There wasn't a working spy in Sunja who didn't.

Clavellus and the Ten had enjoyed Arbin's Row that night. The spy would pass that information along to Bezange, personal agent of Dark Curge.

Later that night, with Goll's permission, Clades left the healer's house and made his way through Sunja's streets, where the torches and street lamps burned low and the darkness hid the drunkards. The drink was still in his system, but he managed walking through the great city's eastern quarters, threading the surest path to his little hovel, nearly indistinguishable from the dozens on the same road. The shadows didn't help much, as most of the street lamps had burned low. In comparison, the starry heavens above brightened with every passing moment.

Kura would be sleeping by then, he knew, and he hated to wake her.

He hated staying away even more, though.

Glancing around and ensuring the street was empty, Clades tried to ignore his heart's quickening beat. With the amount of beer and wine he'd consumed, the first real bout of drinking in years, he knew he would regret it in the morning. He didn't like coming home in such a condition either, but this would be the first and last time.

He knocked on the door, softly.

The streets remained empty. Soft snores ripped somewhere behind him. No one answered the door. The windows were shuttered, barred from within as he'd known her to do. She'd locked the house the very same way for years while he served on the Sunjan-Nordish front.

Clades knocked again, the wood stinging his knuckles. Nervous energy built up inside his chest and legs. Weeks had passed since he'd left, but she'd known he would be away for a while, the only solace he'd given her being that he wasn't fighting some Jackal in the dead of night.

He knocked a third time, put his mouth to the door's seam, and whispered, "Kura. It's me. Clades. Open the door."

No response.

Seddon above. He couldn't remember her having slept so soundly before.

Clades lifted his knuckles for a more urgent knock when the door opened. His wife peeked through the widening crack. She was sleepy eyed, with blond hair tumbling unchecked over her face and shoulders. She pushed her hair back from her narrowing eyes, those blue gems that had hypnotized Clades so many times. She stared at him and saw that it was truly was him and not a dream. Her lips trembled ever so slightly.

She reached out and clutched his shirt.

And pulled her husband in close.

6

Breakfast for the Ten consisted of hard-boiled eggs, cold cuts of honey-crisped ham, apple slices sprinkled with sweet spice, and goat's milk for those who could keep it down. Not surprisingly, Clavellus and Muluk avoided the goat's milk and only nibbled at the food. Muluk's usual exploding bush of hair had been flattened on one side, and his eyes were pained slits. Machlann's eyes seemed deep inside his head. The three of them looked as if they'd been steeped far too long in pisspots and were suffering from the taste. The old taskmaster and trainer took most of their morning meal in the form of water, drinking it often. Clavellus's left hand trembled uncontrollably, but he was in better condition than his Kree drinking companion, who looked as if he'd died sometime during the morning.

Shan's wife fluttered about the room, her gray hair tied back. She wasn't too pleased about her husband's recent absence, but she was the consummate professional to the wounded Brozz and the incapacitated Torello nevertheless. She tended to the men with forced pleasantry, her button eyes casting dark looks toward Shan only when she thought no one was looking.

Goll saw it and knew trouble was near. He said nothing, however. He even left the three drinkers alone, hoping their morning misery would be lesson enough.

He doubted that, though.

With breakfast finished, the house master mustered the group outside, allowing Shan a last moment with his wife. While the men helped Torello and Brozz into their transports, voices rose from inside the healer's house, turning heads. Goll looked at Clavellus, who sipped frequently from a personal water bag. The fluid intake seemed to be working for the old man. He appeared to be in much better working condition than Muluk, who remained unfit to look upon.

The taskmaster noticed Goll's inspection and smiled. "Still alive, Kree. Have no worries."

Goll frowned.

"We'll need to purchase a few strongboxes," Clavellus said, his voice hoarse for reasons he couldn't remember. "With locks."

"With locks," Goll repeated. "Why?"

"For your coin. Unless you want to keep it in a bank."

"Perhaps that would be best."

Clavellus studied his shaking hand and winced as if tasting something foul. "You don't want a bank. Not in Sunja. We're at war, after all."

Goll's eyes narrowed. "What're you saying?"

"I'm saying ... purchase a few stout strongboxes with quality locks. Made by a professional with a good reputation. We can empty those four sacks into the boxes—four heavy sacks that might be far too tempting to the wrong people— and transport them all back to the villa. I'll mark them and store them in my strong room. If you wish."

"How many guards do you have at your villa, again?"

"Including your three once Sujins? Thirteen."

"Will that be enough?" Goll asked.

Clavellus frowned. "You do remember we school gladiators? Only the truly unfit would attempt to steal from us. And if they did, daresay the lads would welcome some live exercise."

"Only the unfit," Goll repeated.

"The truly unfit," Clavellus said and rubbed his belly. "Though I suspect we have one or two amongst us. Regardless.

Strongboxes, Master Goll. We'll carry it all back home. It'll be as safe as anywhere. Unless you don't trust me, of course."

Goll glared, uncertain if that was a jab or not. He looked at Muluk, whose eyes resembled knots scorched from tree trunks. The man exhaled mightily, declining to speak for fear of grabbing his knees and voiding right there.

"All right," Goll said, unimpressed. "Strongboxes. You know of someone?"

Clavellus gestured to Pratos and Valka. "You lads know of a strongbox maker? One who does quality work?"

"I do," Valka answered.

"Then take us to him. Master Goll wishes to make a purchase or two."

"Or three or four," Muluk added, breaking his silence.

"If he wishes," Clavellus said, eyeing the Kree with distrust and taking a step back, for fear of being splashed. "But if he doesn't, I don't think you'd need worry."

"Why is that?" Goll asked.

"Because of him." The taskmaster pointed at the Perician, standing in the house's shade.

Junger frowned at the commotion coming from inside the house as Shan and his wife continued to clash.

"The masses will remember him now," Clavellus continued with a note of sadness. "Especially when they place their wagers with the Domis. We might've won a vast sum yesterday, but we'll never win it again. Not at those odds."

Goll sighed and studied the Ten's gladiator.

Just then, Shan emerged from his home and gently closed his door. He smiled wretchedly before pressing a hand to his chest and walking over to Goll. The healer's face was long and worrying. "Apologies for that. She's not so keen on me staying away for extended periods. We're losing business here."

Goll frowned. "But I'm paying you."

"And I told her. She never was very good at arguing but exceptionally good at sad faces. Those always defeated me."

Clavellus clasped the healer's shoulder. "We'll make it right, won't we, Master Goll?"

"Get everyone onto the wagons," he said, ignoring the question. "And let's be off."

Well before midmorning, the two wagons carrying the Ten rolled their way through thickening crowds. The wheels clattered over the street's fitted stones, rattling those travelling inside. More than a few had missed their morning wash, and as a result, the pungent stink of body odor tormented Goll. The rear flap had been raised and tied, so he glanced out the back, toward the following wagon, and noticed how some of the faces in the fleshy wake watched them. Some of the Sunjans even halted and pointed fingers.

The Kree's lips tightened into a line.

Junger was back there, walking behind the second wagon. Both transports were cramped, so Junger had volunteered to follow behind to make room. Since the man would be well out of his sight, Goll didn't protest the idea in the least.

At the moment, however, he regretted allowing it.

Valka sat in the driver's seat alongside the fat Bagrun and his equally fat moustache. Following the soldier's directions, Bagrun steered the wagons down a side street not as wide as the main road. They stopped twice for Clavellus, Machlann, and Muluk to get out and empty the bulls, something which annoyed Goll to no end. He was especially annoyed with Muluk. The man moved like a sick cow.

In time, the wagons halted before a storefront weathered by years of frequent business. Wide shutters were flung open, and a wide canopy drooped over the entrance. A head bobbed beyond an open window.

Valka pulled back the canvas separating the driver's perch from the wagon's interior. "Here," he said.

"Trouble, Master Goll?" Clavellus asked. "Your mouth looks tighter than a dog's blossom."

"Nothing of your concern."

"Still angry with me?"

"I am."

"I'll buy one of those boxes for you."

Goll looked out the back. "Three."

"Two."

"Done."

Clavellus made his way past Torello's prone figure, actually placing a hand on the man's head. Once at the wagon's gate, the taskmaster lowered himself to the street.

"Get ten," Goll called after him.

Clavellus raised a hand, indicating he'd heard.

"Ten," Torello said. "Seems to me there's a word for that."

"Yes, there is," Goll said, still in a sour mood. "It's called *ten*."

"No, I mean the House of Ten buying ten strongboxes," Torello said, marking the air with his fingers. "There's a word for it. Not good fortune."

"I'll call it good planning."

Torello still hadn't picked up on the house master's surliness. "No, something else. What is it . . . ?"

"When you think of it, keep it to yourself," Goll said and moved to the front of the wagon. "Valka, get below and help Master Clavellus."

The once Sujin immediately stood, smoothed out a graying beard, and did just that.

"I mean it's a good sign," Torello continued from behind. "Of improving fortunes. We're ten, ten boxes . . ."

Goll ignored him and got out of the wagon.

In short time, Clavellus inspected and purchased the strongboxes, hardwood made and bound by iron. Clavellus voiced his concern that Goll didn't need so many, but upon a single black look from the Kree house master, he conceded that being prepared wasn't a bad thing, just in case.

The craftsman, an older man with hands covered in cracked skin, provided keys for the locks. Once the boxes were aboard the wagons, Goll poured the Ten's winnings into three and locked them. Their coin secured, everyone squeezed into the crowded wagons and rolled in the direction of the city gates.

Goll sat beside three stacked strongboxes and smoothed a hand over the wood's fine surface, feeling the grain.

"Cramped in here," Torello noted through clenched teeth.

"No more jumping out the back for you," a nearby Clavellus advised, still recovering from his night of drinking.

"No more alehouses for you," Torello said with a glare.

"I've said that myself several times."

"And yet to listen."

The taskmaster frowned and spoke then, but Goll didn't hear it as the rhythmic pounding of metal hammering metal attracted his attention. He rose, grabbed onto a rib of the canvas-covered wagon, and made his way through the confined interior, eliciting grunts and hard looks from the others. He pulled the sheet covering the back, and a warm blast of moist air penetrated the interior.

The wagons were passing a forge on the left side of street, almost hidden by the shifting mob.

"Stop here," Goll shouted, glaring at the crowded street.

The lead wagon halted, causing everyone to lurch. Torello found himself squished against a bench and hissed with discomfort.

The wounded gladiator and taskmaster looked to Goll for an explanation.

"We need an armorer," the Kree explained. "And a weaponsmith."

With that, he swung one leg over the rear gate and lowered himself to the street.

A forge was nearby, just behind a moving fence of sheep. Goll waited for the animals to pass and strove ahead, not appreciating the tight bustle of the city.

A low wall with a single gate ringed the work area surrounding the forge. Other walls enclosed the space as well, but they were of a sliding variety, easy to shut at the day's end. Three men worked beneath a vaulted roof held up by four stout-looking logs.

An assortment of anvils, work benches, and barrels of scrap metal filled the area before a large hearth. Two of the men were burly sorts, their thick arms soot stained and their faces tanned. Both wore leather aprons heavy enough to stop spear thrusts. One man hammered a length of glowing steel while sweat dripped from his shaved face.

The other apron-wearing man was red-faced, his chin concealed by a shovel of a beard. He brandished a pair of tongs while shouting at the third individual working at a bench.

"You insufferable little pisser!" the man with the shovel-styled beard yelled, jabbing the tongs. "Did I tell you to do that? Did I tell you I wanted a five weave? I did not! I said *four*. *Four* links, you deaf piece of shite. Why are you plaguing me this way? Why? You've wasted a full *day's* material on that mail shirt! A full day! Dying Seddon above. Start again. Again, I say."

The smaller man wasn't very small at all. Bare chested, blocky with muscle, with thick hair and a neatly trimmed beard, the armorer sat and waited, appearing utterly indifferent to the thundercloud raging over his shoulder.

The forge master, as Goll assumed him to be, gathered breath while waiting for a reaction from his initial volley.

Nothing came.

The armorer draped the beginnings of a mail shirt across a work table, next to a metal rod, cutters, and a small hill of iron ringlets. The fellow then straightened in his chair and, with a stoic expression, gazed ahead at nothing in particular, squinting in the daylight.

Goll stood at the forge's gate, waiting for the confrontation to pass.

The Kree's presence distracted the angry forge master. The man huffed, did a double take of the potential customer, and dropped his tongs in a water tub. With a withering glare at the armorer, the forge master walked over.

"Apologies for that," he muttered and slap-wiped his hands. He took a heartbeat to compose himself. "That little punce has been nothing but a thorn in my pisshole since the day we took him on. A *barbed* thorn."

The little punce studied his work, unconcerned with his employer.

"What's he done wrong?" Goll asked as the armorer picked up the hem of the mail shirt.

The forge master followed Goll's eyes and looked back. His face flared red with fury. "*Stop* that, you miserable shite scrub!" The forge master bounded across the floor and slammed the worktable with a hand. Ringlets jumped.

Any other person would have been startled. Some might have been embarrassed. A few would have flashed anger right back at the source while one or two might've even fought.

The man sitting at the table, however, did nothing. Eyes downcast, the armorer sucked on a tooth and waited for the latest barrage to pass overhead.

The forge master retreated a step, shaking with angry bewilderment. "The topper doesn't speak a word of the language," he explained. "If he does, he doesn't pay heed to what I say. Not a lick. Oddly enough, he understands 'done for the day,' which puzzles me to no end."

The armorer reached for a pair of pliers.

The forge master slammed the table again, and everything shivered.

The armorer didn't release the tool. Eyes still downcast, his chin lifted just a fraction. Goll detected the barest flicker of irritation.

"You see that?" asked the red-faced forge master. "You see? Not a word."

"Leave the lad alone," said the smithy as he flipped over the length of steel he was holding and inspected it. "You're only upsetting him."

That mollified the forge master. "*I'm* only upsetting him? *Me*? The ripe little bastard hasn't even *looked* at me since I started shouting at his gurry-rotting hole! He's just—"

The armorer once again attempted to work.

Bam! The forge master smashed the table hard enough for either bone or wood to break.

The armorer stopped and glanced away, at some point farther along the street.

"See!" the forge master shouted, gesturing at the man. "He doesn't listen! He *won't* listen. Saimon *below*."

"Ah, he just doesn't understand," the smithy reasoned. "He's doing things the way he's been taught."

"I know that!" the forge master screamed. "You think I *don't* know that! Dying Seddon! I know! And I don't *care* how he was taught! I only care about him doing what I *tell* him to do. And Seddon as my witness, he understands well enough. He understands. I've already showed him how to piece that shirt together, and what does he do?" Red-faced, he rattled his head to clear it.

"Perhaps Ajik knows of a better way," the smithy suggested, dropping one hammer for another.

"A *better way*?" the forge master nearly shrieked.

The smithy shrugged and focused on his work.

Goll studied Ajik. The man had a familiar look about him and a reserved but sturdy air of dignity. "Where are you from, good Ajik?"

The forge master waved his hands, breaking up the not-quite-yet-a-conversation. "There's nothing good about that tongueless little savage. I believe he's from the Territories. Or the Harudin. One of those damned places. He doesn't speak Sunjan. Or if he does, he chooses not to. I've tried talking to him. Tried talking plenty of times. All I get are grunts. Grunts the best of times and stares any other. Pissy little bastard. He understands firewater, though. Don't you, you unsightly stream of piss? Firewater, yes? You like much much, yes? And any other form of drink, for that matter. From the Black to the Gold and any other brewed cow piss in between, he'll pour it down his gullet."

The forge master fumed. "You know something? I don't need this little shagger. I don't. I've had enough of this git. You hear me? Off with you! Leave! Be gone! *Gone!*"

ABOUT THE BLOOD

The cords on the forge master's neck threatened to burst. He grabbed a second set of tongs and waved them about Ajik's frowning face, backing his head up on his shoulders. Unversed in Sunjan or not, the armorer wasn't unfit in the head. Sensing he'd been dismissed, Ajik stood with a distinguished grace rivaling royalty. He retrieved a gray shirt, pushed his chair in with great care, and looked about his person before selecting the best path.

"That's right, get on!" the forge master yelled. "You unfit *punce*—and don't think I'm paying you a single coin for this! Not one, bloody, gurry-dipped coin!"

Ajik walked into the crowded street.

"So you're releasing him?" Goll asked, keeping the armorer in sight.

"Releasing?" the red-faced forge master huffed, his anger subsiding. "I'm cursing him to Saimon's hells. Any one of them. Or all! That's even better. Hard enough to find anyone to do the work I need done these days, as quickly as I need it done." He thrust his tongs at Ajik's departing back. "*That's* what available. Shiftless rat-pig gurry from parts unknown. I'll tell you this—"

Goll left the ranting forge master and pursued Ajik into the masses of people.

"Ajik!" the Kree yelled. "Ajik!"

People parted, and the little armorer stopped and turned with a frown not entirely caused by sunlight.

Goll stopped before him. "You speak Sunjan?"

The man gave the blankest of looks.

"What about Kree then?" Goll asked, switching to his native language.

Nothing. However, Ajik didn't outright turn away.

"Those are my wagons," Goll pointed and explained, reverting back to Sunjan. "I'm with a house. A house of gladiators called the Ten . . ."

On impulse, Goll ceased talking and mimed working metal. He again pointed to the wagons. Then he signed Ajik joining them. The rudimentary message got through to the man as his attention switched from the transports to Goll. Ajik's back straightened as if he were taking a deep breath. He considered his options and, a heartbeat later, nodded cautiously and walked to the first wagon.

Goll placed a hand on the armorer's shoulder.

Dark eyes regarded the Kree's hand then his face. Releasing him, Goll gestured for the man to follow him to the second wagon.

Ajik reluctantly obeyed.

Goll led him to the wagon. When he pulled back the canvas covering the rear, the men inside stared at the newly acquired armorer.

Ajik, with that gaze of regal indifference, stared back.

"Little space in these beasts as it is," a sweating Muluk groaned from amongst the strongboxes. He glanced from the smaller man to Goll. "Did I hear you bellow? Something sounding like *Ajik*?"

"You did. Dying Seddon." Goll made a face. "Did you empty your guts in here, Muluk?"

"I did not."

"Then what's that smell?"

"I stuck my head outside and emptied my guts," Muluk explained, elbows to knees and his eyes looking dead. "Some might not have cleared the gate."

Annoyed, Goll drew back and inspected the wood. He shook his head. "Make room for him," he said, indicating Ajik.

"We're taking him along?" Muluk asked.

"Aye that."

"We'll have to get another wagon," Machlann added, sitting on a bench during the entire exchange.

Goll didn't rightly know what the trainer meant by that. The space was tight inside the wagon, perhaps even uncomfortably so, but they could make do. A bandaged Brozz sat next to the trainer, holding his midsection and leaning against one of the wagon's ribs. Sweat glistened upon the Sarlander's face, and a concerned Shan hovered nearby.

Goll reconsidered the extra wagon.

"So we're in the business of taking on castoffs, are we?" Muluk asked, drawing an arm across his forehead.

"We're all castoffs," Goll countered as a stoic Ajik sat amongst the men. "But if that man can work metal, then perhaps we can get Clavellus's forge going. With your help, that is."

"You're a hopeful one. I like that."

"I'm determined."

Muluk didn't comment.

Unimpressed, Goll released the canvas, and the men disappeared from sight. He made his way back to the first wagon and pulled himself up over the rear gate.

"Got him aboard, did you?" Clavellus asked.

"Aye that. We're off."

"Not quite, Master Goll," the taskmaster said. "I have a few extra errands to attend to, ones I neglected yesterday, being occupied and all. Nothing much, but I do have a list of purchases to make. Very quick, I assure you. Provisions, drink, clothing. Ah . . . gifts."

"Drink?" Torello asked, brightening. "What kind of drink?"

"Never you mind what kind of drink," Clavellus warned.

"I'll need something for the pain," the Sunjan protested. "To take my mind off my suffering."

"Koba will do that for you."

That silenced the injured man.

"You want to go to market?" Goll demanded of the taskmaster. "Now?"

Clavellus rested his head against the a wooden rib. "You've never been married, have you, Master Goll?"

7

Coin.

One was dead without it, in Grisholt's mind. Riches, so long denied because of woes in and out of the arena, were flooding his person with torrential force. The stable owner didn't allow it to sweep him away, however. He stood as defiant as a boulder in its glorious flow, parting it right down the middle, with fingers spread wide.

Or some such gurry.

Grisholt opened his blue eyes and faced the tailor's open window. The tailor—a well-groomed little fellow, finely dressed—measured off hands and fingers along the owner's outstretched arms. The same tailor had taken his measurements the day before. Grisholt stuck out his chin, little gray beard prominent, and stared. He'd been shopping all of yesterday until he bade his lads good night, providing them all with lodgings, food, and drink—well-earned rewards for their loyalty and their efforts. He instructed his men to enjoy themselves while he retired to a private alehouse room in the city's more sophisticated northern section. There, he feasted upon a magnificent haunch of beef, gravy, and soft vegetables while drinking Sunjan Black and Gold, as well as sweet firewater imported from places he couldn't pronounce.

All the while, he was graced by the company of a young lady he'd hired for the night.

Coin well spent.

That morning, he had awakened alone in his bed and decided he wanted more clothing, proper garments of fine silks and other handsomely colored fabrics that befitted his newfound wealth. What good was being rich if one wasn't willing to spend those riches? He also wanted to make a grand impression on the Gladiatorial Chamber when he met with them later. That was later, though.

Silks. Cottons. Shirts and breeches made of exotic materials from distant lands. He luxuriated in their feel against his skin. Golden chains. Silver rings. The brightest and the best. Food and drink, as well. The best part was Grisholt could afford everything and *more.*

Riches.

The finest drink there was.

"Allow me a little room around the middle," Grisholt said from one corner of his mouth, still staring ahead.

"Yes, Master Grisholt." The tailor fussed about his person like a bee inspecting the sweetest petals.

"Do you have any belts?"

"None at all, good sar, none at all. But there is a fine establishment just a short walk from here. I can provide directions if you're interested?"

Grisholt thought about it. "That would please me."

Brakuss leaned against a wall and studied the developing scene, his expression neutral, though secretly thankful his employer had changed his lavender-scented water for another not nearly as overpowering.

"Brakuss." Grisholt snapped his fingers.

"Master Grisholt?"

"How was your night?"

The one-eyed once gladiator tipped his head. "Harsh. But in the best of ways."

That put a smile on Grisholt's face. He'd paid every man accompanying him amounts owed from months before. He'd also provided an additional ten gold apiece for their patience. He could've well afforded thrice that sum, but keeping the dogs hungry and servile was best.

"We'll need to stop along the way," he said. "I wish to hire the services of some tradesmen. Carpenters. Stone and brick workers. The like. The villa needs repairs. Needs to be restored. To its former glory. I might even purchase a few new strongboxes. And more firewater."

Brakuss didn't mind the firewater himself.

"Remember all of that?" Grisholt muttered, not wishing to move, for fear of the tailor mistaking a measurement.

"I will, Master Grisholt."

"Good lad. Good. Am I forgetting anything?"

"Food, perhaps?" Brakuss suggested.

"You're right. Thank you. We'll secure provisions before we leave."

"Weapons and armor."

"Correct again." Grisholt nodded, inadvertently shaking and causing the tailor to withdraw until the tremor had passed. "Can't forget the very tools of the trade, can we?" the owner continued. "Seddon forbid. We'll stop by the market after the meeting. See what delights are for sale. Anything else?"

Brakuss shook his head. "Nothing I can think of."

"If you think of anything, let me know," Grisholt said with a note of bored nobility and returned to staring out the window, glimpsing passersby. He thought again about his remaining obligations for the day. The season had been extended, much to his delight, and his fortunes had most definitely changed for the better. A longer season meant more coin. Oh, he suspected the odds would no longer be in his favor, but he vowed better control with the potion's usage. He'd restrain himself, using just a sip when the time was right, just to throw off the other houses and the wagering spectators. Even if his fighters didn't partake of the potion, their opponents would still be fearful.

Fear of the Stable of Grisholt and its mighty gladiators.

Fear. Power. Coin.

And the occasional honeypot.

Life was good . . . and Grisholt meant to enjoy it. A dreamy expression fell over his wizened features. He lowered his arms when the tailor instructed him. The little man wrote notes on a slip of parchment. Grisholt shrugged, thinking about his estate and about hiring more servants, shapely young women, mostly, with voices sounding like the strings of hot fiddles.

A mysterious woodsy smell wafted into the store. Grisholt recognized the unpleasant odor right away and rolled his eyes. His peace had just come to a halt.

The ball-shaped owner of the School of Vorish dawdled upon the threshold before wandering inside. An evil smile split Vorish's piggish face.

"Grisholt," the owner said, dispensing with formal greetings. He moved closer, both hands jammed into his pants pockets, jingling unseen coin. That was Vorish. One could hear the wood-smoked asslicker before seeing him.

"Good Vorish," Grisholt replied, already tired of the plum-sized dog blossom.

"Doing some buying, I see."

"I am."

A scowling Brakuss moved toward the door, but Vorish paid him no mind.

A moment later, Grisholt understood why.

The light dimmed as a mountain of a warrior stuck his head inside, ducking to clear the frame. The sheer bulk darkened the room, and both Grisholt and Brakuss noticed how the newcomer blotted out the sun. There the man-mountain stood, on the threshold, replacing the door.

Picking at something in his ear and smiling, Vorish stopped before Grisholt. He squinted nearsightedly at the choice of clothing while breathing hard enough to make one believe he'd just run halfway across the city.

"That's one of my newest lads," Vorish huffed eagerly, staring down his nose at the rival owner.

"Is it?" Grisholt asked, not caring in the least.

"Name's Grigo. A real terror. A chopper if I've ever seen one."

"Hm."

"You've been doing well these past few matches, I see." Vorish huffed, smiling in his happy pig way.

"Been doing very well, good Vorish." Grisholt stroked his beard. "Daresay I'm doing very well indeed. Splendid, in fact. Wonderful. All happening at once. I almost think I'm dreaming."

Vorish nodded, beaming as if he knew a grand secret. "You certainly have poor old Razi in a rage."

"Poor old Razi should realize older dogs bite back."

That tidbit of wisdom brightened Vorish's piggish features, yet his little eyes remained narrowed. "You're doing something, aren't you, Grisholt?"

Grisholt cocked an eyebrow. *Straight to the bloody parts.* One had to admire that.

"You're doing something," Vorish repeated slyly. "In the Pit."

"I am indeed."

"What is it?"

"I'm winning."

"Ohhh, you're winning, all right. Everyone can see you're winning. It's just that... it's you, Grisholt. You hardly ever win. Everyone knows you hardly ever win. Yet here you are. Winning. And winning often. It's quite puzzling."

Feigning boredom, Grisholt shrugged. "Unfortunate. Well, always a pleasure talking."

"Oh, Grisholt." Vorish tsked, squinting as if to squeeze water from his eyes. He leered with secret knowledge, revealing sparse teeth. "We *both* know you're doing something. Trouble is, I just haven't discovered what. Not yet. But I will."

ABOUT THE BLOOD

The coins in Vorish's pocket ceased jingling as he stepped much closer, invading Grisholt's personal space. "As sure as a dog sniffs at a cow kiss, I will."

The words hung in the air, provoking, daring Grisholt to say otherwise. Behind Vorish, Brakuss stood at attention.

"I think . . . I've had enough of you, Vorish," Grisholt said and leaned into the fat man's face, coming uncomfortably close.

Upon those words, Brakuss gripped his short sword's hilt.

In the doorway, Vorish's bodyguard Grigo did the same, scowling at the one-eyed warrior.

The tailor, not three paces away from the unfolding confrontation, glanced worriedly at each man in turn, very much aware of the escalating tension *inside* his store.

"A shame," an unblinking Vorish said. His cheek twitched. A pocket of coin jingled. "I'm very interested in you these days, Grisholt. Very interested. You believe we don't suspect you're twisting these matches to your advantage. You believe we can't see it—probably think you're being clever. That you've fooled everyone. But I know you. I *know* you're doing something wicked. You have to be. You haven't changed anything. There's no way your lads are winning because of your taskmaster or trainers. So what is it, I wonder? I wonder. I'll find out eventually. You just wait—"

"Mind your tongue," Grisholt cautioned with grave sincerity, staring into Vorish's plump face.

The piggish owner didn't heed the warning, though. "I'll find out, Grisholt. I promise I will. Because there's no way a miserable ass licker like yourself could ever win a string of fights. Not like you are now. Not with the half-dead mongrels that lick and sleep at your feet. The sty you call a house, or should I say, a *stable*, hasn't drawn any real talent in years. And recognizing skill is a skill in itself, one that your trainers are *not* aware of. Everyone knows that. *You* know that."

Grisholt studied the other's face, noting hairs in places he'd failed to see before. "My dogs will latch onto yours soon enough, fat man. Then we'll see . . . which breed has the better bite."

"Oh *ho*," Vorish exclaimed, eyes flickering with starlight. "I'll know by then. Well before then, you classless sliver of maggot shite."

That was the absolute end of the conversation.

"Brakuss," Grisholt whispered, barely containing his anger.

Things happened very quickly.

Grigo yanked his blade free before Brakuss could pull his own steel.

The tailor shrieked like a five-year-old boy and bolted for safety.

Brakuss was no small man, and though he was no longer active in the Pit, he was far from helpless.

And more than willing to break a few bones if needed.

Grigo stabbed for Brakuss, but the once pit fighter parried the blade, sending it into the post of the doorframe. Grigo tried to withdraw the blade but lost his grip, disarmed by the close quarters.

Brakuss closed and punched the towering brute, snapping a fist into the mountain's stomach. The big man buckled to his knees.

"Grigo!" Vorish shouted, retreating from Grisholt and suddenly very mindful of where Brakuss was standing in the room.

The one-eyed bodyguard, however, focused on the true threat. He lifted Grigo's head and cracked his sword's pommel across a grimacing jaw, snapping the lout's head to the side.

Grigo toppled.

A large spool of the deepest red fabric stopped Vorish's retreat. He pressed his back against the material, panting and staring like a pig facing its butcher. Ragged squeals escaped the man.

Grisholt folded his arms, delighted at how events were turning out. "I must say, Vorish," he declared, speaking as if he'd expected no other outcome, "seeing you piss your trousers is worth the time spent in your presence."

All color drained the owner's chubby face. For a heartbeat, he sputtered, tangled by what curse to unleash first.

Brakuss did not let him.

The bodyguard yanked Grigo's head up by the hair. He slipped his blade underneath the big warrior's chin and looked to Grisholt for the order.

The old man loved him for it.

Grisholt held up exactly one finger. "Now, now, good Brakuss," he reproached gently. "I'm sure this was all a stupid misunderstanding. Isn't that right, fat man?"

Vorish blinked at the jab. His chest heaved while his brow and cheeks positively sparkled with sweat. A rancid smell was growing around the owner, a pungent, unwashed stink of body odor that Grisholt recognized immediately. *Fear*. He doubted if Vorish's little legs could carry him past Brakuss. If Vorish wanted to try, however, Grisholt would certainly watch.

"Yes, a misunderstanding," Vorish finally said.

"A stupid misunderstanding," Grisholt corrected.

The man didn't reply right away.

"Say it," Grisholt commanded.

"Damn you, Grisholt."

"What did you say to me?"

"You heard—"

"Brakuss?"

"A stupid misunderstanding," Vorish blurted.

Grisholt relaxed, smiling pleasantly. "You see, good Brakuss?" Then his features darkened as he glared at his rival. "Except . . . Vorish insulted me just now. In public." He jabbed a thumb at the tailor, who had retreated to a corner deep within his shop.

"That's something I can't allow," Grisholt continued. "No matter who you are. Who you think you are."

"You insulted me!" Vorish fired back.

"And you accused me of wrongdoing," Grisholt said, badly feigning wonder at the man's gall. "Apologize. Now."

Noises from the street filled that gap of silence. Vorish's face quivered and grew to an even deeper hue of red—from fear or rage, Grisholt didn't know. Didn't care. That fragrant ass-crack stink was certainly growing, however.

Then Vorish composed himself. The effort was impressive.

"I'm sorry, Grisholt," he said, double chins quivering, his hands no longer fiddling with coin. "I'm sorry."

Grisholt sighed, undecided, putting on a rare performance. "I'd believe you except, well, I know what a worm's tongue you have, good Vorish."

Brakuss leered with evil humor, still holding on to Grigo's hair. For good measure, he removed the blade from the fallen gladiator's throat . . . and smacked the side of his head, dropping the man.

Vorish gawked at the brutality.

Grisholt appeared unconcerned. "You listen to me, fat man. You listen."

"I'm listening."

"I'll be speaking with the Street Watch about this incident. You insulted me in public. Your man pulled steel first. I have a witness. Bad form, Vorish. Very bad form. Where do you get these dog blossoms, anyway? Hm? Such savagery. I believe there are laws in place to prevent such acts of violence, aren't there?"

"There are," Vorish acknowledged quietly, guiltily. "There are."

Grisholt didn't believe the man's sullen act. "Brakuss," he asked, "how are you feeling this day?"

The once pit fighter shrugged.

"You're fully within your rights to kill that pig bastard at your feet."

That seemed to brighten the bodyguard's disposition.

The tailor, however, cringed.

"Well?" Grisholt asked his bodyguard.

Brakuss stepped away from the fallen man.

"Well." Grisholt smiled at the trapped owner. "Your man lives. By the grace and mercy of my own. You should thank him."

Vorish's eyes popped open at the suggestion.

Such rare sport. Grisholt thought. He could torment his rival all day. "Thank. Him."

"Thank you," Vorish muttered.

ABOUT THE BLOOD

"His name's Brakuss."

"Thank you, Brakuss. Ah, *good* Brakuss."

The bodyguard didn't bother replying, his attention fixed on the man struggling upon the floor.

"Are we done?" Grisholt asked of the tailor.

The tailor nodded.

"Are *we* done?" Grisholt directed at Vorish.

"Yes."

"Then know this, you unchewed piece of gurry. I look forward to seeing your dogs on the sands. Expect no quarter. You wish to discover what we're doing? You just saw it. *Spirit*, Vorish. Spirit is what we have, and in great amounts. Resolve, as well. And the skill to finish any and all contests to the bloody end. You'll experience it firsthand when my hounds face your maggots. Firsthand. In a more civilized contest of arms. Perhaps you'll have better fortune there. I doubt it, however."

Having said his mind, Grisholt smiled his most menacing smile, the one reserved for true enemies, and stepped away from Vorish's fidgeting person.

"We'll return another day for our clothing," Grisholt informed the tailor. He then regarded Vorish once more, who realized he'd live after all.

"And Vorish? Change your perfumed water. You smell like cat's piss."

With that, Grisholt turned and strolled out the door.

Brakuss stopped, studied the sweating Vorish, and threatened to punch him.

Vorish flinched with a whimper.

Pleased, Brakuss followed his employer outside.

8

Standing between light beams streaming from slits cut into the stone walls, the towering bulk of Dark Curge loomed. Curge glowered at the Gladiatorial Chamber's raised dais and the empty seats there. He'd been staring at that polished panel of red wood for far too long, willing the members to magically appear. Curge despised waiting. It made him irritable. He wore black trousers for the meeting, as well as a white shirt parted at the sternum, revealing a dull gray thicket of chest hair. That broad V in the fabric did little to cool him off, and a sweaty glaze caused everything to cling. Several times, he rubbed his considerable paunch and noted how his shirt—clean that morning—had become damp with his own oozing juice.

The house owner had better things to do than wait for those aging frames of meat to appear. The Chamber members fancied themselves royalty of a most brutal realm and carried themselves as such. They had studied King Juhn for far too long, in his opinion. In any case, Curge wasn't happy.

He wasn't the only one.

Other owners had gathered about the chamber, casting shadows upon the creamy marble floor. No one bothered conversing, perhaps sensing the growing tension. Dark Curge's eyes flickered about, taking in the collection of self-styled rogues and arrogant asslickers fully invested in the games and calling themselves owners. Most of them sickened Curge while others merely annoyed. Gastillo avoided him, standing to the far right while Nexus occupied a space near the back, well away. That suited the Dark One just fine. Sharing a viewing box overseeing the sands was enough for him, but since the fighting season had been extended, Curge would have to endure the gold-faced punce and villainous wine merchant even longer. Gastillo was bearable, but Nexus . . . No doubt he would murder Nexus well before the final eight. The wine merchant's smug arrogance and self-professed expertise on games he was only just embracing annoyed Curge—greatly.

The big owner scuffed a boot, took a breath, and released it with a flutter. His impatience was swelling to dangerous limits. He stopped looking at the others. They'd all received the same message the previous day. The Chamber invited them to their court that morning, to hear and address any questions and concerns regarding the season's surprising extension.

The night had been a long one for Curge. He most certainly had questions, and he'd get answers.

The main doors attracted his attention. He thought he heard a sound, perhaps heralding the arrival of the House of Ten. The Free Trained maggots hadn't yet appeared. Curge wondered why. The brazen he-bitches were about the city. Bezange, with his usual weaselly nonchalance, had brought the news of their drunken adventures to Curge's attention the night before. Clavellus's blatant dallying in the city's drinking establishments had infuriated Dark Curge so much that he sent away his female companionship for the night.

And he enjoyed his female companionship.

The very notion of that old bastard cavorting and prancing about Arbin's Row, boasting, toasting, and otherwise pissing in Dark's Curge's face, caused a muscle to twitch in the one-armed owner's forehead. That bearded topper had defied his warning, and the knowledge salted his innards.

Ancient Tilo wandered over to Curge's side, hobbling along with a walking stick, distracting him from simmering thoughts and dangerous impulses. Of all the owners, Tilo was one of the remaining few who remembered a better age of gladiatorial combat, back when Curge's father ruled the Pit and when Clavellus was a taskmaster in his employment. Vavar Slavol could also recall those golden years, Curge supposed, but that stable owner was not present. Slavol was close to death and constantly bedridden, another old warrior almost caught by time. Lately, his son was overseeing the well-being of the stable and was suffering for it, in Curge's opinion.

Tilo stopped alongside the Dark One's greater frame and gave him a once-over. "Strange business, Curge," he remarked, keeping his voice low, his great beard barely moving.

Curge thought he saw pieces of food speckling that gray hanging mass. "Strange business," he muttered in agreement, not really wanting to talk.

"Something's afoot, mark my words," Tilo persisted, his voice fine and clear and probably capable of carrying a tune. "Never in all my days have I heard of a season being lengthened. Or the rats of the king's dungeons being released in the Pit. Dark days, Curge. Dark days."

Curge grunted and focused upon the door behind the dais, knowing the Chamber members would enter from there.

"Halfway through the season, no less." Tilo rattled his head as he ruminated aloud. "The king's behind it all. Guaranteed. Old Juhn has his hand in this. Right up to the shoulder. And he's holding onto his pisser with the other."

Curge grunted again, a touch distracted, wondering how to escape the ancient topper. Tilo should've died ten years before, but somehow the dusty dog blossom managed to keep living. Even the man's breathing sounded like rusty ass whistles.

Tilo leaned in close and whispered, "Keep staring where you're staring, but when you have a moment, you see that preening kog over there?"

ABOUT THE BLOOD

Tilo was speaking of Grisholt. The lowly owner had entered the chamber earlier with his chin hoisted just a little bit higher, his clothing just a little brighter, reveling in his recent run of fortune within Sunja's Pit. Curge didn't really have to see Grisholt to know he'd arrived. The last time the main doors had opened, a breeze wafted through, carrying the stink of whatever damned perfumed water that walking shite trough habitually wore.

Curge rubbed the dry skin covering the stump of his left forearm. "I try not to, good Tilo."

That brought Tilo's furry face in closer, almost placing an ear to the Dark One's chest, far too close for Curge's taste. He forced himself to not step back.

"That bastard's been doing well over the last few matches," Tilo whispered, his lips barely moving in that foul face bush. "Doing *very* well. Not sure what his trainers have been doing to incite that level of rage amongst his dogs, but they're doing it. Brutally effective as well. Have you ever seen the like?"

Curge scowled and shook his head. Too much was happening this season to keep track of it all.

"My lads have spotted him," Tilo continued, his white grub of a tongue flicking, wetting his lips, which Curge did not need to see. "Him and his pack of scroff meandering about the markets. Strutting like they just sampled the finest honeypots. Spotted them last night and this morning. That one in particular stayed in a very good alehouse last night. All paid in fresh coin. He's tossing gold about like dirt. And here I was, hoping this would be the dog's final season. How Seddon grabs one's bells and gives them a twist, eh?"

Tilo raised a sound point. Seddon did work in strange ways. Curge's nose twitched. The old man's rancid breath assaulted him like some foul black cheese dug out from a dead man's hole. He also glimpsed the sludge gathered between the eroded marbled nubs the old man called teeth.

"Look at him when you have the chance," Tilo murmured, the words damn near poisonous. "Look. Those are new clothes he's wearing. Went to a tailor and ordered an entire new wardrobe. Even purchased buckets of that damned scent he's wearing."

"It's usually," Curge took a breath, "lavender."

"That's not lavender," Tilo whispered bitterly, causing Curge to wince. "That's some other scent. Probably squeezed from some exotic root resembling a rat's topper. Who's he trying to fool here?"

The chamber's side door opened, and the distinguished members filed in, a dull stream of white robes, balding heads, and discolored scars. Their entrance distracted Tilo, allowing Curge to retreat from the noxious hole of the old man's mouth.

The members took their seats without ceremony, appearing somewhat reluctant to face the owners. Master Odant, the recognized speaker for the Chamber, sat and studied the gathered men with all the interest of discovering insect bites upon his ballsack. Odant leaned over the panel low enough that his short gray whiskers almost touched the wooden surface.

"Illustrious owners of houses, schools, and stables," he said and finished with a throaty rumble. "We, the Chamber, are both pleased and honored by your visit this morning. Without further delay, we will get to the matter at hand—the recent decree you all received."

Straight to the meat. Curge wondered if Odant believed he was fooling anyone with his speech. The Chamber members didn't want to be there either, but they were using the pretense of appearing mindful of the owners' time, just to keep the meeting short.

"King Juhn," Odant announced with a throat-clearing rattle, "wishes the season to continue for the foreseeable future, until such a time he deems suitable to conclude the event. In order to accommodate these additional days and to prevent the expected toll upon your resources—meaning your gladiators—the king has graciously allowed his dungeons to be farmed for additional participants. Every thief, cutthroat, and wanderer imprisoned within the king's dungeons, who still possesses the capacity for combat, will be transported to the Pit and await their time before the crowds. We will tentatively schedule ten matches a day, perhaps twelve even, but the house gladiators will be scheduled for no more than half that on any given day. The criminals will be used as meat. A bloody spectacle for the crowds. A prelude to the real pit fighters."

The original role of the Free Trained, *Curge thought with contempt.*

"This is new for you," Odant carried on, "and us."

Piggish Vorish raised his hand.

Odant stared daggers at him before finally, and with great reluctance, nodding. "Master Vorish."

Vorish hitched his hands to his belt, something which he couldn't jingle. "The question that rises to my mind is . . . why?"

Odant continued to stare unkindly at the owner.

"Why exactly is the king doing this?" Vorish asked with a trace of impudence. "I'm curious."

Curge didn't like Vorish, but he appreciated the punce asking the right question.

"Because it's the king's will," the Chamber member replied stoically.

Vorish looked amusingly skeptical at the reply, a gesture Odant clearly didn't appreciate.

Nexus spoke up, his voice a touch impatient. "What about finances, then? This will impact my resources. I haven't prepared for a longer season."

Curge smirked inwardly. Of them all, Nexus would unquestionably be the *least* affected by the games' ongoing costs. The merchant obviously didn't want to crack open an extra coffer when he'd already counted out one or two to cover the season.

"The king will grant extra funding if you require it," Odant answered. "Depending on the nature."

That got Curge's attention.

"What kind of funding?" Nexus asked.

"To be determined. Likely armor, cost of weapons, food . . . anything to aid a house through the longer season. As long as the house's finances are in order."

Taxes, Curge realized, and whether or not the owners had paid them.

"And King Juhn still intends to award gladiators and the houses?" Vorish asked.

"He does." Odant nodded imperiously. "Fully."

"Until this mysterious time when he's had enough?"

"That is correct."

"And our gladiators' records? What of them?"

Odant frowned, growing impatient. "You mean their victories and losses? And how it will affect their standings?"

"For the final eight, yes."

"In the past, only the gladiators with the best records have advanced to the final sixteen, the final eight, and onward. With this extended season, that will remain unchanged. However, in the past, the best records usually belonged to the undefeated. We anticipate some gladiators will sustain losses leading up to the season's final days. As long as he's able to fight when the time arrives and, of course, he's not dead, one or two defeats should not affect a fighter from advancing to the last sixteen. From there, however, one loss will remove the gladiator from competition. Getting to that point will be the challenge. Consider it as . . . a true test of skill. And endurance."

Odant offered a tight-lipped smile, allowing that last statement to sink in.

"What about these criminals, then?" Vorish asked, again taking the floor. "And the Jackals? You have Nordish Jackals in your cells? Underfoot?"

"We do indeed have a handful of our Nordish enemies," Odant answered with a darkening scowl. He cleared his throat. "Captured prisoners of war who have festered underneath the city for some time. King Juhn especially wishes these prisoners to fight. And perish. Preferably in spectacular fashion. He believes seeing a few Nordish heads rolling upon the sands will be uplifting for the audiences."

That set Vorish to thinking, but not before he cast a venomous glare in Grisholt's direction. The look was not lost upon Curge.

Razi, of the House of Razi, stepped forth. "Our lads won't have to lower themselves to fight common criminals, will they?" he asked, lifting the white robes covering his bulbous belly and frame, from shoulders to sandals. "Or even the Jackals? It's bad enough having to endure the Free Trained. There's always a risk involved. Nothing certain in the Pit."

A Chamber member leaned into Odant and whispered in his only ear.

Odant roused his vocal cords once again, as if they'd quickly gather rust if left unused. "We don't know at this time. We are considering it. Especially if a prisoner excels in the games. If a man somehow survives several of the Pit's contests, we may decide to schedule a regular gladiator . . . for the sole purpose of dispatching the upstart."

That bit of news received headshakes and groans amongst the owners.

"King Juhn wishes to see some semblance of sport, not straight-out executions," Odant growled, not appreciating the dissent.

"The king's rarely in attendance these days," commented Burco Ustda, of the wealthy House of Ustda. The man was middle-aged and moderately handsome with well-combed blond hair and, unlike half of the owners, in some degree of physical fitness. His optimism, however, strained Curge's nerves.

Odant didn't appear pleased. "If your gladiators are matched against a prisoner, be it criminal or Jackal, inform them to butcher the man in whatever fashion pleases them. Make it a single thrust to the heart or take their head clean off. Make it exciting. Memorable. However . . . understand that the prisoners *will* be armed. They *will* fight back. To the best of their ability. If your gladiators can kill one quickly, then so much the better, but don't *play* with them. I can't stress that enough. Especially the Jackals. Whatever you might think of them, just remember, above all else, they are *soldiers*. They *will* have training. And probably some amount of experience."

Curge could no longer contain himself. "This all smells like shite, Master Odant. First you grant permission for a rabble of Free Trained to establish a house and now *this*? What direction does this take the sport? Where's it leading? Where will it end?"

Odant's beard lifted in a half smirk. "No doubt you've looked around you, Master Curge, and taken notice there's no representative from that particular house. We are well aware of the . . . tension . . . the House of Ten might cause amongst the games' more established houses and its veterans. Simply put, however, they're here because they paid the fee. And truth be known, we didn't believe they'd actually survive, thinking *your* gladiators"—Odant included all the owners with a nod—"were superior. We still think that way. It shouldn't be a problem for your fighters to decimate the Ten. Decisively. However, that hasn't happened. Has it?"

Odant's phlegmy tone dripped scorn, and Curge didn't appreciate it. Worst, he was embarrassed by the rhetorical question. The Chamber was correct. The House of Ten should've been wiped clean from the games long ago.

"Not yet," Curge granted, his blood simmering.

"In fact," Odant continued, working that dagger into a raw wound, "as of yesterday, I think we were all surprised by the skill displayed by the Ten's fighters. Very surprised. Their numbers defeated a pair of house gladiators. The one called Junger caught our attention in particular. Yes, we're very aware of what he did yesterday. Did any of you know that no other gladiator in the illustrious history of the Pit has ever fought *three* opponents in one day and *lived* to speak of it? Well, you know one now. You might calm yourselves by saying he only defeated Free Trained and a single house gladiator on that afternoon. Some measure of comfort might be pulled from that. From our perspective, it's still a mockery of the games."

ABOUT THE BLOOD

With one scalding breath, Odant reprimanded them all.

"Think of it. A Free Trained whelp has made ... history. Of the most memorable kind. Let it be known we won't record yesterday's episode, but please. *Please*. On behalf of the Chamber"—Odant eyed them all with stony countenance—"don't let it happen again."

The closing remark left the assembled owners silent. Some fidgeted uncomfortably, glancing here and there. Someone cleared his throat. His own face and pride burning, Curge glanced at a wall, wishing he'd never heard of the House of Ten—or a hellion called Junger.

Odant came to life once more. "Now then, are there any other questions?"

No one spoke.

His golden face gleaming, Gastillo raised his hand and cleared his cheesepipe.

"Master Gastillo," Odant said.

"When exactly will these prisoners fight, Master Odant?"

The Chamber member didn't hesitate. "Today."

9

Qualtus, the games' official orator, stood in his podium and contemplated the day's schedule. He was in a sour mood. The very thought of criminals fouling the sanctity of the Pit rotted his guts right and proper. Once again, he wondered why they were bringing criminals to the games. It was beyond his understanding. He didn't mind a longer season. Have them fight right up to winter, was his opinion. The games were his opportunity to shine, to set the theatre, to conjure grand images and quicken the blood. Time crawled by when the fighting season ended, when he retired to tend to his gardens in the east.

Here was where he wanted to be.

Not with *this* rabble, though.

Still, the games went on. Qualtus studied the extravagant viewing box fashioned from rich hardwoods and polished to a very fine shine. Banners of color drooped and waved in the early afternoon breeze, drawing attention to the magnificent platform. King Juhn, however, was not in attendance. The king had appeared at the beginning of the games but was absent of late. Qualtus gave it no further thought. His orders came from the Chamber, who acted upon King Juhn's words.

ABOUT THE BLOOD

An itch took him then, along his ribs, and he scratched them through his robes. After fixing his clothing, he checked the names once again.

Right. Got them.

On with the sport.

And the theatre.

"Good ladies and men of the arena, I bid you *welcome* to the day's events. And I have news to share on behalf of the Gladiatorial Chamber of Sunja and his righteous and glorious eminence, King Juhn. Our wise and magnificent ruler has deemed the fighting season is a most special one this year, exceptional on a scale so grand that he wishes to extend the games past the events gone by. For this, we rejoice."

The gathered multitude of faces cheered weakly. Cloth tarps high above the stands fluttered, providing shade for less than half the people while the sun grilled the rest. A breeze blew across the spectators, but not enough to make the afternoon any more comfortable. Some people coughed, waiting for more.

"And yet, another surprise. King Juhn has decided to rid himself of the lice infesting his dungeons. He has graciously permitted the Chamber to transfer those prisoners most capable of combat to the Pit so that they may die for your amusement. Black-hearted killers. Thieves. Corrupters. Rapists and other villainous gurry. They'll no longer be executed in the dark but will die in the light, upon each other's sword. And axe. And spear. Carnage of a most desperate nature will lead into the formal matches of the day. Enjoy them, good people of the Pit."

Another half-hearted cheer bubbled from the masses, as tepid as swamp water. They were smarter than Qualtus expected. They knew there was no telling what level of sport those caged animals might deliver. Truth be known, Qualtus had no idea himself, but he didn't trouble himself with such negative-minded scroff. He had a job to do.

"It is my greatest pleasure to introduce the first of such matches." Qualtus lowered his voice to a menacing boom and gestured toward the sands. "This man has rotted in darkness for sixteen years. Sixteen years in the dark. Guilty of murder, rape, and thievery. He is, by all accounts, an animal most foul. A leech upon the world's rosy red ass. Is it any wonder we wish to be done with him?"

Another rumble from less-than-enthused spectators.

Qualtus didn't blame them. He had nothing to work with, really. Sorcerers of his particular talents needed much better material. All he had were hellions squaring off against hellions, both equally hated by the crowds. There was no theatre here. Only . . . scroff.

Ever the professional, however, the orator carried on, determined to conjure *something*.

"And now, returned to the light, he is Torric! Of Sunja!"

The iron and timber maw that was the western portcullis cranked upward. A single man stepped through, barefoot, crouched, and wearing only a loincloth. Stained by ash, sweat, and filth, Torric grimaced at the bright sun overhead and jabbed a short sword at the sky. He screeched and babbled nonsense, as if being on the arena floor blasted his murderous mind and made him unfit.

The audience greeted Torric's entrance with a startling roar of undiluted hate and curses.

Even introducing the maggot left Qualtus's mouth with a bad taste. He sighed, barely managing to hide his disdain for the man.

"His opponent," he started once again, back in his orator's role. "A son of Sunja no more. Another killer of innocents and a thief of livestock. He existed in darkness for five years before being pulled back into the light. I give you . . . Nozo!"

The opposing portcullis opened, and an identically dressed prisoner deftly stepped onto the sands. Nozo beheld the majesty of the arena and seemed to enjoy the moment despite the coming fight for survival. He held a short sword angled toward the sands.

"Begin!" Qualtus roared.

The prisoners, however, did not.

The one called Torric regarded his opponent and, still babbling, decided to sit on the arena floor. He thrust his blade into the sand, letting it stand.

Nozo, perhaps realizing what was expected of him, smiled widely and held his arms to the heavens.

More curses scorched the air. A deluge of pure contempt rained down upon the combatants.

Dying Seddon, Qualtus thought, one hand drifting to his forehead. He was barely able to think in that racket.

The two prisoners, however, were not motivated by the angry masses and made no attempt to engage each other. With his legs crossed, Torric rocked back and forth, sometimes clawing at his head. Nozo blew kisses to the people cursing his name, which was the whole arena. He turned in slow circles, kicking sand at times, and took practice slices at the air. Occasionally, he glanced at his foe, just to ensure his adversary wasn't doing anything dastardly.

After a few heartbeats, Torric uncrossed his legs, stood up, promptly unsheathed his manhood, and pissed upon the sands.

That stirred the crowds to an even greater wrath.

Even Qualtus stood in shock and stared. Such actions weren't right at *all*.

"Look!" a voice cried out from the stands. "*Look!* He's emptying the bull! The *bull!*"

"No one wants to see your topper, old man!" another shouted.

"Fight, you bastards, *fight!*"

"Kill him!"

"What's this gurry! Bring out a couple of thrashers!"

"This's bloody unfit!"

And on it went.

Qualtus had no control over the pit fighters once they'd been released, but he was sure . . .

The rising of the westerly portcullis distracted his line of thought.

A single Skarr emerged, impassive, bound in a mail shirt and armor plating. The sun scintillated off his metal adornments.

The crowds cheered, loud enough to startle the Orator a second time.

The Skarr's impassive visor studied the two idle criminals. The soldier's bared sword shone in the sun's dusty glare. For a moment, the Skarr didn't move, watching the pair like a venomous teacher. At the other end of the arena, Nozo noted the cheering crowds and tensed, recognizing the danger. Torric kept his back to the Skarr, occupied with kicking fresh sand over his piss puddle.

The Skarr marched toward Torric, shield hanging off one arm, sword swinging from the other.

The crowds applauded, expecting a fight at last.

Far from it.

For whatever reason, Torric remained unmoved by the cheering. He finally glanced over his shoulder and saw the Skarr, but instead of grabbing his weapon, the prisoner ignored him. He sat, cross-legged once again, and watched the approaching soldier.

He made no move to defend himself.

And the Skarr, once within striking distance, displayed a cold, consummate professionalism and stabbed the man through the chest.

The cheering became deafening. Even Qualtus allowed himself a half smile.

The Skarr yanked his blade free of the dead man and let the body topple. He looked at the second criminal, and the audience's screaming reached an even higher note.

Nozo hefted his sword, meaning to fight.

Like a haunted automaton from a forgotten age, the Skarr relentlessly marched toward Nozo. The soldier crossed the arena's midway point, sunlight gleaming off his armor.

Seeing that formidable figure walking for him, Nozo changed his mind and backed away, to the north of the arena. There, he had a change of heart yet again, as if realizing the Pit's features didn't allow any kind of terrain advantage.

The Skarr marched forward, closing the distance.

ABOUT THE BLOOD

Nodding at the soldier, Nozo smiled and raised his sword, welcoming him.

When the Skarr got within Nozo's striking range, the criminal lunged.

The Skarr got his shield up and bashed aside the clumsy attempt. Nozo landed on his knees, and the crowds exploded with cheers. Nozo raised his blade up to high guard.

The Skarr lopped off that hand at the wrist.

Nozo screamed and fell back.

Wasting no time, the Skarr nailed half a length of steel into the criminal's guts, pinning him to the ground. Nozo bucked, spasmed, and became still. The Skarr pulled his weapon free and repeated the stabbing, through the dead man's heart.

The crowds adored him for it.

Expecting no fanfare but receiving his share, the Skarr walked to the closest portcullis. The gate rose while the audience continued to shout praises on a job well done.

The soldier disappeared into the shadows.

Qualtus decided to put that shameful display from his mind and concentrate on the next pairing.

The next pair of criminals condemned to the Pit weren't much better.

Neither man could handle a short sword. The two combatants circled and flailed at each other well out of arm's length. They danced around the sands while the crowds voiced their growing impatience. The jeers summoned yet another Skarr onto the sands, but whether it was the same soldier as before was unknown.

The prisoners, realizing the Skarr meant to kill them both, quickly joined forces. They stalked the professional. The quick transition from opponents to allies actually interested the crowds, and they cheered for the unexpected twist of events.

The Skarr closed with the two criminals, looking from one to the other.

The criminals attacked.

One man had his sword arm removed at the shoulder in a burst of blood, and while his death cries echoed throughout the Pit, his partner had his cheesepipe opened to the bone. They dropped around the city guard, who waited until they were both dead.

Again, the Skarr departed while the crowd's praises echoed throughout the arena.

A pensive Qualtus, on the other hand, sighed and drummed one finger off his lips. He inspected his schedule, wondering about the next pairing of dungeon maggots. In one way, he supposed it couldn't get any worse.

He prayed to Seddon all the same.

10

Runson possessed half a rack of yellow teeth, which were currently twisted into an offended snarl. He scratched at his bare belly hanging over his belt and below the leather X that crossed his chest. That little bit of armor marked him as a king's jailor. It was bad enough to be sweating below ground amongst a pack of caged savages, but to learn that they couldn't even *fight* well enough . . .

Disappointing. Upsetting even. He felt it reflected badly upon his work.

So Runson sent out the third offering to the Pit, urging them onward with a string of inventive threats, only to later receive word that the maggots had performed quite badly.

Quite badly was being generous.

Unlike the previous two matches, one of the dogs in the third pairing actually managed to stab the other. However, instead of finishing his foe, the would-be victor wasted time by raising his arms and basking in the audience's cheers. Only the spectators saw the left-for-dead man crawl forward and plunge his sword into his killer's ass.

Both bastards died squirming.

Runson took that one personally.

"You worthless piss stains!" he bellowed as he marched up and down the dungeon halls. "*Unfit*. You're worse than unfit.

Maggots are more fit than you. Perhaps you don't understand what's at stake here. You have the *opportunity* . . . to die like a man. A man! Not some lick of gurry who deserves a lance shoved through their dog blossom! You killed and pillaged and Seddon above only knows what other horrors you did to land here. Yet you're swinging steel like a bunch of slack-holed he-bitches! You're going to perish, eventually, you know that, so use your last few breaths and do something useful out there! Fight! Damn you, fight! You brazen, dew-spraying kogs! You sour asslickers! Fight, else I spear the lot of you in your cells, one right after the other, through your staring eyes. So fight!"

And on he ranted, becoming quite red in the face.

"What's he saying?" Heelslik asked in the Nordish tongue, puzzled at the jailor's fury. He lifted his hairy head, black eyes glinting like marble. He couldn't understand the Sunjan tongue in the least.

"Ah." Rullik held up a hand and listened to translate, his bald head wrinkled in concentration. "Ah, he's telling them . . . to fight in the Pit. That the last few matches were, ah, lacking. That if we do not fight, he'll execute us all. By lancing us through our eyes."

"Oh."

Hearing the conversation of his nearest companions, Arrus's forehead rested against the bars of his cell. He scratched at his thick beard and looked to Heelslik across the way.

Head jailor Balazz appeared then, a man much larger than the one called Runson but dressed the same way. Unlike Runson, Balazz had shaved his head down to the quick, removing all hair and leaving no place for unwanted lice. He marched past the glowing braziers lighting the dungeon corridor. A troop of Skarrs followed him. The jailors met and had a brief but heated discussion, the words slinging by Arrus in a stream of gibberish. Rullik, the Norjos Norseman who'd spent enough time in a Sunjan dungeon to learn the sly-sounding language of his captors, had revealed the jailors' names to his Nordish cousins, along with a few other items of note.

It had passed the time.

Now, however, Arrus needed no translation to know Balazz was every bit as furious as Runson.

The head jailor's eyes studied the caged prisoners. He proceeded to Heelslik's cage and pointed. A shout, and a dozen or so Skarrs surged to the cell door.

"They're going to take you," Rullik shouted.

Heelslik laughed, the sound disturbing yet uplifting.

"Arrus," the Jackal yelled over the screech and yank of the iron door. "I'll be back shortly. I'll change the tunes of these bastards."

"Show them hell, Jackal!" Rullik shouted.

Arrus wanted to give his own well-wishes, but a Skarr rapped a sword against the bars of his cell, warning him to step back.

Which he quietly did.

Qualtus scratched his scalp, checked his fingers, then worked on his chin. He peered at the schedule, checked on the tarps flapping overhead, and sighed. In one way, he didn't mind the Skarrs doing the killings. The faster he was through the gurry, the faster they could get to the real fights. *Seddon above*, the Orator fumed with mild disbelief. Those pasty dungeon maggots were actually giving the Free Trained a *good* name. The Chamber would hear about the day's fights. He foresaw changes coming.

"Ladies and men of the Pit," he said, struggling to keep the disappointment from his voice. "We have another match for your enjoyment."

Jeers greeted his words.

"The scutters are better than this gurry stream!" one voice shouted and drew stinging laughs.

Sadly, Qualtus agreed with the man.

"Two fiends of the underworld..." The Orator faltered, wondering why he was painting fancy pictures around these men. Such flourishes did nothing for him or the audience, who knew what they were getting. Best to just sling the gurry out there.

"One is called Anjo," Qualtus resumed, getting to the point, "a Sunjan murderer and stealer of coin. The other, a prisoner from our Nordish war. A captured Jackal."

That subdued the audience.

Qualtus paused at the unexpected hush. Excited murmuring spread through the people, quickly gaining strength. They very much wanted to see their country's enemy bleed in the Pit. Anjo would be hailed as a hero if he killed the Nordish soldier.

That realization caused Qualtus to frown.

A murdering bastard hailed as a hero.

It just wasn't right.

Opposing portcullises cranked open, and the newest pit fighters stepped into the light at the exact same beat.

The blond Anjo wore no armor, displaying a well-built, fair-skinned physique. He studied the sky before settling upon the Jackal across the way. He swished his sword, eager to get to cutting.

The Jackal had no armor to speak of, just an old sword and murderous intentions. Heelslik inspected his weapon and frowned at the dull edge. They'd given him the dullest blade from the rack. His topper had more of an edge to it. With a disdainful sigh, he lowered the weapon to his leg and tapped bare skin. The outing had all the potential to be particularly bloody.

He gazed at the pale asslicker picked to fight him.

Heelslik leered. "You unfortunate bastard."

Some ceremonial kog shrieked something from high above, and the people went mad, shouting that pig language of theirs. The blast startled Heelslik, for only then did he truly realize the scope and spectacle of the Pit, and he took a moment to appreciate where he was. *The games! The legendary games of Sunja.* He'd heard of them around campfires, even joined in the discussions of what manner of man might actually choose such a life.

Killing in war was one thing. But for sport?

Heelslik didn't rightly understand. Perhaps he'd find out.

The Nordish man wasn't one for overthinking. He was direct, to the point, and if given a task, completed it as efficiently as possible.

The Sunjans wanted them to fight.

So he'd fight.

The sun already burning his skin, Heelslik gripped his short sword and approached the man called Anjo. The crowds' screaming damned near burst his ears. Heelslik wondered if the arena's roof might have collapsed from such a sound and the builders had decided against replacing it.

Despite Anjo's time in a Sunjan dungeon, the man wasn't in bad shape. Heelslik could tell Anjo knew how to hold a blade though the Jackal wondered if his foe was any good.

Anjo stalked left and right, content to let Heelslik cross the distance.

Heelslik didn't mind, not after months of walking only the length of his cell.

At the last few strides, however, Anjo lifted his blade and charged.

Heelslik deflected a slash at his head, stopped a thrust for his gut, and parried two quick jabs at his chest.

All good attempts. *Fast* attempts.

With the last strike, however, Heelslik spiraled Anjo's sword to the outside and stepped inside the Sunjan's guard. He punched his sword through the man's gut, the bloody tip bursting from Anjo's back. Dark matter sprayed the air.

The Sunjan wilted upon the steel and collapsed.

Heelslik released the sword and didn't bother taking it back. The blade was a piece of gurry to begin with, the tip as sharp as a boot toe. His shoulder ached from the extra strength needed to stab the man, or maybe he was just out of practice. A long time had passed since he'd actually used a weapon, since he'd had to kill someone.

That didn't interest him, though.

He was in the Pit.

Curlord above. He was *free*.

Jeers and curses rained down upon his person, but he didn't care. He didn't understand any of them and felt strangely armored because of it. His rugged, bearded features split into a harsh smile, and he raised his hands. Enjoying the wide open space, he decided to walk for just for a bit. Heelslik paraded around the bleeding corpse at his feet, taking the hate and even waving to a few of the more attractive faces in the crowds.

"That's the first one, Sunja!" he shouted back in his native tongue, energized by their rage. "That's the first! Give me another, and I'll do the very same again! Hahaaa! Give me your best, and I'll split their buttery holes and make them sing!"

Arms outstretched, Heelslik strolled and whirled, basking in the hot beauty of the day.

"We're *here*, Sunja!" he bellowed. "The Jackals are *here*! And we are *hungry*!"

The angry crowds overpowered his voice.

An opening portcullis stole his attention. Wary, Heelslik decided it best to leave. Just like killing Sunjans at the front—kill and retreat into the darkness. Perhaps if he did a good job, they might give him another Sunjan to kill.

That thought only kept the smile on his face.

Kicking sand, Heelslik turned his back on the squawking masses and walked toward the exit.

After all, he'd been trained to kill Sunjans. Curlord above, it was his *job* to kill them, and he'd lived all his adult life making war against them, terrorizing them. Even though they'd captured him and Rullik had explained their jailors' intentions, a part of Heelslik still didn't believe the Sunjans would actually place him in an arena and give him a sword . . . to kill other Sunjans.

ABOUT THE BLOOD

The tunnel's shade fell across his back as Heelslik entered. He descended stairs toward a group of armed Skarrs, the shadows and firelight playing across their armor.

Heelslik chuckled. Sooner or later, someone would realize their mistake. Until that time, he might as well enjoy himself.

If he couldn't terrorize Sunjans, he might as well make them good and angry.

11

Almost a dozen Skarrs escorted Heelslik back to the dungeon. He was no fool, so he made no threatening moves or dared to resist. When they herded him into his cell and locked him away, Heelslik smiled and gripped the iron bars.

The Skarrs went for another pair of prisoners.

"You live," Arrus said from nearby, a note of surprise in his voice.

"He lives!" Rullik joined in from his own cell and clapped his hands.

"I do," Heelslik answered brightly, leaning against the cold iron. "Do you know there's an entire city above our heads? Watching us kill Sunjans? They really want us to fight up there. Handed me a sword and pushed me out into a great big dish filled with sand. I couldn't believe it. I killed a Sunjan right before thousands of other *Sunjans*."

The Nordish man chuckled. Cell doors opened and closed somewhere down the line.

"Sunjans," scoffed Rullik. "They probably think they're doing something noble here. It's all stupid. All nonsense. Pay heed, Jackals. They're proud and arrogant and stupid, but they'll become wise eventually."

"Perhaps," Heelslik admitted. "But until then, enjoy it. Hear me, Arrus? When it comes to your turn to walk out there, enjoy it. The sun, the fresh air, or what passes for fresh air here. And the fight. Enjoy it. The way I see it, you can only die up there, and that'll probably be quick."

"Were there really that many people watching?" Arrus asked from the poorly lit darkness.

"Thousands," Heelslik answered. "At least thousands. Even some pretty ones, too. I managed to take a walk after killing the dog matched against me. He knew how to hold a blade, I'll give him that. But no real skill. Regardless, the stands were filled with Sunjan women. Flowers just waiting to be plucked. Ah, it was good to see their faces if only for a short time. But angry! Furious! Just because I killed that bastard."

Arrus listened, smiling at some parts, worried at others. He decided Heelslik was speaking the truth and wondered how he would perform under all those eyes, with everyone calling for his death. He was a Jackal, and he certainly followed orders, but that was war, not . . . entertainment.

"I hope they come for me again," Heelslik announced. "That was the best thing to happen to me since being captured."

Arrus couldn't help but smile.

Then he wondered when the Skarrs would come for him.

12

"Who is it I fight again?" an unconcerned Colcus asked as he studied the edge of his battle-axe. A man passed the gladiator a helm fashioned into the face of a snarling lion.

"A Slavol weasel called Sorban," Nexus answered, his normally pallid features wrinkled in annoyance. He wore his silver hair in a horse tail at back of his head that day, to keep it from his eyes.

"Sorban," Colcus rumbled, the sound unpleasant. "Unfit. Who would call their son such gurry? *Sorban*. Balgothan pig."

"Pay no mind to that," Nexus snapped, his black eyes piercing, "Simply make a spectacle of the blossom. Don't just kill him—butcher him. I want an execution out there. For all to see. The bloodier, the better. Instill fear into the hearts of whoever sees you, whoever hears the names Nexus and Colcus. Do you understand my meaning here?"

Colcus stood in the center of the private chamber assigned to the School of Nexus. A vest of worn but serviceable ring mail covered his powerful torso. Exceptionally crafted bracers and greaves of bronze shone upon his arms and legs. He held a battle-axe in one fist, comfortable with the balanced weight. Short spikes protruded from the metal gauntlets protecting his knuckles. Colcus was one of Nexus's better gladiators, a tall bear of a man, black haired and bearded, with wide shoulders and thick arms. He had potential to go far in the games, but after the surprising losses of Malo and Parek—both killed by the ass packer known as Prajus, who fought for Gastillo, no less—Nexus's confidence had been shaken.

Colcus nodded. "Understood, Master Nexus."

"Do you?"

"Aye that, I do."

"Do you *really*?" Nexus fumed, stepping in close and summoning a chill to the chamber's sun-baked interior.

A block of dread descended upon nearby trainers, gladiators, and guards. They paused with their preparations and eyed the school's wealthy owner, uncertain as to what was about to unfold. The wine merchant didn't usually watch the fights from ground level, but that day, he'd remained in his school's private chamber for the majority of the matches, which were mediocre at best but at least bearable to watch, unlike the fights amongst the dungeon scroff.

For the last match of the day, however, Nexus intended to watch the carnage from above, just so he could gloat in Curge's and Gastillo's faces.

However, he had to press his point home to his dog first.

Confused and a touch unsettled, Colcus nodded. He watched the merchant's face, expecting the worst.

Nexus turned away from the warrior and faced Bojen, his well-dressed agent. A light cloak hung from the man's shoulders, and the summer sun had darkened his features, making his white hair and moustache all the more striking.

"I'm in a foul mood, Bojen," the wine merchant warned. "A damned foul mood. The season's been lengthened. Lengthened. Damnation. It's right and proper good to be a king. *It's my wish to extend the games.* Just like that. And the idea of prisoners or Nordish Jackals taking part? That disturbs me."

"Not much one can do if it's the king's will," Bojen said, careful to keep his tone neutral.

Nexus glared at his agent, searching for insult, but found none. He grunted, picked at his sunken chin, and stared off at nothing. "I didn't expect the season to be lengthened, Bojen. It's never been extended in the past. This is different. Which demands the question, why is the king doing this *this* season? You should have seen those other sheep, standing about in shite to their knees and just fine with it. Only one had steel enough to ask why. Only one. And the answer? The king's will. Damnation, that's odd. Is something afoot? And it's not about the coin I've invested into this—though I've dropped a considerable amount. And it's not about my killers meeting up with dungeon maggots who haven't seen the light of day in years. Only Saimon would see the humor in those matches. I want to know *why*. Why would he do such a thing?"

"Perhaps he enjoys the games?" Bojen offered, becoming curious.

"He's barely *there*," Nexus countered with an open palm. "He was there at the very beginning, but I haven't seen him since. No, there's something else afoot here, Bojen. Keep that in the back of your mind in case you sniff something sour around the nobility's cushions you occasionally sit yourself upon. The other maggots weren't so terribly impressed by the decree, but only because a longer season means greater risk to their gladiator ranks. More death. More work later on, to recruit replacements. Otherwise, they simply obeyed. Like sheep. All of them. With bells of shite dangling from their white asses."

Bojen didn't need the imagery.

"Hear me?" Nexus asked the agent.

"I do. And I will."

"And you know what those unfit Chamber pissers said right at the very end? They suggested we *not* kill each other in the Pit. Such gurry. Where's the entertainment if *that* element's removed? Seddon's rosy ass. Gurry! Ripe and rotting. These are games of *blood*! I don't know what those ancient shaggers were thinking to come up with that idea. No killing. Rubbish."

A pensive Bojen nodded. "Ah . . . what did the other owners say to that?"

"I don't care what they say or think," Nexus muttered, incensed to the core. "Not with that bastard Prajus running about. That's one punce I fully intend to have butchered this season. I'll have my revenge on him and any other who crosses the School of Nexus. These games might be the longest, Bojen, but I'll make it the bloodiest. I'll tell you that for nothing. The bloodiest season imagined. I see their noses held high when they see me. I see them. They don't see me as one of them. To them, I'm dabbling here, for my own personal amusement, and for that, I intend to smash some noses. Saimon below will have deep pots at the ready for the dismal rain about to fall. And the first? That shiny-faced topper, Gastillo. He'll regret the day for Prajus. Regret the day. Saimon paddle my hairy ass that I don't make him shiver."

Bojen nodded in silent support, but Nexus's disdain of the other owners bothered him.

"Have you learned anything about that Junger fellow?" the wine merchant asked suddenly.

The change in conversation caught the agent off guard. "Nothing has been revealed, Master Nexus. I have my spies searching."

"I've been thinking." Nexus wrapped an arm around the agent's shoulders and drew him away from the others. "Since you discovered that large brute who was once with the Ten—"

"Sapo."

"Yes, that idiot. He crossed the floor to another house. Curge's house, in fact. I wonder if this Junger fellow could be tempted to cross over? Every man has his price, don't you think?"

"I do, Master Nexus."

"How difficult might it be to make contact with the Perician? He is Perician, correct? See if he might be interested in joining the ranks of real gladiators."

"It's possible," Bojen admitted. "But the Ten are about half a day's travel away by horse or wagon."

"Can you make contact?"

"I can," Bojen asserted calmly. "If not there, perhaps someplace else. Use discretion as usual?"

"Discretion?" Nexus asked, distracted by other thoughts. "Within the city, certainly, but with the Ten? Free Trained shite? Seddon's pink kog and bells. If that young hellpup knows the School of Nexus is courting him, it'll probably be enough to lure him across the floor. Right to Seddon's dewy heavens. Be hard, though. Be hard. Offer it, and make it clear it's a one-time proposal. Make it clear who we are and who he's with. Put flame to his balls. Make him squirm."

"Is it a one-time offer?"

"Of course not." Nexus scoffed with a scowl. "Never close a door on a rare commodity, Bojen. Especially one like that crust of maggot shite. You should know better."

Bojen did know better.

Nexus looked around the room and settled upon Colcus.

"Fight hard, you hellpup," the merchant warned and waved a crooked finger. "Or by my black heart, I'll personally stab you through the eye."

The cloth ribbon went around his hand, pulled tight, then weaved in amongst his fingers. Sorban did that for both hands then stood, pounding his vest of hardened leather and various other black slabs adorning his person. He accepted his helmet, a wild affair with bright plumes decorating the sides and over the crown. The visor was punched with holes, the area about the mouth cup shaped.

Sniffing hard, he fixed the helm over his head.

"Word has it Nexus is becoming particularly . . . agitated . . . with this season's games," said Salwark, son of Vavar Slavol. The handsome owner's son scratched at his head of full blond hair. "*Particularly* agitated. So be mindful of Colcus. Word is he's a punisher. I mean a true punisher. Not just a pretender with a reputation. Just our luck to have drawn him this day, the last fight of the day, but you can defeat him. You can put him down. Just allow your training to—to take control of your limbs as if they . . . they . . ."

Sorban tuned out the owner's son. Like his fellow gladiators, he didn't think much of Salwark's speaking skills. The man should simply shut up and let his silence speak for him. Blacktooth, friend and fellow pit fighter training alongside Sorban in the Stable of Slavol, had said it best. Old Slavol had a gift when it came to words.

Salwark did not.

Simple as that.

Salwark continued to yammer on about Nexus's lad and how good it would be if—*if*—Sorban could defeat him. Sorban pulled on metal gauntlets, the knuckles sprinkled with needles and woefully wicked at close quarters. He held out a hand, and the Marrnite Aidas handed him his quarterstaff—an unpleasant piece of work with metal plates and spikes hammered into the ends.

"Well, anyway, that's all I have to say about that," Salwark finished and looked through the arched window to the sands.

Thank the Lords above, Sorban thought, and waited for the call to go. Salwark mercifully let him be, and in those last few moments, Sorban's thoughts drifted and settled. His season had gone well to that point—five victories to his credit and only one loss, which meant very little since the season had been extended. Faces of gladiators, young and old, dead and living, roamed his mind. Sorban remembered the dead and the mistakes that had led to their deaths. Some of them he hoped to avenge upon the sands. Others . . . He would strive to *not* do as they had done.

A knock on the door broke his thoughts.

"Time," Salwark said, flashing nearly perfect teeth. He slapped the Balgothan on the shoulder. "Fight hard. Fight strong. Fight and be victorious! For the Stable of Slavol!"

Sorban walked away from the owner's son.

The man could right and proper embarrass himself at times.

13

"Ladies and men of the Pit..." Qualtus the Orator paused with his hands held high. "I have for you now a true gift. The final battle of the day will be between two boars of the arena. A pair of thunderheads always willing and eager to roll over any who dare stumble across their path. For years, they have graced the arena floor, smashing skulls. Breaking bones. Releasing torrents of blood. And this day, for the very first time, they will face each other. A pair of tusked animals set to charge each other, ready to gore and stomp. Who will emerge the victor? I wonder..."

Qualtus let the thought hang on the humid summer air, and the audience sucked it all down in gleeful anticipation, already having forgotten the earlier mockeries of the day.

The Orator deepened his voice. "He is a beast set upon two legs. With power enough to fell whole trees. Men fear his axe and whisper his name. He haunts timberlands for all manner of prey. Wars seek his services. Hellions avoid him. Sunjan born and a true monster of the games, I give to you... *Colcus*! Of the School of *Nexus*!"

At the mention of his name, Colcus stepped onto the arena sands. His helm, shaped into a snarling lion, stared across the way. He raised his axe to the sky, acknowledging the crowds.

"His opponent," Qualtus said, swinging a hand to the other side of the Pit, "is a veteran of the games for as long as I can remember. Balgothan by birth, he has decimated his foes, mesmerizing them with his skill before sending them to a most devastating sleep. He feasts on the animals of entire forests and drinks rivers dry. He is a destroyer of men, a ravager of flesh, and a knife stuck deep in the crack of civilization's ass. He . . . is . . . *Sorban*! From the stable of *Slavol*!"

Already standing amongst the heat shimmers of the sand, Sorban stared, features hidden behind his helm's faceplate. He stuck one spiked end of his quarterstaff into the sands and waited.

"Begin!" Qualtus shouted.

Like a smoking, heaving battering ram of legend approaching a castle, Colcus walked toward his foe.

The Balgothan, on the other hand, waited, content to let the larger, more powerful man come to him. When his opponent passed the midway point, he began twirling his staff.

The crowds cheered for the quality of violence to come.

Colcus closed the distance and, at the last few paces, charged. He whipped his axe up and down in a slant, cutting for Sorban's plumed helmet.

Sorban got out of the way and whirled his staff, smashing a hard plate into Colcus's lion snarl.

The blow staggered the Nexus gladiator.

Sorban whipped the staff about and stabbed a spike at Colcus's gut.

The gladiator batted the thrust away. He straightened and cocked that snarling lion's head in a question. Then he attacked again. He swiped for Sorban's head and missed. He chopped at his foe's abdomen and split only air. He slashed for a shoulder, anticipated his foe darting to the left, and swung his spiked fist—

—which flashed through empty space, leaving him wholly exposed.

Sorban bashed the lion's face left, right, left, right before spinning that evil piece of wood and smashing his opponent's armored skull. The blow visibly stunned the gladiator. Sorban then cracked a shoulder, raising a pained grunt from his foe and a cheer from the crowds. He jabbed for Colcus's stomach, but the man deflected the thrust with his axe. Sorban used that force to whip the other end of his staff across the lion's snout, torquing the head violently to the side.

The crowds welcomed that metallic connection.

Colcus took two unsteady steps back, and Sorban pursued.

Crack! The Balgothan bludgeoned a leather-padded thigh. Then another right cut across the lion's head. The impact rang out as blood streamed down Colcus's neck. His guard dropped.

Sorban stabbed and drove half a finger's worth of spike through the tough leather of Colcus's vest.

The lion's face howled, the stricken cry lost in the delighted roar of the crowds. Energized yet livid with pain, Colcus twisted off that painful point. He retreated two steps, reset his arms, and charged back into the fray. He brought his terrible axe crashing down with both arms powering the cut.

Sorban realized he was too close.

The descending battle-axe crunched into the upraised length of wood, breaking it in a lazy, sinewy V. Sorban jumped back, his reflexes saving him from a killing blow to the chest.

The people favoring Colcus cheered.

Sorban retreated and pointed a scolding finger at the Sunjan. Blood dribbled from the puncture in Colcus's vest, staining it. Blood also drizzled down the man's leg, but the Nexus gladiator, true to the lion's guise upon his helmet, did not submit, did not retreat.

Sorban turned his staff over, placed one end under a sandal, and stomped through the remaining fibers, separating the two halves. He gripped the shorter end, wielding it like a club, and walked toward his opponent.

Colcus slashed at his foe's gut.

Sorban parried, the weapons crossing with a *clack*.

ABOUT THE BLOOD

Axe and club parted and clashed again. This time, Colcus got his boot up and snapped his heel into Sorban's lower belly, throwing the man back.

Sorban landed in a spray of sand.

Colcus rushed the Balgothan as he struggled to rise. The Nexus gladiator hacked at the plumaged head with one mighty chop.

The head came away in an explosion of dust. The body rolled away.

Someone in the crowds shrieked.

Colcus's own wounds and momentum ruined him as he stumbled and crashed to the ground in a billowing cloud of dust.

Elation and disappointment erupted from the onlookers.

As the air cleared, a dirty and unarmed Sorban magically stood . . . his head still firmly attached to his shoulders but his helmet knocked clear and free.

Sorban quickly kicked away the axe from the other's grip.

Stained by blood, sweat, and sand, Colcus rolled away from his opponent and regained his feet. He shook himself and raised fists the size of mallet heads. Spikes bristled. The lion's snarling face welcomed a more personal, more brutal exchange, and he gestured for Sorban to attack.

The Balgothan's unprotected face was set, focused. Barely hearing the audience's growing excitement, he beckoned his foe.

Accepting the invitation, Colcus waded in and swung an overhand right.

Sorban ducked and smashed a fist into Colcus's puncture wound. The Nexus man buckled, and Sorban followed through with an uppercut that connected with the lion's chin. Sparks flashed. Needles bent and snapped. Sorban pushed on, delivering a combination of punches, each blow knocking the lion's face back and forth, driving the Nexus gladiator back.

Then one punch smashed the lion's nose, stunning Colcus, and he landed flat on his back.

Sorban mounted him, jerked the helmet from the man's head, and cocked a needled fist. Colcus's face had sustained a terrible beating. The Balgothan had split skin to red bone, and blood seeped freely from purple gashes.

The fog left Colcus's eyes.

Sorban's fist hung in the air, poised like a black rock about to fall.

"Yield," Colcus whispered.

"Bad luck all round, good Nexus." Curge chuckled.

Below their shared viewing box, Sorban the Balgothan stood and lifted his arms to the crowds. Dark Curge glanced over at the wine merchant, who had been a little late joining him and the golden-faced Gastillo, arriving just after the match commenced.

"Oh, I'll have my day," Nexus vowed as the applause for Sorban died away. "And I'll leave my mark."

"Perhaps you'll leave it on Prajus? Hm?" Curge smiled evilly.

That blackened Nexus's face, and the only sound belonged to the spectators as they filed out of the arena. Despite the summer heat, the temperature chilled around the merchant's person.

"I'm sure you'll defeat Prajus when he fights in three days," Gastillo said, careful with his words.

"Three days is, it?" Nexus snapped, his anger bubbling through. "We'll see, then, Gastillo. We'll see."

Curge chuckled and rose from his seat. Nexus didn't bid goodbye to the large owner, and Gastillo saw how the wine merchant's face tightened with contempt.

"I'll be looking forward to that, Nexus," Dark Curge said, his spirits high. "Perhaps something magical will happen with the third attempt."

"Damn your leathery ass, Curge," Nexus muttered. "Go on with you, you brazen, saucy, one-fisted punce."

"Weak, merchant. Weak. I expect better from you. Perhaps that"—he gestured toward the Pit—"was too much this day? I imagine so. Go home and rest your bones. Drink some of that pig piss you call wine. Come back fresh."

Curge departed, leaving the female servant to close the door.

"Ripe and evil bastard," Nexus said after the man had gone.

"Let me be clear here, good Nexus," Gastillo began as spectators continued to exit. "I'm no ally of Dark Curge, but perhaps something good will happen in three days."

Nexus fixed him with a look of undisguised loathing. "What are you prattling on about?"

"Just that. Your fortune might change this coming fight with Prajus. If you still intend to fight him, that is."

The wine merchant's glare deepened even more. "Oh, I intend to fight him. Guaranteed, I'll send someone to stick a length of steel through his unfit head. Just watch and see if I don't."

"I have no doubt, good Nexus."

Attendants with wide brooms appeared on the arena floor to groom the sands. The constant chatter and cheering of thousands dimmed as people continued filing out of the arena, but the two owners remained seated.

"It's not like the wine business," Nexus eventually stated, eyeing the sands. "Or the cloth. Or any other venture I've dabbled in. Though it's become a true passion of mine. A *true* passion. And the more I fail, the harder I'll strive to succeed. And I will, mind you. I've conquered everything else in this life, and I'll conquer these games. Especially when the ruling class consists of a hairless ass licker and a gold-plated prick."

The insult caused Gastillo to sigh.

"I'll have my champion," Nexus went on. "I'll find him, and I'll unleash him upon you and the entire gladiatorial ranks. Dog balls. How I'll crow when that happens. You'll see."

"I'm sure you will."

Nexus regarded him with a look of disgusted curiosity. "What is it you want, Gastillo? Say your peace, and then be off unless you wish to remain and listen to me rave on about how I'll win at these gurry games."

That response set off a warm twinge of hope inside Gastillo as he detected a crack in Nexus's tone. But an opening to what? He wondered how to best approach the wine merchant.

Why not the truth? A voice suggested.

"Good Nexus," Gastillo began, forcing himself to speak in calm, measured tones, "I've grown up with these games. Participated in them and spilled my share of blood. I've fought the day's best and took a champion's title . . . and the coin that went along with it. I've enjoyed the seasons year after year. But now . . ."

He faltered, watching the other man, who didn't say a word.

"Now, I find myself growing weary of these events," Gastillo continued. "I . . . wish to explore other opportunities beyond the games. Try my hand at more civilized interests. Like wine, perhaps. Or grain. Or some other commodity. I have the finances to fund a business venture and leave all this behind, but I lack the wisdom and guidance of peers."

"Peers?" Nexus spat, eyes narrowed.

"Peers."

"You mean me."

"I mean you." Gastillo smiled behind his mask. "Perhaps we could help each other?"

"*Help* each other? Have you forgotten your man Prajus has killed two of mine, you gold-faced teat? How do you propose *helping* me?"

"I'm open to suggestions."

Nexus stared at him for several heartbeats.

Then, as if remembering something, the merchant rose and shooed the one servant out the door. Once she was gone, Nexus glanced around, spying the few remaining people leaving the arena. Satisfied that they were indeed alone, he sat beside Gastillo and leaned forward.

"Then ensure your man *loses*," Nexus whispered, his eyes set and stern so that Gastillo knew he meant every syllable. "Do that. And I'll help you."

Gastillo massaged his throat, absorbing what was being asked of him. "I can't do that, Nexus. Not even if I wanted to. Prajus is somewhat headstrong and doesn't always obey my commands. We've had words in the past. He would be suspicious of me."

"So you refuse to do anything."

"I didn't say that." Memories of harsh exchanges with Prajus ran through Gastillo's head, the most recent having happened just after the insolent bastard had killed Parek, Nexus's most recent avenger. "I'm saying anything I might . . . do . . . to ensure your victory may be suspect. Prajus isn't some senseless animal."

"I mean to kill that man," Nexus whispered, staring hard at Gastillo, who sensed the unspoken words *by any means possible*.

"And," Gastillo struggled to be diplomatic, "I hope you get your revenge. But . . . within reason. You must understand, Prajus is one of my best gladiators. Perhaps even *the* best. With aspirations to be a champion of the games. I have no doubt he will be victorious by the end of this season or the next. He will become a champion. After that, who knows what he'll do. But if you've already sent your best after him—"

"I have," Nexus muttered.

"Then I'm at a loss and wish you best fortune with any further attempts at revenge. I'll admit, truth be known, despite Prajus's success in the arena, if one of yours does strike him down, he won't be missed. Not by me."

Nexus leaned in closer. "Then make it so he injures himself. Have one of your more loyal pit dogs hurt him. During practice. Cut him. Bruise him. Anything that might allow me an advantage. However slight."

The blatant suggestion surprised Gastillo. A part of him almost laughed in Nexus's face for even suggesting such a thing, but he didn't. He sensed he was closing in on an agreement of sorts—an understanding, but he was unsure of what.

Also, he wasn't sure he could do what Nexus was asking.

"No," Gastillo finally said. "I can't do that. Apologies. If I did, I'd be no better than, say, any of the criminals set free upon the sands. Or some street snake yet to be caught."

Nexus leaned back. "Gastillo, you say you're interested in leaving these games behind. In my trade, unfortunate occurrences happen all the time, natural or devised. Even harder decisions must be made, sometimes on a daily basis, resulting in people—innocent people—suffering. In this particular sport, I've done well. Simply because I recognize it's a business no different than any other. That these gladiators are commodities. The owners are merchants. And the same harsh decisions must be made. You freely admit that Prajus won't be missed, yet you refuse to make the decision that would rid yourself of the man. That speaks to me. I question if you have the mind to survive and adapt to a new profession. A business more to your liking. What about this . . . If you *did* happen to find that venture, what would you do with your house? Your fighters?"

Gastillo stopped. *Good question.*

"I'm open to suggestions," he said, sensing an even greater opportunity. "Especially from an established merchant such as yourself."

Nexus wavered, his sunken chin quivering, black eyes twinkling, and finally smiled. "I may be very well speaking out of line here, good Gastillo, but I have a proposition for you. You'll have every reason to laugh once you hear it. Ridicule me, even. What would your thoughts be on an exchange of goods?"

Gastillo forced down the sudden sparkle of hope. "I'm listening."

"Could I not . . . purchase your house from you?" Nexus asked. "Taking control of your current roster in the process? Merge them into my own?"

Once again, Gastillo was ever so grateful to have a golden mask to conceal his dismay. "You wish to purchase my house?"

"If you're willing. You might have ties not easily cut. Sentimental ones. But consider it. If that lad who deserted the Ten and later joined Curge can switch houses, I should be able to purchase and absorb an entire house itself. It would be bloodless and not at all under scrutiny of the Chamber. I'd even offer a small increase in your gladiators' payment. Just to soften any ill feelings your lads might have."

"What about your revenge?" Gastillo asked. "Upon Prajus?"

Nexus didn't appear concerned. "Prajus would have no say in the matter, would he? He'd be under my care then. My control. And have no concern about my dogs. They'll do as I say, for fear of being cast aside. Yes. *Yes*, I like that idea very much. If Prajus is as good as you say he is. If he's a potential champion."

"He is," Gastillo said, his heart thumping. "You've seen what he's capable of."

"I have." Nexus's smile widened even more, reminding Gastillo of an early frost. "Perhaps we should discuss this possibility another time. In more secure surroundings. If you're agreeable." The wine merchant finished with a nod.

Gastillo caught himself nodding in return. "When you're ready," he said, unsure if he'd heard the man correctly.

"My good Gastillo," Nexus said, his pallid flesh aglow. "I'm *always* ready . . ."

14

While the early fights were underway in the Pit, the House of Ten finished their preparations before leaving the city. Once amongst the teeming crowds of the public market, the Ten's wagons stopped, and Clavellus lowered himself to the street. While he inspected dry goods and other valuables, he sent Pratos off to hire another wagon. Seeing they weren't going anywhere soon, the others either relaxed inside their transports or ventured outside, watching the taskmaster buy gifts for his wife or supplies for the house.

If he wasn't buying, he was ordering large quantities of items and materials to be delivered to his gates. In time, he returned and directed the heavyset and wide-moustached Bagrun to load more goods into one crowded wagon.

Goll and a suffering Muluk stood outside during that, listening to Clavellus supervise. The heat was visibly crippling for Muluk, and Goll shook his head at the sight.

"What?" Muluk asked, speaking Kree.

"You look unfit," Goll answered.

"I feel unfit."

"Let this be a lesson to you."

"I will. Next time, I'll rent an alehouse room. And return home the day after." He exhaled mightily.

"Don't you empty your gullet here," Goll warned.

Muluk scowled. "Can't be any fouler than what I'm already smelling," he said, screwing up his nose at the blend of ripe dung, unwashed bodies, and an underlying taint of sewage polluting the air.

"Masters Goll and Muluk."

The two Kree turned.

Valka stood guard nearby, partially concealed by a wagon's corner. The old soldier's eyes flicked in the direction he wanted them to look.

Clades was making his way through the market crowds, pleased that he'd located the Ten. A woman clung to his arm, a lovely woman. She wore a simple red shirt and loose-fitting black trousers. She was pretty, her blond hair tied back, revealing large blue eyes that looked uncertainly upon the two house masters.

Both Krees straightened. Muluk, in particular, made a visible effort to compose himself.

"What are you two looking at?" Clades scolded with good humor. "Haven't seen a handsome couple before?"

"Who's looking at you?" Muluk smiled weakly.

Clavellus walked into the gathering and brightened upon sighting the pair. "Seddon above, I don't believe it. This is your missus, Clades? You've done much better than I gave you credit for. How is it you ever left this flower at all?"

Clades regarded Kura. "I ask myself that question every day, Master Clavellus. That very thing."

"Kura, is it?" the taskmaster asked.

She nodded. "Master Clavellus."

"These sorry punces address me as Master. You, however, you call me by name. No titles." Clavellus gave a curt bow before studying her once more. "He was worried about you, you know."

"I know. And thank you. For allowing me—us—to live upon your land."

Clavellus tsked. "This isn't the Nordish front, and he's yours. Being married myself, I can't imagine walking about without knowing what was happening with my life's chosen one.

Gather yourselves into one of those wagons now. Machlann! See to it the lady has room and that Clades sits beside her. Pratos should be along shortly with that extra wagon."

No sooner did he mention that than the people crowding the streets parted before an arriving wagon. Pratos sat in the perch, next to the driver.

"Good timing," Muluk muttered, a hand straying to his stomach.

"My heartfelt thanks again, Master Clavellus," Clades said. "And Masters Muluk and Goll. This means everything to us."

A stoic Goll acknowledged the guard's gratitude with a nod. If he were married, he supposed he would want his wife nearby as well.

"So many thank-yous," someone with a familiar voice said, turning their heads. "Almost wish I was leaving the city."

There, standing in the narrow gap between two merchant stalls, was Borchus, dressed in a loose green shirt and leggings. The short agent beckoned the masters into the narrow alley. Excusing himself, Clavellus went to the man while Muluk followed. Goll wasn't as quick to follow, but he eventually joined the group. Crammed between rough slabs of wood, the city smells seemed even stronger.

Muluk frowned and checked his sandals. "Think I walked through a piss puddle."

That got the rest of them checking their feet.

"Staying hidden, I see," Clavellus said, crowding in close to the agent.

The man, with his long sideburns and short-cropped graying hair, flashed tired green eyes. "Staying hidden and *alive*," he said and nodded toward their transportation. "Taking in some new people, Master Clavellus?"

"A few."

"Seddon smiles brightly on the kindly."

No one said anything then, but heat emanated from Goll. "You didn't let Shan look at that wound."

"It's much better," Borchus said wearily. "Truly."

"Don't joke with me."

"I'm not."

"At least he's not mucking about like he's been stabbed," Muluk pointed out. "I mean, you wouldn't know unless... you knew."

See? Borchus said with a look.

"What news do you have?" Goll asked, getting to the meat of things. "And who's he?" He stuck out his chin, aiming at the one-legged figure lurking just behind the agent.

The stranger was holding himself up with a pair of crutches and appeared nervous enough for five men.

"This," Borchus said, "is my man Garl. Garl's been very good to me over the years. He's also been very good to us over the last few days, learning things no one else might've learned. All for the House of Ten. But due to circumstances beyond our control, we've decided it best that Garl no longer be in the city. He's a little too obvious, you might say."

"What happened to you?" Muluk asked the one-legged man.

"I was a pit fighter," Garl answered. "Once. Until the Pit took my leg."

"Master Goll," Borchus said, "Garl needs to leave the city. Preferably on your wagon and under your protection. He won't be a bother. He does, however, need a place to live. I was wondering if perhaps you might have some use for him at your villa, Master Clavellus?"

Clavellus straightened and looked down his nose at the one-legged spy.

"This have anything to do with you keeping to the shadows?" Goll asked Borchus.

"Of course not," he answered. "My desire to stay out of sight is... because of another matter entirely. However, there are those who might recognize Garl if they see him. If they do, they might force him to reveal where I am. And then kill him. Possibly me. We both prefer he stay alive, which is why I thought of you."

The agent studied the taskmaster.

"Why not?" Clavellus said. "I'm in a generous mood. Best take advantage of it while it lasts. Any comments, Master Goll?"

He had none.

"You say he's done a great deal on our behalf?" Clavellus asked Borchus.

"He has."

"That's enough for me. Hop along that wagon drawing close, good Garl, and the lads will hoist you aboard."

"That wagon's getting heavy," Muluk noted.

"My concern is turning that beast around and leaving the city," Clavellus stated.

Behind them all, Garl's face dropped with disbelief, for he'd clearly expected to be turned away by the taskmaster. A heartbeat later, he got moving. He stopped beside Borchus and gave the agent a solemn look. Borchus gripped the man's shoulder and gestured for him to go. Without a word, Garl swung himself past the collection of men.

"Any news since yesterday?" Goll asked his agent.

"None."

Goll was about to say more, but Muluk studied him with a pleasant expression.

"What?" Goll asked, not appreciating the look.

"You didn't say a word when Borchus asked about Garl. I'm proud of you."

Goll rolled his eyes. "Seddon above. Clavellus, are you finished with the marketplace?"

"Almost."

"Then please hurry. If we linger much longer, we'll no doubt take half the city back with us." He then looked at Borchus. "Stay well, then. Do what you do."

Borchus nodded that he would.

Goll walked away without another word. Muluk waited a beat before holding out a fist.

ABOUT THE BLOOD

Borchus smiled faintly and pressed his own into it.

Satisfied, the Kree left for the wagon.

Clavellus remained, eyeing the shorter man. "All is well?"

"As well as can be expected. Clavellus . . . Thank you for taking that one."

The taskmaster smiled gently. "Watch yourself, Borchus."

"I will."

A ray of sunshine caught the older man's woolly profile then, and his bald head glistened. Clavellus squinted at the sky before returning to the street.

Keeping to the narrow alley, Borchus raised a hand in farewell to the House of Ten. The men secured themselves and their goods onto three wagons. They tucked Garl within the second one, well out of sight. Borchus wondered if that was Garl's idea and decided it probably was.

The drivers got the horses moving. The crowds parted, and the wagons rolled by.

Once they'd gone, the agent sighed in relief. He watched the crowds moving past the little alley and, keeping his eyes on them, retreated into shadows.

Garl was away.

Time to focus upon his other concerns.

The night before, Garl had provided him with the names of two men Borchus might potentially recruit for his fledgling network of spies. Garl had even agreed to introduce them since Strach had been removed. Deep into the night, however, they still weren't able to find the pair. The spy did meet a beggar sitting against an inn's foundation. Borchus remembered how the wretched man's clothes had smelled of urine and stale beer. As bad luck would have it, the beggar reported that both the lads they sought had been killed by Strach days before.

They left the beggar alone, giving him a coin for his trouble.

Once away, Borchus and Garl got talking. They figured the killings had happened not a day or two before Borchus himself murdered the street snake called Strach.

That still left the agent without spies, but he had one distinct possibility left.

Naulis.

And . . . Sindra.

His heart sank at that prospect.

She would require a little more work to convince.

15

Pig Knot woke in the early afternoon. He was lying on his back in a comfortable bed and studied the bare timbers crossing the ceiling. He stayed that way, feeling the soft blanket underneath him and the straw mattress under that. Beside him rested a comely honeypot by the name of Jana, snuggled into his side like a large leech that had drunk its fill. Pig Knot unclenched his jaw and stuck his tongue between his teeth, feeling an ache about his healing chin. The drawer of the bedside table got his attention. He reached over, pulled it out, and felt around inside.

His fingers touched his leather purse.

Still there. Excellent.

Jana hadn't stolen anything, after all.

He had to admit he hadn't been sure if purchasing Jana's generous curves for the night was a wise idea or not. He wasn't even sure he should have slept in the tavern's room overhead, and he certainly didn't think he should've shuffled his way across floor and steps in front of everyone watching, some even gawking. In the aftermath of the night, however, and seeing the majority of his coin was still his, he relaxed and remembered. The night's activities had been a chore but also a delight . . . and he still remembered most of it.

The stairs. That soured his mood. The stairs had been the worst.

He lifted one half leg and pulled the blanket free. The bandages remained clean. That was good.

Though Pig Knot had been initially thrilled about once again living off Sunja's streets, his mind quickly changed when the smell of cooking food wafted his way. Of course, that led to a tavern, which meant drinking, which attracted female attention. Pig Knot couldn't resist one or the other, and he had to admit that the sympathy he'd received from Jana resulted in some of the most energetic episodes he'd ever experienced in bed.

She stirred. "Mmmmh?"

Pig Knot drew his hand back and stroked her bare shoulder. She'd trapped his other arm beneath her, but he didn't mind. Lords above, she was as soft as she was pretty. And smell—she was as sweet as fresh flowers.

"Is it morning?" she murmured, her lips squashed by his chest.

"No."

She cracked open an eye drizzled with brown hair and smiled. "Then why can I see you?"

"It's afternoon, I think."

"Afternoon?" Her head rose, and her eyes widened. "Oh no."

She sat up with a jolt, blanket falling from her breasts, and bounced off the bed.

"In a hurry?" Pig Knot asked nonchalantly, folding one muscular arm behind his head.

"I have to go."

"I see."

"I have to go *now*."

"Returning husband, is it?"

"Aye that."

Tavern wenches. Pig Knot sighed. As bad as men when it came to lies and truth.

Jana dressed quickly, making him ache all over once again. He reached into the drawer and pulled forth his purse, still filled with coin.

"Here," he said, catching her attention while she pulled on a loose-fitting shirt.

She turned around, white fabric dropping over her privates, and saw Pig Knot holding out a hand filled with gold coins.

"For me?" she asked, eyes nearly popping out of her head.

"If you want them."

She took them and spread them over a palm before depositing them into a pocket. "You're wonderful."

"Well, I *was* hoping you'd undress and then get dressed again."

That summoned a giggle, and she shook her head. "I have to go. My husband will be wondering where I am."

"What is it he does?" he asked through his bandaged chin.

"He's with the Street Watch. He's usually gone all night. If I'm caught away, I tell him I worked until dawn and slept upon a table below. It's not entirely untrue. It's better than walking home alone in the deep of night."

Pig Knot thought that made sense.

"Well." Jana straightened as she completed pulling on pants. She swept back her hair and pinched her shirt away from her chest. "Thank you. I had a wonderful time."

"As did I."

"You really surprised me for a cripple."

That stung, but Pig Knot pursed his lips and didn't let the hurt show. She walked over and kissed him on the head and cheek and gave his flat belly a quick rub, all the way down to his manhood.

"I hope we meet again," she said, breathing foulness into his face.

Pig Knot didn't flinch, but when she turned away, his eyes widened as if he were kicked in the nose.

Jana let herself out of the rented room, wiggling fingers at him as she closed the door. He watched her go with weary wonder, forgetting about the cripple jab. She probably didn't even realize she'd said it. Pig Knot lay there, listening to a chair or bench being dragged across the floor somewhere below. The thought of rising came to him, and he crunched his stomach. He couldn't quite pull himself up, so he pushed himself into a sitting position.

He inspected the room again.

It had been nicer at night. When he was drunk.

And fumbling with Jana's clothes.

Pig Knot found his shirt and pulled it over his head. He then located his loincloth and draped it over his kog and bells. He sniffed at his shirt and decided it could be washed or outright replaced, but he wasn't keen on doing anything right then. Hunger pawed at his stomach, but his head informed him it had escaped the night's drinking unscathed. That was all Pig Knot needed.

And another night like the last.

One more, so he could go to his grave somewhat content.

He lowered himself to the floor, grimacing when his rump thudded against the boards. The pisspot waited, and he pulled it close, angled himself the best way possible, and filled that clay basin. Having done that, he scuffed along the floor to the door, skin rubbing against the planks, thrusting his hips in such a way to lift his bits off the wood. Seddon help him if he got a splinter. Seddon help him if a splinter took him in his topper.

The hallway air was a comforting mixture of beer, mead, firewater, and even that sweet, awful tang of drying piss and stomach juice. More memories flooded Pig Knot. He wished the lads were about. Both Muluk and Halm could down entire pitchers without pause, and while Goll didn't, he still managed to pack away a respectable share.

The lads weren't around, though. Pig Knot didn't expect to see any of them ever again, and the moment's pang of sadness was quickly swept away by the memory of Jana. His first night back in Sunja, fortune had smiled on him. He needed it. Lords above, did he ever.

The stairs greeted him with all the candor of a cliff drop. Pig Knot remembered the climb to the top and knew he wouldn't soon forget the equally challenging climb to the bottom.

ABOUT THE BLOOD

He positioned himself at the edge and sized up the drop. He could perhaps roll onto his stomach and lower himself that way, but he thought he could manage rump first. Gripping the edge of that first step, he pushed himself over, buttocks and back muscles grazing wood, and lowered himself until his arms came close to failing—whereupon he dropped perhaps the last three fingers. He landed partially on one miscued man bulb, which practically squirted out from beneath his thigh.

The resulting pain was brilliant. Nauseating. Enough to topple him. He half tumbled, half slid the rest of the way, the steps slapping the back of his head, right to the bottom. Pig Knot rattled to a halt at the base of the stairs.

A large man with tied-back hair and a straight strip of a beard that reached his waist appeared. "You slip, cripple?" he asked.

"Muh."

That drew a look of confusion. "What's that?"

"Hnnnnnuh." Pig Knot really didn't want to talk.

"You don't want to talk?"

Smart lad. Pig Knot squeaked what he hoped was an affirmative-sounding note. It worked. The bearded man nodded and left him alone.

"He can't stay there like that," a decidedly annoyed woman said.

"I remember him from last night," said the bearded man. "Went off with Jana. Leave him be."

"Someone might come down and trip over his legless carcass."

"There's no one else up there. The rooms are empty."

"Then I might trip over him while going upstairs."

"You won't trip over him." The bearded man sounded tired. "Just let him be."

"Leaving cripples all over your floor. It don't look right. Looks bad."

"He wasn't drinking."

"There's a difference between a drunk cripple and one who's not?"

The bearded man sighed. "Just clean those mugs and scrub down the counters. Then go on up and empty the bedpans."

Pig Knot struggled to pull himself up, and when he did, he adjusted the loincloth that had failed to do its job. Once all was secured for the better, he labored to a nearby bench and table. The alehouse doors remained closed but would no doubt be opened shortly. He turned around, dug his hand heels into the edge of the bench, paused to ensure everything was tucked away, and hoisted himself onto the seat. The effort summoned sweat, and his nearly crushed pearl still ached. Pig Knot realized then the alehouse was warm, humid.

"Barkeep?" he croaked

The bearded man came over while another woman went into the kitchen. The heavily whiskered barkeep looked helpful.

"Anything inside there to eat?" Pig Knot asked.

"If you have the coin, there's food."

"I have the coin."

"Then I think there are a few slabs of cold beef to be had. Or ham. Some cold vegetables—cooked from last night, mind you. And perhaps this or that which I can't rightly remember now."

"How much?"

"A gold piece for a plate."

"Any soup instead?"

"You want soup?"

"It's best for this." Pig Knot pointed at his healing jaw and chin.

"I'll ask my missus to warm up a broth. Same price."

"High, isn't it? For a bit of soup?"

"It's good soup."

"All right." Pig Knot nodded thanks. Food would set him right . . . and perhaps inflate his half-squished plum. He waited, elbows on the table, looking this way and that, lost in a post-morning aftermath of drinking. No hammer rang the insides of his head, and for that he was thankful.

The barkeep returned with a pitcher of water, and Pig Knot gratefully took it. The water hit the back of his throat and kept right on going. When he lowered the pitcher, only a third remained.

"Thirsty cripple," the barkeep chuckled, holding a wet mop in one hand.

That made Pig Knot frown, and he looked at the open windows of the lower floor then the barkeep once again.

The bearded one cocked an eyebrow.

"You always insult paying customers?" Pig Knot asked.

"What?"

"I asked if you always insult your customers."

"You're insulted?"

Pig Knot indicated that he was—just a little.

"You're sensitive? About being a cripple?"

Pig Knot's frown deepened. The barkeep was obviously a punce unfit in the head.

"I'm a *paying* customer," Pig Knot stressed.

"You haven't paid me anything yet."

"I paid you last *night* for the drinks. And the room."

"Ah, aye that. Yes, yes, so you did. You got young Jana up there, too. How'd you manage to do that?" The barkeep leaned forward on his mop as if peering out over a cliff, and a puzzled look hitched his beard. "I mean . . . you've got no legs. So . . . what?"

"I manage," Pig Knot said, not liking the conversation's direction.

"I wager you do. And did. You might be a legless slab of a lad, but not many take young Jana upstairs. Tell you that for free."

Pig Knot's frown lessened at the combination of jab and compliment. He wondered if the man wasn't so unfit in the head after all.

"Well, then." The barkeep shrugged and got back to mopping the floor.

Nursing the pitcher, Pig Knot waited for the soup to arrive. In time, a woman dressed in kitchen clothing and an apron brought a wide bowl to his table. She placed the broth before him none too gently and cracked a wooden spoon down beside it. Then she studied Pig Knot with a withering eye and left with her nose pointed at the ceiling.

Pig Knot wondered what he'd done to deserve that look. Normally, it took much longer for a person to dislike him. He tried the soup and cringed at its saltiness. Small chunks of ham floated therein, along with various diced vegetables bobbing about in a yellowish broth. He remembered the food from the night before tasting much better.

While he'd been drunk.

Then he remembered fumbling with Jana's clothes.

His spirits rose once again.

The soup went down, and while it tasted too much of salt, Pig Knot washed it away with the remainder of the water.

"Barkeep?" he asked.

The bearded man was behind the counter, inspecting tankards.

"A pitcher of Sunjan firewater," Pig Knot said.

"You've coin for that?" the barkeep asked, doubt thick in his voice.

"Aye that."

"Because if you don't, I won't feel right about fishhooking a cripple."

That word picked at Pig Knot's nerves. Annoyed, he reached inside his shirt, grabbed his purse, fumbled for the drawstrings, and pulled forth five coins, holding them in the air. He waved the money at the barkeep before slamming them down on the table.

The kitchen witch appeared as if summoned by sorcery. She looked about, sighted Pig Knot, and shook her head as she withdrew from sight.

The barkeep, however, smoothed out his lengthy chin bush, turned to the tankards lining the back wall, and selected one. He took his time and poured a pitcher from a spout. He glanced toward a window now and then, as if checking on the weather. Once finished, the bearded man came around the bar. Without a word, he placed the brass pitcher right in front of his legless customer.

ABOUT THE BLOOD

Pig Knot realized then the barkeep was a big man with numerous scars crossing his face and arms as if he'd been once cut up by many knives. A harsh scent of soap and water wafted from the barkeep's hands. Pig Knot remained calm as the barkeep leaned over and slowly, precisely, counted away four gold pieces from the five slapped down upon the table.

"That's all for the soup and firewater," the barkeep said. "Cripple."

If he meant to intimidate the once gladiator, it didn't work. As big as the barkeep was, Pig Knot was just as big across the chest and confident in his own abilities. So the two stared at each other for several long heartbeats, neither one breaking away.

Eventually, the tavern man straightened and towered over his customer, sending a none-too-subtle jab that he was taller and had both legs. He backed away slowly and returned to his tankards.

Pig Knot watched the barkeep, sending his own message. The once gladiator picked up the pitcher and started drinking. Ordinarily, he'd take his time, savouring the firewater as it melted his gullet, but the tavern air had become decidedly cold. He believed the time had come to move on.

A short time later, he slammed the pitcher down on the table, receiving a harsh look from the he-bitch behind the counter. Pig Knot scowled back—if the bearded punce wanted to fight, Pig Knot made it clear he was right there.

The barkeep didn't, however.

A sour Pig Knot lowered himself to the floor, made it a point to ignore the hairy bastard lording over the bar, and waddled toward the exit, though not before making certain he dragged both ass cheeks over the freshly mopped floor.

The firewater's full potential struck Pig Knot a short time after he vacated the alehouse, and he welcomed that euphoric numbness. The world became a scintillating bubble. People streamed by him—a flow of faces, waists, and dangling arms. Some glanced his way, but most ignored him. He didn't care. He wore his armor on the inside, he reasoned. However, he realized he needed to do something about being so close to the ground. Sunja's streets consisted of flat, fitted stone and, in some places, brick. The smooth stones were fine to drag himself over, but some had split over time, and twice his hands grazed sharp fragments. The bricks were another matter. Dragging himself over their rough edges was like shaving stubble with a dull blade and not pleasant in the least.

Pig Knot gasped for air and knew he'd drunk the firewater much too quickly. Another thought struck him—a builder, one who specialized in making carts and wagons.

In his glowing capacity, the legless Sunjan hoped he could find one before he came across another drinking establishment.

The memory of the brazen barkeep faded, replaced by alcoholic bliss. He scooted along the main street, avoiding the heaviest traffic and trying to keep to the shade. Despite the wear on his hands, he managed to wobble along, even greeting a few people who stopped to allow him to pass. That was right and proper fine, and Pig Knot slurred his thanks.

Then the worst—but best—thing happened.

He spied an alehouse.

Without hesitation, Pig Knot hoisted himself up a pair of steps and over the threshold. The dark cavern was muggy, though not unpleasantly so, and shelter from the sun. People flittered in and out of his vision like frightened fish though some of the larger ones stopped and stared for a while. Pig Knot didn't care. He even stared back, making faces at times, until the people moved away.

He found a table, and though he didn't remember the transaction, *somehow* a pitcher of Sunjan mead appeared in the center—a whole pitcher, just for him—and all of creation knew that once mead appeared before one, one *had* to down it.

Pig Knot firmly believed that, so he got to drinking.

That's when the world truly began to get interesting.

Feeling damn near invincible at that point, Pig Knot inquired as to where he might find a builder of wagons and got no response. Not many people were frequenting the alehouse, though, so he repeated the question more loudly.

The barkeep, a shorter, pudgier man with a balding head and an empty eye socket, provided directions to an individual called Sanjo.

That got Pig Knot moving, eager to find the builder and give the man some work. He finished off the pitcher and left it on the table.

People, wagons, and animals filled the streets, even more than earlier, if such a thing was possible. The congestion befuddled Pig Knot and obstructed his view. Hands slapped him merrily on the shoulders and he smiled back, even patting a few thighs and rumps in return. He even buried his face into some right and proper fine legs, purely accidental of course. Some people squealed. Some cursed. A dog appeared before him, damn near magically, and he found himself staring into those soft, curious eyes . . . just before the animal sniffed his face and generously licked it. Someone pulled the creature away, and Pig Knot was sorry to see it go. The space around him eventually cleared, strangely enough, which was when he spotted the edge of the street. He shuffled over, not feeling his hands at all, and continued along a wall of shop fronts and gated homes on his left.

He was looking for that someone . . . for that something.

Then he remembered.

Sanjo. The builder. Excellent.

A short time later, Pig Knot found the man, amazingly enough.

Sanjo's work area was a low, single-story building with plenty of open shutters and two wide doors flung open. Sawdust covered the wooden floor and perfumed the air. Pig Knot eased himself through the entrance and spotted a tall, sun-browned man fashioning a heavy door. Two boys in their teens stood nearby, watching him work.

The younger boy noticed the legless arrival and frowned. "Go away!" he yelled.

An off-center Pig Knot glanced over his shoulder. When he looked back, the boy had actually taken two steps toward him.

"I said *go away!*" he commanded in a voice nowhere near a man's.

"I'm here to make a purchase," Pig Knot said, forcing the combined magic of the firewater and the mead out of his voice.

"Are you?" the boy asked, screwing up his face. "Let's see your coin, then."

"I'm not that drunk, you young pissdrop."

The boy's lips became a white line of spite. "Go on, then!"

"Dying Seddon, boy, is that . . . is that your father?"

"Go *on*, I said!"

Sanjo paused in his work, holding a chisel. Sawdust freckled his dark shoulders. The man's eyes narrowed upon seeing Pig Knot.

"Sanjo, is it?" Pig Knot called, his balance wavering at the edges. "The builder?"

"Aye that. The carpenter."

"There's a difference?"

"Just preference."

"Oh. Well, I've come . . . I've come with a bit of work. For you. If you'll call off your young enforcer here."

The boy's face flushed a hot red at that. Pig Knot wondered what had wedged itself into the youngster's crack. As far as he was concerned, he'd been quite respectful to the little dewdrop.

Sanjo approached, dismissing the angry boy with a curt jerk of his head. "You want something done?"

The carpenter looked him in the eye, not paying any attention to his condition. Pig Knot liked the man already.

"Aye that." The once gladiator waved a hand over his stumps. "You see these. I need . . . I need a low-riding cart. A low one. *Low*, I said."

At that point, he placed an open palm not a finger's width off the sawdusted floor, to better clarify his needs.

"One that will roll . . . roll . . . roll over. The stone. And bricks. And keep my lower . . . my lower parts off the . . . the streets. Out of the . . ." Pig Knot struggled to remember the word. "The *shite*. Aye that. Yes. The shite. Filthy shite. Hands deep. But allow me to, ah, push. Push along. Like that. So there. Think you can make something?"

Sanjo considered it. "It'll cost you."

"I have coin." Pig Knot said and belched, bringing up soup and wincing at the taste.

"Seven gold ones, then."

"Ten," Pig Knot countered, placing a hand on his chest where the salty uprising had burned the worst. "If you start now. And finish . . . it by, oh, nightfall."

Sanjo smiled, showing strong teeth. "Let's see the coin first."

Pig Knot reached into his shirt and pulled out the purse. He rattled its weight before opening it and fishing out a few coins.

"Look real enough," Sanjo said.

"Oh, they are," Pig Knot declared. "Been using them all morning."

Sanjo half squinted. "Didn't steal those, did you?"

That took the once gladiator aback. "I look like a thief?" The last word came out as *teef*.

"You might not have any legs, but you've a powerful upper body. I imagine you could club someone out of a few coins if you well and truly tried."

Pig Knot appreciated the compliment. "Well, I could. But no. No, I haven't. These. Are mine."

"No offense meant, good sar," Sanjo said. "Merely run a fair business."

"None taken. I'll stay nearby. If you like. If you think I'll run." Pig Knot chuckled.

Sanjo didn't comment on that as he considered the offer. "Best you slide yourself inside a little further. Show people you're a customer instead of a beggar."

Pig Knot did as told. "Here?"

"That's fine," Sanjo said. "I'll start working on your cart right now."

He called the boys over, using the names Arna and Pindus. Sanjo told them to leave the door they'd been working on. The younger one, called Pindus, looked at Pig Knot with those evil eyes again, causing the legless gladiator to glower back.

Sanjo noticed Pindus staring and slapped the boy upside the head, jarring him.

"Apologies, good sar," the carpenter said. "He forgets his manners."

"Did the same when I was his age."

Pig Knot meant it as a joke, but neither father nor sons cracked a smile. That didn't bother him. He was full of good vibes aplenty—practically falling over because of good vibes. Shame he couldn't spread it around.

The father and his sons got to work.

With his back against a wall and his stumps splayed before him, Pig Knot watched, his hands at his sides. At times, he hummed a tune and glanced outside to appreciate the passing womenfolk. He even nodded and winked at a few and was rewarded with the odd smile.

Time crawled, all to the sounds of metal and flesh shaping wood.

The crowds thinned and slowed.

Pig Knot fell asleep at times, chin to chest, waking with a lurch or just cracking his eyes. The sun hung low on a fence of pointed rooftops, and the sky paled in broad swaths of red and pink. The smell of wood drifted throughout the shop. Sanjo and his boys worked well into the evening, not bothering to eat while Pig Knot's gut grumbled. He'd need to eat something soon—cart or nothing. He'd need to drink as well. The effects of the firewater and mead had worn away, leaving him feeling hollow.

Just before dark, the carpenter finished a few final touches to the project and placed it on the ground. He moved it back and forth with a foot, testing the wheels, and rolled it toward his customer.

The movement woke Pig Knot.

"Finished?" he asked, wiping drool from his lips.

Sanjo presented his work with an extended hand. The boys Pindus and Arna stood off to a side. Pindus still watched Pig Knot with unchecked annoyance.

"Excellent," the once gladiator said and hauled himself onto the seat. He fidgeted until somewhat comfortable, tucking his stumps inside the cart's low walls.

"You should buy yourself a blanket for that," Sanjo advised. "Or a cushion. Something to soften the ride, anyway."

"Perhaps later."

"Those front wheels will turn," Sanjo pointed out, "so you'll have no trouble steering. I've greased the axles, but if it goes dry, just come back, and I'll grease them again. No coin required."

"Many thanks," a red-eyed Pig Knot said. He leaned forward and rolled himself to the carpenter. "Very smooth. I'm just happy to have my balls above the ground once again."

"Suppose so." Sanjo smirked.

Pig Knot paid the man and left with a good feeling, ignoring a sour look from Pindus. He rolled outside and into traffic but realized some of the flat stones weren't as evenly placed as others, which required some effort to pull the cart over them. He pushed himself to the far right, steering with his hands, and rattled along, getting the feel for his newest means of transportation. People walking about and enjoying the evening heat gave him curious looks.

He didn't care. He was above the ground, still had coin in his purse, and had avoided pissing himself. All that made the day a good one.

Pig Knot's stomach rumbled. Time to get something to eat. And get back to drinking.

16

The wagons rattled through the villa's gates well before midnight and stopped alongside torches burning high on posts. The heat of the day had broken somewhat, but the air lacked the coolness needed for a comfortable sleep. Clavellus climbed out of his wagon and stretched. He still felt hung over, despite having drunk water along the way and pissing from the back. He didn't regret the night of drinking, but it punished his body harder with every passing day. It seemed to punish Muluk even more, he recalled. The bump and rattle of the open roads shook the Kree's innards more than the man cared to admit, but he endured.

The others dropped from the wagons behind him. He was about to shout for help when he spied a white-robed Nala emerging from their home. Her face sagged with relief.

"You're home," she said with a little smile. Clavellus delivered kisses to both her cheeks, shielding her from the activity at his back. A fragrance of scented water smelling of wildflowers surrounded her, and he held her close simply to breathe it.

"I'm home," he said. "We're home. How have you been, my lovely?"

"Well," she started, drawing away just a little, "things are wonderfully quiet when you and the lads are gone, but it's also boring."

"I'll have to see if I can do anything about that." Clavellus smiled.

"Saucy. You must have done well."

"Very well."

"Did you win?"

"Everything."

A pair of men helped Torello to the gladiators' living quarters. The sight distracted him for a moment, but then he told her the news of their victories. Then Nala saw the new faces—the woman, a man, and an older one-legged individual who hopped along.

"Ah, we're expanding," Clavellus explained. "Until we can find them homes. Or help build some. Or maybe they'll simply stay in one of the barracks' rooms. That one is called Kura. She's the wife of one of the once Sujin guards. And that one"—he indicated the one-legged man—"is something of a mystery, but I understand he helped the house while in the city. Gathering information on our behalf, I believe."

"A spy, you mean?"

Though gone only a day, Clavellus had missed his wife.

"You have plans for him, I suppose?" Nala asked.

"None yet, but we'll find something for him. Else he perish from boredom."

"And that one?" She indicated the shorter man in the gray shirt.

"He's the new armorer."

"An armorer?" she repeated doubtfully. "He best not be hammering things before midmorning."

"I'll make that known to him." *Or at least try to*, Clavellus thought, aware of the language barrier there.

"Well," she said, "it'll be good to have another lady walking the grounds. If only for a short while."

"An extra person for you to talk with."

"Perhaps she'd be interested in taking on household duties?"

"I'll let you decide that. Oh, and I brought you some things."

Nala's expression tightened then, and her husband knew something had gone wrong. "What?" he asked.

"Something happened while you were gone," she said. "The one called Pig Knot. He slipped away on the wagon delivering wine and such."

Clavellus's brow became a knot. "He what?"

"He persuaded Koba to help him."

That bit of information robbed Clavellus of speech.

"It wasn't planned," Nala explained, "but you'd best talk to him. He feels badly for it, though I see nothing wrong. The man—Pig Knot—simply didn't want to be here any longer. And we are not a prison."

Before Clavellus could respond, he detected a presence nearby. Machlann had stopped at the taskmaster's side, a question upon his weathered features.

"Where's Goll?" Clavellus asked.

Leaving the house masters and trainers to talk in a huddle, the guards and gladiators unloaded the wagons. Under the direction of Nala and a sleepy-looking Clurik, the men stowed the supplies away in cellars and storerooms. Once they finished, most of them retired for the night. Junger and a much-hurting Brozz retired to the gladiators' common room. The Sarlander and the Pericin sat down for a mug of water each, taking the time to cool off before bed.

"A long day." Junger smiled and hoisted his cup. "Your health, Sarlander. May those licks heal quickly. And that wreck you call a nose. That must truly sting."

"Right and proper," Brozz whispered. "Your health, Pericin. And continued success in the Pit."

They drank.

"Day is done," Junger said. "All in all, not a bad showing."

"Unfortunate about Torello," Brozz said.

"Unfortunate, but you saw him in the wagon."

Brozz had. To his and everyone's surprise, before the Sunjan was unloaded and carried to his bed, he'd reached over and taken Junger's hand, thanking him for avenging the death of Kolo.

"I did," the Sarlander said. "Perhaps I'll have another word with him before he's asleep."

"I think he's asleep now."

They listened. The odd voice could be heard outside, around the training grounds, but all was quiet in the gladiator barracks. Not even a snore, not that that was surprising. Not many of them were left.

"In the morning, then," Junger said. "No hurry."

Brozz grunted. A grimace crossed his face, which didn't escape Junger's attention.

"Just wondering," the Perician began. "How is the gut?"

"I'll survive."

"Imagine you will. I was slashed across the guts once. Once. Right nasty cut. Damned near disemboweled me. You don't think much of the word *disemboweled* until your innards are bulging through your fingers. Anyway, I held everything in. Got to a healer. Got sewn back together. A near thing, though."

Brozz listened with narrowed eyes, not feeling better in the least.

They sat in silence then, and all activity outside died away.

Sandals clopped softly across the floor, and Shan wandered in. The healer sat beside the two men and yawned. "All finished," he announced.

"Have a drink with us," Junger said.

"Many thanks, but no," the healer said, chin in his hands and his eyes already half shut. "Busy day tomorrow. And you should be able to sleep for a day and a bit."

Brozz's stern expression softened.

"We may not be here in the morning, good Shan," Junger warned. "Well, suppose I'll be here. Not so sure about the Sarlander. He could very well perish during the night."

"He'll be here." Shan covered his mouth and yawned. Then he glared at the Perician. "Little late in the day to be making jabs at a man. A wounded man, at that, in obvious punishment."

"Just stirring up a little fight in him, that's all."

"There are better ways to help a person."

Junger and Brozz exchanged looks.

"Apologies," Shan muttered. "Tired is all. Many things on my mind. Finally catching me is all."

"Your missus?" Junger asked.

"My missus. I hope she'll reconsider coming here."

"You think she will?"

"The offer's there. And I'm here. She'll think about it."

"What are the other things?"

Shan looked at him as if judging whether or not to say anything. In the end, he decided not. "Nothing. Just that. Well, until the morning, lads . . . Don't stay up too late." He glowered at Brozz. "I'm talking to you."

The Sarlander didn't respond.

"Well," Junger said, "it's one thing to bring cheer to this one"—he nodded toward Brozz—"but to a healer as well . . . Anytime you wish to talk, good Shan."

The healer patted the table and stood. "This is certainly a bloody business," he remarked under his breath and wandered off to his bunk. In a short time, Shan's distant snores reached the two remaining gladiators.

Junger smiled. "The man's in fine tune."

"He misses his wife," Brozz said.

"I imagine he does. That'll resolve itself. Clades now has his wife here. No Pig Knot, however," Junger said, studying the ceiling. "You overheard that as well as I did. It'll be strange not to see him around."

Brozz grunted. "I fully expected to see him drunk. And waiting for us."

"Maybe we'll see him again," Junger said.

"Why did you fight that third fight?" the Sarlander eventually asked.

"Oh. That." Junger looked to the table. Then his smile returned. "Been waiting to ask that one, I suppose. All the way back."

"I have."

"Well. That kind of patience deserves an answer. The Skarrs have orders to . . . persuade the Free Trained if they refuse to fight. The poor punce I replaced, he couldn't fight. The Skarrs would've killed him right there in the tunnel."

"Why didn't you kill them?" Brozz asked.

"The Skarrs?"

Brozz frowned.

"The blood challenges." Junger shrugged. "Why didn't you kill your opponent?"

"There was no need."

"There you have it. You see, Sarlander? We're not so different, you and I. Though I daresay you have more thread keeping you together."

Brozz didn't find the joke amusing.

"It was an easy decision," Junger stated and sipped his water. "Easy to fight one after the other. Goll wants us to be remembered. Well, we'll be remembered—for our mercy as well as our skill."

"You'll be remembered," Brozz corrected.

Junger frowned. "Perhaps. I'd rather not be, truth be known. I fight for the house, so that includes all of us."

"Not many of us left."

"No. There's not."

"Ten," Brozz stated quietly. "Now two."

"Scared?"

The big Sarlander reprimanded his companion with a look.

"Then don't concern yourself with such things," Junger said with cheer. "It's not a war we're fighting. It's organized, scheduled combat. Given the choice between that and, say, a battlefield of thousands, I'll take the arena every time. Just remember, if you can't continue because of wounds, then you can't continue. Or if you had your fill and don't *wish* to continue, then don't. Remember that."

A reflective Brozz inspected himself, placing a hand over his stomach wound. "I wonder what will happen if we're defeated in the Pit."

"I don't think we'll have to worry about that."

"The house, I mean."

"Concerned for the house? Your, ah, menacing glow is weakening, good Brozz."

The Sarlander didn't comment.

"I don't think we'll have to worry," Junger repeated. "If we fall, the house will do two things. The very worst . . . it'll disband. The very best? They'll recruit new gladiators for the next season. We won't care either way. Maybe we'll be remembered on a mural somewhere. I wouldn't mind that. Something fierce."

Brozz shook his head at the Perician. He had to admit, the little man amused him.

"So you let him go." Goll glared into Koba's impassive face.

Clavellus, Machlann, and the two Kree house masters had gathered in the small audience hall inside the taskmaster's residence. Upon a small table was a single oil-burning lamp casting long shadows on the walls.

"I tried to make him stay," Koba said in a clear and guiltless voice, "but he wouldn't listen."

"Perhaps you didn't try hard enough," Goll said. "Perhaps he was becoming a little too close to that girl you've been peeking at. Ananda's her name? Perhaps you wanted Pig Knot removed, and this was the cleanest way to do it."

"No," Koba said. "I . . . favor Ananda, and I'll not lie about not liking Pig Knot's interest in her, but I knew you—all of you—wouldn't be pleased with his leaving. I tried talking to him, reasoning with him, but he wouldn't have any of it. He wanted to return to Sunja. Said it turned his guts rancid watching whole men train while he sat and baked in the sun. Made him feel worthless. I . . . could understand that. Then he said he was a house master and questioned who I was to stop him from leaving. I had no answer. So I helped him. Onto the wagon. He had coin to buy his way."

"Coin?" Clavellus asked, looking at Goll.

ABOUT THE BLOOD

"He asked me for a purse of coin," the Kree admitted. "Said he'd much prefer saving it himself than me holding onto it." He then fixed Koba with a hard, considering scowl. "Did he say anything as he was leaving? Any words for us?"

"He . . ." Koba's head slanted one way, the lamp casting a fearful light across the man's missing ear. "He thanked me. Wished me good fortune. That was all."

"Good fortune?"

Koba set his jaw and wouldn't meet Goll's gaze. The Kree then realized Pig Knot had wished the trainer well in his pursuit of the girl.

"Well," Goll said. "Damnation."

"Pig Knot's right," Muluk muttered. "As much as I enjoyed the shagger's company, he can do what he likes. He's not a prisoner here."

"So why would he want to leave?" Goll asked. "This place has everything he needs. A roof over his head. A place to sleep. Food and water. *Drink*. Lords above, he knows he can *drink* for free here. But he leaves everything so he can return to Sunja? What's he going to do there?"

No one had an answer.

"We'll leave for the city in the morning," Goll declared. "Organize search parties. We'll find that stupid punce. Bring him back."

Machlann and Clavellus exchanged dark looks.

"Sunja is huge," the taskmaster pointed out quietly, "with a near infinite number of holes and cracks a person might hide, especially if one truly wanted to be left alone. Master Goll, the man's gone. He's gone. Let him be. If he found his way to the city, he can find his way back. If he wishes. No amount of searching will recover him."

Goll fumed, lips twisted into an angry pucker.

"Nothing we can do, my son," Machlann added. "Except get ready for our next opponents."

"We might see him in the streets," Clavellus suggested. "You never know. There's always a chance of that."

Goll didn't think so. "We won't. Like you said. Not unless he wants us to. If he couldn't stomach watching our lads train, I doubt he'll be anywhere near the games. He'll stay far and away from the Pit."

"Well," Clavellus said to Koba, "you did what you could. You're blameless here, Koba. No wrongdoing in my eyes. Good night, all. I'm off to find my missus."

With that, the taskmaster left the room. Machlann and Koba followed. Muluk remained, however.

"Far from blameless," Goll said in Kree. "That idiot. That unfit idiot."

"Pig Knot will do what Pig Knot wants," Muluk reasoned. "I'm disappointed he didn't speak with us, but . . . he knew we'd want him to stay. Perhaps that's why he left like he did."

"Stupid, unfit cow kiss."

"We'll see him again," Muluk said.

"But in what state? What state, Muluk?"

"You're not happy about this, are you?"

"No. No, I'm not."

"Why, then?" Muluk asked. "Answer me that. He did everything you asked of him. Why can't you let the man go? You did with Halm."

"Halm will come back. He will. That much I know. Pig Knot's different. If it wasn't for him, we wouldn't have any of this. He should've stayed here."

The lack of light made Muluk's frown all the more intimidating. "So you feel indebted to him? Perhaps even responsible? For what happened to him?"

Goll sighed. "Aye that."

"I see. Well, I think he's released you from that. The moment he left."

Goll's shoulders slumped as those words reached him.

"As you said," Muluk reminded his companion, "he had everything he needed here, but he chose to leave it. He didn't want it. His choice. Not yours. Nothing more can be done."

Goll remained quiet.

"Nothing more," Muluk repeated. "As Clavellus said, if the topper can find his way to the city, he'll find his way back. If he wishes. Maybe he'll find what he's looking for. Maybe not. And maybe he'll return in the end. The best we can do for him, as far as I see it, is to hope he's well. Hope he's not hungry. Or thirsty. And has a safe place to sleep."

A thump from another part of the household, somewhere on the second level, stopped the conversation.

Muluk rubbed the back of his hairy neck and sighed. "Old Clavellus is throwing his boots at the floor. Well, it's late. And there's training in the morning."

Goll regarded the man. "You're wiser than you look."

Muluk's hairy features brightened. "Really? I am? That was wisdom? What I just said?"

"That was."

Muluk seemed impressed with himself. "What did I say, again?"

Goll shook his head. "Thank you, Muluk. I'm fine now."

"*You* might be fine," the other said ruefully, "but I have an armorer who doesn't speak Kree or Sunjan."

17

The door creaked upon opening.

Naulis stepped inside, taking care in the dark interior. He closed the door behind him and swore softly as he groped for a length of wood. He located the plank in short time and slid it through a pair of hooks, barring the door and securing his home for the night. Then he wandered across the floor, stopping at a small fireplace. There, he dropped to a knee and gathered a small mound of grass and twigs. Upon that he dabbed a little oil from a long-necked container. He fumbled for a flint and stone, righted a candle, and scratched for a light.

In short time, he had a small fire going and lit the candle.

The wick came to life, and he turned around, freezing at the sight of Borchus sitting at a table.

Naulis gasped, his overbite and sunken chin making him appear even more surprised. "What are you doing here?"

"I'm here to see you."

"How you'd get in?"

"That's a secret," Borchus said without humor. "One I hope you never find out."

Naulis slumped against a wall, scratched at a greasy head of hair, and composed himself. He walked into an area lined with cupboards one yank away from falling apart. He opened one, which stayed intact, and fished out a bottle.

"What's that?" Borchus asked.

"Mead."

"I'll have some of that."

"You'll get out," Naulis warned, "and be mindful of the damned door on the way."

"I'll leave after we've had our talk."

Naulis faced the man and, after a brief bout of critical thinking, decided to grab two wooden cups instead of one. He sat across from Borchus. "What about?" he asked.

Borchus indicated the mead first.

"You can have a drink afterwards."

The agent didn't approve of that, though. Twirling a finger, he insisted his cup be filled.

Naulis reluctantly did so, and when the drinks were poured, they drank.

"Not bad at all," the agent declared. "Where'd you get this?"

"The market."

"This is truly good."

"I get it when I can afford it," Naulis admitted. "Which is why I'm not so eager to share."

"I can understand that," Borchus said and topped off his cup without asking. "To business, then. Naulis, you've shown you can be very dependable. Reliable. Even trustworthy."

Naulis sat in silence, his mouth open. With his large overbite and sunken chin, he looked as if he were in a constant state of gawking.

"So I've decided to offer you more work," Borchus said. "Steadier work."

"Dangerous work." Naulis muttered with a knowing eye, his mouth clamping shut.

"Only if you get caught."

"Doing what? I don't steal from people."

"Not asking you to steal."

"And I don't kill people."

Borchus paused. "I'm asking you to spy."

That set Naulis back. "Spy?"

Borchus sipped his mead.

"Spy on who?"

"Not spy on who—spy *for*. The House of Ten. The same house you've been running messages to on my behalf."

Naulis's face screwed up in distaste. "I might look like an unfit punce, Borchus, but I do have a brain. Who does the house want me to spy upon? I don't mind running messages out across the plains to a house and then back again. The only thing I have to worry about then are bandits and Dezer. Both of which I can usually see because I'm *on* a *plain*. I can run faster scared than they can angry. No plains in the city. Only crooks and crevices. Plenty of places to get hurt or wind up butchered if one's none too careful. Plenty of places for enemies to hide. And one would have to be very careful about spying."

"Think of it more as information gathering," Borchus said, meeting the other's eyes. "But to answer your question, you'd be spying on everyone related to the season's games. Discreetly, I might add. Leaning ever so slightly towards a conversation at the next table over. A talk in an alleyway or even in amongst the spectators of the fights. Anything about the games and the gladiators within it. Anything related to the House of Ten. Anything that might improve their chances for victory in the arena."

Naulis thought about it. "I'd be only listening, then."

"Correct."

"Who'd be paying?"

"The Ten. Through me."

"Would I still get to ride out there? To the house?"

Borchus frowned. "Why do you ask?"

"They treated me quite well last time. Fed me and my animal. Even gave me a place to sleep for the night."

Borchus thought about it. "I'll probably send you out there when it's called for."

"How much would I be paid?"

The agent shrugged. "Three gold pieces a day."

"Three, eh?"

The agent nodded.

"To listen."

"And the occasional ride out of the city. Which you seem to enjoy doing."

"Doesn't seem like much."

Borchus acknowledged that. "That's still three gold a day, Naulis. Think about it. If you wish, place wagers to fatten your pot."

"I don't gamble on the games."

"Then save a coin every now and then. Tuck it away somewhere. It'll add up quick enough."

Naulis thought about it. "Three gold, eh?"

"Three."

"Not bad, I suppose."

"Not at all. For what you're doing. Even more if you wager here and there."

"Said I don't do that."

"That's right." The candlelight reflection flickered in Borchus's eyes. "You did."

"What if I'm discovered by another house?"

"They'll punish you. Maybe even kill you."

"*Probably* kill me. If they discover I'm with the Ten."

Borchus conceded the man had him there. "Then don't let them know. Don't get discovered. Use those hiding places you mentioned earlier. I'm being honest with you, Naulis. This isn't the kind of work for the meek. Not when there are riches involved. Fame to be had. What of it, then? The work pays well, considering the risks. It isn't plowing a field somewhere. Or hacking down trees."

"Nothing wrong with that." Naulis frowned.

"Or this, for one with the right frame of mind. I think you might have that mind."

Naulis studied the agent over his cup's rim. "Daresay I'm going to get killed for this."

"Daresay."

"How long would this be?"

"The length of the season."

"You know the season's been extended."

That made Borchus stop drinking. "What?"

"The season's been extended. Lengthened. Whatever you want to call it. That's what I heard."

"Where?"

"Just walking up the street there."

"Just now?"

"Aye that. Pair of lads talking about it while sharing a pipe. Nothing wrong with that. The longer season, that is, not the pipe. My first bit of spying, I wager, considering the look on your face."

"The season's been extended," a surprised Borchus repeated. "That *is* news. Any reason why?"

"King Juhn wanted it so. Didn't hear anything more. I didn't join the conversation."

"No, no, that's fine. That'll be your first official task tomorrow. Go to the Madea and ask about that very thing."

"What?" Naulis balked. "Back into the pisspot called general quarters? The very air in that place can kill a person. A dead man's *hole* smells better."

"That's just your mind."

"Well, I'm mindful of going back there. The Free Trained alone are dangerous. And most of them have their own weapons. Look at me. The ladies like me because I'm *not* a savage brute. You don't see the other houses going down there. And didn't you say all I had to do was listen around tables and alleyways?"

"I did."

"Well, there you are, then."

That silenced Borchus for a bit. "Will you do it?"

"Is there more coin?"

"I can free up another."

"That's all right, then. So five gold a day?" Naulis asked.

Borchus sighed. "Four gold."

"Four." Naulis chuckled. "My mistake. Yes, four gold."

"Done."

"Done." Naulis held out his closed fist. Borchus pressed his own against it.

"Now then, that's settled," the agent said, swirling his mead. "Two things. Tomorrow, find out what you can about the season becoming longer. I was talking to our employers just this day, and while it wasn't a long talk, they failed to mention anything about a longer season. That tells me they have no idea of this development. When you do find out the details, leave for the Ten. Tell Goll. He'll be interested in learning this."

Naulis repeated the instructions in his head. "And the other thing?"

Borchus sat back. "Know anyone else interested in working as a spy?"

18

The morning light bore into Gastillo's bedchamber, bringing a frown to his face. He opened his eyes, the sun's brilliance dulled by the mosquito netting his servants had draped over the unshuttered window. Gastillo propped himself up on an elbow and scratched his belly. The pillows were wet from his incessant drooling during the night. With a kick, he sent his blanket flying. He rose and quickly dressed, pulling on a loose summer robe and slipping on sandals. He grabbed his mask, resting on a small table, and left the room.

Today was the day.

One meeting might very well solve all of his troubles—with the wine merchant Nexus.

Before they'd parted company the previous day, the old dealer had asked him to visit his home after the day's games. Nexus didn't care if Curge knew or not, and he told Gastillo as much. Gastillo however, didn't want to mention the meeting with the one-armed owner. He didn't need Curge antagonizing him over dealing with Nexus. Gastillo needed his mind clear.

If he could convince Nexus to purchase his house . . . that would be simply *wonderful*.

He entered his dining room, where the elderly Danshon carried a blue-and-white pitcher.

"Good morning, good Danshon."

"Master Gastillo."

"Another hot morning."

"That it is, sar. That it is. Will you be eating on your balcony this morning?"

"No. Here is fine."

Gastillo sat at a wide table, the surface pitted and scarred. He placed his golden mask beside him, thoughts on the approaching meeting swirling. Without thinking, he prodded at the open hole that was half of his shredded nose. The memory of having his face raked from his skull was long lost to him. All he could recall was attempting to duck from the mace.

Then an explosion of night.

Bandages were covering his face when he awoke, and he supposed it was for the best that he carried on with them in some capacity. He was well aware of what he looked like, a mangled fright marked by rude scars, numerous red-pink lines detailing precisely where the stitches had held his face together for a month.

Danshon brought him whole boiled eggs, toast, honey butter, and sliced apples. A pitcher of water, not the juice pulp of some fruit, lay at Gastillo's right hand. Danshon moved around his employer without comment or fuss. The older manservant was one of the few people who regularly saw the once gladiator without his mask.

"Things are stirring, Danshon," Gastillo said as he ate, always a messy affair controlled by frequent dabs of a hand cloth. "Things are stirring. This day might bring very good winds to our house."

"Excellent, Master Gastillo," the man said, wizened eyes matching his reserved smile. "I hope the day exceeds your expectations."

"I hope so."

Gastillo finished eating and stood, holding a cloth to his lower face. He donned his mask and paused with nearly regal poise. Though his face was scarred, Gastillo remained in good shape, holding back the years through a combination of good food and regular exercise.

He left Danshon to clear the table and walked through his house, to the training grounds. Sounds of wood clattering off wood reached his ear. He emerged outside, before a wide area filled with various tools and apparatuses used to transform men into physical beasts and perfect their fearsome skills to their sharpest.

Sowin the taskmaster, with his bowed back and clean-shaven chin, wandered over to Gastillo's side. "Fine morning, Master Gastillo."

"Fine morning." He then focused on the pit fighters being put through their paces. The men duckwalked, lifted weights, and unleashed multiple combinations upon practice men in a continuous circuit of pain. They glistened in the morning light, chests heaving, their sweat staining the very sands.

"Who fights this day?" Gastillo asked, spotting the hellion Prajus as he duckwalked over a stretch of sand. *No smile upon his face this morning*, the owner thought blackly.

"Kassian. From Marrn."

"See to it he doesn't overexert himself this morning. Just do just enough to get the blood flowing. Can't have him perish in the Pit."

"As you wish. The others?"

"Run them until they drop," Gastillo said, catching the eyes of Prajus as he stood and repeatedly lifted a heavy timber above his head. The insolent pit fighter bared his teeth with every repetition, growling with the effort. His muscular torso gleamed with perspiration.

Gastillo hoped the man's shoulders failed and that terrible weight would brain the punce underneath.

"As you wish, sar," Sowin said, keeping an eye on the exercising. "We'll see to it."

"Any troubles last night?" Gastillo asked.

"None that I know of."

ABOUT THE BLOOD

Prajus groaned loudly, his face fit to explode from exertion. He continued lifting the timber, bellowing from the burn.

Gastillo hoped it hurt.

"Good," he muttered, looking to the other gladiators. "Good."

"If I might say so, Master Gastillo," Sowin said, scratching his chin, "begging your pardon. I know you don't care for the man. Is it truly worth the anguish of keeping him?"

"If you'd asked me that two days ago, I would've given you a different answer. This morning, however, I will say yes. It is. But only for a little while."

The old man's face brightened with sly understanding. "Something planned, have you?"

"When I'm ready to tell you, old friend, I will."

They watched Prajus snarl and drop the weighted timber, where it crashed in a plume of dust. The pit fighter panted and stalked over to a wooden figure. He snatched up a wooden sword, made certain Gastillo was watching, and attacked the target with furious energy, energy that should have been exhausted from the previous exercise. Prajus slammed home combinations that blurred into the upright frame, rocking it, hammering out a tune. Upon completion, he would relax, withdraw a step, reset, and attack the figure anew.

With a different series of attacks.

Behind his back, Gastillo's hands crossed at the wrists and became fists. His mask revealed nothing, but underneath, his features contorted into a frightening scowl. He truly despised Prajus, despised him enough to be rid of the arrogant maggot any way possible without having to kill him.

That thought appealed to Gastillo, however. *Kill him as an example to others.*

Or he could sell him along with the others and profit.

However, a part of him would've liked nothing more than to smash that insolent look from the gladiator's face. Despite the man's obvious talents, Prajus was an ass licker, a pompous, arrogant ass licker. He almost made Gastillo pick up steel again and fight the dog. Fighting him would play into Prajus's hands. Selling him . . . Gastillo allowed himself a smile. Selling him—and the house—was brilliant. The more he thought about it, the more he liked the idea.

Prajus unleashed another combination at the target, glancing over with a sweaty, challenging look of contempt.

"Eyes on that target, you hellpup!" Sowin blasted at the gladiator, startling Gastillo. Sowin was old and buckling about the edges, but he had a voice that could be heard for days.

With a sly smile, Prajus sent the message to the taskmaster that he'd do as he pleased.

"I said eyes on that target, you unfit bastard!"

That got Prajus moving.

"Right and proper full of himself, that one," Sowin commented afterward. "I so dislike that."

Gastillo agreed.

Soon, however, with a smile from Seddon above, he'd be free of the dog blossom.

19

He was called Biljus and had probably killed, murdered, and raped more people than three times his years. He'd forgotten most of the whos and whens of it, but the faces he remembered. They haunted him every night since his imprisonment. He'd run with a blackhearted bunch of bandits that roamed and hunted the area to the south, just beyond Plagur's Reach, where they met their bloody end at the spears of a patrol of Sunjan lancers. Only he survived, later sentenced to a life in darkness.

That was at least ten years before, at least. He'd lost track of all time. Ten years might have been twenty, for all he knew. The jailors didn't talk to him, and his cell was in a secluded part of the dungeon, where only the worst criminals were locked away and forgotten.

He'd had plenty of time to sit and think . . . and regret.

Time had no meaning in the dark—none at all—so when they came for him, opened his cell, bound him in ropes, and hauled his miserable carcass into the light, he fought, screeched, twisted, and spat. When he saw the sun for the first time in years, it nearly burned his eyes out and only deepened his insanity. The Skarrs didn't care. They tied him and packed him into a box with a bunch of other animals.

Then the Skarrs hauled them all off to the Pit.

After all he'd been through, in that deep, disturbing darkness, where things sometimes gnawed upon his skin, he still remembered the Pit. Images of having his head hacked off by a masked executioner haunted him for years, but that never came true.

How they had surprised him.

He didn't know how he was going to fight. Ages had passed since he'd held a blade. He barely had the strength to lift a sword, not that it mattered. Biljus didn't care in the least. He still retained enough sense to know he was finally going to die.

In Sunja's Pit.

The only question was . . . when.

Since he'd lived in the darkness for so long anyway, he supposed a few more days were of no consequence. He'd go when they called for him, for his past deeds, for his sins. A person got a lot of thinking done over ten years—or however long it had been—of imprisonment. He believed he'd been a different person then, and while he wasn't sorry for his crimes, he felt he'd changed, all the same. For the better. At one point, he'd even vowed that if he ever got his freedom, he'd go straight to the Salish and devote the rest of his days to serving the Lords above and Seddon.

Try and do some good in the time he had left.

"You're going into the Pit this day," Balazz had whispered to him from beyond the bars of his new cell. "You remember the Pit, don't you, you pig blossom? You might want to pray to whatever hellion that kept you alive up to this point. You're going to face a killer. Like yourself."

There, in the deepest part of his cell, Biljus's eyes glistened at the news.

"Now, I've got words for you," Balazz continued. "You fight hard. You fight. The man you're facing is a Jackal. A *Jackal*. You remember them, right? You got the hardest reputation of any of these stone lice, and I expect you to collect a scalp or two at these games. Starting from this day forth. You hearing me, you sun-crusted cow kiss?"

ABOUT THE BLOOD

The jailor cracked a club off the cell's bars, startling Biljus.

"You summon up whatever killing fury you got," Balazz went on, "and you put that he-bitch down. Cut him up like you did your victims. Leave him sliced and bleeding in the sun. Just like all the others. You hear me? I see your eyes twinkling back there in the dark. I see you. You better say something else I come in there and break the first bone I grab."

Biljus knew the jailor was speaking the truth. Runson was bad, but Balazz was a creature of the night.

"I hear you," Biljus said.

"What are you going to do when they come for you?"

"Fight in the Pit. Kill a man."

"Kill a Jackal."

"Aye that. Kill a Jackal."

Balazz paused, pleased with the answers. "Good. That's good."

The jailor cracked the door once again and left.

Evil bastard, the once killer thought.

Then he thought about the Jackal he would face . . . in combat . . . after so long.

They'd chosen him because of his reputation. So be it.

His reputation had done him some good after all.

When the Skarrs came for him, he didn't resist. Eight armed men filled the passageway, all armed and ready to gut him there. Biljus could sense them *hoping* he might attack them. He saw how edgy and ready they were when the cell door opened. He saw their eyes. Aye that, they knew his name even though the guards were probably only children when'd he committed all those crimes, when he'd killed all those people . . . or worse.

They surrounded him, swords at the ready. They herded him through the upper levels, pushing him along.

The white tunnel—even that muted glare roused by lamplight made his eyes hurt. Pain—a taste of what was to come. He'd become a creature of the dark. They should have realized that.

Perhaps they had.

A short sword was slapped into his hand, the weight barely manageable. A Skarr faced him, and gray eyes the color of a morning mist rising over Sunja's plains studied Biljus's face.

"Do what you do best, old man," the guard said.

Biljus blinked. Hands shoved him past the gatekeeper, and he almost stumbled upon the stairs leading into the light. *That hateful light.* He shied away from it, the pain already in his eyes and head.

A wall of armor and weapons stood firm behind him, ready to gut him there if needed. There was no going back, only forward.

Just as well, then. Time to return to the light, the terrible, terrible light.

The gate rose with a rumble.

The deepest blue. Freedom, at last.

Or at least a form of it.

Taking a breath, Biljus walked into the closest thing he'd experienced to freedom in years.

The sands warmed his bare feet. The crowds jeered and cursed him the moment he appeared. He looked up and winced, the sun admonishing him for lifting his head. In that brief glimpse, he saw more people than he'd ever recalled, and he'd attended the games before. They shouted and swore at him, shook fists and spat. He set his jaw, straightened his back and took it, knowing he deserved everything . . . and more.

The light gave him his first good look at his own body. His hands had become knotted but soft in the palms. His midsection was emaciated, skeletal even, no longer lean and hard. The muscle upon his frame, well, he didn't need to look anymore. He knew what state he was in.

The roar of the crowds lifted his head.

Blessed Seddon.

The pain . . . He couldn't see but brief flickers. Sun spots danced upon the glaring white sands.

His sword was far too heavy, so he dropped it.

He fell to his knees, grimacing as if the day was crushing the very life from him.

ABOUT THE BLOOD

Biljus thought about his victims, and the guilt was painful enough for him to wish himself dead thrice over. He bent over, eyes squeezed shut, and pressed his cheek into the sand, feeling the heat on his unclean flesh.

He smelled his skin burning under the sun's attention, a little pleasure he didn't deserve.

He'd done bad things, terrible things, and he didn't deserve any chances at life in the least. Locked away in the dark, a person always had a chance to realize what they'd done was wrong. From that point, the question was what could be done to correct the wrongdoing.

The sheer volume of sound threatened to crush him. Biljus opened his eyes. A shadow approached, black and haunting against the scalding brightness. He couldn't quite make the figure out, but it was a man. A Jackal. The one he was meant to fight. Pain lanced his brain and bounced off the back of his skull.

He knew he didn't have much time remaining.

That made Biljus smile, just a little.

"I would've joined the Salish," he said, feeling his throat tighten with regret, hearing the tremble in his own voice. "If they'd taken me. I would've joined the Salish."

The unchecked roar from the crowds pressed down upon him until their voices became a singular note of vengeance. At least, that's how it sounded to Biljus. In his personal darkness, where his skin cooked and beaded sweat, he sensed a presence as if he'd stepped through a tempest and found its calming heart. The ground shivered, if for only a heartbeat.

It lurked above him. Biljus could hear it breathing, if that was possible.

"I've done bad things," he whispered, the sand's heat branding his cheek. "And I'm sorry . . . I would've joined the Salish."

The one concentrated note rose in pitch, as if the very arena was rising, leaving him, until the sound became nothing more than an uninterrupted ringing in his ears.

Odd.

Biljus opened his eyes.

The Jackal split his head open to the jawline.

The Skarrs escorted Noll back into his cell and slammed the door behind him. The veteran Jackal returned to the bars, gripped the iron, and pressed his forehead against the cold metal.

"Still alive?" Dogslaw asked from nearby.

"Still alive. Probably dead tomorrow, though."

Dogslaw grinned at the resignation lacing the man's voice. Old Noll believed he was always on the very cusp of dying, as well as those around him.

"That's tomorrow," Dogslaw reminded him, holding onto the bars of his own cell. "Until then, you get one more night in this delightful place."

A chuckle rang through the gloom.

"Who'd you kill?" Mad Lokan asked from the next cell over. "Tell us, old man, tell us. Did he scream? Did he beg for mercy? Did he drive you to near exhaustion and almost get the better of you? Hm? What of it? Did you have the advantage from the beginning? Was it a slaughter, or was it a fight?"

Noll thought about that. "It was an execution," he reported in a somber voice.

That set Mad Lokan off in a gruesome tittering that sounded as if he were squatting and trying to pass a boulder.

"It was an execution," Noll repeated. "The man wasn't much of it. Old skin stretched over older bones. Doubt if he could even hold up his sword, let alone swing it. He made it only a few steps outside of his gate before he dropped to his knees. I had to walk the width of the arena to get to him, and when I did, he was speaking. Maybe praying. And he was old. Looked terribly old. Older than me. Whoever he was, be it murderer or thief, he'd wasted away to nothing in the dark. Spent. Broken. He wasn't going to fight. And I couldn't return unless I killed him. So I killed him. One chop. To the head. As quick as I could make it. He even opened his eyes at the last instant, just before it all flew apart."

ABOUT THE BLOOD

The telling left both Dogslaw and Lokan quiet. Leave it to Noll to sour the spirits of those around him. In one way, the other prisoners were fortunate they couldn't speak the language.

"Been warring with the Sunjans all my adult years," Noll added after a pause. "Killed my share. I don't like them. But what I did today was an execution. The first I've ever had to do. And . . . it felt like mercy."

"What was it like up there?" Dogslaw asked over the din of other nearby prisoners.

"Bright," Noll answered quietly, changing the subject. The faintest smile flickered across his bearded face. "Hot. Just the barest of breezes, and that was hot as well, like the lightest lick of the Harudin hell winds. Or so I've heard. Even the sands were hot to the foot. Noisy as well. Thousands up there, watching the blood fly. Thousands. Too many to count, perhaps. Excitement hangs in the air like a thunderhead ready to spit lightning. Yes, that's it. All of that."

Mad Lokan chittered that unnatural, straining laugh while Dogslaw looked at the ceiling. All he'd wanted was a quick answer. He should've known better, talking to Noll. He always went the long way around.

"I think Lokan is next," Dogslaw said.

"I'm next," the mad one said, venom in his voice. "I'm most certainly next. Yes. I'll bleed them. Bleed them all."

"And I believe I'm after him," Dogslaw added calmly. "The jailor was eyeing me earlier."

"I see," Noll said in a mournful tone, not bothering with well-wishes or warnings to be careful. "Do what you can, then. Make your peace to whoever's listening. Perhaps I'll talk to you later."

"Perhaps." Dogslaw smirked at Noll's uplifting nature.

Not many stayed in the man's company because of his dour and depressing mood. Locked away in the Pit's dungeons, however, in the fetid dark broken by torchlight, Dogslaw discovered he was grateful for the man's steadfast calm and his willingness to talk, even if it was depressing.

"I'm next, Noll," Lokan insisted, his anger rising. "I'm next. And I'll execute my opponent as well. Won't be quick, however. It won't be quick. If these Sunjan ass lickers want to be entertained, I'll entertain them. I'll amuse them. I'll deliver a banquet of butchery for their eyes. A hot soup of killing. Enough to choke every one of the thousands in attendance and any outside of this place. Just wait. Just wait. I'll blind them with my thumbs. You'll see. Or rather, you'll *hear* of it. You'll hear."

Dogslaw peered across the dimly lit hall, toward Lokan's cell. A torso stepped away from the bars, disappearing into the cage's depths. Dogslaw was glad Lokan was locked away. The man uneased him. His sanity had snapped sometime after he'd been captured.

"What weapon did they give you?" Dogslaw asked of Noll, turning his attention to the right.

"A sword. Short sword. Old weapon. Like myself. Barely had a proper edge to it. My shoulder is still ringing from the effort."

"You're getting older."

"And wiser."

"Plenty of time to do that here."

"Aye that."

"Armor?"

"Just raw skin. Nothing more."

That didn't sound good.

Lokan had quieted in his cell, perhaps not much liking the notion of being naked in an arena. A heartbeat later, Dogslaw noticed the true reason for the man's silence. A column of Skarrs, their mail shirts gleaming in the brazier light, gathered at Lokan's door. They spoke to him, their tone indicating the Nordish man be on his best behavior. Dogslaw knew the man had, in fact, been learning a few words of Sunjan from a prisoner in the previous dungeon, a man no doubt as unfit in the head as Lokan himself.

Locks clattered. The cell door swung open, and the Skarrs swarmed inside, seizing Lokan. They pulled him out by his arms and surrounded him. In such close quarters, the knot of a dozen men or so sent to escort one prisoner seemed excessive. The Sunjans had been like that. Ever since the Field of Skulls.

"I'm going now!" Lokan shouted. "I'm going! Going to get those eyes. Going to choke a neck. Going to do as much killing as I can in the time they give me!"

Lokan didn't resist the Skarrs, which didn't surprise Dogslaw. They were going where Lokan wanted to go.

Even though the man was half insane, perhaps even *all* insane, Lokan was still a Jackal, still a weapon of the Ikull, still Nordish. He was one of the few left alive that reminded Dogslaw . . . that *connected* him to his homeland in the distant northwest.

"Good fortunes to you, Lokan," he whispered.

"Good fortune," Noll said nearby.

The well-wishes surprised the young Nordish man.

20

As Noll had said, they gave Lokan nothing in the way of armor.

The Skarrs pushed him along the passageways, the stairs bringing him closer to the surface. Curlord love him, he could smell the difference in the air, could taste the sandy grit. The passageways became cleaner as well. Lokan looked forward to the fight—looked forward to it very much. Any day he was permitted to fight a sworn enemy of his people was a good day, a very good day. And after so long being imprisoned, Lokan wanted very much to hurt someone.

The Skarrs steered him through a white tunnel, to the base of a final climb of stairs. Above, a portcullis's thick timbers and iron bars cut the sky into blue squares. Shouts came through that barrier, cries eager for the next bout of blood.

The guards ahead of him split apart, and a Skarr faced him. The eyes behind the visor spoke in a tongue that needed no translation. The man grabbed Lokan's arm and slapped a sword into the Nordish warrior's palm. The Skarr glared, clearly not trusting or liking the Jackal, and Lokan sensed the group of Sunjans wouldn't need much of a reason to cut him down.

They might do it anyway.

The guard got out of the way. The portcullis rose.

ABOUT THE BLOOD

Lokan looked at the blade. He looked at the guards. Then he looked at the rising gate above.

He bolted toward the light.

After exploding onto the sands with a wild shriek of glee, Lokan ran barefoot across the arena, his arms lifted to the skies, reaching for it. He cringed under the daylight but endured the discomfort, wallowed in it. He would give it back ten times over to his opponent. Lokan was in the mood for bloodletting. Noll said he'd executed a man. An *old* man. Said the *skolla curnos* was feeble, unable to fight.

An execution didn't bother Lokan. In fact, he felt right and proper *ready* to do a little executing—young or old, big or small.

Angry Sunjans rained curses upon his head, and he lapped it all up and howled for more. He drew his thumb across the scars decorating his bearded face and cheeks. He jabbed his short sword at the contorted faces high above, pretended he was about to sling his weapon into the masses, and mocked their frightened reactions, then he even cupped his manhood and shook it at any daring to look.

The brazen display infuriated the masses, and they yelled and swore, shaking fists and feigning death blows back at him.

Lokan drank it down and gave it back . . . and *more*.

The angry voices rose in pitch. Lokan turned around and saw the distant portcullis crank open in spastic jerks. A deep but phlegmy voice spoke over his head, and the crowds responded with a howl.

Lokan smirked. He didn't care. Very soon, he'd give them something to howl about. Taking a firmer grip on his blade, he waited for the unfortunate *curnos* to appear.

He didn't wait long.

A tall, muscular brute of a man stepped into the light. The warrior, as this clearly was no old bastard waiting or willing to be executed, stood at least a whole head taller than Lokan. The short sword in his hand seemed more a dagger. The man possessed no neck that Lokan could discern, only a chin attached to cords better suited for mooring a heavy ship to a pier. Hair drizzled the fellow's great shoulders like mangy fur, and for a moment, Lokan believed the monster to be the feral offspring of a particularly violent coupling between a man (or woman) and a bear in heat.

Or something much worse.

"Mollo!" the people chanted. "Mollo!"

Mollo. Lokan heard the name on the tongues of thousands.

The arena praised the frightening monster and delighted in how he dampened Lokan's enthusiasm. Mollo didn't acknowledge the crowds. His great bearded face focused on the Nordish man and smiled. No teeth were to be seen.

After a singular, commanding shout, the spectators screamed approval.

Mollo slapped a thick shoulder with the flat of his blade and walked toward the Jackal.

Lokan's eyes narrowed. He shifted from one foot to the other, no longer as confident as when he'd first emerged from the arena's depths. The crowds knew it. They could *smell* it.

Mollo kicked up sand as he crossed the floor, legs working like knotted, moss-covered tree trunks. Sweat gleamed off his hairy torso. His black beard grew in size the closer he got though his hair had been shorn to the skull.

A head taller? As Mollo approached, Lokan realized his mistake. The man was two heads taller and at least that much wider.

The Sunjans might have built a cell around the beast.

Mollo bellowed a harsh line of gibberish then, a nonsensical piss stream of hate and promises of pain, of blood and carnage and bones soon to be snapped across Mollo's knee. His furry smile widened with every step, and the black balls of his eyes became all the wilder.

Lokan rolled his own shoulders and locked gazes with his much larger adversary.

ABOUT THE BLOOD

When Mollo got within five strides of him, the man beast charged with a mighty yell.

The whole of the arena yelled with him.

Lokan ducked under a sweep of Mollo's sword arm, diving headlong into a windstorm that would've blew anyone lesser back ten paces. Lokan slashed as he went under that big arm, cutting a red line across a furry gut.

The cheering faltered, only as long as it took Mollo to whirl about, his hand covering that gruesome parting of flesh. His fingers oozed blood that dappled the arena floor.

Mad Lokan spun as well, dismayed that the monster still lived. He regarded his blade and cringed. His unfit *fingernails* had a sharper edge.

Mollo charged. He swung for the head, chopped for a shoulder, and thrust for the heart. Lokan ducked, weaved, and ducked again, avoiding his largish foe's powerful attacks.

A fist caught Lokan square in the face.

The Jackal landed flat on his back, his face screaming pain. The crowds screamed laughter. Lokan rolled over, pulling his knees to his chest. He remembered he was fighting some half-man, half-mountain bear creature. That much he knew.

The ground trembled. He felt it against his cheek.

Lokan rolled away from a sword stabbing a full hand's length into the sand. The Nordish man barely escaped a foot stomp and skittered away from a second heel slamming down.

With Mollo behind him, Lokan scampered to his feet.

A lick of pain zipped down his back.

Lokan staggered, stood, and winced at the cut. Though he could not see it, he felt it, right down to the right cheek of his ass.

And it stung like fire.

Lokan straightened and nodded, giving credit where it was due, and with a grim smile, beckoned the towering monster closer.

Smiling himself, a bleeding Mollo rumbled forward, bellowing while scarlet ribbons fell to the sands. He slashed at the head, an arm, another arm, and then attempted to grab Lokan's skull.

The Jackal evaded everything, though, and ducked free of the groping hand.

A furious Mollo shouted, froth spraying his beard. He flexed his arms, showing the world how he wanted to break the Jackal's spine in a killing embrace.

No longer in awe of the hellpup's size, Lokan again waved the big man to come closer.

Mollo did.

With a throaty roar that frayed his vocal chords, Mollo chopped and hacked. He slashed diagonally and backhanded for the face.

Lokan ducked and dodged them all.

And when the last one missed, leaving the bigger man wide open and exposed, teetering as if he were about to fall over, Lokan stepped in and slashed Mollo from chest to chin, misting the air with sweat and blood.

That staggered the monster.

Mollo regained his stance. He stupidly punched for Lokan's face.

The Nordish man parried the blow with his sword, half shearing that meaty knob of flesh and bone off its wrist.

Mollo screamed.

Lokan drew two more bloody lines in the Sunjan's torso, backing the man up on his feet. For whatever reason, Mollo dropped his blade and sought to deflect the attacks with his arms alone, as if a plague of mosquitos had enveloped him.

Lokan nicked him with darting thrusts, slashes. Light cuts, they were not deep at all but lightning fast, and they bled. They stung.

And each one slowed the mighty Mollo down just a little more.

Lokan circled the big man. Mollo stood his ground like a grim watchtower on full alert. Blood soaked his hairy frame.

ABOUT THE BLOOD

The crowds no longer cheered. They realized the truth of the matter. The Nordish man, though small, was no slouch with a blade.

Worse yet, the Jackal was *good*.

The blade was nothing more than a length of blunted steel, but it did cut. Even better, Lokan discovered he preferred that distinct lack of bite.

Mollo swiped for the Jackal's head, but Lokan ducked and stabbed a knee, exposing red bone. Mollo dropped with a grunt, landing on that ruined joint. Sand caked the wound.

The Sunjan was now eye level with the Jackal, and even though he was bleeding, dying, Mollo fought on.

The giant backhanded as if drunk.

Lokan parried the arm, cutting it to the bone. Mollo cried out, a loud gurgling, which Lokan silenced with a thrust straight through the big man's throat. Gasps and screams shot up from the audience, startling in the sudden silence. Lokan released his sword a beat before the Sunjan toppled, grasping at the blade left in his gullet.

Lokan let him fall.

While the crowds resumed swearing at him, Lokan stooped and picked up the dead man's weapon.

Not surprisingly, it had a much finer edge to it.

Lokan still needed three cuts to separate Mollo's thick skull from his shoulders.

The Skarrs returned Lokan to his cell without incident. The Nordish man was content, like a blood tick that had had its fill. He offered no resistance to the guards, and when they closed his cell door, Lokan turned and studied the confines with a melancholy eye.

"Ho, Lokan," Dogslaw called. "You live."

"Aye that," the man replied. "You should've seen the Sunjan I put into the ground. Might've been two of them grown into one. A monster. He wanted my skull for a cup, but I took his for a dish. The people who praised him like happy children didn't know what to think. I silenced every one when I took that maggot's head."

Dogslaw smiled with amused wonder. Lokan *hated* Sunjans, hated them with every breath and fiber of his person. He couldn't remember where that loathing had come from or if it had always been there, but it was blazing within him now.

"I think they're taking others," Noll said nearby.

No sooner had the words left him than the Skarrs appeared once more—a dozen of them ready to escort the next man to the arena floor. They stopped at Dogslaw's cell, visors lowered and weapons at the ready.

A part of Dogslaw wanted to smile, but his mouth had gone dry.

He did not resist.

21

When the portcullis rose high enough, Dogslaw stepped outside, into the light. The sun's force momentarily stunned him, stopping him in his tracks, and for a short instant, a few quick heartbeats, he stood and simply absorbed every ray beaming down upon him. A rabid blast of sound came with the heat, but he didn't pay attention to that. Hot, moist air and crushing heat stole his breath, leaving him gasping. Sweat already slathered his back. After months of existing in darkness, where the only light was from a torch or a dish of glowing coals, Dogslaw soaked in the scorching sun and was glad of it.

The Skarrs gave him a short sword and nothing more. As with the others, the only thing he wore was a loincloth, and that was in need of replacing.

Still appreciating the daylight, Dogslaw studied the crowds. Undulating masses screamed, cursed, and jeered. He didn't need to understand the language. The hate radiating from the people rivaled that of the sun. Fists shook. Faces spat. Some even threw their garbage onto the sands.

Dogslaw scowled at those.

Above it all, a single voice called for calm and managed to settle them down for a few moments. That in itself was a feat to applaud. The audience quieted long enough for the other portcullis to rise.

Dogslaw heard the word *Paturo*.

Training had transformed Dogslaw into a Jackal, but the individual standing across the way looked to be a jackal by birth. Paturo was lean and wiry, hunched over at the shoulders with a wild mane of filthy hair. Defined muscles laced his limbs, and he regarded his opponent with an insane light. The man's mouth even hung open, as if about to bite.

Even more concerning was the way Paturo wielded a blade.

He might've been a criminal, but Paturo swung his sword left and right, up and down, practicing a weave that spoke of showmanship and skill. The display drew a chorus of "ohhhhhh" from the onlookers.

Squinting at his foe, Dogslaw tightened his grip on his own blade and casually walked to the center of the Pit. The sand burned his feet, but he welcomed the discomfort.

Paturo the human jackal walked to meet him.

The closer Dogslaw came to the criminal, the more he suspected something was unfit about the man. Paturo was unnaturally pale. He barely blinked. His mouth opened and closed as if possessed by a fit of madness. His tongue rolled and coiled. Sweat drenched the man's beard, but Dogslaw realized it wasn't sweat at all. It was drool—a wild, sopping mess that dripped and sprayed from the man's mouth.

Paturo grinned, revealing a collection of green and black fangs that might've been regular teeth at one point. With his thumb, the Sunjan drew a circle around the scars on his white chest.

Dogslaw stared, not quite understanding the message, but if the man wanted his heart, he'd have to work for it.

The crowds barked and rooted for a quick death.

Paturo raised his weapon and circled to his left. Dogslaw circled the other way, keeping his distance, wondering what the man might do.

He didn't wait long.

ABOUT THE BLOOD

A grinning Paturo kicked sand into the Jackal's face. Dogslaw sputtered as his eyes squeezed shut. Grit still stung them, however, and he cringed at the contact and immediately retreated, much to the crowd's delight.

Paturo attacked, charging through the dust cloud. He slashed for the head, split only air, and split more air on the back cut. Then Dogslaw did the only thing he could do.

He ran.

Scalding laughter rocked the arena as he sprinted across the white sands, diverting his course every so often, wiping his eyes and forcing tears out in an attempt to clear them. The world became a watery, sparkling blur. Dark shadows loomed, and he turned away from the high stone walls, hoping he wouldn't crash into Paturo. The crowds shouted and cursed, confusing him. He slipped once, skidding not three strides away from a wall, and came up spitting.

A ghost pursued him, so Dogslaw ran again, following the brickwork's curve.

When his eyes finally cleared, he saw he'd gone the length of the arena floor.

Paturo had remained in the middle of the Pit, laughing along with the crowds.

Wincing, sniffing hard, and screwing his palms into his eyes, Dogslaw composed himself.

He walked back, and a scathing wall of sound rose from the spectators.

Paturo retreated, matching his opponent step for step, a wild-man's grin spread across his face. He gestured for Dogslaw to come closer.

Dogslaw did.

The Nordish man attacked, three short cuts that Paturo ducked, parried, and spun away from. The Sunjan criminal whipped his fist about, cracking Dogslaw's chin and stunning him. Paturo kicked, planting a bare foot into his foe's chest.

Dogslaw landed on his back.

A shadow fell across the Nordish man, and he rolled away. The spectators roared with glee then disappointment. Paturo didn't press his advantage, and for that, Dogslaw was both grateful and offended.

The Sunjan had deemed himself better.

Stretching his jaw and finding it unbroken, Dogslaw regained his feet, his sword at low guard. He watched the Sunjan. Paturo waved the Nordish man forward, inviting him back for more punishment.

Not so mad after all.

Dogslaw rattled his head, cleared his senses, and stalked his foe. Paturo's eager expression didn't change as the Jackal moved closer.

Dogslaw slashed for a knee. Paturo parried. Dogslaw went high and had that one stopped. Paturo darted forward and punched, missing the Jackal before both men separated and studied each other. Both attacked at some unspoken signal, teeth bared and steel clanging as they strove to gain the initiative.

Paturo opened Dogslaw's left cheek, parting hair and skin in a shocking burst of speed.

The Nordish Jackal responded, zipping a line from Paturo's left hip to his right shoulder. The connection flung the man back. Paturo retreated a few steps and dabbed at the grisly wound. His smile faltered, replaced by anger.

A screaming Paturo charged, sword flashing, cutting Dogslaw across the left shoulder and his left knee. The Nordish man staggered back . . . and kicked a sheet of sand into the man's face.

The crowds protested, infuriated at such poor form, not that Dogslaw cared. The ass-packing Sunjan had started it first.

Paturo rattled his head, grimacing, screwing his eyes clean with a dirty palm. He held his sword at arm's length and didn't run.

Dogslaw quickly closed the space and swung steel, meaning to end the fight.

Paturo parried, and the pair once again skillfully exchanged thrusts and slashes, neither man able to pierce the other's guard.

ABOUT THE BLOOD

They fought on, testing each other. The pace gradually slowed. The grunts got louder. Clearly, neither man could maintain an offensive for much longer.

Paturo sought to break away first.

That was his mistake.

Dogslaw lunged, twisting his torso with audible effort, bringing his blade up in an unexpected uppercut. He cleaved the Sunjan's chin in two with a stomach-twisting *clack* of steel splitting bone.

Paturo staggered away, holding his chopped face. Blood spurted through fingers, covering his chest. He spat and drooled teeth. His features paled even more, and when he again opened his mouth, a great gout of color heaved forth and stained the sands.

Arms burning, his strength waning, Dogslaw slashed, scalping the prisoner's crown to the red bone. A hairy slab of flesh whipped into the sands three strides behind Paturo as he dropped to his knees.

The audience groaned in disappointment.

Wheezing and muttering gibberish, Paturo clamped a hand to his bleeding scalp in a vain attempt to staunch the flow. There he stayed, holding his head together, his frame shaking with exhaustion, his expression alternating between evil glee and rage. If the pain bothered him, Paturo didn't show it. He said something, the sound lengthy and hateful, and got one knee under himself while fixing the Nordish man with cruel intent.

Dogslaw stabbed him through his washboard stomach, the soft *chuff* heard above the raucous hate of the crowds. The Sunjan's last breath grazed Dogslaw's face, just before he collapsed.

Dogslaw studied the dying man for a short while, bone weary and becoming aware of the deep cuts to his person. He inspected himself, flexed his bleeding knee, and discovered it undamaged any further. Blood speckled and soaked his bearded cheek. Dogslaw prodded the cut there with fingers and his tongue.

He winced. Paturo had cut almost straight through to his teeth. A little more, and his mouth would have opened to his ear.

The criminal ceased moving, and Dogslaw left his sword where he'd stuck it. Straining for breath, sweat oozing, and bleeding freely, the Nordish man took in the grand spectacle that was the games. He soaked in every harsh curse aimed his way, and though he hurt, a tired smile spread across his bleeding face, rendering him frightful.

His spine cracked when he straightened it, and with his blood dappling the arena floor, Dogslaw walked toward the rising portcullis.

The lack of light in the Pit's underbelly eased Dogslaw, and he knew then he'd been stashed away underground for far too long. He bled freely, not having enough hands to stem the flow from all of his wounds. Halfway down the stairs, he stopped and placed a shoulder against the wall. The world swayed and knotted, the blasting voices zoning out and becoming far away. Dogslaw felt his stomach knot up, and he braced himself against the wall as if to stop it from toppling over on him.

There he stayed for long moments, taking shallow breaths while his body cooled.

Then he remembered where he was.

Skarrs crept up the stairs toward him, their helmets cocked with uncertainty. He smiled at their approach and raised a hand.

"Still alive," Dogslaw informed them.

Not that the Skarrs understood the Nordish tongue. Nor did they care. He was going to die eventually, in the arena or out. When didn't matter.

The Sunjan guards surrounded him and walked him back to his cell.

Dogslaw was vaguely aware of the door locking behind him. Voices spoke, and when he turned, the jailor called Runson stood there, inspecting him. Runson grunted in satisfaction. He spoke a few words of that nonsense language, smiled, and walked out of sight.

ABOUT THE BLOOD

Dogslaw lowered himself to the floor.

Noll's voice drifted from nearby. "You're back. Thought you'd die for certain."

"I'm back . . . but with new scars," Dogslaw informed him.

He eyed his cot, pressed tightly to the dungeon wall. He stripped the blanket off the bed of sour straw.

"Bad?" Noll asked.

Dogslaw reached over and striped the blanket off the bed of sour straw. "Not bad," he said and ripped the fabric down the middle. "But I'll need something. To stop the bleeding."

"Was that your blanket?"

"Aye that. Got cut. Across my shoulder. And my knee. That one hurt, but I walk fine. Got cut across my cheek. Almost opened my mouth to my ear."

"Lie down," Noll instructed. "Relax. Slows down the blood. Bind your wounds."

"You'll live," Lokan said from across the way.

Dogslaw supposed he would. "Just won't be as pretty anymore."

Noll chuckled in the dark. It wasn't often Dogslaw heard the man laugh.

"Pretty," Lokan repeated with a snort, sounding almost friendly, perhaps sleepy. "Welcome back, Jackal."

The bare straw on the cot didn't appeal to Dogslaw, so he remained sitting. He ripped the blanket into strips, suspecting he'd need them later.

"Are you still there?" Noll asked.

"Binding the cuts," Dogslaw reported. "My cheek is a mess. Grace of Ivus."

"Let those be. Women like scars."

That put a smile on Dogslaw's face, and he immediately regretted it. The muscles flexed in his cheek, drawing that side back with hot claws. Sighing, he folded the cotton over and pressed it against the wound.

"Well?" Noll asked.

"Just finished," Dogslaw said.

"He'll be fine," Lokan remarked across the way.

"Can you talk?" Noll asked.

"I can," Dogslaw said.

A bucket of water lay to one side, and Dogslaw realized how thirsty he'd become. He pulled the bucket over and smelled its contents, mindful of what Lokan had said about the jailors pissing in it. He took a tentative sip. The water tasted fine, so he drank. When he finished, he dipped a rag before applying it to his cheek.

"Dead yet?" Noll asked.

Dogslaw closed his eyes. "Not yet. Bored, are you?"

"I am," the other admitted. "And . . . these are our final days, Dogslaw. I can feel it. In my bones. We'll all perish up there in the sun. Or worse, down here in the dark. Knowing that, I feel the need to talk to someone. Even if it's only for a short while. So if you are able, as long as you're willing . . ."

"All right." Dogslaw pulled the wet cloth away from his cheek. For once, he was grateful for the lack of light.

"My thanks." Noll sounded grateful. "My only other choice was Lokan."

"You could . . . learn the language."

"Of my sworn enemy? Pah. I'd rather scoop out my tongue. What would I talk to them about away? I'm as weary of the war as the next."

A scream pierced the darkness, coming from deep inside the dungeon. Dogslaw barely flinched as screams were common. The combined weight of stone, darkness, and solitude broke everyone down after a while.

"Who did you fight?" Noll asked.

"A right skilled bastard," Dogslaw said. "He knew how to handle a blade. He cut me up, and the crowd loved him for it. In the end, I stabbed him through the gut. Left him dead in the sun."

"Good," Lokan muttered.

Dogslaw suspected he was a little light-headed from his blood loss. Mad Lokan sounded as though he was right beside him.

ABOUT THE BLOOD

"Did you see the people?" Noll asked.

Dogslaw looked up. "I did."

"So many."

"An army."

"Ha. Five armies. All piled into the one spot."

"All hating us," Dogslaw said.

"Aye that," Noll said. "They hate us. But that's important. We need that hate. We need to *use* it. Summon it to our side. Burn it like it was rotting wood and make it work for us."

"And we'll survive this?" Dogslaw's cheek flared with pain, and he reminded himself to talk in short sentences.

"No," Noll said. "We're as good as dead. But when I was up there, Dogslaw, something overcame me. It was the need to live. To survive. For as long as I could. Because all those people wanted to see me die. Maybe even some could collect a few coins at my death."

Dogslaw listened.

"But I won my match," Noll went on. "Worse still, I lived. Lived to fight another day. Lived to piss on the hopes of each and every one of those Sunjan *curnos*. I realize, now, that the longer I live . . . well, that angers them." Silence. Then he said, "And a part of me enjoys that."

As his cheek ached and radiated heat, Dogslaw closed his eyes. Sleep crept in upon his consciousness. He fought against it, needing to do one last thing. He looped a strip under his chin and knotted it atop his head. The bandage was crude, but it would keep the cloth pad against his face.

A part of him couldn't believe he was listening to Noll, the most depressing man he'd ever met.

However, down in the darkness, underneath the stone magificance that was the Pit, Dogslaw agreed with every word the man said.

22

"That's enough, y'frightful hellspawn," Machlann growled, perhaps disappointed in not really having imparted anything new upon the only gladiator standing before him.

A sweaty Junger nodded, placed his wooden sword on a rack, and went for water. Koba watched him walk away while Machlann glanced up at the balcony and the two men overlooking the proceedings. The trainer shook his head, and Goll understood the message.

Junger was a prodigy.

He did everything the trainers demanded of him. He pushed his strength to failing, and even then one had to wonder if he was really exhausted or merely pretending. Junger executed his drills without fault and, at one point, had broken a wooden blade upon a practice man. The Perician worked, and whatever he did, he excelled at.

So the trainers demanded more.

Clavellus and his staff seemed to be no longer preparing Junger for the Pit but trying to determine just how strong, skilled, and capable the Perician actually was, though in such a manner as to not injure the man. With Brozz hurt, Junger was the last active pit fighter remaining to the Ten.

However, Junger had done everything they'd asked for and appeared ready for more.

With the afternoon ending, a pensive Goll stood from his chair next to Clavellus and stretched.

"Going below," he muttered. "Get the blood flowing."

"Go on, then," the old taskmaster said, equally deep in thought. "I'll keep an eye here. Mind Nala, however. She's still gushing over those dyed fabrics I brought her. If you give her an ear, she'll take it. Even show you her designs for robes and shirts."

"I'll be careful," Goll said, but in truth, he liked the villa's mistress. He hadn't had much interaction with her, but the short exchanges they did have left a favourable impression. She seemed to be a voice of reason and calm during a season of madness.

"Check up on that one-legged Garl," Clavellus said, his head half turned. "See if he's settling in . . . at least a little."

Goll hesitated. "You're good to take him in."

"If Borchus said the man helped, the man helped. Only concern now is finding a use for him. Finding a purpose. Everyone needs one. Your man Pig Knot knew that. Why he left, I suspect."

Goll did also. After a night of thinking about the Sunjan, he finally, grudgingly accepted the man's decision to leave even though the idea of a legless house master alone in Sunja's streets bothered him. He wondered what was happening in Pig Knot's head.

Perhaps they'd meet again one day.

Those thoughts rolling about his mind, Goll left the balcony and his surprisingly sober taskmaster. Clavellus had not partaken of any strong drink that morning, nor did he have anything for most of the afternoon. Perhaps he'd somehow sated himself with his wild night amongst Sunja's alehouses. Perhaps Nala had chastised him at length.

Goll descended the stairs, moving past an open doorway where Ananda and Clades's wife, Kura, were inspecting rich-colored fabrics. The pair talked softly, their voices receding as he moved along the hallways and finally emerged onto the training grounds.

Some ten strides away, Junger rested upon the sands, head lowered, his hair dark and wet from a dunk in a nearby water barrel.

Goll didn't disturb him.

Muluk and the sullen Ajik stood under the arched roof of the open forge, just past the row of practice men. Ajik was inspecting tongs, sharp cutters, hammers, and even the curve of the anvils. Two barrels filled with metal rods and scrap pieces stood near a dormant hearth, and Ajik took interest in a rather small bellows. Muluk hung back, rubbing his left hand and the severed fingers there. The Kree had his shirt off that afternoon, exposing a hairy frame and the angry pink of healing wounds. Despite all he'd been through, he still looked formidable.

"Master Muluk," Goll greeted as he stepped underneath the forge's shade. "Looks like your wounds are healing well enough."

"Master Goll," Muluk returned and frowned. "Goll. Really, now. Do I *really* have to call you *master* every time I see you?"

"You should."

"What if I don't want to?"

Goll sighed and nodded at Ajik. "How is he?"

"Him? Can't understand a word I'm saying."

"Nothing?"

Muluk shook his head. "Nothing. Watch. Ajik. Where are you from, lad?"

The man straightened and regarded Muluk and then Goll with an imperious look, slightly irritated at the interruption. His beard had been trimmed right down to the final whisker, it seemed, and while he still wore a gray shirt, he had donned an apron over it. Detecting nothing amiss with the two men, he went back to his inspection of a table filled with metal shards and lengths of thick wire.

"Seems organized enough," Goll observed.

"Oh, he is that. Cleaned and swept the place this morning," Muluk said with an all-encompassing wave.

"So I saw."

"Taking inventory now."

"Hm."

"Quiet lad," Muluk added. "Quiet. Was up before me, and the word from Machlann is the lad was out here before even him. Moving things about and cleaning, Goll. *Cleaning.* That chimney? Had a damn bird's nest inside. A *nest*. Little topper climbed up there with a pole and rooted it out. Then he got about checking on this and that. Testing the blades. Chopping and stabbing and hefting the tools. Rattling the tables and the water barrels. He's the cleanest, quietest smithy I've ever seen on the move."

"Isn't a bad thing," Goll said and glanced back at the training grounds.

Junger was standing, seemingly refreshed, and unleashed a blistering six-strike combination into a wooden frame. He was so fast, so fluid, that even Koba, who was positioned nearby the pit fighter, took a breath to appreciate what he'd just witnessed.

"Ajik, what're you doing, lad?" Muluk asked, drawing Goll's attention back.

Ajik stopped and regarded the man with a stoic yet dignified air.

"Doing?" Muluk repeated and indicated the tables and tools, fingers wiggling as if conjuring magic.

Ajik return to his preparations.

"See," Muluk stated tiredly. "I can get his attention . . . but *holding* it is a problem. It's like . . ."

Goll waited.

"It's like I'm not worthy to be here," Muluk explained, suddenly downcast.

"He's ignoring you?"

"I think. And not just because I can't speak his language—whatever that is—but aye that. He's ignoring me." The burly man shrugged. "I'm thinking this isn't a good idea."

"He seems to be doing fine."

"He hasn't started working on armor or weapons yet." Muluk wondered aloud, "Not certain what or how he'll do, then. What are you going to pay him?"

"A few coins. Food and a place to sleep."

They watched the smaller man putter around the forge. At one point, Ajik stopped and scowled at the walls surrounding the facility. With a grunt, he went back to inspecting a collection of handsaws.

"What was that about?" Goll asked.

"Who knows. Might be about the forge. The walls. The armory is right there, so I don't know."

Goll wondered what was going on in Ajik's head.

"Doesn't look like he'll eat much," Muluk noted as an afterthought.

"I don't suppose."

"What about the firewater?"

"Firewater?"

"That Sunjan armorer said the man understands firewater."

"You heard that?"

Muluk smiled as an answer.

"Of course you heard that." Goll admonished him, "Keep him away from firewater. No firewater."

"But—"

"He's here to work. Weapons and armor. Not to drink himself senseless. Understood?"

Muluk quieted, obviously not in agreement. "What about beer, then?"

Goll glared. "Nothing. No beer, wine, nothing."

"He can't work all the time. Man's not a temple slave."

"Everyone works here."

"I'm not working."

"You're an unfit mess that's on the mend. And you will work once you're ready. Don't argue with me, Muluk. Watch him. Keep him on path."

ABOUT THE BLOOD

Muluk's face twisted in dislike. Before he could say anything, the guards atop the ramparts yelled, alerting all about an approaching rider.

"Watch him," Goll again warned his countryman. "See if you can talk with the man."

"I can't talk with the man."

"Well, figure out a way."

Muluk rolled his eyes at that, and Goll walked off, not wanting to listen. He approached the gates, and two of the house guards pulled them open, allowing a familiar face to enter. Naulis rode in on a gelding, its sides gleaming with perspiration.

The messenger slipped off the animal's back and nodded to the guards.

"Naulis," Goll called. "Any news from the city?"

"There is," the man huffed, rubbing his backside. "The fighting season's been lengthened."

Goll stopped in his tracks.

"Heard word of it yesterday," Naulis explained. "And I checked with the Madea this morning. Damn near killed this unfortunate beast riding here. The season's to go longer this year than any other."

"Why?" Goll asked.

Naulis shrugged. "Because it's King Juhn's will."

On the training grounds, Machlann suddenly lost interest in what Junger was doing and exchanged looks with Koba. On his balcony, Clavellus rose, gripped the railing, and stared.

"This way," Goll said, gesturing toward the common room. As he walked there, he motioned for the others to join him.

The masters and trainers made their way inside, toward a broad table. Even Shan made an appearance, emerging from the doorway to the sleeping chambers. Goll looked expectantly at the same door, knowing neither Halm nor Pig Knot would be joining them anytime soon. A pang of loss shot through his core. The men had been the first he'd befriended in the very beginning, back when he'd been mauled by Baylus the Butcher. Goll remembered meeting all three for the first time, remembered plopping down on a bench and telling them everything he knew about a fighter called Samarhead, from the House of Curge.

He'd been a different person then, but with the same goals—to become the champion of the games, to become a legend.

Seddon above, he remembered.

Once Clavellus and the others had settled at the table, Naulis retold his news, stiffening the spines of the older men.

"Never heard the likes before," Machlann said, looking to Clavellus. "Not ever."

"This is news," the taskmaster declared. "What of the king, then? What was his reasoning?"

"None," Naulis said. "Nothing I was told. The man wishes the games to go longer. His will is law, and all that. They're also bringing in prisoners from the king's dungeons."

"More meat for the chewing," Machlann remarked. "That used to be the role of the Free Trained."

"The houses will look upon them the same way," Clavellus said. "What about regular matches, then? Still house gladiators facing house gladiators?"

"Aye that. Five or six matches a day. Until the end of the season."

"Nothing really changed there," the taskmaster decided.

"But I seem to remember talk it might be increased as seemed fit," Naulis said.

"Why didn't they have a Chamber announcement for this?"

"They did," Naulis reported. "Yesterday morning. All the owners met with the Chamber. That's what I've been told. From the Madea himself."

"Yesterday," Goll said, his face tightening with offense. "We were in the city yesterday. Why were we not there?"

Naulis didn't answer, and no one else spoke.

"You know that answer, Master Goll," Clavellus eventually said. "You—*we're* still Free Trained to them. Still a rabble—and as such, left to hear such news through men like good Naulis here."

"Unfit to grace their chamber," Machlann rumbled, his eyes dark and contemplative. "The gurry of the games."

"We're a house," Goll growled, lips barely moving. The temperature in the common room, especially the air around the Kree, rose noticeably. "We're a *house*. Damnation. We paid the Chamber's fee to be recognized as such. A thousand gold to be recognized. Muluk was damned near butchered for that coin. Pig Knot gave up his *legs*. I've—*we've* earned that distinction. That title. And the damn respect that goes with it. This won't be tolerated. Not while I draw breath. How do the regular houses hear such news?"

"By messenger," Clavellus answered quietly. "Back in my time, that is. They brought the owners a scroll or such. It's been many years, so that may have changed."

Goll stewed in a very personal poison. "I've a mind to go straight to the Chamber. This very moment. Get an explanation *and* an apology. We're a *house*."

No one dared to speak, for fear of drawing the house master's wrath.

"Let's wait a few days for that, Master Goll," Clavellus said, keeping his own voice neutral. "When it's our time to take the sands again. Wait until then. Let the Chamber think all is well . . . until then. And then voice your anger."

"Oh, I will," a red-faced Goll vowed.

"The question now is . . ." Clavellus said, watching the Kree, "how this longer season affects the Ten."

"How will they determine the final eight?" Machlann asked, changing the subject.

"By a fighter's overall record," Naulis explained. "Those with the most victories and least number of losses. They'll be the final eight."

"That hasn't changed, then," Clavellus remarked. "But it won't be the most victories. I have a feeling it will be whoever's left standing."

"Will our gladiators be required to fight the prisoners?" Goll asked, his temper under control once again.

"No," Naulis said with a shake of his head. "At least, I haven't heard of any plans."

"That might change," Clavellus warned. "Houses fight the Free Trained all the time. If they must, they'll fight prisoners. They won't like it, but they'll do it."

"With a longer season, might the wounded be able to fight again?" Goll asked. "If wounds stopped them from continuing in the first place."

"That's a good question," Clavellus rumbled. "Will the wounded be allowed to fight again?"

"P'haps if they recover in time," Machlann said. "Why not?"

"What's Brozz's condition?" Clavellus asked the healer.

Shan thought about it. "Serious. He wasn't so good this morning. Felt hot to the touch."

"Take care of that one," Clavellus said. "But I'm also thinking of the Zhiberian. Would he return? And would there be time?"

"The Zhiberian would need weeks to be fully recovered," Shan reported. "If he lets himself."

"But if he's mended and willing..." Clavellus left the thought hanging.

"The lad's undefeated," Machlann added, warming to the idea.

"Torello?" the taskmaster asked.

Shan shook his head. "Not with that ankle. A month, at least."

"Slap on some of that muck you're always using," Muluk said.

That didn't impress the healer. "That muck is mostly for cuts, and even then, it takes time."

"All right, that means we have just the one dog remaining," Clavellus stated. "Perhaps two or three others."

"I'll fight," Goll said, drawing their attention. "I'm well enough. I no longer limp. And I'm undefeated, with perhaps the most prized of all scalps to my belt."

ABOUT THE BLOOD

That surprised the lot of them.

"You can't fight," Clavellus explained with a disbelieving smile. "You're a house master now. You're above all that."

"I'm a gladiator first. I came to these games with a goal. Baylus robbed me of that goal. King Juhn has given it back. The season's extended. If it wasn't, there would be too much ground to cover. I'd have fallen too far behind the main contenders to make the final eight—the final sixteen, for that matter. Now . . . I have a second chance."

Goll rose from the table, looking at Shan. "I want you to inspect my wounds. Tell me what you think, though I already know the answer."

Clavellus appeared mortified. Machlann was silenced with disbelief. Even Koba stared at the Kree as if he'd suddenly become unfit in the skull.

"You truly mean to fight again?" Muluk asked for them all.

Goll didn't hesitate. "I mean to become champion, Master Muluk."

23

Vonomir of the House of Tilo strutted toward the rising portcullis, already embracing the rabid enthusiasm of the crowds. Vonomir wasn't moved by their calls for blood. No fire rushed through his veins. Taking measured breaths, he stayed calm, unwilling to allow the building energy of the crowds to affect him. The current season marked his tenth fighting in the games. He knew how the Pit could fill an inexperienced gladiator with a frightening vitality, transforming a youngster into a hellion upon the sands, capable of splitting shields and armor with one blow. Such sorcerous energy aided a gladiator tremendously at first, but only for a short time. Then a man's arms and legs became as heavy as granite. Vonomir had seen it many times, where men once battering a foe senseless suddenly had no strength left, their chests laboring for breath, to become unable to defend themselves.

Control was everything. Vonomir was well aware of that fact.

His opponent, Grigo of the School of Vorish, also knew that. Grigo was no youngster.

As the fifth match of the day approached, Vonomir expected the audience was longing for two professionals to display their skills, unlike the earlier dog blossoms marring the arena floor.

ABOUT THE BLOOD

Despite his size and strength, Vonomir wore a hardened leather vest with a chiseled physique. Bronze greaves and spiked bracers covered his limbs. A helmet with a faceplate in the guise of a grinning hellion protected his features. He carried a sword and shield—no nonsense there.

He passed under the raised opening and stopped. Vonomir's eyes didn't go above the stone and brick line, where the spectators yelled and thrashed in a drab patchwork of colors. He kept his eyes on the portcullis across the way, just starting to rise as the Orator introduced Grigo.

"You know him from countless seasons. A beast of a fighter. Born to split skulls. Bred to maul men. Built to bleed all who might oppose him."

The crowds erupted in approval.

Built to bleed all. Vonomir smiled at that one.

Grigo stepped into the light.

"From the School of Vorish, I give you . . . Grigo the Punisher."

The man towered a full head over Vonomir, and he was no small man. A shirt of polished mail hung off meaty shoulders while a rounded helmet with a grill of razors flashed in the sunlight. Drooping from his right arm was a spiked mace the size of a child's head. Protecting his left was a shield that might have been a door ripped from its frame. Despite the impressiveness of the specimen, Vonomir knew all he needed to know about Grigo. A season before, he'd defeated several gladiators in heartless fashion, earning the name of Punisher. Vonomir himself had actually lost to the giant. Grigo was indeed a punisher, a tormentor of lesser men. This season alone, he'd killed three Free Trained hellpups and ended the season for a house fighter. The School of Vorish had done well to recruit and train that well-oiled watchtower of muscle and bone.

But Vonomir was going to defeat him.

Vonomir was determined to ruin Grigo's undefeated record and add yet another victory to his own. Even as the Orator heaped bloody praise upon the gladiator's name, Vonomir took a breath, shut out the crowd's unrelenting racket, and focused on what he'd prepared to do.

Grigo swaggered across the sands, bicep bulging as he raised that awesome boulder of a mace. Sunlight dappled the razor smile. A wide metallic mesh of wires protected and hid Grigo's eyes, giving the man an insectoid appearance. Vonomir felt that cold, impassive gaze and knew Grigo was ready to kill a house fighter if the opportunity arose.

Vonomir sensed it, welcoming the bigger man to try.

"Vonomir," Grigo greeted as he got closer, loud enough to be heard over the voices of thousands.

"Grigo."

"Once again."

"Once again."

"You've done well thus far."

"As yourself."

"Early rounds," Grigo scoffed. The rictus of razors fluted his words.

"As they are for most," Vonomir offered, wary of his larger opponent. "Trako's doing well this season."

"Aye that. Vorish favors him."

"Not you?"

Grigo's head trembled ever so slightly. "Not I."

"Apologies."

"Not needed, but well taken," Grigo said. "I'll spare your life."

"My thanks," Vonomir said and crouched.

"Well, then," Grigo said and hefted his shield. "Let's see where this goes."

The mace ripped toward Vonomir's head. He barely ducked under and away, quickly distancing himself from the larger man. Grigo charged after him, shield held out like a wall. Vonomir bobbed one way then the other, rolling under another swing of the mace. Grigo drew back, expecting a counter.

None came, however.

ABOUT THE BLOOD

Vonomir circled to the center of the Pit, well aware of his position.

"You're *quick*," Grigo huffed, stalking his adversary.

Vonomir saved his breath.

Grigo swung for Vonomir's chest, missed, and quickly reset, but his opponent was already well out of harm's way. Grigo stomped forward and unleashed a two-strike combination, grunting with the effort.

He split only air.

Vonomir backed away from the heavy-handed onslaught, his sword pointed at his foe's chest. Excited cries escaped the onlookers.

Grigo straightened and regarded Vonomir coolly. "You're *very* quick."

Vonomir didn't reply.

"Let's see how you—" Grigo cut his own words off by rushing his opponent. He swung for the head, then a shoulder, and finally a hip. Vonomir ducked, jumped back, and darted well out of range of the spiked ball, stirring up sand.

The spectators voiced their impatience, the noise swallowing Grigo's own grunts of annoyance.

"You can't—" the giant began.

Vonomir lunged unexpectedly, his sword a shot of lightning blurred by a cloud of dust, and nicked Grigo's weapon arm.

A dull ribbon of blood streaked the air. Grigo faltered and lumbered a retreat, cradling his huge shield close as if shutting a door. Screams of victory erupted from some onlookers, but Vonomir knew better.

Grigo was far from finished.

The hulking warrior barged forward. He swung at the grinning hellion and missed, swung again for that taunting face and only fanned it, then smashed his shield's edge at Vonomir's torso, seeking to squash him with one mighty blow. The shield was only a ruse, a screen hiding a well-practiced storm of strikes, each one looking to crush the hellion's metal skull.

That storm flew into Vonomir, who did the impossible.

With dazzling speed, Vonomir dodged or parried every strike before putting distance between him and the giant. He didn't counter, not sparing the effort or bothering to steal the initiative.

Grigo held his monstrous shield out, daring Vonomir to strike it, daring this fish to take the hook. The hellion's mask showed no indication of doing any such thing, as if he sensed his foe's thoughts.

Grigo nodded approval, the razor grin seemingly delighted with the challenge of this particular match. They circled each other then, weapons poised to strike, their bared flesh streaked with sweat and clinging sand. Blood fell from Grigo's arm, but he paid it no mind.

My legs, Vonomir thought, his eyes locked on the giant's grim features. *He'll go for my legs.*

"You're looking to exhaust me," Grigo huffed from behind his shield. "You can try. Many have before."

Vonomir stepped into his larger foe, and the shields clapped together. He twisted at the hips, whipped his sword around the larger shield, and *twang*ed his blade off the back of Grigo's helmet. Grigo's head snapped forward. Unfazed, he pushed back.

That shove nearly planted Vonomir on his rump. He recovered a good six strides away from his opponent.

"Good," Grigo said, taking a breath. "Good."

Good indeed, Vonomir agreed.

They were evenly matched.

Grigo took a mighty breath, one heralding another barrage. The imposing Sunjan stormed forward, and his mace lashed out. Vonomir attempted to deflect the weapon with his shield, but the freakish mace crashed through, connecting with his left shoulder in a sparkling explosion of leather and meat.

The blow bent Vonomir over, off-balance, long enough for Grigo to spin.

The mace flashed out and crunched into that hellion's mask. The helm flew from Vonomir's shoulders, but luckily, his head remained. He staggered, dazed and vulnerable.

ABOUT THE BLOOD

Grigo pressed, seeing blood splashed across his opponent's profile. He swung for that bare skull and missed, but his shield crashed into Vonomir's face with a pulpy crunch, dropping the smaller man to his knees. Grigo reset himself, saw his foe's guard had drooped, and kicked him squarely in the chest.

Vonomir was plied backward with a groan.

The world winked out, replaced by darkness.

The crowds chanted Grigo's name, bringing Vonomir to his senses. He squirmed under a heavy pressure on his throat, seeing a metal plane looming over his head.

Grigo's shield.

It was planted on Vonomir's throat, the pressure robbing him of breath.

"Yield," Vonomir sputtered weakly, patting the crushing shield with a hand.

Grigo didn't appear to hear.

"Yield," Vonomir whispered, his windpipe on the very verge of cracking. Panic replaced pain. His vision narrowed to a single tunnel, and at the end was Grigo. Black motes bloomed without sound in Vonomir's vision. He no longer had the air to plead for his life. Grigo's grill of razors smiled at the fallen gladiator. The eyes became caverns of pitch. Vonomir heard waves crashing on a beach somewhere while Grigo's visor descended, becoming as brilliant as starlight. The shield pressed down, straining Vonomir's vertebrae even more, to the point of snapping.

Then Grigo stepped back, yanking the shield off his opponent's throat.

The sky wavered and deepened, and Vonomir heard the cheers of the crowd.

Still alive, he thought.

"Good fight to end the day," Curge rumbled and slapped the arms of his chair. "For a change."

The Dark One regarded Nexus and Gastillo, both of whom remained sitting. "Something to discuss, do you?"

"We do, actually," Nexus replied coldly.

The admission failed to bother Dark Curge. "Leaving a dog with a snake. Perhaps the best match isn't yet done."

Chuckling, the big owner departed the box.

Nexus waited for a short time, his nonexistent chin pulling the rest of his weathered features down. "Come with me, good Gastillo. I know a place where we can talk. Without fear of being overheard. You have guards?"

"Two."

"Bring them along."

Once outside, Gastillo summoned his guards, and they joined the four armed men waiting for Nexus. With the skies fading into evening, Gastillo allowed himself be led through the throngs of people leaving the arena. Just outside the Gate of the Moon, in the shade of the Pit's high walls, a grand-looking koch waited, surrounded by a dozen armed guards in polished ring mail. The koch's polished wood shone in the evening light. A manservant dressed in fine breeches and a high-collared shirt appeared and pulled the door open.

Once again, Gastillo was thankful for his mask.

Nexus crawled through the doorway, grunting with exertion. "Come on, then," he called out.

The guards encircling the koch allowed Gastillo through but blocked his two men.

Gastillo half turned at the movement.

"Your men will be fine where they are," Nexus said loudly, and Gastillo supposed they would be.

Signaling his men to wait, Gastillo climbed aboard the koch. Nexus gestured for him to sit on the opposite side, on rosy cushions.

With the door and shutters closed, shadow enveloped the pair.

"Now then," Nexus said while reaching for a small cabinet set into the koch wall. "Time for *real* wine. And not the piss they serve here. I swear, Gastillo. Some people have no taste for fine wine. *Superior* wine. Wine that takes years to perfect, prepared by masters. Not some punce with a barrel and grapes. I can barely choke down that arena swill. I'd bring a bottle or two from my own stores, but frankly, I don't need to hear Curge begging for a taste."

"It would be a waste," Gastillo remarked, taking care not to sound sarcastic. He knew full well what the Dark One thought of Nexus's taste in wine.

"It would," Nexus agreed and pulled out two silver goblets. He cracked a bottle and poured, the color as bold as blood. He offered one goblet to Gastillo, who accepted with a nod.

"Ahhh," Nexus said and leaned back into his own cushioned seat. "After planting my ass upon those rocks we sit on in the arena, this is damn near decadent. For a koch."

Gastillo lifted his goblet to his host and then guided it past his mask and to his lips. The wine surprised him, tasting of grape and a hint of something peppery. He liked it very much.

"Expensive, this," Nexus explained, lowering his drink, "but worth it. I sell it all over. The Marrn nobility in particular enjoy this wine. Pay anything for it. Now then, to business. I've been considering what might be a fair offer for your properties, and instead of deciding upon a number, I'll allow you to give me your price."

"My price?" an uncertain Gastillo asked.

"For your house. Your warriors, your property, and especially the contract to Prajus. He is key to this transaction."

Gastillo blinked. "What about the training staff?"

"I have my own."

"They're quite experienced."

"No matter," Nexus declared with a halting hand. "I'll have my own. Too much invested to simply cast them aside. Enough about that. Name your price."

Gastillo's heart thumped as he took a moment to think. "For my property and my current roster."

"Aye that. And your golden balls as well." Nexus brayed laughter. "Apologies. I'm not interested in those, obviously. Sell them to someone else."

The outburst gave Gastillo pause, and if not for the fear of offending the wine merchant, he would've returned with a jab of his own. To avoid souring the discussion, he kept silent.

"And don't worry about the maggots training within your walls. I'll make it so they won't feel betrayed," Nexus said, his eyes twinkling over the goblet's silvery lip.

"You mean to take them on, however," Gastillo said.

"Some. Perhaps." Nexus shrugged. "After a discussion with my own staff."

"I have agreements with those men."

"Once you sell your properties to me, those agreements are finished. I'll take the ones I want. The others will leave."

Gastillo didn't know quite what to make of that.

"Come on, then," Nexus urged him. "It's been a long day, and truth be known, I want to be on the move. Name your price."

"Twenty thousand gold," Gastillo said and then considered his drink. "And a case of this along with it."

"Pah." Nexus wiped his lips. "A case of this is worth five thousand to me, Gastillo. When I said this was fine wine, I was being modest. This horse piss is wrung straight from the best breeds. It takes much more effort to produce. From orchards tended to night and day by masters of their trade. And did I mention the Marrn nobility greatly enjoy it? Regardless, seeing who you are, allow me to think about it."

Nexus settled back and cracked a shuttered window. Gastillo dabbed at his wrecked lips with a hand cloth, catching any spillage. It *was* good wine, perhaps some of the best he'd ever tasted.

"Well, I'm not sure you're worth quite that much," Nexus finally said, rubbing a finger across his chin.

"I assure you my house *is* worth that much."

"I'll give you fifteen," Nexus said, "delivered within two to three days from now. If you're agreeable."

Gastillo blinked. "Fifteen isn't—"

"Fifteen thousand gold pieces," Nexus talked over him. "Delivered in strongboxes. To a location of your choice. When you have it, my staff will enter your house and make the announcement to your men. Whether you alert them of the purchase before then is entirely up to you."

"I don't think—"

"Fifteen and not a coin more," Nexus said, his tone suddenly frosty. "My servants have done research into your pit fighters' history. As well as your staff and your property. Your house is situated closer to the arena than mine, so there's that, but my trainers will have the burden of absorbing your fighters into the fold. Breaking old habits. Forming new. And there are a number of other costs I've taken into consideration. Fifteen thousand. That's a dignified sum. A fair sum. As well as any, say, advice you might require in whatever venture you embark upon next. Wine, cloth, livestock . . ." A smile stretched across Nexus's weathered features, one that could chill the blood of a snake.

"Consider it," the merchant said and reached for the door. He gripped the handle and fixed Gastillo with a steely look. "But know this: it's the best you'll do in this land. Sunja's at war. Merchants are shying away from this place rather than embracing it. It's not so evident yet, but it will be. Sunja once had the reputation of being a prosperous gemstone in these parts, but that's long been covered with mud and shite. Fifteen. Give me your answer when you've decided."

With that, he opened the door.

The guards moved aside to allow him passage, and his own men were waiting just beyond the rest of Nexus's armed force. Stunned, Gastillo regarded them all. In the end, he downed the last of his wine, forcing himself not to hurry, and thanked the merchant for his time.

He got out of the koch.

The door slammed behind him.

At two stout raps from within, the driver snapped the reins. The lavish transport pulled away with the wall of guards walking hurriedly alongside. People in the street parted like curtains for the procession. Gastillo watched the departing koch for a short time while people walked around him, filling the space once occupied by the extravagant carriage.

Fifteen thousand. Was his property and roster actually worth that much? He had no idea. It wasn't twenty, yet the sum left him with a bright tingle in his belly. The coin would keep him alive and in good spirits for several years if he watched his expenses, but he wondered if it would be enough to begin a second livelihood.

Fifteen.

That was the offer. Accept it, and he'd be free of the life forever.

Mulling his future, Gastillo walked home with his two guards flanking him.

The return walk proved to be a hot one despite the deepening evening, and a heavy sweat coated Gastillo's person. Several times, he was close to taking his mask off, but his mangled features prevented him. Better the children stare in awe at his mask than the ruins underneath. The two guards followed him, watching his back. Gastillo walked alone at times as he was still a young man in reasonably good condition, with a gladiator's training and experience. However, he kept a pair of men just to discourage any of the braver gangs that might attempt to rob him of his mask.

They threaded their way through Sunja's maze, crossing main streets and enduring wagon traffic and slower-walking citizens. The three men eventually turned down a narrow lane toward a walled compound. A pair of guards stood outside, before gates no wider than a wagon, constructed of iron bars and thick timbers. Upon seeing Gastillo, they rapped their spears off the entrance. The gates swung open, and the returning owner nodded thanks to his men.

High walls protected and concealed four buildings, one of which was Gastillo's main residence. His escort joined the guards inside the gates and closed the barrier. Gastillo walked alone from that point, studying a sandy training area enclosed by a frayed mat of grass. No gladiators or staff were in sight.

ABOUT THE BLOOD

After the day's exercises and drilling, the entire pack was either soaking in the distant bathhouse or eating in the barracks' common room.

Walking along, Gastillo pulled his mask off and relished the breeze upon his skin. He followed a beaten path in the grass and headed to his own front door. His servants would have prepared a late dinner for him, and he thought of having a bath, believing warm waters would help him think.

Ahead, Jaco, the head of his household guard, stepped out of their barracks, ducking his head to clear the doorway. A pair of armed men flanked him. He spotted his employer and dipped his head. Gastillo waved in return.

"Ho, the master returns!"

The shout stopped Gastillo not five paces from his front door.

"His face might be askew, but there's nothing wrong with his hearing, lads," Prajus remarked and received a round of chuckles.

His mood darkening, Gastillo faced four men just emerging from the bathhouse, their skin glistening in the fading light. They wore only loincloths, and Prajus swaggered toward the barracks with a smiling insolence that offended the house master more than his words. There was no fear in that walk, none whatsoever.

Jaco and his two men glared, already going for their swords. The shout also caught the attention of the four guards just inside the gate. The two forces converged, waiting for the house master's word.

The movement wasn't lost on Prajus.

"Only a jab, Master Gastillo," the gladiator explained with sly sincerity, flashing fine teeth. He smoothed his shock of blond hair with both hands.

The three fighters behind him didn't bother hiding their amusement.

Not in the mood to exchange barbs, Gastillo shook his head at his guards, remembering the offer of fifteen thousand gold pieces.

"I don't think he heard you," said one of Prajus's braver followers.

"I don't think so, either," said another.

"Oh, he heard me," Prajus assured them. "He heard well enough. Those ears of his are quite sharp. All that gold sharpens the hearing. Even now, he's waiting for my next word."

Gastillo stopped at his door, not bothering with the handle.

"Shaddup, you maggots," Jaco slowly growled, his voice carrying across the training grounds.

"Here to defend the *master*, Jaco?" Prajus stopped, unafraid. "Best we get out of sight. The *master's* dogs are barking."

Unchecked smiles and snickers trickled from his pack.

"You know, Prajus," Gastillo said for all to hear, "if your skill with a blade ever matched your tongue, you would've been crowned champion long ago. And the season would already be finished. And I . . . would be a very rich man."

Prajus sighed wearily. "Maybe that's the reason I haven't given my full effort, knowing you would benefit. I'd be free to do as I please, I suppose, and rich myself. But . . . just knowing that you'd be somewhere south, living well because of me . . . the thought bothers me. I know my worth, *Master* Gastillo. I know everyone's worth within these great and glorious walls belonging to you. I even know yours. Tell me, *Master* Gastillo— I'm curious. You're not that far past prime. Does it bother you knowing that the men training within your walls are all younger than you? That they're more skilled and might very well achieve a name greater than your own? Does that ever enter your mind?"

Insolent kog, Gastillo thought, but he didn't respond. *Fifteen thousand* glowed in his mind.

Having enough of the talk, Jaco resumed walking toward the pit fighters, who didn't flinch in the least.

"Fun's over, lads," the mouthy gladiator said. "The Street Watch is here to save the noble master's honor."

Fifteen thousand gold pieces. For Prajus.

Gastillo cocked his head in the familiar way he once had, just before a fight. "Prajus."

ABOUT THE BLOOD

The still-smiling gladiator lifted his chin in a question.

"These walls are mine," Gastillo informed him in a calm but carrying voice. "These grounds are mine. Those guards . . . They're mine. Everything around you belongs to me. And you are standing in the middle of it all. And as long as you live, breathe, eat, drink, squat, and piss inside these walls . . . you're mine. What makes you think . . . I care . . . about what a crust of maggot shite like you . . . thinks?"

Prajus's smile dimmed. The three men at his back fidgeted.

"That's what I like about you, Master Gastillo," the gladiator finally said. "Always moving. Always attacking from another angle. There's a mind underneath all that wrecked skin and pretty metal. It's a shame you're past prime."

"Get to your bunk, Prajus," Gastillo said quietly, looking over his shoulder. "This instant. Or I'll have Jaco tuck you in."

Prajus didn't move, though.

That, more than any amount of verbal sparring, irritated Gastillo the most—the quiet refusal to obey a command. It galled him.

Worse, Prajus's slick smile brightened, well aware of his effect upon the owner.

Gastillo dearly wanted to slap those teeth free. Instead, he pulled the door open, reminding himself that the days of having to even look at that brazen ass licker were drawing to an end.

"Double the guards tonight, good Jaco," the owner said to the head of his household guard. "The pups seem restless. If any get out, you have my permission to discipline them."

Jaco's smile was one of compliance.

Without another thought, Gastillo entered his home and closed the door.

24

Morning had come once again.

Pig Knot wished it hadn't.

The bed beneath him smelled foul. The woman beside him didn't have all her teeth. At one time during the night, Pig Knot had believed she was a princess of some sort. Those magical moments had vanished with dawn's light. He couldn't remember her name and doubted very much if he could escape her arm, draped solidly across his chest, or her face, tucked firmly into his armpit. Thus, Pig Knot did the only thing he could do. He pushed her arm off, receiving a jolt when she unkindly cupped his bells and damn near buckled him in two.

Oddly enough, she held him down while snoring.

When the worst of the pain eased away, he took her arm and hoisted it clear of his goods. Her fingers twitched, crablike, as if wanting to dig into his man pearls once again. Pig Knot got her arm off him and sighed with relief.

Lords above, he thought, this one latched onto a man like a louse to a dog.

He squirmed, his other arm trapped beneath her snoring head. His crotch still ached as he maneuvered his lower half to the bed's edge. He reached for his loincloth and discovered it wasn't where he'd left it. Nor was his shirt. Pig Knot squinted at his surroundings, rubbing the back of his head.

He didn't recognize the alehouse room, didn't recognize anything, and certainly didn't remember the decorative touches of the interior—flowers in vases, candles, bright colors of dyed cloth hanging on the walls.

A frosty chill enveloped him, and his red eyes widened. "Where I am?"

"Mmmhummm," said the woman, her face still plopped into his armpit.

Pig Knot grimaced. He avoided his armpits most times and couldn't understand her attraction.

"I have to . . ." He shifted a little away from her, tugging his arm free while guarding his kog and bells.

Her face slid away and she remained asleep, prompting a double take from him, with the second look being quite incredulous.

Dying Seddon. He sat up, studying her and the bed, her bare cheeks pointing to the ceiling. She might not have possessed all her teeth, but Pig Knot found himself admiring her naked curves all the same. With a yawn, he lowered himself to the floor. Timbers creaked, and the bed frame scraped his back. He landed with a thump, but nothing disturbed his bedmate. A bedpan was nearby, so he used it. A morning trance took him as he relieved himself, his eyes drifting to her back's fine slope.

He finished without waking her. *What was her name?* It escaped him.

"I'm leaving now," he whispered.

She snorted softly.

He spied his loincloth behind the door and his shirt in a corner. Where her clothing had been scattered around the room like perfumed leaves in a tempest, Pig Knot's had been randomly deposited as if forcefully squirted from a dog blossom.

Dying Seddon.

He waddled around the room, annoyed at his best speed, picking up his clothes as he went. His loincloth was suspiciously damp, which drew a weary sigh. A sniff informed him of sour beer. Thankful he hadn't pissed himself, he stuffed the undergarments into a pocket, leaving the shirt to conceal his man bits.

All the while, she didn't wake.

Just the opposite, in fact. Great sinus-clearing snores ripped from her person, signifying a much deeper sleep, and once, perhaps twice, Pig Knot suspected the bed shook from the force.

He quietly left the bedroom and discovered he wasn't even in an alehouse. He was in *her* house. The kitchen he found himself in wasn't huge, but it was well-kept. A fat vase full of white and pink blooms dressed a table. He dug out his purse and left a few coins there, certain she'd find the money. Pig Knot frowned at his dwindling finances. In fact, he'd gone through half his funds in a very short time.

Not that it mattered. Not really.

"Dog balls," he said, more upset that his good times would come to an end sooner rather than later. He tucked the purse away and looked for his cart. His wheels weren't in the bedroom, which perplexed him. Then he remembered pushing himself along the night before—or perhaps he was being pulled. He'd been on it, either way.

He went to the main door and peeked outside.

No cart was resting against the wall.

Then he remembered.

The bed. Pig Knot rolled his eyes. The damn thing was under the bed, which meant he had to go back there. He winced.

A short time later, he exited the house with his cart, placed it on the street stones, and pushed himself along while the sky continued to brighten. Rooftops packed closely together filled the streets with shadows. His stomach rumbled, and he thought of food, which led him to think of drink. He stopped to gaze about, wondering where in Saimon's hell he was. The street looked familiar, but damn if he knew exactly where. The arena lay half a day away—that much he knew, having purposely put distance between himself and the place. Those memories were not welcome.

He smacked his lips and stopped to feel his jaw.

The bandage was gone.

That placed a little smile upon Pig Knot's face. He didn't force it, but his chin felt strong and free of blinding pain. He wondered if old Shan had worked some sort of magic upon him, after all.

"Thank you," he whispered to the healer and resumed rolling, searching for the morning stalls where one might buy a modest breakfast. The previous night had been a stormy one. He remembered friendly and not-so-friendly faces—remembered he'd even punched one. Pitchers. Rows upon rows of pitchers. Laugher and singing. And arm wrestling, resulting in a few more pitchers he won. He'd drunk a *lake* last night, or so his brain and stomach suggested. Then he remembered the woman but not her name. Though she was missing a few teeth, he thought her attractive. He remembered how she'd cuddled up next to him and smelled of spices. That was all he remembered, which was a shame.

Pig Knot rolled into a wider street and turned right. Alehouses lined both sides, but he still had no idea where he was. A large lad, chin down and drooling, sat with his back to a post. He was missing a shirt, and his belly resembled a huge, hairy apple. Pig Knot looked past the sleeping drunk, searching for someplace to eat.

In short time, he found one.

Farther along, someone was opening a food stall, the only one amongst a row of others. A woman, her hair gray and tied back in a large bun, pulled down a pair of wide planks. She stepped behind the stall and sorted through the goods in a nearby cart.

He stopped before the counter and waited.

The old woman barely blinked when she saw him. "Something to eat?" she asked.

"What do you have back there?"

"An assortment of fruit, mostly. Some fresh bread and jams. All easy on the stomach."

"Anything to drink?"

"Water."

Seddon was smiling on him.

"How much for breakfast?" he asked.

She leaned over the counter to get a better look at him, her eyes not going any farther than his chest. "Five silver for two pieces of thick bread with sweet jam. A fruit of your choice. Drink your fill of water."

"I'll drink a lot of it this morning."

"Drink until it dribbles from your ears. I don't care as long as you have the coin. I have a well just a short walk behind me."

Pig Knot fished out a gold piece and received a handful of silver in return. He glimpsed a sizeable bread knife, the steel worn down by the years. The blade might've been a short sword in a previous trade, but she used it upon a fresh loaf, deftly cutting it into slices. She presented the meal upon a wooden plate and left him to eat, which he did, sipping from a mug at frequent intervals.

The street remained quiet and empty. Figures moved across the far ends, some walking as if struck in the head, but no one approached. When he finished his drink, Pig Knot reached up and placed the mug on the counter.

The old woman promptly filled it.

Thankful for the service, he downed the second lot, gasped, and returned it for another filling.

"Either you were drinking last night, or a wench drained you of all fluids," the old lady commented and poured another round.

Pig Knot grunted agreement.

Other merchants slowly appeared, drifting to their own stalls and removing planks from the front. Some wiped down the counters. No one paid heed to Pig Knot. He chewed slowly, mindful of his jaw, and watched Sunja come to life. Wood scraped and rattled every now and again, breaking the morning quiet. The air smelled sweet, as long as one ignored the faintest taint of sewage. Even that didn't smell too bad. It had been that kind of night.

"Were you a soldier?" the lady asked, distracting him.

"A soldier?"

The woman didn't repeat the question.

"No," he said. "I wasn't a soldier."

"What then?"

"I was a pit fighter."

Something *plunked* behind the counter. "Until you lost your legs?" she asked.

"Aye that."

She chopped something unseen, the sound quick and sure. "Unfortunate," she said when she finished. "And now?"

"My work, you mean?"

"Aye that."

Pig Knot finished the last of his bread. "I don't have any."

The woman didn't say anything to that, so he drank some water.

"Looking for work?" she asked.

Pig Knot smiled. "Something to offer, do you?"

"Not really."

"Well, then. No."

"Can you do anything?"

Good question. All he ever did was break heads and bones, bruise hellpups, and perhaps guard pompous toppers too unfit to live.

She leaned over the counter and stared at him. "Don't remember?"

"All I ever did was fight."

"You can't fight now."

Pig Knot thought about it. "No. I suppose not."

The old lady scratched at that hairy ball hanging off the back of her head. "Be careful on the streets. The city's changed. Become desperate. Little by little, but I see it. Every day. Can sense it, too. Becoming dangerous."

"I'm dangerous," Pig Knot said.

She offered a wry smile. "I think you are. One look will tell anyone that. Just be careful. All I say. And if you enjoyed the food, return for more."

"For more bread and jams?"

"And fruit. All I have here. Too hot to serve anything else, especially at midday. Those lads farther along here, those with the meats, they work around small fires all day and into the night. All that sweat and smoke. Not for me. Not that gurry."

"Those meats taste fine, I wager," Pig Knot said, gazing up one street and down the other.

"Who are you looking for?" she asked.

"No one."

"Going anyplace?"

"No."

"You're a friendly sort, to put up with my questions." She puckered up a set of lined lips then. "What's your name?"

"Pig Knot."

"That's a different name."

"Only one I ever had."

"Who gave you that?"

"I don't know."

"You're an orphan?"

"Aye that."

"Sunjan?"

Pig Knot nodded.

"Many of them about," she said and looked in the same direction as he.

"Well, I'm one."

"I'm Vesula. Well met, young Pig Knot."

"Well met, good Vesula."

She didn't smile, but Pig Knot sensed she was somehow pleased. She returned to work, and the unseen chopping resumed.

In no real hurry, Pig Knot lingered, his cart parked before Vesula's stand, and enjoyed the morning calm.

Which lasted only a short while.

Women, men, and even a few children visited Vesula's stall. They crowded the counter, heedless of order. To prevent being toppled, Pig Knot moved himself to the right, just before

ABOUT THE BLOOD

Vesula's cart. She didn't seem to mind him there. The customers noticed him, their reactions differing. Some ignored him outright while some cocked their brows, taking quick peeks at his legs and then his face—always the legs first, it seemed—before going about their business. A couple of men gave him grim nods, as if knowing exactly what was on Pig Knot's mind.

The children, however, were the worst.

They watched him with wide eyes, without shame. Some even smiled wickedly at his condition. One, a tall boy perhaps somewhere in his teen years, actually made a face at Pig Knot, grinned at his companions, and made a face at Pig Knot again.

"Stop that, you little maggot," growled a blacksmith type who'd stopped for a quick bite and a drink. "All of you."

The children scowled back at him.

The blacksmith raised a thick forearm, and they scattered, bolting into the open streets.

"My thanks," Pig Knot said to the fellow, a gruff-looking individual with scarred hands. He was tall, but everyone seemed tall to Pig Knot lately.

"Get on, cripple," the man said. "Do your begging someplace else."

That stabbed Pig Knot to the core, silencing him of a reply. The blacksmith left him with a dangerous glare and walked away, munching aggressively on an apple until other people crowded up to Vesula's counter, blocking the view. Some of them scrutinized Pig Knot, no doubt wondering when he was going to hold out his hand.

His face turned hot.

He looked away from where Vesula was serving people, some shred of dignity keeping him in place while Sunjans bustled by and went about their lives. He wasn't sure if it was the cripple or the beggar reference that cut him deeper, deeper than any physical pain, truth be known. Though crippled he might be, he decided he wasn't a beggar, and being called one scalded him.

The blacksmith's warning spurred Pig Knot to move. No longer comfortable, he rolled away from Vesula's stall, deciding to erase the embarrassing memory with a little exercise. Slapping the stone under his wheels, he bent forward and pushed, feeling the burn in his arms and the sting of the Sunjan's words.

Cripple, Pig Knot fumed. Perhaps, but he wasn't a beggar and didn't intend to be one. He intended to die first—fast or slow, it didn't matter. That begged the question: when did he want to perish? He had come to the city to enjoy his last purse of coin to the fullest and then perhaps get stabbed in an alleyway. Plenty of cutthroats skulked about the city. His problem was, he supposed, staying near the arena. Most thieves didn't like to work so close to the games, for fear of being caught by mobs of people inspired to fight back after witnessing a rousing afternoon of combat . . . or being set upon by trained gladiators or the Street Watch.

Thus far, he'd very much enjoyed the last couple of nights but had yet to manage the dying bit. He'd have to work on that part. Then there was Pig Knot's physical size. Despite having had his legs hacked off, his upper body was still impressive, his physique hard and defined. It suddenly occurred to him that only a truly bold person—or a gang—would consider robbing and killing him.

The southeast section of the city contained the kind of maggots he needed. Most Sunjans looked warily upon the place, and the well-off citizens to the north avoided the area entirely.

Do your begging someplace else, *a voice warned him.*
Wise advice.

People bustled in conflicting currents, ahead, back, and from side to side. Farmers herded livestock to market, and Pig Knot rolled around a wagon filled with chickens. The smell alone stopped him cold. He narrowly avoided a series of freshly spattered cow kisses and vowed to be more careful with his hands and wheels. Several times, people halted in midstep, staring sheer poison at him for blocking the path. Pig Knot kept close to the various storefronts, stalls, alehouses and taverns, and the occasional house. He coasted by actual beggars and understood their plight perhaps a little better.

For whatever reason, he glanced over his shoulder and saw a curious thing.

Some children from Vesula's stall, four of them, were following him. Even more interesting, they made no attempt to conceal the fact.

Pig Knot halted.

They stopped as well, no more than twenty strides back. People passed before them, concealing them at times, but he glimpsed the boys through the moving bodies, seeing their youthful faces, their shabby clothing, and their size. They were big lads. What knotted Pig Knot's brow, however, were the smiles upon their faces, cruel and eager.

The tallest boy, the one warned back at the stall, stood with his friends at his flanks, eyeing Pig Knot with decidedly evil thoughts. The once gladiator scowled back, wondering what the youngsters thought they were about. They all looked halfway to adulthood in age, but that wasn't what truly caught his attention. There was an air about them, a feral posturing he remembered from his own youth.

He spied a nearby alley. Pretending to ignore them, Pig Knot turned his wheels and disappeared between two buildings. Old crates and garbage littered the sides, but he paid no mind to the refuse. A pungent stink of piss fouled his nose just before his wheels splashed through a puddle that wasn't rainwater. He reached the alley's end and saw it connected to another street several strides ahead. On impulse, he glanced back.

The boys appeared at the alley mouth.

A smile spread across Pig Knot's face. The four pups looked as though they were hunting rats.

He intended to show them they were hunting far worse.

Slapping stone, he turned himself around, crashing into a half-crumped wooden crate. By the time he got his cart free of the mess, the boys were walking toward him. Pig Knot checked his surroundings, placed his back to a wall, and faced the approaching pack. On a whim, he pulled his shirt off and wedged it between his thigh and the cart's side.

"You lads want something?" he called out.

The tall one, his hair falling about his eyes as if he'd pulled his head out of a dusty chimney, smiled yellow teeth. He had rat's eyes. The others were no longer so sly, and appeared increasingly cautious. The group stopped a good ten paces away and studied the man with no legs. Two boys glanced back at the alley mouth, as if fearful of being caught doing something very wrong.

"You've got coin, cripple?" the tall one asked, trying hard to deepen his voice.

"And if I do?" Pig Knot asked, genuinely amused. He drew himself up on his cart, placing his muscular torso on display. Legless he might have been, but his upper body was far from crippled.

The boys filled the width of the alley and crept forward. A fat one hung to the tall one's right while a lad with a face as pale as a pearl was on the left. A fourth boy brought up the rear. The fat one actually seemed much too happy, in Pig Knot's opinion. The pale one kept looking back toward the main street, but his face was drawn and hungry looking—not for food but for violence.

The tall one jerked a knife free of his shirt.

Pig Knot scowled. These rats weren't about to be easily scared away. He expected to be preyed upon sooner or later, but not by . . . *youth*s.

"When I was your age, we grabbed the food from the carts," he said. "Or tugged coin ever so gently from pockets. We never used knives."

The fat one pulled another knife, as did the boy with the complexion of a ghost. The fourth boy stayed in the rear, but Pig Knot knew he probably had a weapon as well.

"Give us your coin," the tall one whispered bravely. "And we'll leave you with your life."

"Maybe even your topper," the ghost said and broke into giggles, trading looks with the other pack members.

"Boy," Pig Knot warned, "I don't like it when children pull steel on me. Point that knife at me, and I promise you . . . you'll hurt for it."

The smiles disappeared. The boys didn't like the threat.

The tall one lifted his chin, and his face darkened. "You give us what you got, and we'll let you live."

The pack was only six or seven paces away. They could rush him, but they hesitated to do so, becoming very much aware of Pig Knot's size.

"Let me be clear," the once gladiator said in an all-too-calm voice. "I'll break the nose of the first punce who swings at me. If I catch an arm, I'll snap it in two. If I catch a knife, I'll use it. You look like you've done this before, but you've made a mistake this day. I don't frighten easy. I'm certainly not frightened by youngsters . . . thinking their knives . . . make them men. My legs might've caught your attention, but you won't notice them."

On that note, Pig Knot put his fist through the side of a nearby crate. The sound got the boys' attention, even whipping the head of the fourth boy around. Pig Knot pulled away a jagged shard and brandished it with unscathed knuckles.

"When I shove this . . . up your dog blossoms." Pig Knot glared at the gang leader.

Despite the threat, the tall lad didn't back down. The boy was a brazen one, and ready for the dirtiest of work.

"Jurnos?" the fat one asked.

Jurnos—the tall one—slowly shook his head and lowered his knife, and Pig Knot thought the situation was all but finished.

The tall boy lunged, a steel coil snapping forward, the knife slicing for an eye.

Pig Knot slapped the blade away, grabbed the lad's filthy shirt, and heaved Jurnos into the crate he'd punched. Wood crackled. Pig Knot lost his balance with the effort and fell from his cart. Jurnos quickly recovered and scrambled onto the legless man. He tried to cut Pig Knot, but the once gladiator punched the boy in the face, crossing his eyes. Jurnos collapsed against the alley wall.

The three others tensed, eyes and ears and, most of all, mouths opened wide. Their blossoms drawn tighter than three knots on a string.

Pig Knot righted himself and tossed his wooden shard. He picked up Jurnos's knife, and grabbed the pack leader's shirt. Muscles visibly flexing, he dragged the boy from the crate's ruins, got behind him, and held the blade to the youngster's throat.

Pig Knot gave the other three his most dangerous look.

The boys broke, raising dust clouds as they fled the alley.

Letting his breath go, Pig Knot chuckled.

Jurnos stirred.

Pig Knot straightened his arm, serious once again, and cocked the knife. "Stay still, you little maggot shite," he whispered against the boy's temple. "Stay still. Anger me, and I'll cut you. Truly anger me, and you'll wake up without a kog in Saimon's hell."

A defiant Jurnos showed teeth red with blood but didn't move.

"You made a mistake today," Pig Knot whispered. "Remember that. And remember you were this close," he held the knife to the boy's face, "to losing your life."

Jurnos fumed, lips tight with rage.

For an instant, Pig Knot thought it best to kill the lad and be done with it. The youngster had that look, that feel of evil encased in flesh, but the once gladiator hadn't gone that far yet, not enough to kill boys, even though Jurnos was perhaps fourteen or fifteen.

He released the lad and shoved. "Get on," Pig Knot said, nodding at the alley entrance.

Jurnos crawled a few paces before standing. When he did, he checked the distance, and his fury came loose.

"I'll find you," the boy swore, red-faced and venomous. "You legless pile of horse shite. You think I made a mistake?

You made the mistake, you stupid-assed bastard. *You* did. I'll find you. I'll find you, and I won't hesitate next time. I'll gut you and leave you bleeding in the ditches..."

Jurnos emphasized his words with a pair of quick, underhanded stabs at the air.

Pig Knot didn't appreciate the rant, not after his very generous act of mercy. He pulled back his cart while keeping an eye on the boy. He kept the knife, as he had nothing close to a weapon and had to admit the blade wasn't a bad one.

"You're *dead*, cripple," the boy whispered and pointed. "You're *dead*. I'll open you up and leave you for the rats to nest in. I'll leave you in the streets so everyone can see my work. You're not the first. I've killed six men already. *Six* men."

"All while they're sleeping, no doubt."

That enraged the lad.

"I'll kill you! Seddon above, I'll kill you!" When Jurnos saw Pig Knot was unmoved, he changed his tune. "Tell you what, give me that blade, and I'll consider killing you quick when I find you. Quick. One stab to the throat."

"You want this?" Pig Knot asked, holding up the weapon.

The boy tensed, suspicious.

"Here," Pig Knot said and shuffled forward.

Jurnos backed away.

"*Here*," Pig Knot said, continuing to move toward him. "Come closer, and I'll give your knife back. I've got no legs. You said so yourself. So why are you afraid?"

"Not afraid of you," Jurnos said, but he retreated all the same.

"You're the worst kind of coward." Pig Knot smiled. "One that talks loud from a distance but whimpers when face-to-face."

He propelled himself toward the youngster, who ran for the alley mouth. An instant later, the boy disappeared around the corner.

"Thought so," Pig Knot grumbled with some measure of satisfaction.

Shaking his head, he returned to his cart and climbed aboard. He left his shirt off, not wanting to wear it right away.

However, he pulled on his damp loincloth, not wanting to frighten anyone. He realized then he'd facd the youngsters while naked. Perhaps that was the reason the other three held back when Jurnos lunged. Thoughts of the lad soured his mood. He wasn't sure if he would've killed the boy or not, but he wasn't opposed to delivering a right and proper beating. *Young street rat. Nothing worse or more annoying.*

Sensing nothing good would come from the encounter, Pig Knot hung back from the teeming traffic of the main street. Not one person had come to his aid while he faced the street rats. *Sunja,* he thought. *You haven't changed.*

Wanting something powerful to drink, Pig Knot wheeled himself into the hot daylight and stayed close to the road's edges, enduring that sweaty, smelly mob. Figuring that distance was the best option, he decided to leave what he believed was Jurnos's territory. Southeast might not be in his future at all. He'd go east, perhaps near the great lower lake, where the city's naturally occurring spring water pooled. At current speed, he thought it would take him half a day to get there.

Children.

He wanted to die—that was a given—but the thought of being knifed and robbed by a pack of budding street rats turned his guts rancid.

25

Sunja smothered Pig Knot with trapped heat, smells, and parasitic crowds. The sun bore down on his meaty frame as he maneuvered his little cart through the bustling streets. Feeling that fearsome heat, he put his shirt back on. Sweat quickly soaked the cloth. He frequently looked over his shoulder, scanning the tangles of people for Jurnos or any of his pack. The boy's face and fury bothered him enough to make him doubt releasing the teenager had been the right thing to do.

"Six men," the boy had said. He'd killed six men. The troubling thing was it didn't sound like a lie.

Pig Knot avoided the alleys and the backstreets, not trusting them. He didn't stop for anything to eat, wanting to be well into the eastern part of the city before nightfall. A wagon with pigs wrinkled his nose, and people clogged the street sides in order to get around the animals. The congestion caused tense moments for the once gladiator as a deluge of waistlines and hopping children flowed by him. Hundreds of voices melded into gibberish. Pig Knot struggled to see everything at once. Hidden hands concerned him the most, as they might belong to youths looking to sink a blade into him. Annoyed faces loomed overhead, some surprised at seeing him, others quickly glancing away. Pig Knot reached a set of wooden stairs and parked himself alongside, placing his back against a wall. Yells peppered the air, calling on the farmer and drivers to get the animals out of the street. An old man with a cane climbed the nearby stairs, the wood creaking with his effort. When the crowds finally eased up some, Pig Knot wheeled himself out and away.

He didn't see Jurnos or his lads.

Either the boys had left him alone, or they'd become more careful at hiding.

Enduring looks of pity and contempt in equal amounts, along with one or two smiles that seemed oddly out of place, Pig Knot continued east.

By early evening, he stopped before a small tavern that looked somewhat respectable. A single-story affair made of dark-stained timbers, it had none of the festive trappings of the fighting season adorning the front. Two tables were positioned on a raised deck on either side of the main entrance. Three men were drinking at one of those tables. Shuttered windows were thrown open to allow the smell of smoke and cooking roasts to waft into the street.

After the day Pig Knot had endured, a good meal would improve his spirits.

Two broad steps stopped him, so he parked his cart alongside them and dismounted. He landed with a grimace, glad that he avoided crushing his plums. He hoisted himself up and over the steps, drawing the passing interest of the three men. They spared him only a glance before returning to their conversation, muttering about the ongoing war and the politics of Marrn and Vathia.

Upon reaching the deck, Pig Knot stretched and pulled up his cart. He mounted it and rattled inside. Pipe smoke clouded the interior. Wood carvings of hawks leered from roosts fixed into thick columns. Tables and benches lined the main floor in a thoughtful, organized maze. A broad counter had been built in the very back, with a row of stacked goblets and mugs behind it, shiny as if plucked from a dream. An impressive wall of kegs rested behind the goblets.

Pig Knot liked that very much.

He aimed for the table nearest the bar and, once he settled in, waved for the barkeep's attention. He ordered two pitchers of beer and a plate of whatever was cooking. The barkeep took the order without comment. He was a tall individual with long locks tied at the back in a style similar to Pig Knot's. The once gladiator liked the man's silent demeanor, and when a serving wench placed two pitchers on the table before him, he had already forgotten his morning encounter and the rest of the day.

There was drinking to be done.

"You say you scared them off?" A burly individual called Pline asked.

Pig Knot held onto his sixth pitcher of the night—that one being mead—and nodded with the patience and philosophical wisdom of a person well and truly pickled.

"Scared them off," he slurred and winked at one of three serving wenches working the floor. "Youngsters. When I mean youngsters, I mean boys. Perhaps, perhaps no more than sixteen." Which came out as *sheexteen*. "Not fit. To hold a blade. Yet brazen. Oho. Brazen enough to mark me as an easy peach. Really, now. Do I look like an easy mark to you?"

"Not at all," Pline agreed with a frown, leaning in over substantial forearms. Pline had a crow's beak of thinning hair, which had been slicked back with something as shiny as slug slime. The man possessed a long face—or the lack of hair gave him the illusion of having a long face—and Pig Knot tried hard not to make comments about it. Pline, while affable enough, looked big and powerful, even bigger than Pig Knot back when he still had legs.

"S'all unfit," Pline stated with a sad shake of his head. "Unfit, I say. Everything's going bad these days. All bad. No insult intended, good Pig Knot—but when the youngsters are robbing the, ah, less physically limbed, then I know it's time to go. Where was the Street Watch when this was going on?"

"Never saw a hair," Pig Knot replied with a slack face. "Nothing. Not that . . . I wanted them around. I scared those boys right and proper. One lad was—was a true hellpup. Right nasty. All the while I was—excuse me—I was threatening him like, like with the knife, right? He was just festering with anger. *Festering*. Oh, you never seen the like. Could see it plain as day. As that one standing right there against the bar. And you could smell it. Could *feel* it, plain as fire. Shocking. Purely shocking."

"Shocked just hearing it," Pline said. "And a little angry, myself. You would've been right to end one of them. Just as a lesson. Too many of them sorts around Sunja these days. Don't know what's happening to our fair city, but the streets are becoming more dangerous with every nightfall. And the watch are stretched thin. What with the games going on and all. You watch the games?"

Pig Knot paused for effect and took a shot of mead. "I fought in the games."

"You fought in the games?"

"Aye that."

"That the reason . . ." Pline trailed off, nodding at what *wasn't* below the table.

Pig Knot nodded.

"Unfit. Just unfit."

"You know, I was a house master."

Fat lines resembling worms creased Pline's forehead. "*Whaaat?*"

"I was. The House of Ten."

"The Free Trained one?"

"Aye that."

"So you're here with them?"

"No. I left them. Behind. Not with them now."

That struck Pline speechless, and he struggled to understand.

"Time to leave," Pig Knot explained. "I was . . . hating. Having to watch the lads. Seeing them train. Reminded me. Too much. Of when I had legs. You see. When I was whole. Had to leave. Return to my city. See if I can"—there, he decided it wise to hide the truth—"do anything here. Anything not with the games."

"But you were a house master! Couldn't you just have gotten used to it? Saimon's black hanging fruit, man. Anything's better than on the streets, I daresay."

"Not for me," Pig Knot declared. "Not for me at all."

"The House of Ten," Pline said. "Heard they've got only a couple of lads left in the games. All the rest are dead or can't continue. But there's one lad who's a right and proper bastard with a blade. Doesn't even unsheathe his sword when he fights. Pounds his opponents into submission."

"That would be Junger. Perician. Perician Weh . . . Perician Weh . . ." Pig Knot belched. "Weapon."

"Aye that, that's the one. He's the talk of the city after the other day."

That made Pig Knot curious. "What happened the other day?" he got out and was immensely pleased with the lack of hitching.

"You haven't heard? That man fought three fights in one day, one after the other. Last one was a house gladiator. The Perician beat them all. All *three*."

"Three?" That was impressive . . . and practically unheard of, at least to Pig Knot.

"The lad's a terror. A terror, I say."

"He was a terror on the training sands," Pig Knot said. "I can . . . tell you things. Why, there were days . . ."

And into the night, the once house master regaled the Sunjan with tales from the House of Ten's training grounds. Pline ordered more drinks for them both, and Pig Knot repaid the man by ordering yet another round. When the lamplight grew low, Pline bade the legless gladiator a good night and stumbled off to the latrine before heading out the front door. Pig Knot had already made two such stops—quite thankful the latrine was just a wooden trough set into the floor—and decided he would finish the night with one last visit to another tavern or such.

He slid off the bench far too heavily and flipped his cart, causing the last few faces to look up from their conversations. Pig Knot smiled and waved as he righted the cart, loaded himself aboard, and wheeled himself to the front door.

A hard-looking enforcer type stood there and regarded him with a knowing leer.

"Had your fill?" the man asked.

"Barely," Pig Knot sputtered and wiped his mouth. "I was . . . I was going to . . . to have a go at that honeypot. In the white dress . . . but I daresay she's none . . . she's none too . . . too pleased with me."

"I know the one. Don't concern yourself with her. She fancies another."

"Ah. Well then, no rooms in this place. I saw no stairs."

"No rooms. The barkeep doesn't want the headache. Cleaning those things is a chore in the morning. Especially after those who can't hold their drink. You can imagine."

Pig Knot could, easily. He made a face. "Well," he said, "I'm off."

The door guardian nodded, and Pig Knot wheeled forth into a moist summer night that offered nary a breeze. The streets were deserted, and a wall of humidity stole his breath. He looked up into a black field of stars as bright as diamonds. The heavens twinkled with a magical intensity that set his heart aflutter.

Until he misjudged the length of the front deck and his tipping cart flung him into the street. He crashed, rock raking the side of his head. He felt no pain, just contact. He stayed there for a bit, hearing a few chuckles around him, which didn't bother him in the least. He'd be laughing too. With a grunt, he rolled himself over and sat up.

The door enforcer was gone.

"Need a room," Pig Knot croaked, clumsily dusting off his shirt. He looked about with glassy eyes, checked himself as an afterthought, and was quite pleased he hadn't pissed himself in the tumble.

ABOUT THE BLOOD

Task in mind, he righted his cart and got aboard. He pushed himself along in a line that veered to the right. He stopped, straightened his course, took bearings, and started moving again, following a string of oil lamps that shimmered in the night.

Hands grabbed him and hurried him into a nearby alley. Pig Knot didn't resist, not understanding why he was going into that beckoning void between two buildings, and when he did, it was too late.

"Brazen—" he slurred, reaching for his knife and finding it gone. *The tumble. Must have dropped it.*

A hard knock to the side of the head dazed him. The ground crashed into his senses, and he raised his arms, glimpsing stars through his fingers. Someone slapped his hands away. A foot kept him down while he was roughly groped and searched. Hands ripped away his shirt, the sound of tearing fabric rousing Pig Knot's anger. He lifted his head and got it knocked back. Then he got it knocked back a *second* time.

Foul breath then, right in his face, and a moon of pitch that contained a single hooded eye.

"Stay still," someone whispered, "and you'll live." The voice was a man's that time, not a youngster's.

Pig Knot scowled. "Get on—"

A grip of iron fastened itself around his mouth, shoving his face back. His jaw protested with a star-bright warning of pain. As drunk as he was, Pig Knot knew how frail his chin was. He grabbed the hands and got his face slapped—twice—hard, crashing blows that rattled him to his bones and left his ears ringing.

Mutterings then:

"Thought you said he had coin?"

"He did have coin, unless he drank it all away."

"Not all," said a third voice, gruffer than the others. "Here. What's this?"

"Seven pieces."

"Bah, barely worth the effort."

"No effort at all."

"Barely. Worth. The effort." A hard slap to Pig Knot's head punctuated each word, damn near driving him to unconsciousness.

"Kill—" *me* he tried to say, but a vicious boot to the stomach emptied him in a rush.

"Check them wheels he's got," someone urged.

Shadows picked up the cart and flipped it about, searching. To Pig Knot, the very night seemed to clutch the little cart. One of the thieves placed it against a wall and put his foot through the bottom.

The sound animated Pig Knot. He reached for the wood.

More kicks to the body while the world cracked and splintered.

"Stay right there," a shadow said, "or I'll gut you."

"Seems like he almost wants to get gutted," another said.

"Nothing," the third person reported, picking through the wreck of the cart.

"Get him up."

Hands grabbed Pig Knot and pressed him against the wall. Fingers as tough as spikes clutched his throat, nipping off his air.

"All you got on you?" a shadow demanded, punching Pig Knot's stomach. "This all? Seven gold?"

Two more slaps to the head.

"Aye that," Pig Knot finally gasped.

"You drank it all?"

Still held between those fingers, Pig Knot managed a weak smile.

"Nothing in the wood. Nothing hidden," the third one repeated.

"Check his loincloth."

"*You* check his loincloth."

Pain exploded in Pig Knot's crotch then as his kog and berries got rudely squashed one way and then another. He nearly lost the night's investment right there in one soupy heave.

"Nothing."

"Bad for us," spoke the man holding onto Pig Knot's chin. "And for you."

A fist rocked Pig Knot's head. When he failed to fall over, the attacker truly got into his work. Three savage blows slammed into the once gladiator's skull, pounding Pig Knot to the ground. A parting boot to the gut triggered all that liquid merriment to leave his person in a series of gasps.

It worked out for the better, however, as the thieves stopped striking him.

"Dirty bastard," someone said, repelled by the stomach juice.

"Got it on my foot."

"I just stepped in it."

More talk, but all Pig Knot saw was a field of stars.

The voices receded into the night.

Lying on his back and no longer able to see, Pig Knot drifted sideways until everything went black.

26

Two gladiators crossed blades while eyeing each other behind their guards. Neither man wore armor, and the sun put a glistening polish to their dark skin. Both were finely chiseled with muscle, but one man was much more powerful looking and noticeably taller by a few fingers. Wooden swords clattered against targets in the background, and those gladiators strained with various exercises meant to strengthen and improve their endurance. That noise faded out, becoming distant, to the point of barely being noticed.

"Ready?" Sorban asked, holding his wooden blade.

The other gladiator—a Sunjan called Urson—nodded.

The Balgothan lunged, stabbing that fat splinter of a blade past Urson's upraised sword, and slapped the man's shoulder.

Urson gasped and jumped back, his free hand immediately grabbing the point of impact. Unchecked shock exploded on the Sunjan's face as he examined his hand for blood. None was there to be seen, however.

Sorban, not pressing the attack, relaxed and stepped back from the warrior. He frowned and pointed at the shoulder. "Damnation, Urson. You move like a sick cow."

"You didn't cut me," the man exclaimed in wonder. "How is that?"

"Skill, you young shite. Skill," a trainer, Mal, explained in a neutral though schoolmasterly tone. He tapped one sandaled foot on the sand. "Something which we can only hope you acquire one day."

"Bit harsh," Urson grumbled, offended.

"The truth," Mal said, squinting and inspecting the gladiator's shoulder. "Come on, now. Sorban only tapped you. Not even. A tavern wench wouldn't notice that. Sorban?"

"Master Mal?"

"What's your opinion on Urson's speed?"

The Balgothan frowned. He hated being put on the spot in such a way.

"Could be improved upon," he managed, inspecting his wooden sword.

"Diplomatically said," the trainer noted. "Very much appreciated. You hear that, young Urson? 'Could be improved upon.' And that was given without a drop of blood. Without losing a match in the Pit and certainly without damaging your future. You do well to listen, especially from that man. He only used a sword on you this day. A wooden one, at that. Seddon forbid he takes up that staff of his. As of now, I wouldn't want to see you try and evade that. That's a lesson and daresay a spectacle for another day."

"My thanks, Master Mal. Sorban," Urson said in a low tone, accepting the advice with only a slight bruise to his pride.

"Pick up one of those heavier sticks," Mal directed. "The heaviest you can find. And hit that man over there two hundred times. Or as close to it as you can manage. Off with you."

Orders received, Urson nodded and went to a rack of wooden weapons. Just beyond that was a line of wooden targets, where several other gladiators were hacking away at outstretched limbs and headless necks. Mal and Sorban watched the young Urson select a sword.

"Not headstrong or stubborn, you understand," Mal said out of the corner of his mouth. "Just moves like a sick cow."

Sorban didn't comment.

"There's a shift in recruitment these days," Mal observed. "A fundamental change in thought. I was discussing it with Thurlo and Irva the other day. Owners are letting speed slip away. Nowadays, it's becoming strength. Might. They want their men to be able to split shields with one blow. Take heads off with one cut. Mind you, the masters could do that. Sadly, there are very few masters at these games. Those hellions developed a near-perfect balance between speed and power. A level we strive to achieve but rarely reach. These days, it's as if some of these dogs expect you to stand still and let them swing at you. They would better spend their time hacking down forests. It's one thing to strike a man once and hope he falls—it's another to strike four or five times in rapid succession and know he will."

Sorban listened. "Different schools of thought, Master Mal."

Mal studied the gladiator with a contemplative look. "Exactly, good Sorban. Exactly. Now, then. Seeing we're of the same mind with regards to speed, and that you're willing to give your time in helping the others . . ."

Sorban smirked inwardly. He knew what was coming.

"What about going over there and helping Punder with his stance?" Mal asked.

"His stance?"

"The man walks like he's about to let slip a cow kiss."

Sorban spotted the gladiator amongst the others. was right. The man did walk around as if in dire need of a shite trough.

"Now's the time to fix it," Mal said.

Sorban wasn't so sure.

"Do it, and Master Thurlo will let you head home this evening to your wife."

That lightened the gladiator's expression.

"Not so bad now, is it?" Mal said, looking at his feet.

Nodding, Sorban walked through the training grounds belonging to the ailing Vavar Slavol, owner of the House of Slavol. The old man wasn't present that day—he rarely was—but

ABOUT THE BLOOD

Sorban glanced toward the raised platform just before the man's private residence. A carpet of greenery surrounded the stage, and upon the wooden floor were two chairs. Sometimes, Vavar would sit there, under a high canvas shade, and watch them. Not this day, however. Sorban didn't want to think about that. The others were a superstitious lot. They were already of the mind that any day where Vavar wasn't watching them, bad fortune would follow.

Sorban didn't disagree with his sword brothers.

"Ho, Punder," he called out, turning the gladiator's head. Like them all, Punder was dressed in only a loincloth, enough to cover his man bits and nothing more. Like them all, he shone with a terrible sweat.

Punder, of a smaller build than Urson, turned away from his practice and squinted at the approaching Sorban. "What did I do?"

"Nothing."

"All right. What is it I'm *not* doing?"

"Master Mal wants me to help you with your stance."

Squinty grimace in place, Punder looked over Sorban's shoulder and met the steely gaze of the watching trainer.

"My stance?" Punder asked.

Sorban nodded.

"What's wrong with my stance?"

"He says you walk like a sick cow."

Punder sighed. "And he sent you to fix it."

Sorban smiled in answer.

The sky darkened, lit by jagged streaks of purple and pink. Sorban came out of the bathhouse refreshed and smelling much cleaner than before. He straightened out the leather skirt he wore, pinched the sleeveless white tunic from his wet chest, and started walking. A few others followed him out and wandered toward the common room at one end of the training grounds. Punder stopped and watched the older gladiator go.

"Sorban," he called out, "you're passing on the rabbit?"

"I am."

"My thanks for today."

Sorban lifted a hand.

"Sorban," someone new called out.

That stopped the older gladiator in his tracks. He recognized that voice.

There, standing upon the platform of Vavar, before the old man's chair, was his son, Salwark. The man was waving him over.

With just the barest twinge of reluctance, Sorban went to the acting owner of the house.

"Master Salwark," the Balgothan said, stopping well away from the man.

"Good Sorban." Salwark smiled, flashing that awesome set of teeth that no doubt inspired envy amongst the royal family themselves. He was a handsome fellow—no denying that—with his long hair in a daring knot at the back and a light in his eyes brighter than most. Salwark wasn't a bad person, certainly not ill-mannered, but he could talk, and not in a good way, like his father.

Worse, the young man's breath could kill five paces out.

"Taskmaster Thurlo and Trainers Mal and Irva have spoken highly of you this day. What I mean to say is they speak well of you *any* day, truth be known, but they were particularly pleased by your patience and generosity with your time. Schooling the younger lads, hammering out a few issues, getting them well and ready for their upcoming matches. I just wanted to let you know that I also value your time, good Sorban. Very much value your time."

The Balgothan stood and listened, well out of range. He kept his face neutral, but with a flicker of gratitude. He was about to reply when Salwark started up again.

"These games are a challenge for all of us these days. All of us. Especially with Father stricken as he is. But regarding you, he and I are of the same mind. You're a fine one, Sorban. A boon to the stable. A standard of the games. And undefeated this season. *Undefeated*. Not many of those left. Taskmaster

Thurlo and the trainers all agree that you'll take that one easily, if and when you face him. That's, ah, inspiring. At least, I find it inspiring. You'll go far. *Truly* far. Ah, how do you feel?"

Sorban realized he was being asked a question. "I'm well, Salwark."

"Off to see your wife?"

"I am."

"And a well-earned reward for a long day," Salwark said. "Well earned. Give the others something to think about when they're practicing tomorrow, eh? What does she think of you participating in the games?"

"She doesn't like it," he answered truthfully.

"None of them do, I suspect." Salwark became quiet then, thinking of the next thing to say no doubt, and burning Sorban's time.

"Ah well, good evening to you," the owner finally said. "Enjoy yourself. See you back here in the morning."

"Thank you, Master Salwark."

"Eat well. Sleep peacefully. All that."

Sorban nodded that he would indeed.

"I hope you appreciate this gesture. From me. To you. For your time. In helping the lads." The man finally ran out of words, but he fidgeted as if containing one last thought. In the end, Salwark smiled, releasing the full glory of those teeth, and gestured for the pit fighter to walk on with a grand flourish of an arm.

Puzzled, Sorban walked away from the platform. He cleared his mind of the encounter and focused on the closed gate of the Slavol property. Three guards stood there, dressed in leather armor and helms. Swords hung from their waists in sheaths. A rack with at least two score throwing spears was propped against the wall.

With every step, Sorban expected Salwark to call out to him with "one more thing," but then he was at the gates.

"Letting you loose, eh?" one the guards asked him with a lewd smile. "Fortunate."

Sorban didn't comment.

"Master Mal was here earlier," the guard explained. "Have yourself a fine evening, good Sorban."

The guards opened the smaller door set into the gate.

There stood Zelia.

Her anxious look dissolved into one of relief upon laying eyes on her husband, pleased with his surprise. Sorban blinked and slowly smiled at his lovely wife. She was an eyeful, short and shapely yet not quite overweight. She wore tasteful robes of green and yellow that were tied off at the waist. She had blue eyes, and a round face freckled by the sun. Her hair, light and long, was pulled back, uncovering a high forehead, and flowed halfway down her back. At least, that's how she wore it that day, knowing full well he liked the style.

"Husband," she said.

Sorban got over his surprise. "Wife."

"Master Salwark thought you might enjoy seeing me at the gates. His lads fetched me not too long ago."

That was it, Sorban realized, now understanding the owner's posturing. He glanced back toward the raised platform.

There, Salwark could be seen by the glow of his teeth alone. Sorban would have to thank the owner again in the morning. He stepped into the street and nodded thanks at the pair of guards who had escorted his wife to the gate. The guards stepped around the couple and entered the grounds. They closed the gate door behind them, leaving the couple with their secret smiles.

"You shame the evening, lovely one," Sorban said in Balgothan while staring into her eyes.

The compliment pleased her, and she stared right back at her man. "You look clean," she said.

Sorban knew what she meant. "I was coming home. I made sure I washed."

"Smart lad."

"Very smart lad," he agreed.

ABOUT THE BLOOD

Zelia looked him over for injury, something she always did when he returned to her. Inspection complete, she stepped closer and wrapped her hands around his arm.

"Did you eat, then?" she asked him.

"I did not."

"Excellent. Master Salwark provided me with a small but unexpected purse."

"He did?"

"He did. Six gold coins. Enough to enjoy a nice meal this evening."

"A very nice meal."

"You must have been a good boy in there, today," Zelia said, her head touching his arm as they walked along a not-so-crowded street. The cut stone shone under the setting sun, and dust motes rode the air. Yellow flowers and other greenery flourished in large clay boxes lining both sides of the road. People walked by the husband and wife, unconcerned with them.

"This way, then," she said and led him away from the Stable of Slavol.

He didn't resist.

"The season goes well for you?" she asked.

Sorban knew she hated the season. "It does."

"And that's as much as I'll speak of it."

He thought as much. She despised speaking of the games, not wanting to hear anything about the dangerous sport. She refused to even speak of birthing children until he left the games entirely, as she believed children would only attract the worst of luck and leave her a widow.

Sorban knew that, knew she wanted him to leave, having pleaded with him not to continue at the end of last year's games despite the coin he'd won and passed on to her. Coin, she'd said many times, was cold comfort in a bed meant for two.

The games had ruined the lives of many couples.

"Where are we going?" he asked her, seeking to avoid any arguments that night.

"Somewhere."

"How have you been?"

"Since a week ago?"

The last time he saw her. "Aye that."

"Well enough. The household finances are well. The days are boring, but I suppose that's a good thing. No one's attempted to rob us. Or rape me."

Sorban frowned. "No one would dare."

"No, I don't suppose. But that's one more reason to come back home. And stay. To protect me."

"I thought you weren't going to speak of the games."

"I didn't. I'm talking about me and our home."

Sorban sighed. "You don't give up, do you?"

Zelia pulled away from his arm and studied him with innocent eyes.

"Evil woman," he muttered.

She gripped his arm all the more.

They stopped into a small, secluded alehouse not far from the nobility area. They ate roast chicken and vegetables set in a spicy gravy and drank Sunjan Gold. Sorban watched her eat and listened to her stories of the week. He did not speak of his victories or any aspect of his gladiatorial life.

"What?" she asked him at one point, a silver goblet not far from her mouth.

Sorban didn't answer. She already knew.

Zelia smiled before taking a drink.

Located north of the stable but still a good walk from where Sunja's nobles roosted, was Zelia and Sorban's home, a one-story affair with a tall roof and a strip of grass that surrounded the property. The neighbors were only an arm's length away, but the area was quiet, regularly patrolled by the Street Watch, and well-kept. Zelia produced the key for the front door and fitted it into the lock. Moments later, they were inside, and Sorban fitted two planks across the inside of the door.

When he finished, she'd already struck a flint and lit candles, not bothering with the fireplace. The place was small but comfortable, and that's what Zelia appreciated the most. She said she didn't want large grounds or thick gardens, not while he was away at the games. Those features would be sought after in their next home, in their native Balgotha, when it was time to leave Sunja. So while they waited for that day, Zelia tended to the house's three rooms: a modest kitchen, a sitting area, and a small indoor bath—a luxury in Sunja. A set of stairs led to the loft, where a soft mattress of sheep wool and feathers waited.

"What's that I smell?" Sorban asked.

Zelia tsked and looked cross.

"What did I do?"

"We're here, alone, behind closed doors, and all you can ask is 'What's that I smell?' Have you learned nothing?"

She stood in the center of the room, holding her hips.

"You're right," Sorban said and went to her.

She stripped him of his tunic and slid his leather skirt off his hips. The undercloth came free with a tug. Her hands ran over him while her eyes locked onto his.

"Honeywood," she whispered, feeling the cords of his flat stomach.

"What's that?" he asked, holding his breath.

"The scent. It's honeywood."

"What's that?"

"Incense. I bought it at the market."

"I see," he whispered then grunted. "It's nice."

She smiled and stepped closer to him. His arms folded around her.

"Husband," she murmured.

Then his mouth was upon hers.

The night went too quickly, and when the crows cried out somewhere in the distance, Sorban awoke in annoyance.

They were in their bed, the sheets thin and clean and half off them both. Zelia slept next to him, her head at his shoulder. She made not a sound. Her leg straddled his, and one bare breast pressed softly against his arm. Spent honeywood lingered on the air. Sorban didn't move for fear of waking her though he could hear voices outside their home, somewhere in the street.

The moment was one of those when, with every rise and fall of her back, he wished time would simply stop.

Later, while he had his nose in her hair, she stirred and snuggled in closer.

"Don't go," she whispered.

Sorban smiled sadly and didn't answer.

"If you do go," she said, "take me with you."

He nudged the top of her head with his nose.

"I've been thinking," she continued, her words soft. "You know how we agreed not to have children before the end of the games?"

"Yes."

"I've changed my mind."

"I see."

She waited for his thoughts.

"Let's talk more of this . . . later," he said.

She sighed against his arm. "You won't change your mind."

"No. Probably not."

With another sigh, she lifted her head. "We no longer need the games," she whispered. "We've coin enough. We could leave today."

Sorban couldn't leave the games, though—not yet—so he kissed his wife's sleepy head, hugged her, and got out of their bed.

27

Goll bent over, hands to his knees, and gasped for breath.

Sweat ran down his face and dripped off his nearly naked frame from heavy exercise. His short sandy hair was saturated into clumpy spikes. His frame trembled, the sun already turning his pale back to a sore red.

Machlann nodded in approval of the house master, liking the man's effort, even though his motivation was clearly rage fueled, not that Machlann cared. Whatever started the fire was fine in the trainer's mind, and thus far that morning, the Kree had performed admirably for a person who'd not trained in a month.

"You're a tough one, Goll," Machlann crooned in that frayed voice of his. "*Eeeee* a right and proper tough one. Aye that, my missus. You didn't hear me call you master just then. None of that gurry. Not while you're standing on my sands. *Eeeeee*. Not on my sands. You take that breath. Take a few, why don't you? You make them count. I'll even call Shan over there and have him check on you, just to make sure you won't drop dead this day. Or have something important fall off."

Machlann glanced toward the barracks and spotted a concerned Shan standing in shade. Muluk stood next to him, his swarthy features dour and pensive. The trainer's blue eyes then met Clavellus's gaze, who was observing the spectacle from his balcony. A worried Nala stood behind him. She'd cringed many times during Machlann's drills, much to the old trainer's amusement. He'd promised plenty more cringes, and he aimed to make good on every one.

Goll had surprised them all earlier in the morning when he strutted from the living quarters in just a loincloth and bare feet—surprised them even more when he announced he would be training with Junger that day. Even though he'd declared his intention to be champion of the games the day before, it was still unexpected to see the Kree duck walking, lifting timbers, and any other exercises Machlann could put him through.

"Weapon Masters of Kree," the old trainer muttered, disdain dripping from his words, his mouth obscured by his beard. "You're not in Kree anymore. And if they were any good, you would be still in the games, wouldn't you? But you're not, you misplaced half shite. You were damn neared gutted and left to brown in the sun by a certain famous butcher. Now you're in the tender care of another, not-so-famous butcher, but one very bit as fine with the cutting. *Eeee* I guarantee it. I guarantee."

Machlann looked at Clavellus for approval. Just on the far side of the training grounds, Koba was putting Junger through his morning paces.

"When you finally drop, my missus," Machlann growled, "then I'll have a mug of something wet. Something sweet. For a morning well done."

Goll glared at the trainer.

"Don't you be looking at me with love in your eyes," Machlann snapped. "Seems you're all done. Clades!"

The soldier stood next to the rack of wooden weapons.

"Toss me one of those," Machlann said, snapping fingers. Clades selected a sword and lobbed it to the trainer, who caught it deftly.

"Now then," Machlann said, his voice carrying over the clatter of Junger tearing into his target, "you unfit he-bitch who calls himself a weapons master. Take this."

The trainer threw the sword into the sand at Goll's feet.

"You're *hot* now," Machlann explained. "So you take that stick and you hammer out a five-stroke combination on that practice lad right over there. Aye, you see it, right below Master Clavellus there. So he can have a good look at you and have the best line of sight when I finally break your miserable carcass . . . and fishhook you by the unfit hole."

Goll glared. He picked up the wooden sword and studied its length. A practice man waited, its wooden arms outstretched and casting a slanted shadow upon the sands. The Kree approached it, examining the target.

"You show us what them weapon masters taught you, *Kree*," Machlann taunted. "You show us that you're well and truly ready for the hell of the Pit. Because it bled you once. *Eeeeee*. It'll damn well bleed you *dry* a second time."

Blinking away sweat, Goll waited for the command.

"Begin!" Machlann bawled, startling Nala up above.

Perhaps it was the heart-bursting routine Machlann had driven the Kree through before he even picked up a sword. Perhaps it was the trainer's mocking tone. Maybe it was lack of activity in weeks gone by or just the heat. Perhaps it was the sum of everything. In any case, Goll struggled with striking the target. He hacked, rested, then hacked again. A heartbeat later, he stopped, regarded the wooden man's arms and headless neck with contempt, and shook out his shoulders.

"*Hit that punce*!" Machlann shrieked with a single foot stomp, stirring up the sand.

If he didn't look angry before, Goll did right then.

He surprised them all by flowing through a ten-strike combination and simply battering that wooden frame. He allowed his limbs to remember the routine, to do what had been beaten into him for years. Goll whirled and slashed arms and legs, a neck, and stabbed deep until the cross guard hooked into the target. He didn't relent but added an additional five strikes to what he'd shown, and in the final flurry, he smashed the wooden man's neck on the left and right. The entire frame shivered and chips flew—until his sword broke and the upper half twirled end over end to land in the sands.

Gasping for breath, Goll stood back from the target and met Machlann's contemplative gaze. Without a word, the Kree held out a hand, and snapped his fingers for a second sword.

High above, Clavellus chuckled, unable to contain himself, and grabbed his wife somewhere below the railing, causing an unimpressed Nala to slap his shoulder.

"Clades," Machlann said, gesturing first for another length of wood then at Goll. "Get that man another stick. Show us again, Kree. Show me something. Leave me speechless."

The once Sujin tossed a second sword to the panting Kree, who deftly caught the weapon. Goll twisted and with an exhausted bark, he broke the new sword over the practice man's arm with one brutal chop.

The crackle of breaking wood hung on the air, silencing all else.

Nowhere near finished, Goll discarded the ruined half he held and gestured impatiently for another sword.

That time, Machlann traded looks with Clavellus. The taskmaster leaned over the railing and propped his head up with a hand.

"Impressive, Kree," Machlann said in a much quieter tone. "But that's enough for now. Take a rest. You'll wish for death tomorrow morning, I wager, just to be spared the soreness. And I'll personally tickle Saimon's taint if any bathhouse waters or healing shite will stop that particular rust."

"Again," Goll demanded, his hand unwavering in the air.

That got some attention from the watchers.

"No," Machlann said, his scowl deepening. "Now do as I say, or by Seddon's rosy ass, I'll make your last moments here as painful as I can devise. Go!"

"You've proven your point, Master Goll," Clavellus cut in, his voice a soothing balm in itself. "Do as Machlann says. Take a few moments. When he feels you're ready for another round, he'll be the first to tell you."

ABOUT THE BLOOD

With a withering glance in Junger's direction, Goll relented. He walked, on sheer stubbornness alone, to the edge of the training grounds.

Whether or not he saw the pleasant glow upon Clavellus's sun-baked features was another matter. The taskmaster stood and beckoned Machlann to join him for a talk.

"He did well just now, didn't he?" Nala asked her husband's back.

"Very well," Clavellus replied before disappearing into the shady interior. *Very well indeed.*

For a man who'd limped his way into Clavellus's life, Goll had displayed remarkable speed and power in his first training session in over a month.

He met Machlann at the base of a stairway, and the trainer's expression mirrored what Clavellus already knew.

"The lad's a hellion," Machlann quietly stated. "You see what he did? You see?"

"I saw."

"And that was after he'd spent a good part of the morning waking those muscles up. He'll be as stiff as an iron bar come tomorrow, but Seddon above, Clavellus. Is it possible we've come across *two* hellpups in our return to the games?"

"Why not?" the taskmaster asked and led Machlann deeper into house, away from anyone who might overhear. "Why not? Not as if we haven't paid a price all these years. Lords above take me now if that's not true. He broke two sticks over that target's hide. *Two.* Split the second one right on the first blow. Who does that? Who do we know who's *ever* done that?"

Machlann's bushy white beard didn't move as he shook his head. "No one. Not ever. I've seen lads split wood like he did with the first, but not the second. Not when he should be exhausted."

"And he was exhausted. And ready to go again."

"All push. And damn all else."

"And did you see the look he gave Junger?" Clavellus winced.

"Aye that. Wasted, though. The Perician didn't even notice."

"He might've," Clavellus countered with a trembling finger. "He just might've. We were all too stunned by what Goll was doing to truly pay attention to the lad. We'll have to ask Koba for that matter, but I wager that first broken sword got his attention. Maybe even the second."

Machlann smiled. "Daresay I'll keep my thoughts about Kree's weapon masters to myself from here on."

"As will I," Clavellus agreed, stroking his beard. "As will I. *Two*, Machlann, two. The Sarlander is no slouch by any means, but Goll . . ."

Machlann nodded, understanding the taskmaster's line of thought. Brozz was good, but Goll just showed them perhaps why he'd been so critical of the Perician. Perhaps the Kree believed himself equal . . . or superior.

"Watch him," Clavellus instructed his trainer.

Machlann nodded he would indeed and marched back into the sun.

Thoughts whirling, the taskmaster returned to his balcony. At the top of the stairs, he met Nala.

"Is all well?" she asked, eyes clouded with worry.

"All is very well," he assured her and clasped her hands. "Very well, indeed. I tell you, Nala. There was a time neither I nor Machlann ever thought much of this Ten. Never thought there was any potential. They were paying coin for our property and experience, and I was lured by the chance to return to the games. Well, these past few weeks have been a pleasant surprise. I feel whole again, as if that which had been cut from me had been replaced. Even better, I think the house—*this* house—has potential beyond our expectations. Anyone's expectations."

"So what do you mean?" she asked.

"I mean . . ." Clavellus searched her face, organizing his own thoughts. "Even though the Ten might be reduced to three, or perhaps even two—those two are exceptional. Better than a good many I've seen over the years. If they get the right fights, the right opponents, and if they can avoid any potential blood matches, then . . ."

ABOUT THE BLOOD

He couldn't finish, the notion far too much to hope for, not with Dark Curge lurking in the background and the rest of the houses no doubt looking to finish the Ten's chances. The house was still Free Trained at its heart, and far too many were eager to stomp on it.

So he shut his mouth and gazed upon her with bright and loving eyes.

"Well," she said, pulling at his beard, "if you're happy, then I'm happy. Even if it means the season will be longer this year."

"It might be to our advantage."

Nala studied his face. "Clavellus, dearest."

He winced, knowing what was coming.

"I'm not planning on staying home this day. I'm going to travel to Pynn's Brook and stroll through the public market there. You did well with the items you brought back to me the other day, but there are a few more things I wish to purchase. And we are doing well with coin, are we not?"

He was having his fun, and the time for hers had come.

"So aren't we?" she asked again. "Doing well with money?"

"We are. We most certainly are. The best in years, I believe."

"Then I'll take a wagon and leave right away."

"Take a few guards with you," Clavellus said.

"I will," Nala said and began descending the stairs. "I'll return later this evening."

She fluttered fingers at him, and Clavellus watched her leave, enjoying every movement.

Once she was gone, he returned to the balcony.

"What in Saimon's blue pisspot was *that*?" Muluk exclaimed when Goll stopped less than a dozen strides away from where he and Shan were standing. "*What was that*?"

"That . . ." Goll huffed. "Was training."

"Breaking wooden swords?"

"Don't be saucy."

"You certainly don't look like the man who's been hobbling about on crutches," Shan said. "Your recovery's complete, except for a few wayward scars. Any pain?"

Goll flexed and rolled his shoulder, the same one Baylus the Butcher had stabbed through. "None. Thanks to you. My shoulder feels as it should. I'm slower right now, but by the time I fight, I should be more than ready."

"You should train easier for the rest of the day," Shan cautioned. "Machlann's right about what he said. You'll be stiff enough in the morning."

Goll nodded, but Shan suspected the man wasn't about to listen.

"It feels good," Goll said, studying the training grounds.

Junger lashed into his practice man with combinations, and while the speed and power of the Perician was still formidable, he wasn't breaking any wooden swords over his target.

"Very good," Goll stated. "I'm looking forward to returning."

"Fool," Muluk scoffed and shaded his eyes from the sun. "Well then, I'll leave for Ajik. The little man's working at something over there."

Over there was the forge, where the newest addition to the house toiled away at various chores.

"He's not lazy, I'll tell you that," Muluk said. "He didn't leave it until nightfall, and he was up before me this morning."

"We're all up before you," Goll said.

"Now *you're* being saucy. Ajik was working hard this morning, getting that whole area in order. Straightening rods and inspecting tools. He filled the water basin this morning as well. If only I could speak with the little topper."

"Go on, then," Goll said. "Watch him. Have him take a look at our weapons as well, put edges to them all. Then perhaps get him started on some armor."

Muluk hesitated. "You realize any armor is a long way off. It takes time."

"I know. So get him started on something today."

Muluk walked off toward the forge.

Goll studied his countryman's back for a few heartbeats. Then his face darkened as he turned his attention upon the Perician.

Goll finally did listen to Shan and, with Machlann's dismissal, retired for the day. He relaxed in an early bath and emerged from the bathhouse feeling exceptionally weary but in a good way, the way one feels after vigorous exercise. Wearing only a short cloth skirt around his waist, Goll stepped into the sun.

The gate guards waved to Clavellus, roosting in his balcony. Four riders approached the villa.

"Clades," Clavellus called out, "go see what it is, would you?"

The once Sujin joined the other guards at the closed gate. In short time, faces appeared on the other side. Clades talked with the visitors. When he faced his employers, he looked none too pleased.

"Master Goll," Clades called, "perhaps you'll want to hear this."

"What is it?"

Clades nodded toward the visitors.

Goll walked along the brick walkway, smelling his scrubbed skin warming in the daylight. Four newcomers waited. Three were guards outfitted in toughened leather and sheathed weapons. Sweat ran down their faces as they sat on their horses and sized up the villa's defenses. The last man was different. Perhaps in his forties, he waited with a dignified air. The day's heat and ride had stirred up dust that clung to his fine clothes. A head of white hair had been slightly tousled, and he dabbed a hand cloth around a carefully maintained moustache and beard.

"Greetings good sar, from the School of Nexus." The man smiled, revealing teeth that were quite feral looking. "I'm called Bojen, messenger for Nexus himself. We've travelled from Sunja to humbly request a meeting with the house masters and the gladiator called Junger. Of Pericia."

Leather creaked. A bee buzzed nearby. Metal tinkled from the direction of the forge.

"What's this about?" Goll demanded, squinting at the messenger.

Bojen studied him in turn before unleashing what he probably believed was a pleasant smile. Goll thought it condescending.

"I wish to talk with your house master, good sar," Bojen said.

"I'm the house master."

"Begging your pardon, good sar. You're much younger than I expected. You must be the one called Goll, then?"

"I am."

"Well met, Master Goll. I bring greetings and well-wishes from the School of Nexus on this hot summer day. We've traveled from—"

"Yes, yes, I heard all of that," Goll said testily. "And I heard you mention our man Junger. What is it you want?"

Bojen paused, his smile fading. If there were rules regarding pleasantries between the heads of houses and such, Goll was unaware of them. Truth be known, the Kree had no time or patience for such gurry.

"Master Nexus has been greatly impressed by the extraordinary skills displayed by your man Junger. So impressed that he has decided to respectfully inquire about the gladiator and make a proposition, to you, to purchase the rights to your warrior."

"Purchase?" Goll asked, cocking an eyebrow.

"Yes, indeed. I've been instructed to offer both him and your house a substantial sum of coin if you'll release him to the School of Nexus, honorably of course, with legal paperwork."

A breeze whistled through the gates. People approached Goll from behind, their feet scuffling through the training sands. All the while, the weight of the words sank into his head, causing his guts to roil and bubble.

In the background, a sudden flourish of activity caught Bojen's attention. The messenger craned his neck to see. "Ah," he said. "There he is. Magnificent."

Goll didn't share that sentiment. "You say you're from the School of Nexus?"

"Ah, yes," Bojen said, distracted. "I am that. Master Goll, wouldn't it be better to discuss matters within? Out of this blistering sun?"

"No."

The curt answer surprised Bojen, but he quickly recovered. "It is customary—and courteous—to entertain messengers from other stables and houses. Perhaps offer food and drink while having an open dialogue. To better understand each other's position."

"I don't need to invite you inside," a stoic Goll countered. "And I won't extend any such courtesies."

Bojen's features sagged. "But—"

"But you stand there and lecture me about customs with that weasel's smile in place. You mentioned respect? Where's the respect in attempting to sway one of our remaining gladiators to leave us for another house? That's not respect. That's pure envy. Tell me, what would happen if I met Nexus with the same request?"

"Master Nexus would most graciously invite you—"

"Dog balls," Goll interrupted. "Talking to you is annoying. You've wasted enough of my day. And no, in case I'm not clear, you will *not* be invited inside. Get gone from these gates. Tell Nexus the House of Ten will remember this slight. When our gladiators meet in the Pit."

Bojen's eyes fluttered as if he'd been slapped repeatedly.

"You tell him." Goll finished with a louder note, "Now get out of my sight." The house master regarded Clades. "Keep watch here until they've gone. If they're not gone by the time I pass the gate again, muster the lads, and we'll drive these dog blossoms away."

With one last scalding look, Goll walked away. He marched inside Clavellus's house, and eventually joined the taskmaster sitting in his balcony. The Kree stopped in the doorway and looked toward the gate.

Bojen and his guards had departed. The man wasn't an idiot after all.

"What was that about?" the taskmaster inquired.

"Arrogant ass lickers," Goll growled. "They wanted to buy Junger from us. If it's not the damned Madea or the unfit Chamber, it's the rival houses."

Clavellus frowned in puzzlement. "Odd."

"They were going to offer us coin to give him up to the School of Nexus. And offer him coin as well."

"Nexus," Clavellus said. "I don't know much about him. One of the newer owners."

Goll peered over the villa's wall, attempting to spy the departing men.

"It's common courtesy to invite them in," the taskmaster said.

Goll fixed him with a dangerous look.

"Though not entirely necessary," Clavellus quickly added. "This wasn't unexpected."

"It wasn't?"

"Oh no. Happens from time to time."

"And?"

"Ah, some houses profit from such a bargain. Others don't. It's a question of coin. How bad one house's finances are, the finances of the gladiator in question, and how much the other house would be willing to pay for a particular fighter. Such dealings are rare, but they're viewed upon much more favorably than say, a warrior deserting a house entirely midseason to fight for another. That's bad form. There's no resentment if a house is sufficiently compensated. And the fighter."

"We won't engage in such practices."

"Not ever?"

"Not ever."

"It's your house," Clavellus conceded and gestured to a nearby plate of half-eaten cured meats. "Care for something?"

"No." Goll marched off toward the stairs.

With a contented smile, Clavellus returned to eating.

28

Pig Knot swam in the darkness, aware of movement at times, then blissfully oblivious. He occasionally felt hot then cold, but those instances were fleeting, and he never fully surfaced from his unconsciousness to see where he was. Once, he had the sensation of being struck again, across the jaw, but he felt hardly any pain.

He was well past that threshold.

Cool stone finally roused him, and he forced open his eyes. Daylight was casting shade into the alley, revealing a broken slab of wood wedged between him and the very close foundation of a building. Pain flooded him. *Seddon above.* He winced, facial muscles barely responding. He'd only just recovered from nearly dying, only to have everything undone in one night.

Worse, he still wasn't dead . . . despite what he considered to be a very fine effort.

Pig Knot pushed himself up, breaking the bloody bond of skin stuck to stone. He frowned at the sight of his gruesome profile upon flat rock. One jaw tooth gleamed like a dull crown on the street, the red roots visible.

"Dying Seddon," Pig Knot groaned, pain flaring along his right side.

He slumped against the wall, inspecting the incredible display of purples, blues, and reds blotching his torso.

"Dying Seddon," he repeated, having never seen such colors upon his person.

He prodded the worst of the bruises with a finger, exploring the hot tightness of his skin, discovering egg-sized bulges. Then he felt his mouth and discovered two back teeth missing. One tooth was accounted for, but he couldn't see the other.

"Oh Dying Seddon," he whispered and tentatively touched his eyes, swollen like a pair of plums. He pressed those inflated mounds of flesh, gently, the pressure restricting his vision to slits. Blood covered his face, hands, and everything else. He scanned the area the best way he could and spotted his shirt. He leaned toward it, spikes of pain lighting up his frame.

When he pulled the shirt back, it came away in shreds.

Miserable, Pig Knot grunted and inspected the damage, realizing his loincloth was especially damp. After a quick check, he let loose an exasperated sigh. Battered, bruised, and practically naked, he'd also pissed his underbits.

"Lovely," he whispered.

Even though he knew better, he searched for his purse—gone.

Pig Knot dabbed the cloth in a nearby puddle, which he hoped wasn't piss, and wiped away sticky blood. He stopped, cursed himself for doing things backward, and sniffed the rag. A slick chunk of something went down the back of his throat, and Pig Knot gagged before swallowing. He sniffed again, nasal passages that much clearer, and took a weaker whiff of the water. It wasn't piss, but it wasn't the cleanest, either. He continued cleaning himself, eyeing the broken wood that used to be his cart.

That hurt.

A dagger of poison went through his heart.

Why did they break the cart? He whined to himself, dismayed at the thorough destruction. They'd taken his remaining coin so there was no need to break the cart. Where could he hide extra gold on the thing? Whoever had beaten him within a lick of his life had thought otherwise, leaving Pig Knot without coin as well as a means of travel. The money bothered him, but it wouldn't have lasted anyway. He'd only planned to be drinking, eating, and rutting until being robbed and killed.

The thieves had only half finished the job, though.

Pig Knot groaned and took in the mighty blue overhead . . . before passing out a second time.

With a snort and a chin dip, he awoke much later. He glanced around to see if anyone was nearby. No one was. The alley wasn't well traveled. It was long and cluttered with refuse. The thieves had chosen well.

He needed water. His drinking had left him parched.

"Never again," he swore but wished for a pitcher of anything.

People walked by the alley entrance, not bothering to stop and gawk at the once gladiator. For that, Pig Knot was grateful. Tonguing the holes where his teeth had once resided, he dragged his soiled rump across bare stone. His hands weren't the only things developing callouses.

Daylight loomed like a blinding portal, periodically halting him. He knew how he looked and how he smelled, and he knew the reactions he'd soon be receiving. He took shallow breaths to avoid the sparkling pain in his ribs and waddled to the nearest corner, into sunlight.

Faces morphed into expressions of shock and hostility as he eased into view. He moved a few paces and stopped against a wall. He smiled weakly, the bruises and swelling distorting his face. Still, not bad for a man left for dead, he figured. People passed by, and Pig Knot kept his blackened eyes downcast.

Sandals and boots swished by him.

"Get on with you," someone commanded.

Pig Knot looked around. There, standing before an open doorway, between two piles of timber, was a man—perhaps a merchant—wearing tailored breeches and a bright, yellow-dyed shirt. "Get on, I said. And don't you dare bleed on my property."

"Do you . . ." Pig Knot croaked, "have any water?"

That infuriated the merchant. "I'll give you my boot if you don't drag your legless ass away from my property! *Go!*" He took two steps toward the once gladiator and shooed. "Go, or I'll summon the watch!"

The merchant raised his hand to slap Pig Knot's shoulder, but he stopped with a grimace, revolted at the thought of making contact. "Go, I said!"

So Pig Knot went . . . slowly, and not before adjusting the soiled cloth that irritated his nether bits, just so he wouldn't frighten any decent ladies of the day or make their husbands jealous. That made him smirk, which brought the entire gurry weight of the morning down upon his head in a deluge of madness. Pig Knot chuckled at his wretched luck. He stopped and rested against a stone foundation of what might have been a house. The chuckling became a laugh, which died away in a painful wheeze.

He wiped his face and saw fresh blood smearing his hand.

People avoided him, shunning his space. Some spied him, only to quickly look away. Pig Knot didn't know what was worse, being seen or being outright ignored.

Not one person offered to help.

Giggles rattled him, sinister in their sound, and Pig Knot held out a hand. He didn't see the harm. He'd seen it done often enough. His palm trembled at times, reminding him of a certain old taskmaster, and that made him chuckle until the weight of his arm became too much. His arm dropped. He stayed where he was, no doubt frightening the children.

A boot nudged his thigh, getting his attention. Pig Knot glanced up, knowing he looked unfit.

The leer melted from his face.

Street Watch—an entire column of the armored bastards.

"Well, then," Pig Knot said to the Skarrs. "I might look like a dead man's hole, but I still know my manners. Greetings, good watchmen, greetings. And, please, when you have a moment, I invite the lot of you he-bitches . . . to lick the dew off my man pearls. They're right here." He pointed, a smile creeping back into his devastated face.

The nearest Skarrs exchanged glances, their visors hiding their expressions.

One lifted a very solid-looking club.

Pig Knot groaned. He preferred a sword.

The hardwood slammed across his head, dumping him into yet another bottomless vat of unconsciousness.

Pig Knot's hearing returned first, signaling that he was indeed awake. He discovered he was lying on his side in a cell. He was above ground, or so he believed, since a barred window was just above him. The mat he was lying upon stank of smoke and unpleasant sweat. He rolled onto his back, grunting at the pain, and stared at a low ceiling. Bare, solid-looking timbers loomed above.

Dying Seddon.

The day just kept getting better.

He caught a whiff of water. He propped himself up on an elbow and spotted a bucket, just inside a small grate inserted into the bigger cell door. Brick walls surrounded him while the window's iron bars allowed daylight to mark the opposite wall. Sounds of the street reached his ears, a low steady rush not unlike the roar of waterfalls.

It sounded peaceful—relaxing, even.

Pig Knot pulled himself to the bucket and cupped water to his mouth. When he'd drunk his fill, he splashed some over his face and body. He was still wearing the soiled loincloth, so he stripped that off, poured water over it, and scrubbed at his unmentionables.

Once finished, he considered the rest of himself and regarded the loincloth. He hadn't planned his cleaning well enough. With a shrug, he hefted the bucket, emptied it over his head, and cleaned himself as best as he could.

The noise attracted attention.

A door opened and closed with a bang. Feet shuffled along, approaching Pig Knot's cell, making him pause while rooting around an armpit. He finished his wipe-down, shook out the cloth, and draped it over his manly bits for modesty's sake.

The jailor appeared at the cell door. He was a large man, with twin belts of studded leather crisscrossing his broad chest. A short-cropped beard hung off the jailor's chin, and blue eyes the color of the open sea focused upon Pig Knot.

Never had the sea uneased him so much.

"Well," he muttered. "Greetings, good jailor. Pleasant day out there?"

The jailor studied his prisoner with all the indifference of an animal studying a piece of meat.

"Ah," Pig Knot said. "Not in the mood. I understand."

No response.

"Well, when you're ready," Pig Knot carried on, weakening just from talking. "And willing. Please refill the bucket. Let me clean myself. A little more. Before I fall unconscious. Again."

"What happened to you?" the jailor asked.

That took Pig Knot off guard. "What's that?"

"What happened to you?" he finished and pointed. "The Skarrs do all that?"

"Ah, no, no," Pig Knot answered, surprised the man was talking to him. "I was robbed. At night. Maybe last night. Thieves took my coin, ruined my shirt and a cart I used to wheel myself around in. Then they paddled me senseless. Foul luck all over."

The jailor listened.

"I . . ." Pig Knot hesitated, "might've been a little harsh. In my explanation to the Skarrs. The ones who happened upon me."

"What was it you said to them?"

"Ah. You heard about that."

"I might have."

"I don't remember. Not the exact words. But it was enough to bring me here."

"It was," the jailor said. "Skarrs usually can't be bothered with beggars. Unless given good reason."

"I might have given them good reason."

The jailor smiled. He walked away then, only to return a short time later with another bucket filled with water. He also had a thin towel. The bucket went through the smaller grate while he threw the towel into Pig Knot's face. It smelled clean, at least.

"Stay quiet in there, and don't annoy me," the jailor stated in a reasonable tone. "Do that, and you'll be fine."

He walked away.

Still surprised at the man's relatively good nature, Pig Knot completely missed the chance to ask about how long he was going to be imprisoned.

A door closed with a bang.

"That's Sharo," someone said from the next cell over. "Not a difficult man. Fairly honest. As far as I can tell. Treated me fairly, anyway, thus far. And by that, I mean he hasn't taken a club to my head."

Pig Knot ripped the towel in half. He draped one piece over a knee then dipped the other into the water. He applied it to his forehead and squeezed. Water rushed over his face.

That was the best thing to happen to him all day.

"Who're you?" Pig Knot asked wearily.

"Zepedos."

"Pig Knot."

"Well met, Pig Knot."

Pig Knot chuckled, the sound a wheezy rattle. "Well met."

"You say you were robbed?"

"Last night. I think it was last night."

"You were dragged in here early this afternoon and just awakened."

Pig Knot smiled. "And only now, you're introducing yourself?"

"I don't usually speak to my fellow captives. Most times they're brazen gits or killers. Killers only wish to intimidate you. Not very interesting to talk to."

"Why are you here?"

"Caught stealing coin from a merchant. Three days ago, just so you know I wasn't involved in your . . . ah . . . bad fortune."

"I see," Pig Knot said, taking care while wiping his face. The aches and pains leached his energy. "They didn't execute you?"

"They don't execute thieves. They imprison them. Until such time they grow weary of them. I'm fortunate in a way. This is the first time I've ever been caught. They say a good thief needs to be caught at least once. Twice, well, you're not so good. Or smart."

Pig Knot grunted.

"For a thief," Zepedos clarified. "The underworld isn't very fond of thieves that get caught."

"You could move on to killing."

"Pah," Zepedos said. "I'm a thief. Not some cutthroat. I've yet to kill anyone over a few coins. Or for any other reason. And it would have to be a damn fine reason. Luckily, I haven't been in any such situations. No. I just rob others of a few coins. Nothing more."

Nothing more. To Pig Knot's eyes, the cell seemed to turn.

"Zepedos, you say?" he asked.

"Aye that."

"The room is taking on . . . a slow spin."

"Oh?"

"Just so you know. I won't be talking. For the next little while."

"I see," Zepedos said, sounding pleased with the explanation. "Thank you for telling me. I would have figured it out. Rest then, Pig Knot. I caught a look at you when they dragged you in. Not a pretty sight. I didn't think you'd live. Truth be known, I was as surprised as Sharo. You rest. We should have plenty of time for talking later."

But Zepedos's words became a whisper, as Pig Knot's senses began to spin. He closed his eyes, and the cell still spun, the sensation sickening to the guts. Worse, it seemed to speed up.

He slumped onto his right side. Cold stone kissed his cheek. Then . . . nothing.

*

ABOUT THE BLOOD

He woke in a cold sweat. Pig Knot could barely open his swollen eyes, so he licked a finger and rubbed them. That helped a little, allowing him to see. He remembered where he was while his ribs twinkled with pain, warning him to keep his breaths shallow. The rest of him wasn't much better. He push-crawled off his mat to the far corner, away from the cell door, and found the hole in the floor. There, he relieved himself, gasping at a stream of red that lasted a moment before clearing.

That one fright set his heart beating and his ribs afire.

A door opened, somewhere out of sight.

"Here," Sharo said and tossed in a few pieces of bread and an apple.

The food fell about Pig Knot's mat. "Thank you."

But the jailor was already gone.

A door closed.

Grimacing, Pig Knot hauled himself to the food and ate what he could. The apple had just as many bruises as he did, half of them brown, but he downed it all the same. After eating, he retired to his mat and rested against the wall.

"Zepedos?"

The thief didn't answer right away. "Yes?"

"You finished eating?"

"Aye that."

"What was the best meal you've ever eaten?"

"Ahhh." The thief recalled a tavern in the western part of the city. He described a honeyed ham complete with sweet vegetables and a dark, rich gravy that one could drink straight from the dipper. "And you?" he asked after finishing.

"Can't remember right now," Pig Knot said. "But I know I've had a few. And I've eaten some terrible ones. This . . . is one."

"This?" Zepedos scoffed. "This is nothing. Sharo treats us well, you know. The bread is fresh, the water's fresh, and the fruit isn't rotting. Some jailors will piss in the water before they hand the bucket to their prisoners. And the poor bastards drink it. It's that or perish of thirst."

"That's harsh."

"Harsh enough. I'll never be caught again."

"Going to give up the life, are you?"

"Hardly," Zepedos said. "Just be more careful, that's all."

"I hope you are." Pig Knot quieted then.

"How did you lose your legs?" the thief asked. "If it's not too . . . painful a question."

"I was a gladiator."

"Really?"

"Free Trained. At first. Then as part of the House of Ten."

"I've heard of them. Yes, yes. The Free Trained one."

"Aye that."

"I imagine the other, more official houses despise you."

Pig Knot smiled. "They do."

"So how did you get here? Didn't you have a house to take care of you? They should do that at least, for their warriors."

"It's a long story."

"The only thing I might do here is sleep or die. And I'm not tired in the least."

Pig Knot supposed he had little chance of dying while imprisoned. "Very well then . . ."

He spoke of everything, from the first day of the games, from meeting Halm the Zhiberian and the Krees, Muluk and Goll. In halting sentences, he told the thief about the band of cutthroats who'd tried to kill Muluk and steal their savings. He talked of Goll ordering him to lose a gladiator match in order for the House of Ten to come into existence, the very reason that cost the Sunjan his legs and nearly his life. He talked of watching the training sessions at the villa of Clavellus, how he gradually hated being there, and how he convinced a trainer called Koba to help him to leave.

"So they didn't want you to leave," Zepedos assumed.

"Ah, I don't know. But truth be known, Koba surprised me. The bastard tried to persuade me to stay. But I wanted no part of it."

That silenced the thief for a beat. "You wanted no part of it."

ABOUT THE BLOOD

"That's right. Unfit, eh? But I couldn't stand sitting on a mat, watching whole men prepare for their matches in the Pit. I felt useless. Less than useless. Wretched. Worthless. I wanted to live as I did before. When I still had legs. So I came back to Sunja."

Zepedos said nothing to any of that.

"I'd rather be here," the once gladiator stated. "Even if it's in a cell."

"Why?"

Pig Knot pondered the question. "It's more like living . . . than back at the Ten's house."

"You mean you felt more free, somehow? Even locked up here?"

"Aye that."

That set the thief to chuckling. "I've only just met you, Pig Knot, and I'm not one to judge another so quickly—especially a man who's in the cell next to mine—but I think you made a mistake coming back to Sunja. Perhaps Seddon wishes to show you your mistake."

"Perhaps."

"You don't sound convinced. I think you will be, however. In time. How much time is the question. You came here to live? As you did before? I don't think that's possible. Not at all. You strike me as a stubborn man, Pig Knot. Perhaps your time here, in a cell, with me as a neighbor, will soften your ideas on things. Maybe change your thoughts."

"You think I made a mistake?"

"I'm not you," Zepedos said. "Let me be clear about that. And I suspect there were other things pushing you to leave. But I'll tell you this. The streets of Sunja are harsh. You know this. Day and night, but the night can be especially deadly. To anyone. There are those who'll prey on the weak and the crippled and leave them dead. Or worse. I think . . . when you do leave this place, you should reconsider returning to your house."

"How long will I be here?" Pig Knot asked.

"I don't know. You say you only insulted some Skarrs. That could be just a day. Maybe a week. I don't know how they do things around here. Maybe ask Sharo."

Pig Knot grunted. He would do that.

A spider crawled up and over the raw, knotted skin of his stumps. Pig Knot raised a hand to kill the thing but didn't. The creature crawled up his thigh, all eight legs working, until it reached the crook of his hip. He could barely feel the contact. Pig Knot frowned at the insect traveling up his side, ignoring his wounds entirely, as if they didn't exist.

When the spider reached his belly, he pinched it dead.

Time moved on.

Daylight faded and dimmed. Sharo appeared with the evening meal—more bread, more bruised apples, and a change of water. Pig Knot asked when he might be released.

Sharo didn't know. That was up to the Street Watch to decide.

Pig Knot continued talking to the man called Zepedos, whose company wasn't offensive in the least for a self-professed thief. Sometime in the night, however, not long after the sun had left the sky, he grew tired and thus, excused himself.

Sleep came quickly.

The morning arrived with a door slamming and the irregular cadence of many boots upon the floor. The sound jerked Pig Knot awake, from a dream where he was actually sleeping upon his cot back in the Ten's barracks.

"That's not him," someone declared.

The footsteps resumed, getting closer.

"You."

That one frigid syllable informed Pig Knot that all wasn't well. He propped himself up on his elbows, blinking sleepily while his swollen eyes watered. Skarrs stood outside the cell door. A tall city guard exhibiting an air of authority gazed through the bars. The Skarr's visor studied the once gladiator with an intensity that brought Pig Knot to his senses. The stare worried him.

"You have no legs," the soldier said.

The man's quick, Pig Knot thought but kept that to himself. He wasn't that unfit in the head.

"What's your name?" the visor questioned.

Pig Knot hesitated.

"Answer me," the Skarr demanded.

"Pig Knot."

"Pig. Knot," the man said, hate dripping from the words. "Interesting. Not too many like that around. You enjoy the ladies?"

Danger ripped up Pig Knot's spine and sizzled at his skull's base, but his mouth was too fast. "I do."

"You remember a woman called Jana?"

Pig Knot's mouth went dry. His stomach clenched and frosted over. His voice deserted him, and Jana spoke in his head, talking about her husband.

He's a Koor with the Street Watch. He's usually gone all night.

The bruises on Pig Knot's face kept the color in place, but he swallowed nervously, all the same.

The Koor saw everything. "Yes, you know her. Probably think of her with every passing breath."

Pig Knot licked his lips. He wouldn't say *that* but wisely chose to not answer.

"When I told her we'd caged a man with no legs," the Koor explained, "well, her face betrayed her. Happened so quick I had to ask what was wrong. Was she ill? 'No,' she said. But I could smell the lie. 'Why show any concern for a cripple?' I asked. It didn't take long to get answers from her. Not long at all. Apparently, you're quite memorable."

The Skarr moved closer until his helmet tapped the iron bars. "And a legless man with an interesting name has stayed in my memory up to now. So you see, I don't have to ask you anything." The Koor's eyes crinkled with building rage befitting a husband. "Unfortunately. For you."

Pig Knot's breathing quickened while his skin turned cold. He swallowed, hearing the dry click of his gullet.

The officer waved a hand, and Sharo hurried forth. The jailor unlocked the cell door and quickly got out of the way. The Koor waited a few menacing heartbeats then pulled the door open. Hinges whined.

Nothing lay between the officer and Pig Knot's battered hide.

"Seddon has deserted you, *Pig*," the Skarr Koor declared and entered the cell.

The other soldiers followed, filling the small space.

Pig Knot pressed himself against the wall. The slits of his swollen eyes widened.

Then they were upon him.

Outside and watching the walled compound of the Street Watch, Jurnos stood and thought he heard a scream over the din of the crowds. He shifted from one foot to the other, straining to hear, but the sound was lost.

"You hear something?" Nolbin asked from the right, a sour smell of body odor hanging about him.

"Thought I heard someone scream," Jurnos muttered, hoping to catch another note.

"That could be anyone," Nolbin said.

"When do you think they'll let him go?" Pot asked from the left, leaning against the stone wall they were all sharing.

"Soon."

"Yes, but when?"

Jurnos eyed thickset Pot with that same feral look he'd given the legless cripple. "You have something to do?"

"No, no," Pot replied quickly, his features slack with fear. "Not a thing. Just wondering is all."

"Just wondering," Morott added, his pale skin sweating under the scalding sun. He was standing to the left of Pot.

The memory of being held by the cripple, who'd scared off his companions, rankled Jurnos. He had a reputation to uphold, a reputation he'd killed to earn and killed to maintain. No one placed their hands on him and made him look weak in front of his pack—no one. Certainly not some cripple with a horse tail of braided hair hanging off his head. Jurnos had vowed to find the pig bastard, and he had. He'd never expected the cripple to actually stay in his territory, but Jurnos had to admit, that was smart.

Jurnos was smart too, though . . . and patient.

He'd recognized an opportunity to build further upon his street name: a story of vengeance, one that he liked the more he thought of it.

"We'll just keep watching," Jurnos said, eyes set upon the gates of the soldiers' compound. "Until they do. In shifts. From dawn to dusk. They'll release him sooner or later. When they do, he'll come out of those gates. Easy to see. Easy to follow. When that happens, we'll follow him. Track him. Wait until he's someplace quiet. Somewhere out of sight."

Jurnos's mouth hitched into a sneer.

"And then we'll gut that brazen ass licker."

29

A new day came, and with the afternoon fights about to begin, Gastillo walked the Pit's outer passages. He didn't care for watching the criminals hacking away at each other in the opening matches. They were worse than the Free Trained, if that was possible. The owner possessed a distinct spring in his step as he walked along, dabbing a hand cloth at the drool underneath his mask, catching it before it dropped.

Fifteen thousand gold pieces. He'd given a lot of thought to Nexus's offer. The more he thought about it, the bigger the sum became, but Gastillo felt it wise to haggle a bit more with the wine merchant. He saw no fault in countering the offer with a price of seventeen, still lower than his original ask of twenty but not that much higher than Nexus's offer.

This time, the wine merchant would not cut him off in midsentence. Gastillo would be firm.

After all, Nexus was gaining a potential champion of the games, as much as it twisted Gastillo's guts to admit it. Prajus trained hard and possessed not only the skill but the mindset of a champion. More than any other in the house, Prajus believed he would conquer all this season and be triumphant.

Furthermore, Gastillo believed him.

ABOUT THE BLOOD

The trouble was that Prajus enjoyed harassing others and was an insolent and brutal killer who thought himself of noble birth. To be so close to ridding himself of such a burden lifted Gastillo's spirits immensely.

Nexus recognized the man's value, which explained the sudden switch from wishing for the man's death to potentially embracing him as one of his own. The only thing that bothered Gastillo was if Nexus discovered Prajus's true character before the completion of the bargain. If he did, that would dampen things.

He decided not to think about it and focused on the counteroffer.

Seventeen was a fair price. *Seventeen or nothing.* The merchant might squirm a little, but Gastillo wouldn't budge from that number. If, for whatever reason, Nexus wouldn't commit, then perhaps some other owner might.

Calming himself before he entered the owner's box, Gastillo opened the door. Daylight stabbed at his eyes as a blast of heat engulfed him. A robed manservant stood with a silver tray clasped in both hands. Goblets rested upon the metal. Gastillo took a drink and nodded at the man, who bowed in return.

Ahead, Curge and Nexus sat at opposite ends of the box. A single chair waited, situated between them. Gastillo rolled his eyes. He hated sitting between those two.

A distant wall of shifting bodies and waving arms lay beyond the box's stony rim as spectators struggled to reach favored places. The terraced seating teemed with featureless flesh and cloth already giving strong voice to the scene. Some hanging tarps provided limited shade for the masses, but those sitting closest to the action baked under the sun.

"Ah," Dark Curge rumbled and scratched at his chest, wrinkling the white shirt he wore. "Gastillo's here. See, Nexus. I said you had nothing to concern yourself with. Your man has arrived."

"Saimon's black hanging fruit," Nexus replied, exasperated. "You're a tormentor, Curge."

As an answer, Curge drank from his goblet.

Anticipating a long day, Gastillo sat between the two hellions. He nodded at Nexus, who gave a curt dip of the chin in return.

"How are the day's fights thus far?" Gastillo asked.

"I only watched the final pairing of the earlier ones," Curge said, leaning on one elbow while peering into the Pit. "Criminals. They're well and truly terrible. There's no poise, no style and certainly no skill. Murderers and thieves are *not* trained pit fighters despite what some might think."

"I watched all the matches to this point," Nexus said, annoyance in his tone. "Nothing worthy at all."

"The real matches begin shortly," Curge added, addressing no one in particular.

"One of yours will fight this day?" Gastillo asked.

"Aye that."

"Anything to say of the man?" Nexus asked with heat. "Any boasts? Or shall we wait for the Orator?"

"You can wait for the Orator," Curge said and drank.

Nexus's lips twisted into a hateful button.

"Well, then," Gastillo said, seeking to defuse the tension, "perhaps we'll see something special this day."

"I'm hoping for blood," Nexus said and sipped his own wine. "And plenty of it."

"I imagine you'll see enough this day," Curge muttered cryptically and half turned in Gastillo's direction. "Perhaps even something special. There's always something afoot at the games."

The big man's eyes twinkled. Unease gripped Gastillo. Dark Curge had agents and spies about, as did they all. He wondered if the Dark One had learned about his meeting with Nexus. Gastillo dismissed the notion, remembering the number of guards surrounding the koch. Even if Curge knew they'd met, he had no way of knowing the details. Far too many guards had been about.

The Orator began the introductions, describing the gladiators in typical fearsome fashion, capturing the audience's attention.

ABOUT THE BLOOD

Trako from the House of Vorish would fight that day, and his opponent would be Habol, from the House of Razi.

Habol watched the wraithlike form of Trako pacing back and forth, coming closer with each pass. He had a strategy for this particular fight and knew he'd have to be at his finest. Trako was a beast, a hellion born and brought to life by some dark sorcery Habol didn't want to understand. The day before the match, Master Razi's spies had spoken of the Vorish man in cautious tones. They believed Habol destined to lose. His sword brothers offered encouragement, but even they'd failed to hide the doubt in their eyes.

That bothered Habol.

They were marking him as doomed even before he stepped onto the sands.

He wasn't, however, and he was far from dead.

Those thoughts energized Habol. Focused him. He was determined to not only defeat this unchained animal set loose within the Pit, but also send a message to the others. Habol was no one's meal, and if anyone was going to put down Trako, it was *him*.

The black iron helm considered Habol with evil interest. Trako stood shorter by a few fingers to Habol, but he was bulkier, possibly stronger. His leather vest had been fashioned into an abdomen better suited to a statue. Spikes bristled from his shoulder pads. Trako's weapons consisted of a long-shafted mace in his right hand and a single-bladed axe in his left. Bristling, spiked cups protected his fists, and Habol knew Trako would use them if he got in close.

Habol's own ring mail would absorb a few punches, being of a more practical design. His helm was fashioned to fit his skull and allow him ample breath through several holes in the visor. A long, narrow slit provided a wide field of vision. The head protection was plain in comparison to other gladiators' exquisite pieces of metalworking. Both men wore greaves and bracers to protect their limbs. Where Trako was hunched over like some corrupted hellion, Habol stood tall, his round shield and sword lowered. Where Trako resembled a Zuthenian beastman freed from chains, Habol was the noble Sunjan poised to kill the invader.

He was the light to Trako's darkness.

Trako had amassed five victories thus far and suffered no losses, projecting an air of invincibility.

Habol had enough bruises underneath his armor to resemble a ragged quilt. A huge gash over his right eye had taken over twenty stitches to close, which would later become a scar to draw the interest of the ladies. His last fight, against a brute from the House of Ustda, had almost broken his shield and the arm with it. The limb still didn't feel right.

No matter.

Habol was going to put this topper into the ground head first, ass up, so the whole world could have a kick at each brazen cheek . . . or simply sink a toe deep into the offered crack.

The Orator shouted for the match to commence.

Taking a breath, Habol went to the center of the arena, where Trako met him.

"Well met, Habol," Trako said in a metallic voice.

The pleasantry surprised Habol. "Well met, Trako."

"I know of you," the man continued. "You've done well this season."

"As yourself."

"Have you recovered from your clash with Orzata?"

Habol raised his weapon and shield, not trusting Trako in the least. "Not at all. I still ache in places. But that's the season, isn't it? Like old bones in winter."

"That it is."

"Have you recovered from your last fight?"

The grinning iron helm didn't move, and for the first time, Habol realized he couldn't see Trako's eyes at all, just those dark slits framed in iron.

"Good Habol," the Vorish man said coldly, lifting his weapons to guard, "I've never felt better."

Trako attacked, weapons churning forward like the mighty cogs of some great, infernal machine, and Habol immediately parried the mace and war axe. His shield splintered with a crack. His arm shuddered. Habol strove to slip to the side and nearly had his head removed by Trako's axe. Trako swung for a right shoulder then a left before whirling into a backhand spin, whipping that iron moon of a mace across Habol's face.

The impact rang out within the arena and crumpled Habol to his knees. Black motes swirled and winked before his eyes, tantalizing him with their brilliance while a rising gale reached his ears.

In one frightening instance of clarity, he realized that sound belonged to the crowds, screaming at him to stand.

He lifted his shield, blocking Trako's shrieking war axe as it descended. The axe split the barrier in a jagged thunderbolt, right down to the metal bracer protecting Habol's forearm. The Razi pit fighter attempted to pull back, but Trako put a boot to the ruined shield and shoved him off in a squawk of iron and wood.

Habol stumbled away, holding up his shield as if it could withstand another blow. It would not.

Trako circled to his left, taking his time, studying Habol as he shook off the ruined shield and let it drop. Habol took a wider stance, grasping his broadsword with both hands.

Seeing an opportunity, Trako rushed his opponent.

Habol parried the mace, parried the axe, and parried the mace again before jabbing for Trako's eyes. The broadsword clanged off the black iron helmet, startling the faster Trako and backing him off almost immediately. Habol charged, chopping for a head. Trako ducked. Habol hacked for a shoulder, but Trako dodged out of harm's way. Habol pursued and slashed at the Vorish man's left arm.

He missed entirely.

Trako stopped, set his feet, and whipped his mace around like a black rock circling the sun. The iron head crashed into

Habol's helm, bashing him to the earth. Habol landed in a heap, tried to rise, and had his face slammed into the sands.

The arena erupted into excited wailing.

Habol sensed something was wrong, *dreadfully* wrong with that side of his face and jaw. He tasted blood and spat red teeth. Reality shimmered, sparkled, and became painfully clear.

Seddon above.

The mace was *embedded* in his helmet.

Spikes had perforated both metal and meat to knock free a pair of lower-jaw teeth. Another spike had punctured his upper jaw, removing a molar and piercing the roof of his mouth. Habol clenched his jaw, and his face lit up in agony.

Then his vision became skewed as Trako planted a boot to Habol's ribs and yanked, trying to free his face from the spikes. Trako jerked the mace left and right, rattling the man's head, all to the crowd's morbid delight.

Trako failed to free the weapon.

Then he remembered his axe.

The weapon flashed high in the sunlight as Trako appeared intent on solving the puzzle with one blow.

Habol lashed out with his broadsword—a wide, desperate slice that cut Trako across one knee, splitting the leather bands holding the greave in place.

Blood spurted. Trako toppled and landed on his back.

Hope surged through Habol then, and in that singular moment, when the eye and limb act as one, he rose to his knees—mace still stuck to his helmet—and looked to take Trako's head off with one executioner's chop.

As Habol's broadsword came down, Trako spun on his back and kicked. The boot caught Habol hard in the midsection, buckling him, causing him to fall to the side.

Mere heartbeats later, a dazed Habol looked up . . . as Trako grabbed the shaft of the mace still stuck in the helmet.

He yanked.

ABOUT THE BLOOD

Trako stretched Habol out on the sand, facedown and off-balance. The Vorish gladiator cranked his war axe into Habol's head with a *clang*.

The mace came free, red ribbons cutting the air.

Trako cast the mace aside, no longer interested in the weapon. He mounted his opponent's back, poised to smash the helm of the unmoving gladiator.

But Trako didn't strike.

He paused in the apex of his swing, axe quivering as if stayed by an invisible hand. Some onlookers screamed for him to kill the fallen man. Others pleaded for mercy.

The axe steadied, wavered, and dropped to Trako's side. The Vorish gladiator stood. He nudged Habol's still form with a boot.

Habol's hand rose weakly and dropped. Dark blots stained the ground. Sand caked the defeated man's punctured face.

"Your victor!" the Orator shouted.

Trako raised his arms.

30

"Much better than the gurry before it," Dark Curge commented, greatly entertained by the performance. "Much better. We need more of that."

"I need more wine," Nexus said as if coming out of a trance. He snapped his fingers for the manservant.

"Your man is next, I see," Gastillo said, glancing at the schedule.

"He is," Curge said. "You should watch this, Nexus. See what a quality fighter is. I don't believe you've been present for his past four victories."

"How will I calm myself?" Nexus asked, gazing off while holding his goblet to be filled. "And yes, I've been present for his fights. Even the one he lost."

"Your man Gair fights the House of Vandu?" Gastillo asked, diverting the conversation.

Curge scanned the audience. "Aye that. A man called—"

Sergur checked the bindings of his leather vest and saw they were tightly knotted. He retrieved his helmet and studied the visor's gleaming metal, shaped in the likeness of some hellion, fangs wide and howling into a storm's fury. Metal war braids hung off the sides and back, which he regarded with pride and fear because the face reflected his inner self, or so he thought. *These savage games. Why do I still partake?*

No answer came forth.

Sergur suspected it was the training. He enjoyed pushing himself to his physical limits, dropping face-first into the sands, exhausted, only to rise stronger the next day. The practicing and honing of techniques and multiple combinations intrigued him. He also enjoyed the Pit, savored the smell of spent battles, and loved the violent anticipation upon the air. Facing an opponent provided a heady mixture of fear and exhilaration—far superior than any wine or hypnotic herb. He also enjoyed the company of the other pit fighters. The crowds, however, he despised, hated their fickle hides one and all.

However, deep down lurked the real reason he enjoyed the games. The real reason he'd fought for seven years in the Pit was much more sinister.

He fought because he liked hurting others.

That knowledge both shamed and disturbed him just a little, though not enough to make him leave the profession.

Those thoughts ran through his mind while he stood in the private viewing chamber of Vandu. His fellow gladiator, Curn, was standing nearby and held out Vandu's twin short swords. The Free Trained calling themselves the Ten had handed Curn his first defeat of the games only days before. The loss had plunged the normally confident man into a mire of depression and anger, but his spirits had brightened with the announcement of the season's extension—enough that he'd accompanied Vandu to the Pit for Sergur's fight.

Outside, the crowds stirred, their collective voices becoming as harsh and beautiful as an ocean's surf.

"Time," Curn said quietly, his black eyes intense.

Sergur nodded and ran a hand over the visor's fearsome visage. It was indeed time—time to become the hellion. He donned the helm, and a tingle stropped the length of his spine. It always felt that way when he pulled on the armor and tightened the chin strap.

He became the hellion.

As unfit or eye-rolling that statement might sound, Sergur didn't care, for he believed the mask he wore unlocked a greater power within him.

"This is Dark Curge's lad," Vandu cautioned quietly, barely audible over the craving for violence the crowds so vocally demanded. The fat owner stood with his back before the arched window, the light framing his person. He was an older man, short, with a trio of scars across his right cheek. Once, he had been a hard trainer but left that role and assumed the mantle of both owner and taskmaster. Those were two reasons to avoid signing up under his roof, he would tell young prospects. He believed himself taxing but fair, and he strove to treat his lads with respect if they deserved it.

Vandu hooked his thumbs on his thick belt, shrugged thicker shoulders, and regarded Sergur with sleepy eyes.

"But you . . ." he said, continuing the thought, "you're going to defeat that man. You're going to pound his head into the arena floor. You are a monster among men, Sergur. A monster. And those are your claws."

Vandu indicated the pair of short swords.

Curn slapped Sergur's iron-studded shoulder pads.

"Curge thinks he knows what you're about," Vandu explained. "You show that one-armed pig bastard that you're different. You show that dog pisser of his you're different. And you summon everything you have to put that lad down. Make an example of him. If you can't do that"—Vandu shrugged—"then just butcher him. You are superior . . . in every way. You are not to be defeated. And anyone facing you on the arena floor is to be punished. Understood?"

The hellion mask nodded with evil intent.

"Go on then," Vandu said. "Bring us a victory."

A pit fighter opened the chamber door. The white tunnel beckoned.

Sergur went.

*

When the portcullis allowed enough of an opening, Sergur stepped into the Pit. The heat attacked his armored form. The air was hot and tasted of grit. He crossed his swords and held them up to the audience, soaking in the thunderous applause. They knew who he was. They knew what he was capable of.

The Orator finished introducing the man Sergur had come to destroy, Gair the knife fighter.

The sun beamed down upon a muscular V-shaped figure, a student of Dark Curge himself and no stranger to the games. Gair wore black breeches and greaves about his lower half. A band of leather protected his midsection to his chest, to keep his guts inside in case of a fatal slash. A red iron faceplate covered his features. A monstrous silver jaw with short, troll-like tusks hung off the mask beneath black eye ports. A bundle of white-and-red cloth had been wrapped around the rest of his head. Gair held a pair of thick knives the length of a man's forearms. They shone brightly, matching the gleam of the lower jaw.

Gair had lost once during the season, and his chances of continuing to the end had improved with the extension of the games. Like Sergur, Gair was back in contention.

Also like Sergur, Gair would be looking to make an impression with this fight.

"Begin!" the Orator shouted, the words drowned by the spectators' roar.

Sergur strode toward the middle of the arena, swords flashing, the sun reflecting off his hellion's face.

Gair lifted his deadly knives and assumed a puncher's stance. Spiked gauntlets and bracers twinkled with malice.

As Sergur closed the distance, the audience's cries rose to a staggering level.

Sergur slashed and sliced, the sword edges scintillating, attacking the knife fighter at a speed too fast to follow.

As swift as Sergur was in his strikes, what truly impressed the onlookers was the reflexes of the knife fighter. Gair bobbed and weaved, his knives deflecting any attack he couldn't evade.

At times, Sergur swayed left and right, noted by a slight pause in his stabs and cuts. Openings appeared when Sergur dropped back to compose himself, but Gair didn't pursue. Instead, the knife fighter respected the distance, shook out his arms, and assumed a guarded stance.

Sergur took his time, studying his adversary while sometimes locking eyes with the man. Sergur had spent countless days strengthening his endurance. He possessed power enough to keep swinging until the sun dropped from the sky. He circled the knife fighter, at times quickly changing direction, sizing up Gair like a stubborn roast of meat.

The knife fighter held his ground, matching his opponent's every move.

Sergur the hellion detected a possible weakness. He stomped forward, cocking his right sword while stabbing with his left at the same time—a move meant to confuse.

Gair wasn't so easily fooled, though. He spun away from the killer thrust, whipping a spiked fist into Sergur's ribs as he went by, breaking at least a pair. Sergur backhanded, sweeping a scything arc at Gair's neck, but the knife fighter ducked, popped up within Sergur's guard, and rapid-punched the swordsman's abdomen. The final blow crunched into the hellion mask, hard enough to drive Sergur back, his arms spiraling as if he was teetering at a cliff's edge.

The crowds stood and applauded.

Regaining his balance and angered at the vocal support for his adversary, the hellion ignored the mounting pain. He straightened the mask and regarded the waiting knife fighter in a new light. Sergur decided he was going to hurt the man.

The gladiator powered forward and unleashed a blistering series of slashes, thrusts, and over-the-shoulder chops that crashed into Gair's twin knives and sparkled the air. The onslaught forced the knife fighter back.

Sergur's left blade licked a red line across the meat of Gair's shoulder. The cut energized the hellion. He attacked Gair with renewed determination and unleashed a flurry of strikes that went as high as fifteen before he cut the knife fighter on the outside of his right bicep. Sergur hacked into a metal bracer, driving Gair off-balance, and slid his blade along the man's silver jaw.

A retreating Gair spun away, showing his back for an instant. Glittering sweat and blood flew from his shoulders.

Sergur went after him... and walked right into a counterstrike.

Gair unexpectedly dug his feet in and sprang back into the fight, right into the charging Sergur. His knives crammed and swatted the swords away, opening up Sergur long enough to get close and unleash his fists.

In that one instant, Sergur realized the true purpose of the knives.

They were shields for Gair, shields that could potentially cut and kill, but shields all the same.

The real danger lay in the knife fighter's fists.

An unchecked barrage of spiked gauntlets battered Sergur's person, snapping his head left-right and left-right again before Gair diverted an angry drum roll to the midsection.

Sergur buckled and lost his left sword.

Gair uppercut, mustering all the power of his arm and hips behind it, and slammed a fist into the gladiator's hellion mask.

The blow lifted the mask a full four fingers high, blinding Sergur.

Gair hammered Sergur's head. Iron rang out against iron. Sergur dropped to one knee. Then a knee and a hand. Then all four.

One last punch drove the gladiator flat.

Sergur did not rise, did not attempt to rise.

Holding his knives above his head, Gair kicked Sergur's remaining sword away and placed a foot upon his chest. With a quick knife salute in Curge's direction, he pointed his other blade at Sergur's unmoving head.

He held the pose until the Orator proclaimed him the victor.

*

When the fight had been favoring Sergur, Curge hadn't said a word, and he maintained his silence even when Gair began battering the man without remorse, sending the Vandu gladiator crashing to the arena floor. When Gair saluted him, Curge nodded and drank a mouthful of wine while the audience heaped praise upon the victor's name.

"That's a gladiator, Nexus," Curge finally growled. "*That's* a pit fighter. And Seddon's my witness, that's the man who'll win this season. No matter how long it will be."

"Not if I can help it," Nexus retorted, the color rising to his pallid cheeks.

Gastillo shifted uneasily, stuck between a mountain and a storm front. His attention wandered from the fight below, and he realized he wasn't watching them at all. His mind was on facing Nexus afterward and the haggling destined to take place.

And there were two more matches to watch . . .

Two more gladiators emerged victorious.

Red Mane from the House of Tilo soundly trounced a man called Trydas from the House of Ustda. Curge, Gastillo, and Nexus watched the near death of Trydas, and while the wine merchant vocally dismissed the battle, the other owners felt the stirrings of fresh, though begrudging, respect for old Tilo's warrior, who remained undefeated. They'd heard their agents' warnings about that pit fighter.

The day's final match had a man called Punder emerging victorious. The Stable of Slavol gladiator won his fifth match, defeating Bozzen from the House of Vandu. Unlike most, the match had been a long and dreary battle, carefully fought, and Gastillo hoped every swing would be the deciding blow. A cut to Brozzen's sword arm and a quick bash to the head ended the fight, and by that time, Gastillo was ready to burst.

With a weary look that suggested he should've left earlier, Curge checked his goblet, drained it, and waved for the servant to take it away. The big owner stood with a groan and applied his hand to his back.

"Another day," Curge rumbled and glanced at the other two owners, who were making no move to rise. "And another conversation, I see. Seddon above, Nexus. You're almost making me curious about what you two are talking about. Perhaps it's something to do with the games?"

The one-armed owner scratched his bald head. With a derisive wave, he left the box, unconcerned with the pair.

"Wait a few moments," Nexus advised Gastillo, glancing over his shoulder. "Let that pig bastard walk on. Then we'll leave for my koch."

"He doesn't seem interested in our talks."

"Really, Gastillo?" Nexus frowned. "You've been at this longer than I have. He doesn't seem interested means he's *very* interested in our conversations. And truth be known, it tickles my dead heart that the brooding one-armed punce is puzzling over us. All right, this way, then. It's time enough to leave. Bloody day at the games. Some very good contests. I enjoyed it if not for that brazen pisser."

Gastillo kept his thoughts to himself as he followed Nexus out of the box. As before, his two guards joined Nexus's larger escort, and they walked back to the waiting koch, parked outside the Gate of the Moon. Another dozen armed guards surrounded the vehicle, the polished wood gleaming in the early evening light. Gastillo's men stopped before the merchant's guards and were not permitted beyond the ring. Leaving them behind, Gastillo followed Nexus to the koch, where the same smartly dressed manservant pulled open the door.

The two owners climbed aboard. The door closed with a click, and the interior appeared a little different to Gastillo, or so he thought as he shifted upon the red cushions.

He faced the merchant. "No wine this day?" he asked, a smile accompanying the question though Nexus didn't see it.

"No wine this day," Nexus replied and studied his mask. "How much did you pay for that face?"

"This? It was made from the gold of a little over two hundred pieces. Another hundred to hire a craftsman skilled enough to make it."

Nexus examined the work with even deeper scrutiny before blinking, as if awakening from a sleep. "Well, your decision?"

Gastillo didn't move. "I think you've valued my property too low."

"Too low, you say," Nexus growled, hard eyes staring.

"Aye that. Much too low. You can have it at seventeen thousand gold. Not quite as high as twenty and a little less than half the difference. That's quite fair for—"

"No," Nexus said in a low tone.

That flat answer surprised Gastillo, rendering him speechless. "No?" he eventually asked.

"No. I'm surprised at you, Gastillo. You think I've just arrived at that offer on some sparkling revelation? Or maybe I pulled that number from the very heavens? Perhaps you think there was no thought behind the sum? That I have mountains of wealth where I can simply fill a pot or two and hand them over? I'll tell you different. There's always thought behind what I do. What I say. I'm not one for quibbling over a potential purchase. *Fifteen* was more than a fair price for your property. More than generous. I'm insulted if you think you can raise the number upon a whim. You believe because I'm successful in my other ventures you can wring a few more coins from my aging carcass? Well, you're wrong. In fact, you're so wrong, I withdraw my offer. Our business is concluded."

Though his mask hid his face, Gastillo's stomach clenched and dropped. "But—"

"Concluded," Nexus said forcefully. With that, he reached for the door and threw it open. "Get out. Seventeen thousand. Pah. To think I was going to offer my knowledge of the trade to you."

Gastillo remained sitting, his stomach somewhere deep in the private latrine he suspected was lurking under his cushion.

"You'll be lucky to get *twelve* thousand," a red-faced Nexus carried on. "Twelve and not a coin more."

"Perhaps I have been too—"

"I *know* you've been too quick. I offered fifteen out of respect. Respect, you greedy punce. For all you've put into your name and house. Daresay you think me an idiot for even offering that sum at all, and now you're about to sweeten my cheeks for a savage dart of the tongue? Don't even consider swaying me back to fifteen. It's twelve now or nothing, and it *is* nothing since we're done here. Done! Remove your gurry hide from my koch!"

The interior seemed to shrink. The manservant appeared in the doorway, a mild question wrinkling his brow.

"Get out!" Nexus commanded.

Two of the merchant's guards glanced over their shoulders. The servant held the door, his eyes downcast.

Defeated, Gastillo slid out of the koch, his mind paralyzed and unable to put forth an argument. Truth be known, all fight had left him. He stood on cold legs and glanced back at Nexus, livid and shooing him away before retreating within the interior's shadows.

The servant got aboard the koch and closed the door.

Reins cracked, and the koch rattled away, the wine merchant's guards moving at a double pace to keep up.

Gastillo and his own escort were left in the street.

The koch disappeared into a tide of people and livestock. Gastillo watched the shape drift away, along with the helmets of Nexus's private guards. He remained that way until they disappeared.

A growing sense of loss and confusion would've been easily spotted upon his face—if not for his mask of gold.

Well past the evening meal, Gastillo finally returned to his residence and house. His two guards behind him, he'd wandered Sunja's streets in a morass of anxiety, weariness, and a gnawing sense of missed opportunity. The more deeply he contemplated

Nexus's reaction, the more he wished he could have the entire conversation again. Perhaps the merchant was correct. Perhaps he had been a little greedy after all. In the end, Nexus had thrown down an offer that wasn't quite an offer. Twelve thousand gold was still a large sum of coin, a small treasure. Such an amount would easily buy Gastillo a small manor near the nobility residences in the city's northern district. He could get even more if he wished to purchase something beyond Sunja's walls. Furthermore, Nexus had expertise in producing and selling wine and other commodities, which Gastillo knew nothing about. Having the merchant as an advisor in such matters would be priceless.

Perhaps if Gastillo agreed to twelve thousand, Nexus might still take Prajus off his hands.

Then his mind went the other way, wondering if the merchant was playing him for a fool.

Twelve thousand. Lords above.

Jaco and a handful of his house guards greeted him at the main gates of the house. Gastillo wearily acknowledged them as he passed by, his mask covering the pensive expression underneath. When the gates closed, he stopped and regarded his property as ribbons of purple clouds stretched across the evening sky: wide open training grounds, already groomed for the next day; practice men and targets; timbers for increasing one's strength. His own private residence was a two-story affair, the stone painted a sky blue with long timbers stretching from the roof and over the balcony, creating shade on the hottest of days. The servants' quarters was next to that while the bathhouse lay at the far end of the property. The barracks for the gladiators was the largest building within the walls, comfortably housing the men. Ample room existed for weapons, food, a deep well accessing clean water, and the dozen or so servants and support staff beyond the modest household guard he employed. The staff he'd probably take with him if they were willing, but the rest . . .

ABOUT THE BLOOD

Was it all worth twelve thousand?

More importantly, was it worth Gastillo's peace of mind?

He decided it just might be enough . . . to be well and clear of the trade, to be well and done with—

"Ho, lads, look! Master Gastillo returns at last."

A handful of men sat outside the common-room entrance, relaxing after a hard day of training. Prajus sat in the middle of his little group, taking aim at Gastillo with that aggravating leer of his. He wore little except white breeches, his upper body left bare.

The house owner steadied himself. An impulse to strike that annoying expression off the man's face came dangerously close to the surface.

"Fine evening for a walk about the streets," Prajus loudly observed.

Catty grins sprang upon the faces of those closest to him.

"While the true gladiators strain and bleed under a hot sun. And now he's ready to retire, but not before an evening of chasing the servants about for a quick tickle, eh? Perhaps even a bath later on. Ah, the life. The life you have, Master Gastillo. Must be quite nice to be so unconcerned with house matters, eh?"

A few soft chuckles escaped Prajus's pack.

Perhaps it was the heat of the day, the long walk home, or the subsequent disappointment with the meeting with Nexus, but for whatever reason, Gastillo decided he simply did not have the interest or strength to engage the mouthy Prajus.

"Prajus, shut up," he said. "Or I'll shut your mouth for you."

That silenced the man.

Gastillo kept walking to his home.

Then Prajus said, "Anytime you wish to try, Master Gastillo."

That stopped the house owner on his front step. He turned at the much-too-close jab. Jaco and the house guard approached from the gates, but Gastillo waved them off. *Twelve thousand gold,* he thought, the number burning in his brain.

That included Prajus, an insolent fleck of dog shite if one ever existed. For a dangerous moment, Gastillo wondered how much his property might be worth without the mouthy fighter.

"Prajus," he said, the word hanging in the air like an executioner's axe. "Your friends must enjoy these early evenings under watchful guards. Jaco?"

"Sar?"

Gastillo reached for the latch of his front door. "Clean up that cow kiss. And the whole lot around him. Ensure that none of those lads leave the grounds tonight. Congratulations, Prajus. I don't know what Sowin and the trainers have planned for you tomorrow, but I'll make sure it's doubled in difficulty."

That removed most of the smiles but not that of Prajus, who leaned back on his elbows and crossed his legs, shaking his head in disappointment.

"Anytime you wish to try, Master Gastillo," the man repeated, brazen and enjoying it.

Upon hearing his name, Gastillo tightened his grip upon the latch and pulled the door open. The house owner waited a few heartbeats, his body temperature rising, becoming increasingly angry at the total lack of respect from the dog. If the man were anyone else, Gastillo would have him driven from the house.

He eyed Prajus, weighing his options, ignoring the suddenly attentive pack of pit fighters. Jaco wavered at the very edge of his vision. All he needed was to say the word, and the house guard would make quick work of the man. The guard made it clear that he was more than willing to pull steel upon the gladiator.

Twelve thousand.

Thus, in perhaps the greatest display of willpower ever, Gastillo entered his home and closed the door.

He didn't look back.

If he did, he was certain Prajus would be still there, leaning back with that saucy smile. If he saw that, Gastillo wasn't exactly sure what might transpire next. His breath was hurried, his pulse raced, and his fists clenched and unclenched. In the dying light of the foyer, he silently cursed the day he'd brought that hateful maggot into his fold. The day was approaching, Gastillo knew, when he would have to deal with Prajus . . . one way or the other.

Twelve thousand.

His hatred for the man bubbled over the sum. He hated that dog blossom more with every passing breath. The pit fighter could be butchered in the Pit, and Gastillo realized he'd applaud whoever did the deed. Truth be known, he'd sell Prajus off for twelve gold or less. At that moment, he would even consider trading him for a sick goat—anything to be rid of the pig bastard.

A cold realization overcame him. Gastillo would kill the man for nothing, just for the satisfaction of killing him, just for the peace of mind.

Twelve thousand, his mind whispered again.

Thoughts churning, nagging, he retired for the night.

The manor's door closed without so much as a click, which struck a lounging Prajus as extremely curious. Gastillo had been acting quite strange lately, and that encounter seemed odd as well.

Jaco approached, stern and with the promise of violent affection in his eyes.

Prajus was unconcerned with the guard. The house master interested him more. Gastillo was on the verge of pulling steel, or so he suspected, but somehow the man managed to suck that anger back inside and sheathe it. Certainly, Gastillo had said he'd have old topper Sowin and his ilk double up on the day's drills, but that didn't bother Prajus. He would welcome the burn.

He wondered if he had almost taunted the house owner to the edge of no return. So many times before, he'd mocked the man but never sensed the raw tension the likes he'd felt only heartbeats earlier. Prajus knew his worth, knew Gastillo needed him for the season as he was considered, rightly so, to be the best in the house—the entire games even, which he supposed gave him a certain amount of grace in these exchanges.

But directly challenging a house master? Prajus had to admit his voice had surprised even himself that time, not that he would ever withdraw the invitation. However, after daring the unspeakable, in front of others no less, Gastillo did very little. He even held back. Curge would certainly not have held back. In fact, Curge would have commanded the entire roster to kill him, and he would've been justified, in Prajus's mind.

Not Gastillo, however.

He wondered why.

"Thought he was going to pull steel on you, Prajus," one of the others whispered, just as the shadows of Jaco and the house guard fell across them all.

"I thought so as well," Prajus replied.

31

The day had ended, once again.

The long-bearded rabbit-eating healer—the same healer Borchus and Halm had visited upon surviving the Iron Games—puttered about his house, placing jars of ointments, remedies, and medicinal herbs in their correct places after a day of work. His name was Ivalo, and the day, he reflected, had been rather slow, with only three paying customers and the fourth wishing to trade chores for the treatments. Ivalo didn't mind that. He had a roof in need of repairs before the winter, and he was already contemplating where to purchase building materials.

After thinking about shingles, thoughts of supper filled his mind—something quick, but he hadn't a clue. He could sew up a cut without hesitation, skillfully set bones, banish hellions from a person's head and heart, and correctly diagnose and treat any number of illnesses, including mild cases of gut binding, which had plagued one of his visiting patients that day, but when it came to cooking, Ivalo shrugged in defeat. He did what he could. He lived alone after his wife of thirty-one years had died three years earlier, and mealtimes weren't terribly special for him anymore. Eating had become more of a routine, where the ingestion of food merely kept the body going and the head thinking.

He stripped a blood-speckled sheet off one table, remembering the stitches he'd had to place in a young woman's thumb where her kitchen knife had bit her. *Beets*, he realized. He'd been paid in bottled beets just the day before—sweet, thick-sliced chunks with juice, excellent for moving one's bowels and providing energy. Supper's puzzle was solved.

The front door creaked open, breaking his thoughts. He turned and stared as two men entered his healing house. One was short and stocky while the other loomed over his companion and even Ivalo himself. It was quiet outside as if the people living nearby had seen something monstrous slinking through the streets.

"Yes?" Ivalo muttered in a scratchy voice, his beard barely moving. Out of habit, the old healer ran a hand down his chin whiskers, smoothing their length.

The short one ensured the front door was closed while the tall one nodded at Ivalo. He smiled, his chin thick with greasy-looking stubble. "Greetings, good healer," he said. "We need to speak with you. For just a moment."

Scrunching his face, Ivalo stared down his nose at the pair—he was growing increasingly nearsighted. A quiet, deadly air of dread descended upon the room.

Ivalo didn't bat an eye. "Well, I'm about to close for the evening."

The short one stayed at the door while the tall one moved closer, past the tables and chairs with nary a sound. Ivalo detected the muscular bulk of the tall one. Waves of menace emanated from the man, and as he approached Ivalo, the old healer felt his dog blossom pucker up tight.

"Suppose I could answer talk for a few moments," Ivalo offered weakly, lifting his chin as the bigger man came closer.

"We're looking for someone," the tall one slowly explained. "A short man. Called Borchus. Graying hair with sideburns down to here." When he indicated the sideburns, he slipped a finger to the left side of his face and drew it down, under his chin, and across his throat.

ABOUT THE BLOOD

That disturbed Ivalo.

"Strong-looking fellow," the tall one continued, stressing the *strong* bit and very much unconcerned with the healer's discomfort. "Had a knife wound that might've needed tending to. We're very interested in finding him. Has anyone visited you these past few days?"

Ivalo struggled to keep his face expressionless. "I . . ." *usually don't discuss my patients*, he was going to say, but in that instant, with that tall brute of a man standing only two paces away and appearing to fill the whole room, what Ivalo actually said was, "think I do remember a lad like that."

The tall one's brow knitted together, and he became much more interested. "You're certain, good healer? You remember someone matching that description?"

"I do," Ivalo said, warming to the idea of revealing everything he knew, talking more than he had all day. "Short man, you said? Long sideburns, deep voice. A learned man. Or at least sounding that way. Yes, a few nights back. Came in holding his side. Been cut with a blade. Quite possibly a knife."

The tall one didn't immediately reply. Instead, he exchanged looks with the shorter one positioned near the door. The shorter one's eyes seemed sunken deep into his skull, making their light all the sharper.

"He said he'd been cut with a knife?" the tall one asked.

"No," Ivalo answered, genuinely uneasy. "No. He . . . he didn't say that, not exactly. But after years of being in this work, one recognizes a knife wound."

"You're sure it was a knife?"

Ivalo hesitated. "I'm sure."

"Did he say anything to you?"

The healer was thankful his patient had not. "No."

"Did he say his name?"

"Ah . . . I don't rightly remember."

The tall man scowled with disappointment. "Do you know where he lives?"

"No. I'm sorry."

"Does he come here often?"

"No. Only the once."

The tall one examined the healer's face, searching for untruths. After a short time, he nodded, accepting the information. He stepped back from the healer. The tall one's expression became thoughtful, and he ran a hand over a table's surface. At one point, he even studied the ceiling's bare timbers before turning to his shorter companion.

"What do you think?" the tall one asked.

The short one nodded, his eyes never leaving the healer.

The tall one digested that answer and regarded Ivalo again. "One last question, good healer. One that is very... very important. Do you think he'll return?"

The urge to blink was a powerful one, but Ivalo strained not to, to not do *anything* that might bring about extreme pain at the hands of these two brutes. Then he realized he had an honest answer after all, unlike his last one.

"No idea," he said, his throat clicking. "They come and go here. Morning, noon, evening, and night. Some with minor ailments. Some with... more serious problems."

The tall one studied Ivalo for a long time, picking through the words for any signs of untruth. Then he said, "Our thanks to you, good healer. We think you've met the man we're searching for. You might see us again around these parts. If you do, rest easy. We're looking for him. Not you."

Relief flooded Ivalo.

Message delivered, the tall man backed away. Once a few steps had been placed between him and Ivalo, the tall man turned. The short one opened the door, and the tall one passed through. Ivalo watched the two men leave, the short one taking care in closing the door without a sound. The short one didn't smile, but that wasn't what caught Ivalo's attention or frightened him.

As the man closed the door, metal gleamed atop his hand—his thumb, in particular.

Though Ivalo couldn't tell for certain what that was, he suddenly didn't feel like supper anymore.

ABOUT THE BLOOD

*

While Sunjack, the tall one, and Bardal, the other one, discussed what to do next with a third member of their party who had remained outside, supper was being devoured in another part of the city.

A meal of roast chicken with vegetables damn near drowned in thick gravy had gone down well. Brejo leaned back in his chair, rubbed his nearly bursting gut, and was about to comment when a moment of melancholy seized him. He cleared his tightening throat and focused on his beer, played with his shirt's white sleeves. For that meal, they'd all worn shirts, covering the fearsome ink that colored their arms, shoulders, and chests. A brooding silence hung over the table. Calagu and Jaro sat nearby and tended to their own tall mugs. Neither man spoke. At times, however, Calagu's eyes flickered to the chair where Strach would've sat, between the other brothers. That skeletal piece of furniture haunted the room, making it feel unusually empty.

Brejo hadn't talked much since learning of his brother's demise. The loss of Strach greatly bothered him. Even Calagu was downcast—not Jaro, however, which only confirmed what Brejo had long since suspected, that their brother hadn't really cared for Strach. Brejo thanked Seddon above Calagu had ample stores of Osgarman snow orchid. The bud eased them through the unexpected grief over their brother's death. Truth be known, Brejo would've preferred some of the Zuthenian white tar, but none was to be had, so they made do with the snow orchids . . . and firewater . . . and several bottles of wine. Difficult though the time was, Brejo endured, and after a final stabilizing meal with his remaining brothers, one to end their period of mourning, he decided to return to ruling the realm.

"Well," he said, his voice crackling, "I'm ready to speak with him."

"As I," Calagu said with a nod. "Let's get this done. The Iron Games happen this night, and I have to oversee."

"Jaro?" Brejo asked his enforcer brute of a brother. "Bring him in."

The big man nodded, one hand playing with the point of his graying beard. Jaro stood, wood shrieking on wood, and left the table. He returned a short time later, leading the handsome Linfur. Linfur stopped in the doorway, dressed in well-made gray pants and a white shirt, his sad face a little too theatrical.

The man's appearance offended Brejo, but these were trying times. "Dressed well this day, I see," he said, face drawn and dark.

"Out of respect," Linfur replied.

"Respect." Brejo sighed but held his peace. "Linfur, the lads and I have decided a thing or two about the business. Since Strach is no longer amongst the living, and we're reasonably certain you had nothing to do with his death, we've decided on one or two items. From today, you'll be watching over the beggars."

Linfur's expression tightened in concentration, as if he'd been expecting something else entirely. "The . . . beggars?"

"Aye that. We need someone to keep them in line. Keep the coin flowing. You can be ruthless, I understand?"

"Ah, yes, I can," Linfur admitted. "Yes, yes, I can. Most certainly. Ah . . . the beggars."

"The beggars," Brejo repeated, enjoying seeing the man's noble air punctured and bleeding. "Down with the street lice and the rats."

He had to applaud Linfur. The well-dressed asslicker managed to maintain an outward calm.

"Ah," Linfur looked at the floor. "*Those* beggars."

The badly concealed disdain didn't please Brejo. "There's another kind?"

"Now, Linfur," Calagu interrupted, pointing a finger at the dapper henchman, "listen. This is an opportunity for you. Keeping a lot of beggars in line won't be easy, but if Strach managed it, then you will. We expect a certain amount of coin to come from the streets, and Strach never failed to deliver. With him gone, that task falls to you. Keep them under your control. Keep the coin flowing. Be ruthless. Even kill a few if you have to, as warning to the others. Do well, and rewards shall be had."

"Yes," a smoldering Brejo croaked in his harsh voice. "Rewards."

Linfur looked from one man to the other.

"You were expecting something else?" Brejo asked. He knew the dapper, well-cut punce thought himself destined for finer things.

"No, no," Linfur quickly replied. "The beggars are quite unexpected, by which I mean I'm honored to manage them for you, especially in these difficult times. Dare I say it, I'm pleased that you've chosen me for the task. I shall strive to do well. As well as Strach."

"Listen now," Brejo said, locking eyes with the younger, well-groomed man. "I know you think you're meant for noble courts and the love of a princess. Know this. As of this day, you have control of a kingdom, a particular kingdom with subjects who must be controlled, must be taxed and, when needed, punished. On our behalf. Understand?"

"I do," Linfur said solemnly. "I most certainly do."

"Then work. Establish yourself. Strach usually worked alone in the streets, but he was Strach. A right and proper murderous bastard if there ever was one. Now you, you might need a few lads to go along with you. We'll give you a handful. Some rules to follow. Don't be pestering the merchants for drinks or meals or the like. Don't be showing the ink on your arms to everyone in public. Only ones in private. Be intimidating without overdoing it. You'll only have to do that once or twice in the beginning, then they'll remember you. Word will spread soon enough. And if not, cut a throat."

"Or two," Calagu added.

"Or three," Jaro muttered and returned to brooding.

Nodding at each suggestion, Brejo gestured for Calagu to speak.

"We expect the beggars to bring in at least a hundred gold a week," Calagu explained. "At *least*. Remember that. With an iron hand, you could probably increase that sum. You will receive a percentage of that amount, small to begin with, becoming generous as you prove yourself capable."

"If . . ." Brejo stressed.

"If," Calagu agreed a tad testily, not appreciating being told his business. "But Linfur, don't think about keeping an extra coin for yourself. Don't do it. We'd find out eventually, and if we do, you're aware of what will happen to you."

Linfur appeared mortified. "Of course not! Never! I'd never do such a thing."

Calagu waved a hand, shutting the pretty bastard up before he truly began to sing. "Just be aware that we'll find out eventually. Now then, the beggars are yours. There will be times when they'll produce double what we've asked. And there will be times where they'll barely scratch together a pair of coins. It all depends on how hard you wring those coins out of them. Learn your limitations, be wary of the Street Watch, and best of fortune. Perform well, and you might one day sit at this very table."

That earned a dark look from Brejo.

Sensing the lecture was over, Linfur looked at each of the brothers in turn. "Many thanks. Many, many thanks for this opportunity. I'll not disappoint you. Ah, who are the lads who'll help me?"

"Jaro will pick a few."

"Ah, excellent. Excellent!"

"I'll speak with you in a moment," Jaro rumbled. "Wait for me inside the main entrance."

"I will. Thank you again, good Brejo and good Calagu! I'll have those riches flowing soon. I promise."

He disappeared through the doorway. Jaro made certain the man was gone before closing it.

"That man sprang out of the wrong honeypot," Calagu said, pursing his lips.

"Aye that," Brejo rumbled in agreement.

"He'll do what you ask," Jaro assured them. "And more. You just wait."

The two brothers exchanged looks.

They would wait and expect results.

32

Thunderheads prowled the morning sky, granting a reprieve from the usual summer heat. Somewhere over the villa's walls, a deep rumble rolled over distant hills.

Goll rose, opened the shutters of his window, and smiled faintly. Those thick clouds would keep the sun off his back as he continued preparing for his return. Securing a gray wrap, which he draped around his hips, he left his sandals and emerged into the barracks hallway. Snores ripped from behind closed curtains. He wouldn't disturb the others, not yet. He went into the empty common room. The outer door had been left open just a few fingers, to allow a breeze. Goll stepped outside and inspected a threatening sky.

The air ached for rain.

His thoughts traveled back to his days under the Weapon Masters of Kree. What would they think of him now? Him. A master of his own house. The road was still long, but Goll's determination was an iron spear, and since the season had been lengthened, not only could he return to the games as a gladiator and resume hunting for a title, but he could do so with a second goal in mind, further establishing the Ten as a force amongst the existing houses.

Headless wooden practice men greeted him, their hides battered, chipped, and scarred yet still standing. The targets and Goll were similar that way. He'd been mauled by Baylus the Butcher, the man who'd finished his season before it truly began.

However, he had a second chance. He intended to make the most of it.

He walked past the practice men, the racks of wooden swords, and the heavy timbers for strength training. Goll approached the forge area and stopped at the edge of the grounds. There, he turned around and walked back toward the living quarters, faster this time, shaking out his arms as he went. After a brief pause, he bounced along as he walked, forcing blood into his thighs, making them burn. A stiffness lingered there, but thanks to Shan's medicinal salves, it wasn't too concerning. In fact, he felt wonderful, invigorated, as if his entire body was finally returning to him. Blood flowed through dormant muscles and forced them awake. His mended bones held and felt as strong as steel.

Sweat covered his brow as he stopped at the weapon rack and selected a wooden sword. Goll swung the blade around his head, loosening his arms, shoulders, and sides. He stitched the air with thrusts, each one a little faster than before. No pain hampered him. Satisfied, he turned and slashed at an imaginary foe, moving forward. He flowed through a complex series of strikes and defensive stances, completing the exercise in thirty-three moves. When he finished, he found himself facing the gladiators' barracks, whereupon he turned around and began a different set of strikes and defensive poses—moving even faster.

The Kree summoned a damn-near-sorcerous spectacle of swordplay underneath a gray sky. The wooden blade whisked and pricked and weaved all manner of complicated tricks against imaginary foes, both singular and multiple. He spun and slashed and repelled attacks from all quarters, and when he finished, he turned around once again and performed yet another different set. He moved with confident grace, slowly in some places, lightning fast in others, his stance perfect, his guard impenetrable, and his limbs remembering. The sword never missed and didn't waver.

After the completion of a fifth set, speeding through well over two hundred movements, Goll abruptly stopped as if hit midchest by an arrow. Torso heaving, bare skin coated in a glaze, he listened to his breathing, inspected his weapon, and did a mental check of his performance.

He allowed himself a little smile.

On impulse, Goll looked up and met the eyes of Clades's wife, Kura, watching him from the corner of the main house. She startled at having being seen, boggled in place as to what to do, and finally settled upon nodding in his direction.

"You're up early," the Kree said, breathing hard. "Quarters aren't comfortable?"

"Begging forgiveness, Master Goll," she said, not coming any closer. She inspected the green robes she wore. "The quarters are fine. A . . . bit smaller than what I'm used to, but I'm with my husband, and we're both away from the city. So I'm happy."

Goll walked a few paces toward her. "Don't care for the city?"

Kura shook her head.

He didn't disagree. "How do you find life in the villa?"

"Still new, truth be known," she said. "I've spoken with mostly servants thus far. Ananda. And Clurik, who seems to do most of the cooking around here. I've had a few words with Lady Nala—although she insists on me not using her title. She's very pleasant."

"But . . . ?" Goll asked.

The woman looked around and shrugged. "But it's not home," she said flatly. "It's not mine. It feels more like an in-between place. Please don't say a word of this to my husband. He knows. And he wouldn't care for my speaking my mind to you."

"I appreciate a person who speaks their mind. There's no wrong guessing, then."

"I suppose not."

Goll studied the training grounds.

"I'll leave you, then," Kura said. "To your fighting. You seem very skilled with a sword."

He didn't comment.

"Good day to you," she said and disappeared around the corner, in the direction of the servants' quarters.

"And to you," Goll said as an afterthought, realizing she was gone. Frowning, he replayed their conversation in his head.

In time, he started pacing about the grounds.

Overhead, the gray brightened as the sun struggled to break through. Ajik appeared, flicked a casual glance toward Goll, and paid no further mind to him. The armorer stopped before the forge and looked about as if wondering where to start. Then he stooped beside a small wood pile and loaded his arms, indicating a busy day.

Goll slowed to watch.

Feeling eyes upon his back, Ajik straightened and met the house master's gaze.

"Good Ajik," Goll greeted.

Ajik returned to work.

Not surprised, Goll resumed pacing, thinking about what combinations to practice next. The sun split the cloud banks at multiple points, checkering the grounds with light and shadow. Goll looked at the wooden practice man. Sword in hand, he went to the target.

The time had come for the rest of the house to rise, anyway.

Naulis rode into the villa by midafternoon.

Goll and Clavellus met the skinny messenger near the forge.

"News from the city?" the taskmaster asked.

"Aye that," Naulis said, his huge overbite making him appear in a constant state of awe. He glanced at Junger, practicing combinations upon a practice man. "Where's the others?"

"Resting," Goll said. "That news?"

"Oh, right. Well, you have two fights the day after tomorrow. Junger will fight a house gladiator called Brontus. A rough lad from the House of Ustda."

"And Brozz?"

The messenger climbed off his horse. "One called Sapo. From the House of Curge."

The taskmaster and owner exchanged pensive looks.

"That's it?" Clavellus asked.

Naulis slicked his greasy hair out of his eyes, revealing a forehead gleaming with sweat. "That's it. Not much else."

"Two days," Goll declared in a stern tone. "They'll be ready."

"Left the city at dawn," Naulis said. "Becoming dangerous to travel alone. City Skarrs told me there's been stories of the Dezer riding about. All I need is the risk of running into a pack of those animals."

"Dezer?" Clavellus asked, concerned. "Where?"

"East, northeast of the city. They looted a small village. Put most to the sword. Heard they also attacked one or two groups of wagons bound for Sunja's public markets."

"The season's wrong for the Dezer," Clavellus said.

Naulis shrugged. "That's the talk, but perhaps the Dezer know that as well. Maybe they decided to be . . . What's the word? Unpredictable?"

"Grim news. The only predictable thing about them is the fall."

News of the roving marauders didn't really interest Goll though he knew the Dezer's reputation for marauding. His knowledge of Sunjan history wasn't the best, but he knew that in the beginning, the plains and forest had sustained the earliest Sunjans before the people split apart. One group built upon the mountain plateau, eventually becoming the city. The Sunjans who remained upon the plains evolved into the horse culture called the Visigar, who resented present-day Sunja laying claim to their territory. Then there were the Dezer, the third group, who separated themselves from the Visigar's passive attitudes. The Dezer took to more murderous methods of diplomacy and, in time, fragmented into smaller, divided tribes of barbarians inhabiting both forests and open plains.

The Visigar inhabited Sunja's northeast. The Dezer, however, roamed wherever they wanted, claiming territory as it pleased them and terrorizing anyone not of their tribes. The turning of the leaves and the cooling weather marked the days when groups of armed horsemen would emerge from hidden valleys, pillage the weak, and return to their secret homes before winter.

The Visigar could be hostile at times but could be reasoned with.

The Dezer had descended into savagery.

"Which way were they moving?" a concerned Clavellus asked, breaking Goll's thoughts.

"West," Naulis said. "Or so I heard."

Clavellus didn't like the sound of that. "Any sight of those murderers is troubling. Heading west, are they? If we're fortunate, they'll run into the Nords. Jackals against a pack of Dezer. That's a fight we all win."

"I have a message for you," Goll said to Naulis, "for the Madea. I mean to fight again. The man that killed Baylus the Butcher. You tell him Goll of Kree will fight on the same day as the others if he has someone to fight."

"Done," Naulis said, scratching an armpit. "As long as I don't run into a pack of Dezer on the way back."

"You're not going to run into a pack of Dezer."

"Those hellions might be striking west, but they just might change direction and come south," Clavellus muttered, perturbed at the thought. "Damn hellions. Bloodthirsty he-bitches, each and every one. The Klaws should have rooted out and killed the lot of them years ago."

"Trouble was finding them," Naulis said quietly. "Hills are thick with timberland just over the marsh plains. Rises and hollows. Fog and mist. If they settled down somewhere, it might be possible, but you know as well as I they're always on the move. Then there's the war going on . . ."

"What's Borchus doing?" Goll asked.

"Ah." Naulis scratched his other armpit and sniffed his fingers. "The man's moving about. He's become very careful these past few days."

Borchus. Goll wondered if he should dismiss the agent. If that other concern overshadowed his duties for the house, he would find someone more reliable.

Clavellus sighed heavily. "Well, rest up a bit. Take a fresh horse, and head back when you're ready. The days are still long enough to make Sunja by nightfall."

"Ah"—Naulis cringed—"does that rest include a bit to eat?"

Clavellus pointed toward the common room.

"Many thanks." The messenger brightened and walked off.

When the spy was out of earshot, the taskmaster faced Goll and took stock of the gladiator. "You really mean to fight, eh?"

"Master Clavellus," the Kree replied, "I mean to win."

33

Torchlight illuminated the small audience chamber of Dark Curge. The one-armed owner sat near the back, opposite the room's entrance, and gazed upon his collection of old weapons adorning the walls. Short swords, daggers, maces, and axes hung from nails, their edges and points still sharp, still deadly. Formidable face cages and dented helms also hung on a wall, creating an intimidating collage of weapons and armor. Curge had utilized every piece at one time or another during his career, and he kept them after every fight. Each piece had its history, its battles to the death. No truer friends could a man ever have, and he trusted them completely. Curge hadn't been in the best of moods lately, not after receiving word of Clavellus and his dogs prancing about the alehouses, staggering from one drinking hall to the next, spreading the word of the Ten's victories and pissing in his face.

The man continued to defy him, daring him to respond.

And Curge would have to respond, lest he lose face—lest the former taskmaster think him gone weak. In the absence of Old Curge, his father, Dark Curge found comfort in his weapons and armor. The torchlight on the scratched metal calmed him, helped him think, or when needed, transported him back to better days, when his father and mother were still alive and he was crushing wooden heads.

Beyond the door, the clearing of a throat caught his attention.

The youthful Bezange entered with the grace of a ghost, his soft boots barely heard. Curge quietly marveled at the agent's light step. The man damn near floated over the ground, he moved so stealthily.

Not so, the pit fighter who followed him.

Like a bull with four twisted hooves, Sapo lumbered into the chamber, looking a little uncomfortable at being summoned so late. Since having crossed the sands, Sapo had done little to impress Curge and his training staff. The man was powerful—no one would dispute that—but he was a graceless brute, relying too much on his strength rather than skill. He was still young, with the stubborn air of knowing better than his elders, but that wouldn't protect him from Curge's wrath if he refused to work under his trainers' instruction.

"Good evening, Sapo," Curge rumbled.

"Master Curge," Sapo replied, clasping his hands in front then behind before finally settling on holding his hips.

"Not too late, I hope," Curge asked.

"Not at all," Sapo replied without a trace of humility, a touch too familiar with Curge. The owner didn't like that.

"You will fight in two days, you understand?"

Sapo took a mighty breath. "I do."

"Against your former house."

"The Free Trained shite, yes."

The comment amused Curge. Since having been taken in, Sapo quickly disassociated himself from the ranks of Free Trained and started calling himself a true gladiator, as if he'd never spent any time at all within the Pit's general quarters. It irritated the house's veterans, men who had trained and participated in the games for years, and the friction had already resulted in two incidents upon the training grounds.

"Are you ready?" Curge asked plainly, his fingers picking at the end of his chair's arm.

"I am. I won't disappoint you, Master Curge. I've been looking forward to this since I've joined the House of Curge. I'll kill their man Brozz. I'm not afraid of him."

"Never was a question of fear," Curge rumbled, "but of preparation. Of mind and will and skill at arms."

"I'm ready," Sapo said, his chin rising. "And, as I've said, I look forward to the contest."

"You know of the bounty I've placed on the Ten?"

"I do."

"My bounty applies to those under my roof."

"And I'll earn it," Sapo said confidently. "The Sarlander's dead. He's a corpse about to have the ground swallow him whole."

Torchlight flickered, casting long shadows upon the floor and wall. For long moments, a contemplative Curge stared at the young man while Bezange quietly stood at attention near the door. In the shadows, the agent's face appeared even more untouched by time.

"That will be all, Sapo," Curge finally said. "Get rested. Soon, you execute an old friend."

That stiffened the big man's back. "They're not my friends." Sapo huffed and bowed curtly at the waist. "Good night, Master Curge."

Sapo turned and plodded out of the room. After waiting a few beats, Bezange reached out, checked to see if the man had gone, and closed the door. He placed his back to the wood and regarded his employer.

"What do you think?" Curge asked his agent.

"The man's a force, there's no mistaking that."

"He's an unfit lout."

"He's an unfit lout. Yes."

"And ill-mannered at that," Curge rumbled and rubbed at the stump of his left arm. "I was ready to strip a length of skin from his hide about his training, but I'll wait until the match is finished. Not impressed with him thus far. He has as much skill as a battering ram. As a falling mountain. All force. No thought. I have my doubts about this coming match. I've seen the Sarlander fight."

"There's no loss if the Sarlander kills the man," Bezange pointed out. "You're only losing a brute you never really invested in. Even better, you gain the right to a blood match with the Sarlander. You can choose who kills him, then."

Curge grunted, his eyes drifting to the armaments on the walls.

"I have news," Bezange said, getting Curge's attention. "Our spies confirm that the man called Halm has left the villa of Clavellus. They report that he's taken up residence in the small village of Karashipa."

That caught Curge's interest. "He left?"

Bezange nodded. "And our lads report that he looks near dead. Far too many beatings. Far too much inflicted damage. His season's over."

Curge ruminated upon that. "The season's a long one now. The Zhiberian might have left it, but if he heals, there's the chance he might return."

"Always a possibility," Bezange agreed. "Word might reach him about the games. And he is undefeated. One of the remaining few."

"I want him back," Curge said flatly. "I want him killed in the arena. So all might see the wrath of the House of Curge."

Bezange wisely kept silent.

"I sense what you're thinking, Bezange." Curge smiled with malice. "I know I've had ample opportunity to dispatch the man, and yet he still lives. The fact is . . . the Zhiberian is good. Skilled. A raw, undisciplined nature, mind you, which will fail him in the end, but it's kept him alive to this point."

"Word is he seems, ah, occupied with a woman in the village," Bezange reported.

"What about her?"

"She owns a small tavern there. There's not much else to tell. The Zhiberian is there, seems taken with her, and apparently appears a day away from dying."

"A woman," Curge muttered and studied his helmets. "Is the Zhiberian courting her, perhaps?"

"He is staying at her residence. A good match, I believe. The man has a reputation for the taverns and alehouses."

"It serves nothing to have him killed in Karashipa."

Bezange didn't comment.

"Let him have his time, then," Curge said. "Until I choose to bring him back. I'll bring him back when I see my time. Daresay it'll be easy enough. The man's a pit fighter. He lives for the games as much as any of us. He'll return. And when he does . . ."

Curge let that part go unspoken.

"I want you to do something else for me," he told his agent. "Learn what's going on between Nexus and that gold-plated teat Gastillo. I've seen them talking. Recently, however, they've been quite cold toward each other. Nexus more so than Gastillo. Gastillo's hellpup Prajus fights tomorrow, and he's been a hook in Nexus's skin, but I'm not so certain that's the root of it."

"I'll alert our spies," Bezange said with a dip of his head. "Nexus will be a challenge, however. The man keeps a wall of guards about his person."

"Do what you can. You have spies at the gates?"

"I do."

Curge shook his head with hateful contemplation. "That pig bastard Clavellus will return. I know it. I've made it clear he's unwelcome in the city, and he defies me. What do I have to do to uphold my father's words, Bezange?"

The agent didn't comment.

"That one . . ." Curge rumbled. "I find myself having no issue at all with killing that one outside the Pit. Not in the least. Make it known."

"He's another that never strays from his pack."

"So you've said," Curge acknowledged. "But his appearance at an alehouse suggests he's growing bolder. No doubt from being in the games once again. It's in his blood. No question of that. The alehouses drew him in once. They'll do so again. What's a day at the games if you can't enjoy the taverns afterward? Just let your spies know. Have someone ready to strike. Make it look like a street stabbing. And just to be clear, his death doesn't have to be within the city limits. Anywhere will do."

The torchlight reflected in the agent's eyes. "As you wish, Master Curge."

"I wish. Now then, other matters. What have you learned about the Perician?"

Bezange shrugged. "The man has no history. It's as if he's wandered out of the wilderness and started competing in the games. No one knows where exactly he's from or if he has friends. Or family. No one knows anything. It's quite unusual. In the past, my network has managed to scratch information for even the most foreign fighters... but not this one. What we've seen in the Pit is all we know, I'm afraid."

That didn't sit well upon Curge's mind. "Keep searching. Sooner or later, we'll be matched against that hellion, and I know the outcome already. Saimon's black hanging fruit, the man hasn't even bared his sword in a contest yet. He keeps it in his scabbard."

"I'm aware of that," Bezange stated. "And quite intrigued. I'm nowhere near your level of expertise in these matters, Master Curge, but the man *is* a mystery. And the troubling thing is ... I suspect he's capable of so much more."

"Saimon take me," Curge said, unease creeping into his voice, "I think the very same."

34

Two days later, under a morning of white gold, the House of Ten piled aboard three covered wagons with the house masters and trainers in the lead. Canvas covers were hooked back to allow air to pass through the interiors. Once aboard, they departed for Sunja. Clavellus leaned forward on a bench, his frame shaking from the ruts in the road, and regarded a piece of parchment Nala had given him.

"A list?" Goll asked, sitting across from him.

Clavellus's beard turned upward in a faint smile. "Yes. The lady has given me a list. Items she wishes me to purchase. Today or tomorrow if we can't return right away. Don't worry, Master Goll. I'll not venture into the taverns or alehouses this day. Curge will have his spies watching every place between the gates and the arena."

Though he didn't reply, Goll's unease leaked away. He'd been worrying about that very thing. All he needed was an old taskmaster wandering the city, emboldened by a few victories and energized by more than a few pitchers.

"Where's your list?" Machlann asked of Koba, bringing knowing smirks all around.

Sitting near the back, the scar-faced trainer frowned and looked at the tall grass of the open plains.

In the wagon that followed, Junger also gazed at the far-reaching emptiness of the plains. The air was warm, but not uncomfortably so, and the flies weren't the biting kind.

After a time, he looked at his traveling companions and frowned.

"Lift your faces, lads," he said to Brozz, Shan, and Clades. "The day's a beautiful one. Take that breath and savor it. Pity poor Torello, who had to stay behind."

Shan's face tightened as he nodded at the Sarlander. "It's a pity this one insisted on fighting."

With his nose bound and bandaged, Brozz sat on a bench, his long legs dividing the wagon floor in two. His chest and midsection were covered in tightly wrapped bandages. The stitches in his left cheek gleamed with medicinal ointment, and a faint smell of onions hung around his head. His dark, sullen eyes flicked to the great paws that were his hands. He didn't look at the healer, sitting just behind the wagon's driver.

"You heard me," Shan warned. "This is a mistake. A huge mistake."

"You got into the wrong business," a sardonic Clades remarked.

"*I* didn't get into the wrong business," the exasperated healer said. "I'm in the business of *helping* sick or hurt people. I fix them and send them on their way, and usually, they have the sense to avoid the very thing that brought them to me in the first place. *These* people came to me. I'm still not certain how I became employed by the house, but I can tell you it's becoming hard watching good people being stupid on a daily basis. I've sewn enough skin together over the last few weeks that if someone provided me with the cloth and the line, I'm fairly certain I could put together a shirt."

A frown crossed Junger's face. "Bit harsh."

"Well, it's frustrating," the healer complained. "Very frustrating. Especially when I have patients like Torello arguing he's fine to travel when he's clearly *not* fine to travel. He shouldn't be muddling around with that twisted ankle. It'll heal faster if he's stationary. You know what I had to say to him? I said, 'If your ankle becomes strong enough and you still wish it, there's still a chance for you to fight in the games at a later point.' *That's* how I convinced him to remain behind, by promising him a chance at further butchering himself. Unfit, I tell you. Unfit."

"I think good Torello will want to return," Junger said, almost apologetically. "He seems a changed man."

Shan thumped his head against a wagon post.

Brozz eyed the Perician. "There's a few lads who've changed."

"No doubt," Junger said. "Not in my mind. Just weeks ago, I thought you were no more than a tall, imposing brute with some strange hatred for birds. Now I *know* you're a tall, imposing brute with a strange hatred for birds . . . but also someone who will mutter a few words around mealtime."

Brozz's great moustache partially hid his smile.

"Why exactly do you wear that thing?" Shan asked him, gesturing at the necklace of crow heads. "It's unsettling."

"I'm very glad you asked that question, good Shan," Junger said pleasantly. "Very glad. Yes, good Brozz. Why do you wear that thing?"

Not particularly keen on addressing the subject, the Sarlander put elbows to knees and inspected his hands. "Wherever I traveled, people would eventually start talking to me. I'm not a talker. Never was. Never will be. So I decided to look more like a killer. Grew the beard. The moustache. That didn't work."

"Hardly think why," Junger remarked casually, squinting at the daylight.

Brozz gave him a good-natured look of warning. "So I decided something more was needed."

"And killed a few crows," Junger finished. "Took their heads and threaded a length of twine through their eyes? Just to keep curious people away? That's a bit harsh as well, isn't it?"

Brozz didn't answer, but his eyes twinkled *yes*.

Shan looked mortified. "That's . . . unfit. Those poor animals. They're quite intelligent, you know."

"Can't be that intelligent," Junger muttered, eyeing the Sarlander's handmade jewelry.

"I don't like crows," Brozz said, inspecting his hands again. "They're scavengers. Of the dead. And living. Seen them . . . pluck the eyes from dying men. Then call out to other crows. To let them know there's food to be had. Hateful things."

"Always thought they looked rather noble myself," Junger said.

"They are a handsome bird," Shan agreed, thinking on the Sarlander's story. "But you're right. They'll pick apart the dead. Or the helpless. Nature's way. Life and death. Death giving life."

Brozz's features tightened. "Death gives only more death."

That quieted the healer.

"Wonderful, Brozz," Junger observed drily. "You just unsettled the one man keeping you together. Not to mention convincing him even more that this is all madness, which makes me sad because he's clearly the only other one willing to have a conversation aboard this wagon. Now, I'll have to listen to myself on this trip since you're not a talker. Clades there is obviously thinking about his wife—and rightly so, I might add. So thank you for that, good Brozz. You leave me with no choice but to entertain myself on this trip. Believe I'll start with a song. I've been told I carry a decent tune. Listen now . . ."

Brozz lowered his head.

Shan straightened against one of the wagon's high ribs. "Please don't," the healer asked. "Let's just enjoy the, ah, peace of the moment. And the view." He pointed out the openings as the wagon rolled along the ruts in the road.

Junger studied each face in turn. "Not one for song, are you?"

"No," Brozz said flatly.

Shan rattled his head. Clades frowned, unsure if the man was serious or not.

"I see," the Perician said.

In the awkward silence that followed, Junger leaned back, clasped his hands, and crossed his legs at the ankles.

He looked at the plains.

*

The wagons carrying the Ten labored up Sunja's mountainside and entered the city by late morning. The drivers navigated the streets to the arena, splitting the crowds and avoiding locks with other wagons. In time, they reached the Gate of the Moon and unloaded their passengers. Clavellus eased himself to the stonework, grimacing as his feet touched the ground. Koba got out behind him and immediately strapped on a blade. A handful of guards, led by Clades, dropped to the streets and took up places around the taskmaster. Stiff from the morning's early rise and the long trip, the men stretched and groaned.

Civilians gathered outside the arena's high, majestic walls watched the Ten emerge from their wagons. The spectators noticed one man in particular and were quick to point him out to others.

Brozz saw them. "Perician," he called out quietly.

Junger turned, a question upon his face.

"You're attracting a crowd." Brozz indicated the onlookers.

That put the slightest frown upon the Perician until he saw Brozz spoke the truth.

The small gathering of onlookers was studying Junger with great interest. One woman waved.

A hesitant Junger waved back and faced the Sarlander. "Not something I was expecting."

"Enjoy it," Clavellus said, seeing the crowds. "While it's there. You'll miss it when it's gone. Like that morning air just before we entered the city."

"Let's move," Goll told them all. "Get below before the heat fries our tender hides." The house master glanced around and noted the people. "Seems we're gaining something of a reputation," he said, pleased with the recognition.

"Not us," Clavellus pointed out. "It's him."

Goll's features hardened. *Junger.* The people were fixating upon the Perician. That irked the Kree.

"Come on," Muluk said in Kree. "He's one of ours. Don't look like that."

"I'm not looking like that," Goll replied without emotion and walked toward the open gate. The rest of the Ten followed.

"The Perician fights this day!" someone yelled from the masses.

"Bring them hell, Perician!"

"Good fortune to you! You've made me some coin!"

"Crack some heads, man!"

"You're the best this season!"

"*Pull steel*, lad! Pull that steel, and do some *cutting*!"

On it went. The words of praise and encouragement drove Goll into the tunnel depths to escape. The others increased their pace to keep up.

"Slow yourself, Master Goll," Clavellus called after him. "Some of us don't walk as well as we used to."

"I've business to attend to," Goll replied, his words taking on a slight echo. "With the Madea."

That concerned the taskmaster and trainers. Muluk shared a look with Clavellus.

"He doesn't mean to have words with the man, does he?" the taskmaster asked.

"He does."

"Best you get after him. Tell him not to yell at the man too much."

"Why's that?"

Clavellus frowned. "Because the *Madea* is the last person you want hating you. If Goll pisses in the Madea's face, the man *will* remember it. Especially when he's scheduling our fights."

That hit Muluk hard, and it showed on his face.

"Perhaps we can have him removed, then?" he asked.

"The Madea?" Clavellus asked in surprise. "No one removes the Madea. He's the right arm of the Gladiatorial Chamber. *He* does the removing. In the Chamber's name. He'll make our lives miserable for the remainder of the games if Goll tears into him. Go on, now. Slow that Kree down. Take Clades with you. No one is going to bother us with the likes of Junger and Brozz and this one-eared brute standing over me."

Hearing his name, Clades stepped up alongside the Kree house master, and together they hurried after Goll.

"You think that'll make a difference?" Machlann asked, watching the men go.

Clavellus shook his head.

Passing through areas of torchlight where the odd sliver of straw or mouse bone decorated the floor, Goll, Muluk, and Clades smelled general quarters long before they arrived there. The stench of foul air and excrement slowed their pace as if they were wading through a knee-deep cesspool.

"Seddon above," Muluk swore, holding a hand to his mouth and nose. "Did someone die down here?"

"Someone probably did," Goll said. "The air never was good."

"But this . . ."

They entered the hive of activity that was general quarters. Lamp and torchlight cast long shadows and created wells of darkness. Outlines moved in those caves of brickwork and stone columns, passing through the shadows. Hundreds of pit fighters occupied the area, waiting for their time in the arena. A few warriors studied the new arrivals, sizing them up as potential opponents. Other gladiators walked unhurriedly across the Ten's path, fixing them with glares. Some men had their backs turned as they stood, legs spread, voiding into the designated shite and piss troughs.

Through the shifting tides of warrior flesh, Goll spied the familiar wall of Skarrs guarding the great desk and matchboard. The soldiers' armor gleamed in the meager light. The Madea was nowhere in sight.

"This is foul," Clades choked out, his hand covering his nose. "Worse than unfit. How'd you ever survive down here?"

"Watch for cow kisses," Muluk warned.

"And piss puddles," Goll muttered.

That unnerved the once Sujin, who immediately looked at his feet.

Goll studied the massive underground chamber. "Seems to be more here."

"There's more men here?" a horrified Muluk asked, looking around.

"Aye that," Goll confirmed. "Makes sense. The games will need the extra bodies. They'll have to come from somewhere. Unless they have an unlimited supply of meat in their dungeons."

One brute a full head taller than Muluk bumped into the Kree and staggered him. The larger man stared a sleepy warning before walking away, ignoring Muluk's annoyed expression. Before he could say anything, another figure caught his attention. From out of the gloomy soup of torchlight and shadow came the white-robed Madea, as imperious as ever, with four Skarrs surrounding his person. The guards escorted the arena official to his high desk, where the soldiers joined the others. The Madea stopped and paused, surveying the controlled chaos just beyond his station.

Goll started toward the arena official, but Muluk grabbed his shoulder.

"Remember what I said," the hairy Kree warned, referencing the conversation the two Krees had before descending beneath the Pit. "What Clavellus said."

Goll didn't comment. Muluk released his companion's arm, and together, the three men approached the Madea's desk. The older man spotted them right away and straightened warily, sensing a confrontation on the unpleasant-smelling air.

"What... do you want?" he asked with authoritative contempt.

"Do you remember me?" Goll asked in a hard voice, stopping before the Skarr fence. Muluk's jawline twitched upon hearing the question, and he knew right away his countryman wasn't about to heed Clavellus's warning.

"I do not," the Madea replied.

"I'm Goll. House master of the Ten. The newly formed House of Ten."

Pit fighters lurking nearby stopped and listened, also sensing confrontation.

"Ah, yes," the Madea replied softly as if remembering an old joke. "The Free Trained house."

That rankled Goll. "Free Trained no more, good Madea. We're a house. Paid for in gold and more than just a little blood. We've been formally recognized by the Gladiatorial Chamber itself, which means *you*, good Madea. So, please," the house master stressed, as if talking to an unfit temple slave, "address us properly."

The Madea didn't comment.

"Do you recognize us?" Goll demanded, looking past the stoic visors of the dozen Skarrs present.

What Goll didn't see, but what Muluk, Clades, and the Madea were fully aware of, were the dozens more Free Trained warriors paying attention to the conversation, drawing closer like vultures smelling meat on a battlefield. Torchlight revealed curiosity on scarred and dirty faces.

The Madea eyed them all, taking his time in replying. "I do."

He didn't sound as if he did at all, though. Nor did he offer an apology.

"Then, once more, good Madea," Goll cautioned, "use our right and proper name from this time forth. I'll take offense at anything less."

The man gave no indication of doing such a thing.

Goll stepped closer to the wall of armed men. "Now then, why weren't we informed of the recent changes to the games? And why weren't we informed of a meeting for houses and schools? We were in the city when all that happened."

The white-haired official showed no emotion. "I've no idea what you're talking about."

"You aren't aware the owners gathered before the Chamber to discuss the extended season? I find that hard to believe, Madea. What about the criminals being included in the games. You know about that, don't you? Every house and school met with the Chamber about the matter. Except us. Why weren't we notified?"

The man didn't bat an eye. "Messengers were dispatched," he replied with a cold calmness. "Perhaps they weren't aware of your house."

Goll glared. "Are you saying a messenger's responsible for that mistake?"

"Possibly."

"Is that all?"

"I suspect."

"'Possibly,' 'I suspect.' You're not well informed, are you, good Madea?"

Muluk winced.

Goll wasn't finished. "How is it, then, that other houses get their notices?"

The Madea paused for a heartbeat. "We send messengers bearing scrolls."

"To their residences?"

"No. Scrolls are delivered to their private chambers here at the arena, either given directly or left outside their door."

"We did not receive any such scrolls."

"Unfortunate," the Madea replied with that stoic calmness.

"He's not sorry in the least," slurred one of the pit fighters watching the scene. "I can smell the shite already."

"That's the Madea for you," muttered another unimpressed voice.

"We're all scroff to them anyway."

Others muttered agreement.

The arena official's face darkened at the grumbling.

"I expect a better effort in the future," Goll continued, his voice carrying. "From this day on . . . please . . . deliver everything to the Ten's chamber door. I don't wish to see you again, good Madea. I'm sure you don't wish to see *me* again. If I have any further issues with your management of the games, then I'll go straight to the Chamber. They let us into the games for a few coins. I'm sure they'll listen for a few coins more."

The Madea's stony exterior hardened a discernible fraction.

"Understood?" Goll leaned forward, and Muluk caught the subtle, dangerous tensing of the Skarrs, who had remained inanimate until that point.

The arena official glowered at the younger man. A dozen sword arms appeared poised to pull steel, and surprisingly, the surrounding pit fighters weren't quite ready to disperse. In fact, Muluk sensed that bloodshed was but a single word away.

Perhaps the Madea shared that same thought.

"Understood, Master Goll," the arena official said in weary voice, as if tired of being lectured. "From this day forth, you'll receive any and all notices at your door, or if you are not present, within your private chamber. Arrange it so one of your people checks on a regular basis. It'll be placed on a bench or such."

Goll wasn't finished. "Another thing."

Muluk's blossom clenched tight.

The Madea waited, his mouth becoming crooked with impatience.

"Since the season has been extended," Goll said, "and since my wounds have all healed, I find myself capable and willing to enter the games and resume fighting. Consider me active once again."

That caught the watching gladiators off guard. Heads turned.

"You're fighting?" the Madea asked with mild surprise, not disagreeable in the least.

That uneased Muluk.

"Aye that," Goll replied. "Any issue with that?"

The official struggled to suppress a smile. "None at all . . . none at all. It's just that . . . house masters usually don't fight in the Pit."

"That's because they're too old or too scared," Goll said.

"Or too smart," Muluk muttered.

That earned him a powerful glare from his countryman. Goll faced the arena official once again. "The Ten was born in torchlight, good Madea. Right here. This is where we first gathered, first met, and later recruited. I'll never forget that. Neither should you. But I was a gladiator first before I was a house master. I came to these games to fight. And fight I shall. I'll fight this day if you have a slot open."

The Madea's white eyebrows arched with interest. "Today?"

"Today."

"You'll fight this day?"

"If you have someone available."

The Madea's eyes widened, as if mildly insulted, then narrowed to black slits as he consulted his scrolls. The haste with which he studied his notes was not lost upon Muluk.

"Return to your quarters, Master Goll. I'll see what I can do. Remember, however," the official warned without looking up, though his scowl was evident, "*you* asked to return this day."

"I'll remember," Goll said. He turned and marched toward the white tunnel.

Any Free Trained in his way quickly moved out of his path.

Muluk looked from the Madea to Goll's retreating form and then back to the Madea once again before hurrying after his countryman. Clades followed a beat later.

A baleful Madea watched them go. When they were out of sight, he considered his charts and notes. The official turned and consulted the match board on the wall behind him, searching for names. A distinct dislike for the one called Goll grew within his breast.

The Kree wanted a fight.

Seddon above, the Madea would give him one.

"Saimon's black hanging fruit," Muluk whispered as he caught up to Goll. "I thought the man was going to unleash his dogs upon us back there."

"With all those pit fighters around us?" Goll asked. "He'd do no such thing. Besides, we're in the right. You saw him. In his eyes, we're not a house. But that's going to change."

Muluk wisely kept his mouth shut.

"You see how he looked when I asked for a match this day?" Goll asked.

"I did. He damn near pissed himself."

"I'm going to fight today."

"What's that?"

"You heard me," Goll said as they walked along a familiar stretch of brickwork. "I'll be fighting. That man will make *certain* I'm fighting, even if he has to hobble some unfit bastard to do it. And I'll wager coin that I'll be facing a Free Trained lout eager to claim Dark Curge's bounty."

In the torchlit glow of the white tunnel, Muluk quieted with worry.

They soon reached their decidedly crowded chamber, and Goll glanced around at the familiar faces. "No Borchus?" he asked.

Clavellus shook his head.

"The man's a ghost."

"He'd be here if he could," Clavellus said. "Don't worry about him. What about the Madea, now?"

Goll retold the conversation. Muluk stood nearby to emphasize parts with nods or disbelieving shakes of his head. When Goll finished, Clavellus looked at Machlann, standing near the window.

"What do you think?" the taskmaster asked.

The trainer smirked. "I think Master Goll has picked himself a fight."

35

The day's first matches were painful to watch.

The criminals weren't the trained professionals of houses. Even the Free Trained displayed a better degree of skill than the gurry released into the arena. The sun was particularly intense, as if the day wished to scorch away the unpleasant stains left by the condemned men. The highlight of the afternoon was a match between a Jackal and a Sunjan Lancer that had been branded a deserter. The horseman was no slouch with a blade and took the fight to the Jackal, but the Nordish man, all quickness and sinew, weathered an early storm of steel before wounding his opponent. He then continually nicked the Lancer, taking his time and bleeding the man with a cut to the forearm or the thigh or even a quick lick of steel to the cheek.

The match ended with the Jackal stabbing the Lancer through the midsection, hard enough to lift the Sunjan off his feet.

From where they watched in their private chamber, Clavellus patted the sill of the arched window. "No surprise there," he said dourly. "That Jackal might've been imprisoned for a few months, but there was no weakness with a blade."

"Should've given the Lancer a horse," Machlann remarked.

"Would it have made a difference?"

The trainer grimaced. "Jackal would've only killed the animal as well, I daresay."

"Daresay."

With the fifth fight consisting of another pairing of prisoners, Clavellus sighed and turned away from the window. He regarded Goll first and then Brozz. The tall Sarlander stood with his head down, mentally preparing himself for his moment in the Pit. The leather vest he usually wore had been laced in front, covering his wounds. The helmet had been painful for the man to fit over his broken nose, which could be seen through the face cage. A set of metal gauntlets covered his hands, the knuckles spiked. The necklace of crow heads hung around his neck, each one threaded through the eye and screaming because of it.

From a distance, the man they called Crowhead looked no different than he had any other day.

Up close, however, he was unfit.

"You look even more the fright with all those cuts and bruises," the taskmaster remarked.

Brozz didn't respond, his profile solemn.

"Are you ready?" Clavellus asked.

The Sarlander nodded.

Clavellus lifted his head as if smelling blood. "He's fighting for Curge now, so no holding back. He'll be looking to make an example of you."

A smile flickered across Brozz's battered face. "Don't worry, Master Clavellus. I never really liked that Sunjan."

The taskmaster smiled at that.

"Pitiful," Curge said, shaking his head at the poor display he'd just witnessed.

"You think your lad will do better?" Nexus challenged.

Curge didn't answer, mainly because he had his doubts. He ignored both other men, who sat on either side of him. Unfortunately, he'd been the one arriving late at the games that day, which resulted in the new seating order. The arrangement didn't surprise him. While Gastillo had made attempts to engage the wine merchant over the past couple of days, Nexus kept his comments curt, not interested in the least with talking to the other owner, and even leaving the games early, almost with theatrical timing.

Children, Curge had decided.

"How did you manage to get a fight against the Ten so quickly?" Nexus asked with his usual unpleasantness. "With the very one who deserted them?"

Curge scoffed with a shake of his head, not dignifying that question with an answer. "I'm curious, myself, good Nexus. Are you two still at odds today? Or will the ice finally melt?"

"We're not at odds," Nexus snapped. "And it's none of your concern."

"All right. Other matters, then. Has anyone discovered anything about the Perician called Junger? My eyes and ears have not."

That was the one topic that was decidedly safe to discuss. As expected, the question drew the two punces into a conversation.

"Nothing," Gastillo said though his mask was focused upon the arena. "My spies have found nothing."

"As mine," Nexus grumped, his attention also on the bright sands. "The man's a ghost. A ghost without a history."

"Pericia's a four-day journey," Gastillo noted. "And it's a large parcel of territory that just happens to be a country. I didn't send anyone that far. If we don't know anything by now, chances are we're not going to."

"A near-perfect mystery," Curge observed.

"He has a past," Nexus said with a sneer. "He has one. Somewhere, someone knows him. Knows something about him. The challenge is finding that person before the season finishes."

"With him in the final eight."

Truth be known, if no one could discover the man's past, Junger would be in the champion's match, and Curge couldn't think of a man who might defeat him.

*

Away from the owners discussing the puzzling Junger, in the private chambers of Dark Curge, where his gladiators waited for their call, the man called Baris, who held the title of both taskmaster and trainer, stopped before the tall, muscular bulk of Sapo. Baris was squat and thick necked, with the stomped-on face of a pug, but his mind was as sharp as a rack of polished spears. He inspected Sapo one last time.

The big Sunjan had been a challenge, as the taskmaster had discussed with Dark Curge. Sapo had been getting by on sheer power alone, and he didn't apply himself in learning the skills, techniques, and combinations needed to be a true gladiator. Baris advised Curge he'd need a full year to drill the first month of basic instruction into the man's head. Curge, however, had ordered him to make do.

So Baris made do.

Sapo stood with a huge helm already in place, transforming his skull into a spiked barrel. Grillwork covered the mouth area, allowing the man plenty of air for those big lungs. Preparing decent armor for Sapo had been a challenge for the house armorers. The end result was both frightening and impressive. A leather vest covered Sapo's torso while a high collar protected his corded neck. The usual greaves and bracers adorned his limbs. Heavy gauntlets spiked with nails adorned his hands.

The axe completed the nightmare.

Huge and double bladed, well balanced and also sporting a spiked head, the weapon looked like something wielded by a death god. Sapo's biceps bulged as he hefted that frightening chopper. With just the right amount of muscular flesh showing to intimidate, Sapo cut a terrifying figure, and he knew it.

Still, Baris knew appearances were only part of the battle, especially in Sapo's case.

"Are you ready?" he asked.

"I am," Sapo said, mouth and eyes hidden by the helmet.

"What are you going to do out there?"

"Kill a man."

"How long will it take you?"

"Two cuts only."

"And what are you to bring to Curge?"

"The dog's head."

Scowling, Baris stood in Sapo's shadow and didn't budge, sizing up the gladiator's killer bulk. As good as expected, he supposed, but at least the lad's thinking was in the right place.

"Go on then," Baris said, "and butcher me a cow."

Behind the grill, Sapo allowed himself a smile.

"You're with the Ten, aren't you?" the gatekeeper asked Brozz as the gladiator stood and waited for the portcullis to rise.

The Sarlander nodded.

"I remember you," the old man said. "You look good. Good."

Brozz didn't feel good. Stitches strained and pulled with every step, threatening to burst. He didn't think he could swing his weapons without ripping himself apart. His face and jaw ached dearly, and when he could draw a breath through his smashed nose, all he could smell was sour onions. Shan had smeared that healing salve all over Brozz's person.

"Word is you're fighting the one who left your house?" the gatekeeper asked.

Brozz nodded.

"Unfortunate I won't be able to watch," the old man said in disappointment. "Blood's bound to fly in this one." With that, the gatekeeper yanked down hard on a nearby lever.

As the portcullis cranked upward, Brozz supposed blood would indeed fly.

He hoped it was Sapo's.

The stairs were a chore, but he managed to climb them, feeling the stitches move underneath his armor, keeping him together. He entered the arena to lukewarm applause and more than a few curses. The Orator prattled on with introductions, but Brozz paid little heed to those.

Across the way, Sapo emerged from the shadowy maw of his entrance. The Sunjan had found someone to stitch together a proper suit of leather for him. *How fortunate*, Brozz thought wearily. Few men stood eye to eye with the Sarlander. Even fewer were bigger. Sapo was only a finger or two shorter and outweighed the Sarlander by perhaps the weight of an entire man, most of it muscle.

The Sunjan was huge and swinging a battle-axe designed to turn a man's bowels to watery scutters.

"*Begin!*" the Orator finally shouted.

Brozz tuned out all distractions, and the screaming crowds became a low buzz in his ears. He clenched his short sword and hand axe and went forth. Sapo's bulk seemed to enlarge with every step. As they closed the space between them, Brozz detected the smile behind his foe's protective grill.

"You're the first," Sapo said when he was about five paces away. "Maggot."

The battle-axe flashed in the sun, a flat cut meant to slice a man in half, swung with brutal intent. The force of the blow would have taken down a tree if it had connected.

Brozz yanked himself back, avoiding the edge by a finger's width. His sewed-together skin stretched and strained.

With dramatic grunts, Sapo chopped and swung three more times in a surprising combination that had Brozz ducking and weaving. The mighty Sunjan hacked at an arm and a neck, then attempted to split Brozz's helm right down to the jaw.

All missed.

The Sarlander avoided the blows rather than parrying, well aware that deflecting Sapo's heavier blade would only rip his own weapons from his hands, perhaps even breaking his wrists in the process.

The Sarlander backpedaled, and Sapo charged, grunting with every swing. The Sunjan sliced at an arm then a knee, and when Brozz jerked his leg away, Sapo quickly recovered from the arc of the falling blow and stabbed with the axe spike.

The point pierced Brozz's leather with an alarming prick of pain, stabbing skin and the wall of muscle covering his stomach. The crowd roared at the connection, some even jumping to their feet and shaking fists.

Brozz jerked himself off the dreaded spike, knocking the weapon away, unfortunate enough to see a bloody line spewing from the hole. Sapo reset and swung for Brozz's head once again. The Sarlander ducked, but when he straightened, his wounded midsection flared in agony.

Sapo slashed at Brozz's left side, but the Ten man deflected the blow off his hand axe. When the two blades collided, the heavier steel ripped the smaller from Brozz's hand. The contact brought Sapo in close, and he punched his foe's head. Three times he struck—short, powerful blows punctuated with hateful barks of breath and the crinkle and *skraw* of spikes on helmet. The armor absorbed a terrible pounding. Metal dimpled and dented. The stitches holding Brozz's cheek together burst, spitting blood and revealing pink meat.

Dazed and desperate, Brozz shoved the bigger man away and stabbed, sliding a length of steel along Sapo's own profile. The connection startled the Sunjan, who broke away, one hand going to his neck. A quick inspection later, Sapo nodded at his opponent.

Brozz stayed behind a wary guard, pointing his sword at the pit fighter stalking him. His midsection screamed at him. He pressed it and drew away a palm wet and slick. A fire had started down there, burning away his strength. His limbs became heavy.

"You're the first." Sapo leered through his grill, teeth glistening. He hunched over, bobbing his axe left and right, up and down, with the odd thrust that kept Brozz guessing. "You're the first," Sapo repeated. "The first, Brozz. The firs—"

The axe's spiked head stabbed for Brozz's gut.

Suffering as he was, the Sarlander parried instead of dodging, bringing his blade across while twisting at the hips, attempting to sweep the axe away to his left. With a *clang*, the weapons locked and Sapo yanked back with all his might.

The short sword flew over the Sunjan's shoulder.

Brozz stood without weapons.

"You're the first, Sarlander, and you know what that means?" Sapo taunted from behind his upraised axe, which moved side to side before jabbing. "It means I'll split you down the middle. And when I'm done with that, I'll finish off the Perician and any other that pig bastard Machlann might've trained. I mean to split each and every—"

Brozz lunged.

Sapo had committed a grievous error, talking when he should have been swinging, all while Brozz was eyeing the timing of the battle-axe. When Sapo jabbed, the man called Crowhead lashed out with a metal-clad fist, slamming a set of spiked knuckles squarely into his opponent's grill.

Destroying the smile behind it.

The impact took Sapo off his feet, and he landed flat on his back to the collective *OHHH* of the crowds.

Amazingly, Sapo kept a hold of the battle-axe.

Brozz spotted his own hand axe two strides away as Sapo crunched his stomach, pulling himself up into a sitting position. Dark eyes focused on the Sarlander while a dented grill squashed Sapo's mouth into a messy pulp of lips and shattered teeth.

The Sunjan struggled to rise.

Brozz dropped upon the fallen man, punching that ruined helmet a second time, driving his opponent into the sands. Brozz mounted the Sunjan's midsection, putting a knee into the valley of the man's elbow, trapping the weapon arm.

Then he rained spiked fists onto Sapo's helmet. The big man bucked and lurched, attempting to rise, absorbing horrific damage.

In short time, he stopped moving.

The surrounding sands became blinding fire, and the crowds' screams crackled with heat and fury, cursing Brozz for attacking a dead man.

At some point, Brozz paused and took stock of what he was doing. Through the sunken eye slits, Sapo's eyes flickered and squinted against the blood flowing into them. Gasps of air sprayed droplets of matter through the ruined grill. The sight stayed Brozz's poised fist. Just then, dazed and bleeding and far from defending himself, Sapo didn't look like Sapo anymore. Sapo looked like a young father, one of many Brozz had been ordered to execute in the Sarland foothills, upon the command of the Grand Vir. The man's wife and two daughters had already been killed by other Gorsha, the unit in which Brozz served.

The resemblance between Sapo and that long-dead farmer took all the fight out of the Sarlander, and he lowered his fist. Leaving a man like Sapo alive would be a mistake. Brozz knew that to his core.

Brozz had no intention of killing him, though—not this day, and certainly not this way.

Gasping, his wounds burning, Brozz slowly stood and ignored the vocal crowd. He spotted the arched window of the Ten's private room. He wavered, just a little about the shoulders, and gave a solemn nod.

The faces there lifted hands, indicating the message received.

Taking his time and growing ever aware of his hurts, both new and old, Brozz picked up his weapons.

To a mixture of praise and stinging hatred, he walked to his gate, leaving Sapo's twitching husk behind him.

"Oh, how unfortunate, good Curge," Nexus said with feigned sympathy so thick it offended Curge much more than the fight's ending. "So sorry to see one of your men fall to the Ten. So very sorry."

The yelling crowds prevented Curge from answering immediately.

When he did, however, he did so with a smile. "He wasn't one of mine, good Nexus. He was one of *theirs*. One of mine would not have made the mistakes he did. So don't you worry about this fight. The season's long, and I'll have another chance at killing that tall hellion staggering off the field. One of my seasoned hellpups will shove a length of steel up his dog blossom and set him squealing."

At that point, Curge regarded the wine merchant with a contemplative look. "But I'm curious. Does your face hurt when you tighten it like that?"

Back in the Ten's private chamber, Koba and Muluk led their returning gladiator inside, to a waiting bench. Wounded and drained, Brozz sat down heavily and leaned against a wall. With medicinal materials nearby and waiting, Shan pulled the battered helmet from the gladiator's head, grimacing at the sight underneath. Muluk helped, attempting to free the Sarlander from his punctured armor and the crow necklace. The rest of the House hovered nearby, ready if needed.

"Get me those bandages," Shan instructed as he produced a knife and cut through the knots lacing the leather vest. When the armor came free, blood spattered the floor.

The stitches across Brozz's chest had split apart at some point, in addition to the sewing of his cheek. Two ghastly red mouths parted and dribbled wine, but the most disturbing was the puncture wound in his gut.

"More bandages," Shan told Muluk, who nodded his hairy head and complied. The healer took the thick compresses and pressed them to Brozz's belly and upper chest.

The gladiator sighed at the contact. Blood reached the floor. Shan had Muluk maintain pressure on the bandages before applying another cloth wad to the Sarlander's cheek. The aged healer worked quickly, surely, sneaking peeks at the hole in the Sarlander's midsection.

"Might have cut some of the muscle there," Shan said as he worked. "I'm not sure how serious. Does it hurt?"

Brozz nodded.

"Lean back, then. Sit still."

The taskmaster loomed, appearing over the hunched forms of Shan and Muluk.

"You did very well, Brozz," Clavellus said. "You did very well."

Goll chewed upon the inside of a cheek and met the eyes of the taskmaster. Brozz had done very well indeed, but he knew sparing Sapo might have consequences. Though the Kree wished Sapo dead, he had to admit he was grateful that the House of Curge would not be pursuing vengeance—or so he hoped.

"You put that punce down," Muluk gushed, smiling in Brozz's face as the bandages slowly turned scarlet. Muluk then frowned at Goll, urging him to speak.

"You did well," Goll finally said, wondering if Brozz's season had just finished.

36

The next two fights were between the lesser houses.

Morric of the School of Vorish was soundly defeated by the Balgothan Sorban, from the Stable of Slavol. Then a gladiator called Korzo, from the House of Razi, punished Ithas, from the House of Tilo. Korzo hurt his opponent badly enough that the man had to be carried to a healer.

"Season's over for that one," Machlann commented grimly.

"Fortunate he's still breathing," Clavellus added, glancing back at an uncomfortable-looking Brozz.

Shan had trussed the man up in fresh stitches and bandages during the matches while Koba brought in a bucket of water to clean up both flesh and blood. Brozz looked less of a mess at the moment, but the taskmaster wondered if the gladiator would be able to continue fighting.

A knock at the door interrupted Clavellus's thoughts. He glanced at Junger, who stood without a helm or armor, his chest bare. Clutching a sword still in its scabbard, he nodded he was ready.

"Do what you do," Clavellus said.

Unconcerned, Junger walked to the door, passing Brozz. He stopped and patted the Sarlander on the shoulder, getting a faint smile from him.

"Make them scream, lad," Machlann said.

Clades opened the door to allow Junger passage, revealing an arena attendant standing there.

"A message for Master Goll," the attendant said.

"Yes?" Goll asked.

"You'll fight after Junger and Brontus. You'll face a Free Trained called Sarvil."

Outside the arched window, the audience's rumbling voices rose upon some unseen signal.

Goll didn't seem to notice. "I'll be ready."

The attendant looked at Junger. "It's time."

"I was already on my way."

The attendant frowned, perhaps thinking that if all gladiators did such a thing, he might very well be out of work.

Junger departed among a second round of well-wishes.

"So," Clavellus said to Goll, "you have your fight. Seems the Madea took a liking to you."

"Or he despises you," Muluk suggested.

Goll ignored that. "I'm just glad to fight."

"A Free Trained," Machlann pointed out. "Not a house gladiator."

"The Madea might not have even troubled them," the taskmaster thought aloud. "No matter. Put down this Free Trained, and you'll get all the attention you want from the houses."

With grim concentration, Goll crouched near a cloth sack and started pulling out slabs of armor.

When Junger stepped into the day, the crowds remembered him.

They cheered his name. Women tried to capture his attention. The Perician lifted a hand to acknowledge them all, and the very world trembled at the resulting blast of sound. Junger didn't think much of the noise, but he admitted with a flicker of guilt he was enjoying himself far more than he thought he should be. He looked above the multitudes of people, above the heat-shielding tarps and the towering brickwork of the arena. Thin clouds stretched across the deep blue, heading south. Perhaps he'd go south one day.

One day.

The Orator delivered his speech of theatrics. Junger didn't listen to it. The sun baked his skin, drawing sweat, and on some unseen signal, almost mystically, he turned and faced his opponent standing at the arena's far side. The Orator introduced the warrior called Brontus, from the House of Ustda, and the name received a fair share of cheers, enough to let Junger know the man had a reputation of sorts.

Brontus chose to ignore the Orator's prattling and walked to the center of the arena.

Junger went to meet him.

"Greetings," the larger man said, dipping a helm. The headpiece had a chain-mail beard attached to the visor's lower portion. The mesh encircled the neck, granting some measure of protection.

"Greetings," Junger answered, appreciating the height of his adversary. "You're a tall one."

"They tell me that. This to the death?"

"I don't believe so."

Brontus made no move to lift his own mace and shield. The man was not only tall but also thick, with a layer of fat coating a powerful frame. He wore leather, complete with a crenellated skirt. Greaves ended at spiked knees. Light glinted within the helmet's dark eyeholes.

"Good," Brontus responded, tipping his helm in approval. "You've done well thus far, good Junger. The crowds favor you, the likes I haven't seen or heard of in a very long time, truth be known."

That didn't really surprise Junger. "Thus far. I've been fortunate. It could all change any moment."

"I mean to test you," Brontus informed him stoically. "See if what they say is true."

Junger thought about that. "It probably is true."

"Ha!" the helm barked. "No pride there, eh? I'd say more, but there's not a mark on you. Dying Seddon, man. Your hide's as fair and untouched as a babe's cheeks."

Junger smiled, a touch sadly.

"Come on then, Ten man." Brontus nodded. "You've come this far. Let's see you pull that steel."

"I haven't yet."

That puzzled the big gladiator. "And what's the reason for that?"

"Hasn't been a need."

Brontus stared down at the smaller man. "No need? *Ha*. Some might think that's the height of arrogance, Junger of Ten."

The larger man extended his long-shafted mace, the spikes dull in the light. "Best we get on with it. The crowds grow impatient."

Junger lifted his sheathed sword and tapped the offered mace. "Well met, good Brontus."

"Well met, good Junger."

Then the big man attacked, breaking into a frenzied combination of mace swings and shield strikes. The house gladiator moved swiftly despite his size, and Junger figured that when one faced a wall crashing down, getting out of its way made good sense.

Junger dodged and ducked, slipping through the strikes like a sandfly buzzing through raindrops.

Nothing touched the Perician.

Nothing came close.

After that short but intense barrage, Brontus broke away to catch his breath, keeping the Perician in front of him.

Surprisingly, Junger didn't attack—didn't leap into a dazzling cross cut or lunge into a brilliant thrust to the heart or jaw.

"Tired, are you?" Brontus asked, shuffling to the right.

"You're a skilled fighter," Junger told him and very much meant it.

The big man chuckled . . . before he lunged, attempting to knock Junger's head from his shoulders.

The Perician bobbed, passed on the opportunity to counter, and backed well away. Brontus pursued, heaving all his considerable strength into a series of attacks. He swung his mace at his foe like a prickly comet, aiming for the head, a shoulder, the head again, then a leg.

Junger evaded everything.

At times, the Perician made his opponent appear far too slow, as if he exactly knew the pit fighter's every move, every thought. Several times, he backed away from a combination of strikes, rendering the outburst ineffective and leaving the audience marveling in disbelief.

A gladiator of note was attacking the Ten man—a Free Trained warrior—and could not touch him. Couldn't come *close* to hitting him.

More than anyone else in the Pit, that lack of contact frustrated Brontus.

The sun roasted the big man. Sweat flowed due to his concentrated efforts. Brontus gathered himself and peered over his shield's edge at his elusive adversary, upset at his lack of success yet every bit as amazed as the spectators.

"Time to end this, good Junger," Brontus huffed. "It's becoming too hot."

His guard raised and unwavering, Junger checked on the sun and nodded agreement. It was becoming too hot.

As Brontus swung his mace, Junger shot forward with a speed impossible and jabbed his foe squarely in the abdomen, catching him above the belt line. The house gladiator buckled like a door smashed by a battering ram. Brontus crumpled, dropping everything. His head touched sand. Struggling for breath, he clawed his helm free and, red-faced, cradled his lower half.

Perceiving the match all but over, Junger knelt beside him, gently rolled him onto his back, and dropped a knee onto the big man's chest. He extracted a hand's length of steel from his scabbard and held it to the fallen gladiator's throat.

ABOUT THE BLOOD

A gasping Brontus nodded his intention to yield.

The crowds erupted with mad delight.

Junger leaned in close to the defeated gladiator and placed a hand to the man's face. "You rest for a few days, good Brontus," he advised. "You fought well. Remember that. You'll do well in these games of blood."

The stricken Brontus couldn't speak, but his brow scrunched in confusion.

Junger patted his adversary's head, stood, and backed away from the fallen man.

Once he was safely clear, he lifted a hand in victory.

The cheering tripled in intensity.

In the crowds, an old man's eyes widened in disbelief, and his heart banged against his ribs. He'd lived upon the world's back for a good seventy-eight winters, and every day he doubted he'd see another, but his memory was still as sharp as the edge of a pit fighter's blade. He'd attended the day's games at the urging of his oldest son, who knew his father enjoyed the blood sport. His son was next to him as everyone around them cheered and chanted for the one called Junger.

Junger.

He covered his mouth with a shaking hand, but he didn't doubt his memory in the least.

He'd seen a man move like that before, fighting dozens more and cutting them up with damn-near sorcerous ease, making whole packs of killers appear sick with age. The man called Junger strolled the arena sands, enjoying the crowd's attention, and Seddon above, Junger even *walked* the same, the carefree stroll of one without a fear in the world.

Then the old man saw the Perician's face.

His knees trembled, and his legs went numb.

It was impossible.

The old man would always remember the face as clearly as the sun in the sky. He *had* to remember it since it was a face that had saved him and his village years before, saved the lives of his mother, father, and sisters, even. Such a memory had been etched into the back of his mind, even visiting him in his dreams, where the deepest sleep led him over the glowing pastures of his youth, where the sky was the happiest blue and he was still a boy filled with wonder.

He remembered that face.

And that face was Junger's.

But the old man had to be wrong. He *had* to be.

That man—Junger's twin—who had saved so many lives back then, could not have been older than twenty-nine. Perhaps thirty.

The old man had only been seven when he first saw him—a stranger then, but two weeks later, a stranger no more. Junger's twin had even smiled at him once and shaken his shoulder. At that time, that swordsman had become a right and proper hero.

That had been seventy-one years before.

And the hero's name was Arco.

37

When Junger finally left the field, Goll turned away from the window's arch and slapped on his helmet.

"Anxious, aren't you?" Muluk asked.

"I am."

"Wait for the man to get back, at least," Clavellus said, distracted by the spectacle outside.

"He knows the way," Goll said.

"That's not what I meant," the taskmaster said, lowering his voice. "A few words of congratulations will be good for him to hear. Besides, the attendants need to groom the sands for the next fight. It won't take long."

Goll reluctantly decided to wait, but he didn't think Junger needed to hear any such congratulations from him. Goll looked at Brozz, who sat with mottled bandages applied to his person, appearing as though he'd just fallen off a mountaintop. A concerned Shan hovered nearby, dabbing cloth and sewing skin together.

When Junger returned, everyone else congratulated him. Koba slapped the man on the shoulder, and even Brozz managed a weak smile.

"A fine display," Clavellus told the Perician. "You moved like a fly waved off a cow kiss."

Goll, however, did not lavish such praise upon Junger, sensing something strange about the man.

In short time, the attendants knocked at the door, summoning the waiting house master.

"Well done," Goll said as he walked past Junger.

That was all.

He wanted to add, *"and now watch how a real warrior fights,"* but truth be known, claws of nervous energy were digging themselves into the Kree's spine and limbs. He believed nearly two months had passed since that first time in the arena, sixty days since he'd killed the man who'd all but defeated him upon the sands and then spared him. The Kree gladiator had trained nearly all of his adult life to reach the games, convinced he was the best, and upon his first fight, he'd nearly died. Baylus had embarrassed, shamed, and humbled him.

Yet there Goll was, about to enter the arena once again.

He wouldn't be bested a second time, he wouldn't underestimate the opposition, and he wouldn't forget killing Baylus the Butcher in one merciless act born of anger, the one man who had defeated him.

In Junger, Goll saw the potential to lose once again.

And truth be known, it uneased him.

With sweat beading upon his brow, Qualtus wasn't happy in the least to announce the day's final fight. The last few matches had been astounding, with the Perician once again stealing the attention of the Pit. That put a smile on the old orator's face. He imagined more than one owner was watching and damn near pissing themselves.

Junger was a spectacle to behold, and Qualtus doubted anyone in the games could challenge the Perician gladiator.

He read his scroll, and his mood brightened . . . to a point.

"Women and men of the Pit, we have one last conflict to witness upon the arena floor. A ghost has returned from the past, good people. A ghost who had nearly died at the beginning of this deadly season. Trained by the venerable Weapon

Masters of Kree, this man faced a much admired butcher upon his opening day and lived to speak of it though the encounter nearly killed him. Badly wounded, his season was finished. He has a second chance this day, however, and he's able to fight again. Healed and eager to once again pursue that coveted crown sought by all, and this time as a member of his own house, I present to you . . . the slayer of Baylus the Butcher, *Goll* . . . of the House of *Ten*."

Within the private viewing chambers of the Stable of Slavol, Salwark, son of Vavar Slavol, blinked and swallowed in mute shock upon hearing the name. His throat visibly worked, and he gripped his chin in nervous thought. Since having taken over duties from his stricken father, Salwark struggled with talking to his gladiators. He knew he didn't have the gift of speech his father possessed, but he tried, despite that painful awkwardness.

This revelation, however, was something else entirely, completely beyond Salwark's abilities. He wondered how he was going to tell his pit fighter that the man who'd killed an old friend had returned to the games. He turned away from the window and met the eyes of the one Balgothan who had, upon learning of Baylus's death, sworn vengeance upon the killer—a vengeance denied since the gladiator had disappeared from the games.

This day, though, Goll had returned.

Staring at the Balgothan, Salwark realized he wouldn't have to say a word. Sorban had heard Goll's name, had heard the glowing introduction of the Orator. A hateful intensity colored his face. He glowered for one long heartbeat before joining Salwark at the window.

The angry heat radiating from the man caused the owner's son to step back.

The sun was bad enough.

"Not many would dare face this killer of champions," the Orator continued, "but we have found a man. A pit fighter willing to face him in the arena. A man seeking to carve out a name for himself at these games. He is a mauler amongst the Free Trained ranks, on the very cusp of greatness. He knows no fear and possesses a very bloody set of skills, as demonstrated by his last two victories. I give you . . . *Savril of Marrn*."

The man called Savril lifted his arms and turned in a slow circle, embracing the crowds as they cheered his name. Goll noted they hadn't cheered *his* name, but that was because they'd forgotten him. He'd make them remember.

"Begin!" the Orator shouted.

Savril immediately walked toward Goll. The man wasn't as tall as the Kree, nor did he appear overly strong of limb. Spiked bracers protected his forearms while his biceps were bare. A poor leather vest covered his torso. Savril didn't bother with a helmet, preferring to let the wind blow over his shorn crown. The man possessed a low brow squatting over a set of intense gray eyes.

He carried a shield and sword, the weapon curved and sharp.

Goll went to him. He didn't offer greetings. He didn't say anything at all.

The Kree pulled back his blade as if about to stab straight from the shoulder while his shield flashed ahead, the edge aimed for Savril's eyes. Savril barely deflected the unexpected attack with his own shield. He then parried the sword thrust meant for his chest and then the other aimed at his head.

He twisted away, placing his shield between him and his attacker.

Goll followed, swinging as he went. The Kree's sword crashed against his opponent's shield, then Goll was jumping back, parrying three savage countercuts meant to open his neck or head. Each connection tinkled over the arena sands.

They separated and circled, studying each other for weakness.

"Perhaps if I kill you," Savril said, "they'll take me into the House of Ten?"

Goll attacked, a succession of deadly jabs and slashes. Savril parried the first before avoiding the others, taking a shot to the shield as he parted.

ABOUT THE BLOOD

Goll did not pursue.

"Too slow, Kree!" Savril mocked and charged. He chopped for a shoulder, which Goll darted away from. Savril waded in, looking to lop off limbs, grunting as if every strike could fell a tree.

Goll evaded every attempt, cringing at times, but fluid and sure on his feet. He stepped outside of Savril's range, taking a few heartbeats to study the man.

"I'm going to butcher the topper who butchered Baylus," Savril panted from behind his shield, his eyes just visible. "Going to take that head from your shoulders and nail it to the arena wall."

Goll lunged.

Savril stopped the attack flat upon his shield. They grappled, trying to establish dominance over the other and became snared in an uneven dance. Goll stomped for toes and missed. Savril cracked his shield's edge across Goll's cheek, raking his visor before crashing the barrier downward and narrowly missed a knee.

They broke free of one another.

"You killed Baylus the Butcher?" Savril jeered. "How did you manage that? The man must've been pickled."

Breathing hard, Goll peered over his shield, sword poised and ready, and stalked his foe, closing the distance. He'd had his fill of Savril's voice and waited for the man's shield to drop just a finger. Just a sliver below his chin. That was all the Kree needed.

"Pickled," Savril shook his head. "You're going to d—"

Goll lunged and slashed. A line of red erupted across Savril's throat, and his words became a mangled hiss. The pit fighter's face paled in a heartbeat, and he dropped his sword and shield. He grabbed for his neck as his life sprayed from between fingers.

By the time he fell to his knees, Goll was already walking back to his portcullis.

Having seen the house master in action for the first time in the Pit, Clavellus cocked an eyebrow and exchanged looks with his trainers.

"Imagine that," Muluk said as Goll marched off the sands. "We have another hellion amongst us."

Clavellus liked that idea.

The games needed more hellions.

38

Goll walked back to the Ten's chambers, looking for the house's familiar door. The victory had lifted his spirits immensely though he appeared calm, if not winded. He'd sustained a bruise or two, but nothing serious. Sweat saturated the cloth under his leather vest, and Goll cringed at being unable to bathe until he returned to the villa.

His thoughts returned to the fight just won.

Damnation, he thought. *That* was the start he should've had at the very beginning of the games.

Just then, a shadow led a man along the torchlit tunnel. He slowed to a stop and regarded Goll. He wore armor—a leather vest—and a full scabbard hanging from his waist. The stranger had his hair pulled back into a war braid that hung over a shoulder, reminding Goll of the missing Pig Knot.

"Goll of Kree," the man called in a deep voice. "Weapon Master. House of Ten."

Goll stopped not twenty paces from the individual, with the Ten's chamber door roughly at the midway mark. "Who are you?"

"An impressive return," the man said, ignoring the question. His eyes, extremely angry eyes, warned the Kree of some unknown danger. "But not so much when one realizes you killed a Free Trained. Of course, you know all about them, don't you?"

Goll placed him as a gladiator, older than most others within the games. "I don't know you."

"You knew Baylus the Butcher."

A jagged spear of ice went through the Kree then, but he kept his expression blank. "What of him?"

"He was Balgothan. As I am."

Goll gripped his blade's pommel and kept his hand there.

"And he was my friend," the man finished.

"So?"

That brought a skull smile from the gladiator. "I expect nothing less from the likes of you."

"What's this about?" Goll demanded.

The Ten's door opened, and Muluk eased into view. Koba and Junger followed, taking in the newcomer. The Balgothan gladiator ignored all three, keeping his eyes upon Goll as if the Kree might disappear.

"Revenge, Goll," the man announced. "In Balgotha, we take revenge very seriously. You killed my friend. I'll kill you. In the arena. Before the whole world. I'll cut your heart from your chest. If you're fortunate, and I know you are as you bested Baylus, you'll die quickly. Without much pain. Before you hear the snapping of your ribs."

The threat left Goll speechless, his mind clawing for traction. "I . . . didn't mean to kill Baylus."

The Balgothan's stony stare didn't relent, as if he hadn't heard, but then he glanced a warning at the men emerging from the Ten's chamber. Goll became aware of footsteps approaching him from behind. A complement of Skarrs arrived to ensure peace was kept.

"I'm called Sorban," the man declared, his hand tightening on his sword's hilt. "And I'm pleased this day. Because I've found my friend's killer, and when I cut your heart out, I hope he'll be there, to throw you into the dark."

More gladiators and armed men appeared behind Sorban.

"Don't disappear again," the Balgothan warned, pointing a finger at Goll.

His message delivered, Sorban turned away from the gathering crowd and parted the onlookers at his back. Some of the pit fighters followed while others stood their ground, quietly hostile toward the Ten.

Muluk looked from Sorban's departing person to Goll.

Both Krees were at a loss.

After the Skarrs and scowling gladiators dispersed without incident, the Ten regrouped behind a closed door.

"His name's Sorban," Goll stoically informed his companions.

"Sorban?" Clavellus repeated and scowled. "This is why we need Borchus."

"Doesn't matter about Borchus," Muluk said, standing nearby. "The man made his point. He's Balgothan, and he wants Goll dead for killing Baylus."

Goll sighed. "Sorban has been waiting for me to appear. Now I'm here. I'll fight him when he wants it."

A faint smiled flickered across Junger's face.

"What?" Goll asked.

"Nothing."

"Oh I saw that, so explain yourself."

"Just thinking that was very brave of you, Master Goll," Junger quietly explained. "You put down a man friend's at these games, and you'll give him the chance to avenge that death. That's admirable."

"I'm glad you think so."

"Well then," Clavellus said and wrung his hands together. "I believe it's time to leave this place."

"This man shouldn't travel just yet," Shan announced, gesturing to where Brozz sat upon a bench. "I'd suggest moving him to my house until the morning."

"Will your wife be angry at the short notice?"

"Well, Master Clavellus," the healer said, "perhaps when you have the time, I might ask you about building a small house upon your land. If I'm going to remain in your service, that is."

Clavellus looked at Goll.

"Why not?" the old taskmaster said brightly, barely concealing his delight at having three more victories for the House of Ten, credited to himself and his trainers. "You've caught me in a good mood, good Shan. Now then, why don't we wait here for a bit, just to allow the crows to scatter, and then we'll go see the Domis. I think I made myself a little coin this afternoon."

39

When the cheering died down and attendants arrived upon the sands to drag the Free Trained fighter away, Dark Curge slapped the arms of his chair. He rose with a bear's growl.

"Day's done, you unpleasant toppers," he announced with weary satisfaction. "Until tomorrow. Perhaps if I'm fortunate, it'll rain. Save me the pleasure."

"I was thinking the same thing, you miserable pisser," Nexus said with unconcealed dislike, but Curge was already halfway out the door. The wine merchant stood and turned to follow.

"A moment of your time, good Nexus," Gastillo said, the golden mask muffling his words.

Nexus rolled his eyes. "I've nothing to say."

"I wish to discuss your latest offer."

"What latest offer?"

"The last one . . . when we talked."

"I thought I made it clear there was no last offer the last time we talked."

That robbed Gastillo of all speech.

The wine merchant waited, however, brow furrowed. He studied the shining mask for moments. With a sigh, he motioned for Gastillo to walk along with him.

"Say nothing until we are aboard my koch," Nexus warned. "Say nothing, and I'll give you a moment. But just a moment."

"My thanks, good Nexus,"

A short while later, they were aboard the merchant's koch.

"Well, speak your mind," Nexus said with a cranky pout. "I've other matters to attend to this day."

Gastillo spread his hands. "I'll be brief. I've thought about your offer and believe it's more than a fair price. I'll accept the twelve thousand gold pieces for my house and my fighters."

The wine merchant stared with grave offense, eyes slitted and cold, studying Gastillo for fault.

"Twelve thousand?" Nexus seethed as if releasing a blast of foul, pent-up gas. "Are you unfit? That was two days ago. Do you think that shiny face you wear somehow impresses me? That moment has long since passed, and I've moved on to greater things, you understand. You're no longer in my thoughts at all, Gastillo. Not in the least."

"I beg you to reconsider," Gastillo interrupted, not bothering to check the desperation in his tone.

"What's to consider?"

"Please, good Nexus."

That screwed up the wine merchant's face. He glanced at a shuttered window as if hearing the voices of Sunjans lingering just outside, beyond the ring of his personal guardsmen.

"I've no interest in purchasing anything from you," Nexus said.

Gastillo felt his stomach drop.

"For anything more than, say . . . nine thousand gold."

The number shocked Gastillo. "Nine—" His voice fluttered.

Nexus locked gazes. "And not a piece more. You said it yourself. Twelve thousand is more than a fair price. Well, now you have the absolute final worth of your property, Gastillo. Nine thousand. See how you should've taken fifteen? Hm? When I so generously offered it to you? See what a flicker of greed will bring a man? Consider this your first lesson in trade, lad. Remember it."

Gastillo struggled to find his voice.

"Nine," Nexus repeated. "And not a single coin more. I'll have the sum delivered to you by koch. In strongboxes. Twist and whine at this final offer, and there'll be no more."

"I'll approach the other houses."

Nexus rattled his head with disdain. "You think they can match my price? Or offer something *better*? And that you'll actually have your coin in a day? A *day*? Go, then, Gastillo. That'll be your second lesson. You'll be back here within a week, and I'll take that golden face of yours just to listen to you plead. And then I'll offer you seven. *Seven.*" Nexus's eyes widened with the threat. Then his expression calmed and returned to normal—or as normal as could be with his sallow features.

"I can't accept that," Gastillo whispered. "My reputation alone—"

"Is worth half that offer and no more. My spies have been asking about you. About your potential champion called Prajus. A regular hellion he is, isn't he? Both in the arena and upon the training grounds? Even likes to piss in the odd alehouse? Eh? For amusement. Insolent one, isn't he? Far beyond what you are willing to tolerate. That's the main reason you want to sell, isn't it? To be rid of that right and proper bastard. A rat-pig dollop of spit that hasn't been scuffed under a boot like he should've been the very instant he discovered a backbone. He's the reason, isn't he? He's poison to your ranks and your authority, but you can't do anything with him since he's *the best you've got*. And if *I* know about him, you can be certain the *others* know. Nine thousand gold, Gastillo. Now be off with you. Return to your house. Think on my offer. See if it fits you."

Nexus rapped on the koch's door, and it came open. The wine merchant indicated with a look that the time to leave had come.

Stunned, Gastillo stepped out, the koch trembling in his passage. When his feet touched the ground, he sought to get one last word with Nexus, but the satisfied smirk on the wine merchant's face stopped him cold—glimpsed as the door slammed shut.

Nexus's manservant regarded Gastillo with a question, but the owner ignored it. That fleeting peek of Nexus's smug smile blazed in his mind, enough to rot Gastillo's guts to the coiled core.

Nine thousand gold.

It was an insult, a right and proper insult.

Then it struck him.

Nexus had been schooling him in the art of haggling from the very beginning, whittling him away to nothing. He was a wine merchant—a merchant straight to the core of his black, deceiving, putrid heart.

Nine thousand gold.

Reins snapped, and a voice hollered. The extravagant koch pulled away from the arena gate, the circle of guards moving with it at a brisk trot. Gastillo stood behind, watching the transport vanish upon making one turn down a street, leaving only people in its passing. His own guards, two men that usually watched his back, crept into the edges of his awareness.

"Master Gastillo?" one of the men asked.

The house owner didn't respond.

A part of his mind played over Nexus's not-quite-final offer, and Gastillo hated himself for it. He'd been played, perhaps from the very beginning, by a master, and the trouble was everything Nexus had said was true. No one would take Prajus off his hands. The gladiator was poison—potentially the best of the games, but poison all the same. If Gastillo drove the man out, that would only significantly lessen the value of his property, but if he kept him, no one would bother purchasing the property anyway, not with Prajus attached to it.

Gastillo realized he'd gone over those facts before with very little satisfaction.

"Master Gastillo?" one of his guards asked.

"Yes?"

"Will we be heading home?"

His face burning underneath the mask, Gastillo nodded.

He intended to have a drink or two along the way.

ABOUT THE BLOOD

*

The compound gates opened, and Gastillo huffed across the far-off walkway, head down, shoulders hunched, and making straight for his front door.

Prajus watched the house master return home. He sat among a few of his companions—he didn't think of them as friends, not during the games—and eyed the gold-faced topper march across the grounds as if in dire need of a lengthy squat. The gladiator didn't like the way the man carried himself. Certainly didn't like the air of entitlement that hung about the character. An aloofness there was only magnified by that golden faceplate. The more Prajus gazed upon that pretentious piece of jewelry, the more it bothered him. Dark Curge had had one hand chopped off and wore that battle wound like a crown—not Gastillo. His pretty face had been raked from his skull, and as a result, he replaced it with an even prettier one.

A once champion didn't sulk along darkened walkways with his head held low as if he'd just been kicked in the skull. Gastillo wasn't a champion, wasn't deserving of respect.

Prajus sighed. There he was, still fighting for the golden punce.

He should've left long before. He knew that now.

As Prajus sat outside the bathhouse, the sight of the house owner scurrying along the training grounds turned his guts rancid. He wondered if Curge would run to his private house in such a way and decided the man would not. *Weak.* Their lord and master was weak.

With a wink and a smile to his sword brothers, he gestured at the skulking Gastillo.

"Just look at that," Prajus remarked. "You'd think he was running for a shite trough. Or in need of a good scrubbing. You hear me, *Master* Gastillo? You look like a cat who's just been pissed on by dogs."

Three of Prajus's five followers chuckled. The newest pair smiled nervously.

Halfway to his home's front entrance, Gastillo stopped walking. He straightened his spine as if removing a crick, and looked to the purple-and-pink heavens.

"He heard me that time, lads." Prajus smiled. "Any of you who don't want extra exercise tomorrow or his rations reduced best leave now. If you stay, I'd say it's all that, plus a cursing. Maybe even a whipping, which wouldn't surprise me, but I don't think Master Gastillo would do such a thing."

Gastillo remained looking at the heavens. House guards walked toward the lounging gladiators, ready to apply force if necessary. For some odd reason, Prajus wasn't impressed by them either.

"Well?" the gladiator shouted and stood. "What is it? *Master* Gastillo? Pissed on by dogs or maybe mounted by one?"

The smiles dimmed upon the newest faces of Prajus's gang. The three regular members fidgeted with unease, their own leers fading.

Prajus had clearly crossed a line with that last jab.

Even more unsettling, something was different about Gastillo that night.

Before, it had been strictly a jab and jab until Jaco and the other house guards stepped in or the house master summoned them. That evening, however, Gastillo was taking far too long in responding to Prajus's insults. No haughty jab came in return, or a promise of taskmaster Sowin drilling them into the sands the following day. There was a deepening silence, a reckoning, with all eyes centered on the poised house master in dreadful anticipation. Some of the lads had wondered about such a time, when the house master would decide he'd had enough of Prajus's mouth. They'd wondered what the punishment might be that fateful day, only to have Prajus himself dismiss such talk, explaining at length how Gastillo was too old, too fearful, and too *smart* to risk injury or release such a prize from his roster.

But now, at that last lightning strike of words, the very air hummed as if gathering power. All life beyond the property's walls seemed distant. A child squealed in the distance. The guards slowed to a stop and waited for a command.

Gastillo, however, made not a sound.

With a saucy question upon his face, Prajus glanced at his gang.

After the passing of several long moments, Gastillo faced the speaker. Three cups of firewater lit up his person, adding even more fuel to his growing anger. The golden mask hid that rage, but Gastillo knew—as he'd *always* known and perhaps even feared—that he'd been vastly too kind in punishing Prajus, that he'd exerted nowhere near the level of discipline needed to straighten out the mouthy warrior. Gastillo had worked and trained and bled on his own journey to become a champion of the games, and no champion would tolerate disrespect from unproven hellpups. Prized fighter or not, a gladiator held a line of decorum, of respect, for his house master and peers.

Prajus had failed to show that respect, perhaps even refused to, and despite all the discipline forced upon the man, he'd only become worse, to the point where Prajus had actually possessed the swollen balls to mock Gastillo as if the owner were one of his little band of ankle nippers.

That realization embarrassed Gastillo—enraged him.

He studied the four faces still smiling at him, knowing he wasn't about to let that last jab pass.

No more.

Perhaps it was the knowledge of Nexus having played Gastillo in their negotiations. Maybe it was because Gastillo knew deep down the wine merchant truly wanted the gladiator after all, at any price, but it amused him to torment Gastillo with ruthless bargaining. Or it might be Gastillo simply didn't have the patience or the mind to endure any more gurry from anyone, especially one wet curl of shite called Prajus.

"What did you say to me?" Gastillo asked quietly, his golden mask bright in the fading evening light.

Pleased that Gastillo was finally up to playing, Prajus smiled broadly. "I think you heard me."

From the doorway of the training staff's living quarters, old and faithful Sowin finally emerged. Berlis and Pius, the trainers, followed.

"Prajus . . ." Gastillo said, a tremble to his voice. "You go too far this night."

"Apologies," the gladiator said, smiling and bowing ever so slightly.

"No."

Prajus cocked a brow and slowly straightened.

"No," Gastillo repeated and gripped the neckline of his tunic. Fabric ripped as the house master pulled the material from his still-muscular chest. The sound tensed Jaco, and he approached cautiously, one hand holding his scabbard, the other on the sword's hilt.

Gastillo tossed the clothing to the ground and motioned Jaco to remain where he was.

"No," the owner said, heat rising to his voice. "The time for apologies, *sincere* apologies, is over, you unfit bastard,"

That wiped the smile from the gladiator's insolent face entirely.

Even Prajus's stout supporters appeared worried.

Gastillo walked onto the training grounds, his torso gleaming, rippling with strength. He took his time, not hurrying for anyone. He selected a wooden sword from the rack and appraised it. *Strong wood*. Gastillo hefted the training weapon, judged its weight and length acceptable, and proceeded to the center of the grounds. Jaco and Sowin made to move, but the house master stopped them both with a hand.

Standing as he was, Gastillo addressed Prajus again. "Get yourself a sword, you miserable maggot."

"To what ends?" Prajus asked, intrigued by the challenge.

Gastillo reached up and removed his mask, exposing the hideous void where a chunk of skin had been clawed from his skull by an overhand mace so long before. The blow had removed half his nose as well, leaving only a frightful black hole. Pink-and-white flesh covered most of that facial wreckage, but not the nose or the mangled lips that constantly drooled.

The humor upon Prajus's face drained away.

"Now you understand," Gastillo said, teeth gnashing into a smile. "Only at the end do you understand. Get a sword from that rack."

"Why not real ones, then?" Prajus fired back, warming to the idea.

"You're not worthy of real weapons," Gastillo said, right eyelid dropping only halfway as the left completed the blink.

Prajus wore only a loincloth, having bathed and eaten not too long before. The Sunjan pit fighter didn't look at his companions as he knew their eyes were upon him. More gladiators stepped out of the main barracks, their expressions drawn yet full of wonder. Men lined the edges of the training grounds.

"All of you," Gastillo said in clear voice, "you all stay back. This dog has insulted me, repeatedly defied my command, and dishonored my house. He's done so for the final time, and I mean to kill him tonight."

Stunned silence met those words.

"Not if you were *twenty* years younger, old man," Prajus grinned and snatched a wooden sword from the rack. He swished it left and right and walked onto the training sands, a little faster than expected, as if he feared Gastillo might change his mind.

"But if you wish." Smiling cruelly, Prajus stopped not five paces away from an unmasked Gastillo and spread his arms in a *Well, here I am* gesture.

Faces looked toward the house master.

"Nine thousand," Nexus's voice rang out in Gastillo's head. *"Nine."*

For this.

The wine merchant's flicker of a smile burned in Gastillo's mind, and he was tired of being thought of as a fool. Gastillo hunched over into a low guard, summoning all his arena experience and knowledge, accessing training untouched in nearly a dozen years. If muscles truly did remember, then Gastillo hoped his would as well.

Because he meant to brutalize this unfit he-bitch.

Prajus regarded the owner merrily. "What's that? You mean to stab me like that?"

"No," Gastillo said coldly. "I mean to beat you to death."

That doused Prajus's humor.

"But first," Gastillo continued, "I'll scar that pretty face of yours. So you'll no longer be tempted to creep over my walls at night. In search of wine and women."

"Come on, then," the gladiator snarled, all business. "The sooner I finish with—"

Gastillo slashed for Prajus's mouth, missing it by a hair and lighting up the man's features with surprise, but Gastillo wasn't through, by any means. He pressed forward, releasing a ten-strike combination upon his youthful adversary. The wooden sword came alive in his middle-aged hands, and a dozen years seemed no longer than a dozen days.

Prajus, however, parried the slashes and avoided the thrusts. He ducked under a backhanded fist aimed for his head and blocked a cut for his knees, kicking up sand as he did so.

When Gastillo broke away, Prajus followed and released all of his training and experience of more recent years. He drew a line across Gastillo's good cheek, nicked a shoulder, then split the right thigh of the owner's fine breeches—all too fast for the eye to follow. The hits pained the owner, backing him up with each connection. Blood seeped from cuts as if Gastillo had rolled around in a briar patch.

"Wait, Master Gastillo." Prajus laughed. "Wait. I'll show you more."

Then he did.

The younger man utilized everything he'd learned under his taskmasters and trainers, every trick and tactic meant to obtain an advantage and break down the will of the opposing warrior. Prajus prodded with his sword relentlessly, feinted, and at times, scratched at Gastillo's bare flesh at will, slowly bleeding the owner. He opened Gastillo's cheek under his bad eye, actually stabbed and punctured the meat of the left cheek, and followed up with a heavy fist crashing across the owner's face, toppling him, and leaving him in the sand.

That punch tensed the gathered household guards.

Stepping away, Prajus lifted his arms and circled the master of the house.

"Right and proper!" he bellowed. "Nothing more than a fresh cow kiss in the dirt. Get up. Get *up*, I said."

Gastillo lifted his head, spat dust, and did as commanded. Sand stuck to his bleeding wounds while pure undiluted hatred twisted his face. He waved off Jaco and the other guards. Taking a few deep breaths, he lunged for the younger Prajus and sliced for a leg, seeking to slow the pit fighter down.

The gladiator danced away with infuriating grace, pointing with a sword.

"This is the kog that lorded over us," he cried.

Chagrinned, Gastillo didn't look at his staff, didn't meet the eyes of Jaco. He felt them, heard the mental pleading to end the fight, to show that brazen punce that Gastillo was once a champion of the games.

But, Lords above, the man was *fast*, faster than he'd ever expected.

He slashed for another leg and had the attempt parried. He cut for an arm and Prajus parried that. The gladiator darted out of reach, shaking his head at the effort.

"Too slow, Master Gastillo," he said and pricked Gastillo's ear as an afterthought, the wooden sword flashing across a distance the owner thought of as out of reach.

The house master retreated a few steps more.

"How did you ever become champion?" Prajus asked and lunged, far too fast for Gastillo to react. Prajus stabbed the man's right breast.

Gastillo winced and crumpled.

Not content to wait, Prajus cracked the owner across the skull, dropping him in a heap. Confident the fight was his, Prajus didn't skip away. He lingered, enjoying the moment.

The gladiators crowding the edges watched, some amused, some anxious, most of them concerned. Old Sowin with his crooked back stared on, holding a cane for support, silently urging Gastillo to get to his feet once again.

"Yield, old man," Prajus said, considering the lateness of the day. "Yield, and maybe I'll spare your life."

That put fire underneath the owner. Gastillo got to his knees, then his feet. Blood streamed from numerous pricks and gashes, covering the owner's body. A fleshy bulb the size of a plum grew on his scalp from where Prajus had struck.

But Gastillo didn't submit.

His sword wavered as he fixed blood-rimmed eyes upon his hated foe.

"I'll kill you . . ." Gastillo panted.

Frowning, Prajus regarded his wary supporters, the other gladiators, and finally the household guard. He shot them all a look of *can you believe this one?* Then, he walked to his house master.

Gastillo lunged, wrapping both arms around Prajus's midsection as the pit fighter staked him through the back. Gastillo hissed at the connection, picked the gladiator up by the waist, and threw him down in a fleshy clatter of dust. The owner jumped on the lad and punched, punched hard, driving fist after fist into the man underneath him. Prajus's unspoilt face reddened, burst apart in places, and his expression changed from pain to an eyes-squeezed-shut grimace.

Then Gastillo's hands slowly lost power.

They drooped, much to his puzzlement, for he believed himself in better physical shape. His breathing became labored. He wheezed and spat, spraying Prajus with red speckles. He continued hammering the face beneath him until Prajus opened his eyes. Blood traced the gladiator's smile.

ABOUT THE BLOOD

An excruciating bolt of pain seized Gastillo in the back, and he faltered before rolling onto the sand.

Something dug deeper into his flesh, preventing him from lying flat.

Prajus sat up and grimaced. "Ah, *now* he feels it."

That got Gastillo's attention, and he realized the thing robbing him of his strength was the wooden sword still in his back. He felt that toughened grain rub against bones when he moved an arm, felt his heart flutter against it. Gastillo coughed, disgusted at what sprayed forth, and looked toward the west wall, where the sun hung in the sky like a great baleful eye, watching his every movement.

"You heard him," Prajus shouted and spat a gob of red into the sand. He walked around the fallen former champion. "He challenged me. He meant to kill me. I'm not at fault here. I'm *not* at fault."

The words sounded much farther away to Gastillo before becoming dreamy echoes. A hand clutched his shoulder. Someone moved him and laid him on his side.

The wooden sword in his back no longer hurt.

Red sun.

Glaring.

Blinding.

40

A ringing sounded in his ears, digging claws into Pig Knot's brain and dragging his consciousness back to the light or, specifically, the glow of torchlight. He opened his eyes, slits really, as the last beating Kelmo had given him was truly a thing of morbid beauty. Pig Knot didn't quite know how bad he looked, as he could only see himself properly from the neck down. His torso was a mire of welts and bruises, and every breath he took brought on a fire that enveloped his entire body. He figured his face was worst.

He still clung to life, though.

Miraculously, Kelmo hadn't broken Pig Knot's jaw yet. The Street Watch Koor—who was also Jana's exceptionally vengeful husband—had been punching his face to a point where he felt one of the plum-sized contusions burst, and a warm wetness spattered his face.

That had been just before Pig Knot passed out.

Torchlight flickered, and he lifted his head toward the cell's door. It was nighttime, and someone had left a torch in the hallway beyond.

Pig Knot grunted. He tongued the gaps where missing teeth had once been moored. Four more had departed in the most recent session—a pair of jaw teeth as well as two more near the front, an incisor and one to the right of it. Eight teeth were gone from his head in total since Kelmo and his lads had taken a punishing interest in him. The Koor might've been collecting them except Pig Knot had glimpsed him kicking them into the latrine. He didn't know why the officer did so. If Pig Knot had been doing the beating, doing the extractions, he thought he might actually collect them, if only to show them to his prisoner at a later date, as a way of warning upon being released. *"Don't come back here,"* Pig Knot would warn. *"We took these last time. We'll take the rest if we catch you back here again."*

Eight teeth. Down the shite hole.

Something was . . . humorous about that.

The door creaked, alerting the legless man of another visit, possibly a very painful visit. Zepedos remained in his cell on the other side of the wall, but the Koor had no interest in him. That surprised the thief. He'd said so himself.

Pig Knot had been receiving the beating from five men. It felt like more, in fact, until he lost his senses.

The torchlight flickered as a passing shape disturbed the flame.

Pig Knot sighed and lowered his head to the floor. Water dripped somewhere, spattering stone. A presence that could only be described as all wrath filled the entrance of the cell. He knew it was there and thought remaining still was the best course of action.

"Awake?" Kelmo asked.

That word frightened the once gladiator. He didn't look up. He was neck deep in a vat of constant hurt and didn't want to acknowledge Jana's very jealous man. Truth be known, Kelmo was a hellion, possessing all the righteous outrage of a husband intent on punishing the man who'd bedded his wife—not that Pig Knot blamed him, not at all. He'd have been upset as well.

The admission made it hard for him to hate the punce.

"You're awake," Kelmo said. "I can see you're awake. Look at me."

That sent a spike of fear through Pig Knot. He really didn't want to do that.

"I said *look*."

Reluctantly, the battered man did as ordered, fearful of what might happen if he refused. The tall and powerful Koor loomed in the waning hue of torchlight. The man looked clean, sober even. During one of the beatings, Pig Knot had glimpsed his blood in Kelmo's beard—not just speckles either, but dollops as thick and bright as berry jam. The Koor had cleaned himself nicely.

"All alone?" Pig Knot managed, his words muffled though nothing was in his swollen mouth. Uttering those two words made him light-headed.

Water dripped and spattered stone again.

Kelmo tossed a blanket at him. "Use that."

The fabric fell across Pig Knot's lower bits.

"My . . . thanks."

The Koor studied his prisoner, taking in the injuries from one angle and then the other, ruminating on thoughts as black as pitch. The officer didn't show any sign of regret, not a flicker of mercy. He was quite cold in that respect, and that thought alone froze whatever remaining piss Pig Knot had in him.

"I'm not . . . entirely detached from your plight," Kelmo said, unexpectedly.

Pig Knot sighed. He didn't believe a word of it.

"But I must admit." Kelmo placed a shoulder against the cell bars. "I like having you here. Seeing you . . . trying to heal. Before I give you another paddling. Almost like . . . your body retains hope. Well, you should have hope. You should. Hope's a good thing."

Pig Knot kept his breaths shallow because of his broken ribs. "That's the most . . . you've said to me."

"I've said more. You just don't remember it."

Pig Knot grunted. *Suppose so.*

"A man can only punish another for so long"—Kelmo fiddled with the lock—"before it becomes wearisome. Even pitiful."

ABOUT THE BLOOD

The cell opened.

Kelmo stood there, his hand by his sides, unarmed, glaring at the legless man.

Pig Knot wasn't about to rise, but his temples thrummed, and his heartbeat sped up in morbid anticipation of the beating to come.

"Why not escape?" Kelmo shrugged. "At least *try* to escape. The way is open. There's no one beyond that door. No other Skarrs. Just me. If you can overpower me, you're free."

A tempting offer.

Instead, Pig Knot listened, as if confirming that, indeed, no one was waiting beyond the door, which supposedly led to the rest of the Street Watch's jailhouse. He eyed the Koor, then the area past the officer, before carefully clutching at the blanket. He pulled it toward his side, using his right hand instead of the left. Someone had stomped on his left hand earlier, breaking the last three fingers there. Those poor digits presently resembled fat, purple sausages.

"Why don't . . . you just kill me . . ." Pig Knot groaned weakly, not even certain it was he who spoke. "And be done with it?"

"Good question," Kelmo said and studied the ceiling. "Why not? Why not just wring that neck of yours until something pops? Or pull steel and slip it across your throat? Why not? I'll tell you why. I'm angry with you, Pig. Very angry. The rage of an insulted husband. You're not married, are you? Well, the pain I experienced upon learning my Jana had . . . bedded you . . . was much, much worse than your hurts now."

Somehow, Pig Knot doubted that.

"You weren't even the first, it seems," Kelmo went on. "But fortunately for me, you *are* the one I caught. And I mean to wring every drop of life from you. Until there's no more—either your eyes roll back into your head or your bones snap. I mean to hurt you. For a while. Unfortunate for you. Even more unfortunate, I'm Street Watch. A Koor. I'm . . . the law. My men know what you've done, so every punch, every kick I give you is serving several purposes. Punishment for you. A warning to others. Instilling fear in my own men."

Seddon above, Pig Knot thought, an insane giggle almost rising to his lips. He wondered if Kelmo thought his own men were going to bed Jana as well. He clamped down on that, going as far as rubbing that split plum upon his forehead. That watery, broken blister stab of pain concealed his laugh in a flustered squeal.

Kelmo smiled at the sound, thinking it something else entirely.

"Just kill me," Pig Knot whispered.

The officer was silent then, as if considering it. "No," the Koor said with a noble air. "I'll release you, eventually. When I get bored, perhaps. There's only so much physical punishment a man can inflict upon another, and truth be known, the sight of you now, well, almost sickens me."

Almost.

Pig Knot snorted in amusement. That tiny movement aggravated his broken nose and brought water to the slits of his eyes.

Kelmo became a blurry hellion.

"Yes, almost," the Koor said and stepped closer. Fists as wide as shovels clenched and unclenched. Water plunked again outside of the cell. "I'm not a cruel person, Pig. I'm not. But there are consequences for every action. You bedded my wife— that's an action. I catch and crush the life from you at leisure. That's a consequence."

Pig Knot sighed.

"Tell me," Kelmo asked quietly. "Before I slam your face into the floor. Repeatedly. Was she worth it? Was she worth all of this?"

Dying Seddon, no, Pig Knot thought blackly. He shook his head.

Kelmo's face darkened then, and his mouth tightened into an angry knot. "So she isn't worth any of this?"

The slits that were Pig Knot's eyes widened as far as possible, which really wasn't far at all. The legless gladiator shook his head, damn near rattling it off his shoulders. He'd absorbed far too much punishment at Kelmo's hands, too much damage over a very short time. If he were in a sharper state of mind, Pig Knot knew he could talk with the Koor, probably even convince the man that he had intended no harm and was sorry for the indiscretion with the officer's wife. He hadn't even known Jana had a husband until after the deed.

That wouldn't have bothered Pig Knot at the time, but he could put forth a convincing lie *now* to protect himself . . . if he were in a proper state of mind, which he wasn't.

"You unfit bastard," Kelmo whispered, white fury in his voice as taut as a strangling wire. "I'll break your skull apart and patch it back together with candle wax. Someone mentioned you were a gladiator once. You should try and escape. Overpower me. Try and kill me even. You're still a strong man. Even I can see that. Resist. Fight back."

Fighting back was the *last* thing Pig Knot was going to do, but then something occurred to him. If he did, perhaps Kelmo would kill him on the spot. If Pig Knot could get him angry enough, maybe the Koor would make a mistake. Pig Knot wanted death, after all. This would be the quickest path.

"Come here, then," he muttered to the blurry shadow. "Come down here, and I'll fight. Maybe even tell you things about your missus. Things you don't know, but I certainly do."

That spot of night about Kelmo's shoulders darkened all the more. The Koor stepped deeper into the cell, and when Pig Knot tried to face him, the soldier slapped him across the head with an open hand. The blow landed like a thunderbolt. Pig Knot collapsed, all fight gone from him, the world slanting one way then the other, as if he were caught in a riptide of ink.

Kelmo steadied himself and drew back a pointed boot, one that would connect with Pig Knot's midsection. The door to the outer chamber opened with a clatter, and a voice sounding as if it was speaking underwater reached Pig Knot's ringing ears. The words were fast and distorted, but he caught them all the same.

Gladiator. Killed his master. Gastillo.

Kelmo stopped, and for a heartbeat, he ignored the heap on the floor. A look of lethal annoyance crossed his face and he retreated, barking orders. Pig Knot didn't understand a word of it.

Gastillo. The name sounded familiar.

He had no control over his closing eyes.

Outside the Street Watch building, the pack leader Jurnos saw the Skarrs rush forth from the entrance and march double-time down the street. The tall gang leader held his breath, uneasy at being so close to the city's only body of law. The soldiers gradually disappeared into the night. Jurnos supposed a fight had broken out somewhere, maybe at a tavern or such.

Settling back against the wall of a merchant shop, one that stitched together articles of clothing, he steadied his breath, drew a hand across his face, and got comfortable once again.

The Skarrs hadn't released the punce without any legs yet, but Jurnos knew they would eventually. When they became tired of him, they would throw him back into the streets.

Memories of being beaten and humiliated by the legless one tormented Jurnos, but he endured them, weaponized them. He intended to make an even greater name for himself when he finally caught the legless bastard that embarrassed him. He meant to catch that muscular dog blossom as soon as the Skarrs threw him away.

Whereupon Jurnos would catch him . . . then kill him.

41

Sunlight glowed around curtain edges, waking Curge. His morning stare was a thing of stone, and at that time, neither of the two women nestled into his sides stirred, their naked skin dark and smooth. He sighed and felt rested, his body fit to rise. The smell of perfumed water drifted across his nose—roses and some other flowers he had no knowledge of but his lovers adored. He stretched just a little, enough to make one woman nudge his arm with her nose and chin.

On impulse, Curge glanced to the door and saw Bezange, standing just inside the bedroom.

A scowl creased the owner's features. "How long have you been there, you damned weasel?"

"Not long, Master Curge."

"Get out."

"I have urgent news, Master Curge," Bezange blurted, his youthful features actually showing some age that morning. "Gastillo of the House of Gastillo is dead."

That stunned Curge. He sat up, letting a thin sheet fall to his lap. The women in his bed uncoiled from him like snakes. "You're—"

"I do not joke," Bezange said, uncharacteristically cutting the owner off.

The cogs in Curge's head rattled to life. He remained in bed, absorbing the news. A hand slid up his arm to his shoulder, and he remembered the women.

"Get out," he commanded. "Now."

Hearing the iron in his voice, his bed companions rose in a hurried rush, treating Bezange to an eyeful. They gathered up their clothing and ran to the door in a flutter of bare feet and dark hair, barely noticing the agent.

"Tell me everything," Curge ordered when they were alone.

Bezange didn't waste any time. "Upon your wishes, my spies have been watching the interactions between Gastillo and Nexus. They met again in the wine merchant's koch yesterday, after the games. No one could approach because of the combined guard force. Gastillo was quick to leave Nexus's company, however, and he even appeared in a daze before walking home. Walking home in a very determined manner, I might add. He stopped in a tavern and quickly drank three cups of firewater, as if something was bothering him."

"That does sound odd," Curge said, having never heard of Gastillo partaking of any amount of firewater before, or with such speed.

"Upon returning home, the gladiator called Prajus taunted him. This had been a reoccurring event between the two as of late. Last night, however, Gastillo had no mind to tolerate any further nonsense, perhaps due in part to the firewater."

Probably due to the firewater, Curge thought.

"He challenged the gladiator to a public fight," Bezange continued, "declaring his intentions to kill Prajus, and got himself killed instead."

Curge scratched his brow. "Prajus. Gastillo died at the hands of his best fighter?"

"Apparently so. The Street Watch were summoned to the household, and they questioned the staff and gladiators. Several described Prajus having a history of making jabs at the owner despite being frequently punished. Gastillo evidently had enough and fully intended to kill him, beating him to death with a wooden sword, no less."

"Seddon above."

"The Street Watch found no reason to arrest Prajus as Gastillo had challenged and threatened the man."

"Even though the dog taunted the owner? Provoked him?"

"They are grown men," the agent explained. "If there was a slip of control, it was on Gastillo's part. Banish the fighter if necessary, but to challenge him as he did, threatening to kill him as he did . . ."

Bezange frowned with grand disdain.

The news dumbfounded Curge, nailing him to the bed's edge, a single sheet puddled around his navel for decency. *Gastillo was dead? Lords and Seddon above.* The man had a pair of bells after all, but he'd chosen the wrong man to challenge. Prajus was a recognized beast and Gastillo slowed by years.

Curge wondered what had pushed Gastillo to such a confrontation. He knew the man hid behind that mask of his, to a degree, but he had never suspected such an ending for the once champion, being killed by his own gladiator in a fight upon his own property. The idea left him at a loss.

"Word from the Chamber?" he asked.

"It's too early to know, but in light of all I've learned, there's very little the Chamber can do. Even if they are willing to somehow punish Prajus, his defense will be Gastillo openly challenged him in a fight to the death. This wasn't a cutthroat stabbing in the dark. It was honorably done."

Honorably done! Curge marveled. *What a way to wake to a new day.* He looked at the curtains and the light threading the edges, imagining the viewing box without that gold-faced shagger. He briefly brightened at the thought, but only until he realized he still had to share the space with Nexus, and Gastillo's place would be filled next year, probably by someone even worse.

That soured Curge's mood.

"The house will probably disband," Bezange reasoned. "Gastillo wasn't known to have any appointed heirs to assume control. Without that or any other claim to the property, there's no formal backing. The king's legal entities will assume control over the assets, and they'll cut the staff and fighters loose, who will then seek other houses to support them. With the recent extension of the season, it's fair to assume the more talented of the lot will be snapped up by other owners. Who's to say what will happen to the rest?"

Curge grunted agreement.

"But that won't happen for Prajus," Bezange concluded. "His career is finished."

That drew a grim smirk from Curge. The man's *life* was finished. Once news of a gladiator slaying his keeper reached the other owners, the hunt would commence in earnest. Talented and vicious Prajus might be, but even if he had escaped being arrested by the Street Watch, he would face consequences for killing Gastillo. The immediate one would be reprisal from Gastillo's own gladiators, the vengeful ones, and Curge wasn't exactly sure if those seeking Prajus's blood would wait for an official pairing in the arena. Then there was anyone close to the deceased: staff, friends, lovers . . .

Curge looked toward the ceiling. He knew what Prajus's fate would be, though perhaps not that day or the next. Truth be known, he might very well look into putting the man into the ground, himself. Perhaps even have Demasta look into it. None of the owners could allow a gladiator to kill another owner and let it go unpunished. Such happenings might inspire the more unruly of their ranks and place deadly thoughts into their heads.

"That man is dead," the one-armed owner rumbled. "Well and truly. Honorable challenge or no challenge. Threats or none. He was dead the moment he took up arms against Gastillo. Anyone with eyes knows Prajus is an insolent bastard. The man's more trouble than he's worth. We can't have curs that bite their masters. And Gastillo wasn't disliked amongst the owners. Dying Seddon. Prajus might be skilled in the Pit, but the man's no doubt realizing what he's done this morning. Realizing the consequences. Dead. Right and proper dead."

"He could carry on as a Free Trained," Bezange pointed out. "If he truly wishes to continue."

"A man like Prajus? A dog groomed for greatness? He won't cast himself in with those maggots. No. His days are done. If, by Seddon's intervention, he survives the coming wrath, he'll still be an outcast. Probably making plans this morning to leave Sunja, never to fight in the Pit again. Maybe he'll make a name for himself in the lesser games of Vathia, and that'll be his living. Until he dies or grows too old. If my father were alive, he'd make it so not even the hellpups of Vathia would take in Prajus's hide. Bad form to kill the one preparing you for the games. Very bad form. Unfit stupidity, truth be known."

"I agree."

Curge studied his agent. "Foul news this morning, but you did right to bring it straight to me. I'll hear more of it as the day grows old. This story strikes me as being far from done."

Bezange remained silent, his face long from constant frowning.

Curge covered his mouth, mulling the night's events. "Whatever happened in that koch between Gastillo and Nexus put Gastillo in a foul mood, foul enough to try to kill his best and die in the attempt. And Nexus won't speak a word of it, not unless I manage to question him in my private chambers."

That visibly brightened Bezange for a moment before his frown returned. "I don't think that will happen, Master Curge."

"No, I don't think so either. But a man can hope. Go on and see if you can scratch any more details from the dirt. There might yet be more to this story."

"I'll try, Master Curge."

Curge looked toward the curtains, indicating the time had come for the agent to leave. "Bezange."

The man paused.

"Those women just now. They're in a room just down the hall. Send them back in before you leave."

42

In another part of Sunja's countryside, while the afternoon sun baked bone and stone alike, Grisholt stood inside his villa's aging walls and adjusted his newly bought finery. The clothes weren't tight, but the weather was just too damn hot for so many layers. He fidgeted, feeling as if he'd tucked his lads into a pouch of boiling leather, a mistake he'd realized only after he'd stepped out into daylight. Once done with his fussing, he directed his attention to the progress on his roof. A group of six carpenters labored, summoned from a nearby village by his cook, Marrok. Under that hot bauble in the sky they worked, replacing worn shingles and making repairs as needed. Hammers rang out, as did the subtle smell of tar and wood, all held together by a low undercurrent of conversation amongst the workers.

Grisholt didn't envy the unfortunate bastards in the least, eyeing their half-naked frames made both shiny and red by the heat. He wasn't one for pounding nails, despised carrying heavy weight, and scoffed at the notion of taking simple measurements. Supervision was more to his liking.

"Take a look for rot while you're up there," Grisholt bellowed, his hand straying to his pointed beard. "Check those timbers. And be mindful that I'm paying you upon your work's completion and not before."

Faces turned and listened to the stable owner before getting back to work. Four of the villagers kneeling upon the roof resumed hammering without any indication of having heard. That tickled Grisholt the wrong way.

"Where did Marrok find these toppers?" he muttered as one-eyed Brakuss leaned in to listen.

"Whitewood, Master Grisholt," the guard replied.

"Are they all deaf in Whitewood? Or merely dense?"

Brakuss snorted amusement.

Grisholt wasn't finished. "What about the stone workers?" he asked and looked down his nose toward the open gate. Another handful of men toiled there, churning a barrel of mortar, readying it to apply to the crumbling sections in the villa's outer wall.

"Pynn's Brook."

"That's a far way to travel," Grisholt noted without any real interest.

"A day at least on foot."

"No doubt the entire lot is related somehow," the owner observed but then smiled. "Village idiots. My father once said, when you fetched water in Whitewood, you did so with your blossom facing the waters. And if you were in Pynn's Brook, one didn't bend at the waist to pick something off the ground. One knelt and did so quickly."

Brakuss chuckled at the foul humor. "Marrok did say they were able tradesmen."

"Marrok would. You should've seen him when I told him *not* to bring any of his relatives to work on my property. He was fishhooked. All I need is more of Marrok's blood running about. Where is that insufferable topper?"

Brakuss looked about.

"No matter." Grisholt grimaced at the sun's face. He was in good spirits this day. An order of firewater was due later in the afternoon, along with a wagon of wine and beer. The beer he'd give to Brakuss to distribute amongst the lads. Taskmaster Turst and the trainers could indulge as well if they so desired. Grisholt didn't care. With his recent success in the Pit, he had coin enough to fling off a cliff and enough goodwill to allow his minions a day of respite from the games. His family's property was in a state of repair and restoration, and he'd placed an order to Marrok to find him some unmarried women willing to work as servants within the house—pretty ones with flattering figures and no objections to the occasional petting. The very thought made Grisholt stand on his toes.

Wealth was an infection much to his liking.

The main gates were open wide to allow the village idiots better access to the hinges. The guards posted outside the gates saw fit to allow a rider through, drawing Grisholt's attention. The owner quickly recognized the man.

"Caro," Grisholt said fondly and lifted a hand.

"Master Grisholt," the once gladiator panted, reining in his brown gelding. He steered the slick animal to a water trough and slipped off its back. The sun had visibly exhausted him, and the horse appeared all but ready to collapse in its drink.

Caro had traveled hard.

He nodded at Brakuss. "I've news from the city."

"News, eh?" Grisholt said. "Well, we'll have someone see to your horse while we discuss it over some wine. I've still a bottle remaining. Truth be known, I've ordered a whole wagon of some—"

"Perhaps after the news, Master Grisholt."

The owner paused, smiled, and shrugged, thinking the man foolish. One didn't pass up freely offered wine. "All right. I'm listening, then. Let's hear it."

"Gastillo of the House of Gastillo has been killed."

The pleasant expression upon Grisholt's face disappeared as if sprayed with cat's piss. "What?"

"He was killed by one of his own men."

ABOUT THE BLOOD

"*What?*" Grisholt placed a hand to his resplendent chest as if to calm his heart. No love was lost between him and Gastillo, but to hear of an owner dying at the hands of one of his own people . . . *The unfit bastard!* His crooked mouth opened as if about to croak.

The powerful-looking agent went on to explain the night's events as related to him by his spies. Gastillo had been killed by Prajus, a name known to Grisholt. Grisholt remained quiet as he listened to the details, sickened at how Gastillo had exposed himself to such danger, threatening and challenging a pit fighter in front of witnesses. The very notion seemed unfit. Unless gold-faced Gastillo had very loyal men, the chances of punishment were scant. Grisholt wouldn't be surprised in the least if the Chamber itself didn't do anything. They would no doubt let the houses take care of matters themselves. As for Gastillo's staff and roster, a frenzied picking of the bones might very well begin, until only the scroff remained. The games would grind on to their relentless but glorious end.

Prajus, however, was a dead man.

"That savage he-bitch," Grisholt fumed, immediately suspicious of his own lads. The thought that a hellpup would turn upon its master boiled his guts. Gastillo should've stomped on the dog's plums at the first sign of insolence and stomped hard.

"What was he thinking?" He asked no one in particular while hammers pounded wood.

"I don't know," Caro admitted, taking a moment to inspect the ongoing work around the property. "I'll ask about, but as of now, it seems that gold-faced topper simply had enough of the dog's barking."

"Why didn't he simply toss the man to the streets?" Grisholt asked, but then he connected Prajus's name to the man.

"The man's an exceptional fighter, Master Grisholt," Caro said, voicing the owner's memory, "perhaps the best Gastillo had put to field this season. Cast him out, and his house loses its best chance to win the games. Then there's the possibility of a rival house recruiting Prajus. Without hesitation."

"Perhaps that was Prajus's intention," Grisholt furthered the thought. "Get cast out and then throw in with another house."

"Perhaps." Caro didn't sound convinced.

Grisholt mulled over the matter. "Prajus." The owner sighed with grand remorse, much better suited to a Perician stage, and looked at the sky. "And Gastillo is no more. Well, well. I'd have chosen one or two others to perish before him. Unfortunate. Very unfortunate."

Grisholt ruminated on how the incident would affect the season and saw no reason why it should. "Anything else, then?" he asked his agent.

"I've learned when you will fight the House of Ten."

Grisholt's eyebrows jumped. "The Zhiberian?"

"No, Master Grisholt. He's not returned from that village."

"I'll have his head and more. Who, then?" The owner's breath suddenly caught in his throat, and his eyes fixed upon Caro. "Not him."

"Aye that."

Grisholt smiled evilly. "The one they call Junger."

Caro nodded.

Tingles sparked and traveled throughout Grisholt's person. *Junger of Pericia.* He knew the man, knew him very well. He wasn't the maggot shite Zhiberian, but he'd be a trophy kill all the same, a tremendous victory and, more importantly, a crippling blow to the Ten's quickly dwindling ranks.

"Yes..." Grisholt whispered, already warming to the matchup. "Excellent. Who's he scheduled to fight?"

"Barros."

"Even better," the owner rumbled with wicked delight. "Even better. Razi didn't press for a blood match this time?"

"He did not."

"Wise, Razi, very wise," Grisholt said and reflected upon what needed to be done. The lack of hammering caught his attention. The men tending to his roof had paused for some unknown reason. One withering look from Grisholt prompted them back to work.

"Brakuss," the owner said, "if any of those kogs stop working, you have my permission to paddle their collective balls."

The one-eyed bodyguard nodded curtly.

"Also," Grisholt continued. "Inform Barros of his next opponent." The owner's smile returned and damn near reached his ears. "Tell him he'll get to kill a Ten man."

43

"Now, remember, don't try to match him strike for strike. Just wear him down. Wear him down, and when you see the opportunity, put him into the dirt. But don't kill him. Don't do that. Not if you want to fight that Ten man, the one that killed Baylus. I'll have a talk with the Madea about that. He might be willing to do something. I doubt it, but I'll see. In the meantime, focus on this lad and win. You can do it. I know you can. I *know* you can. You have just as good a chance as anyone here. Win! For yourself and the Stable of Slavol!" Salwark grinned mightily then, his horrid breath of wine and fish almost crossing Sorban's eyes.

Sweet Seddon. The gladiator braced himself against the blast but still retreated a step, scowling as he did so. Sorban wished Vavar was able to attend the games, but the old man remained sick and bedridden.

Salwark was standing in his place.

The jittery son nodded and withdrew, as if interpreting the Balgothan's expression of disgust as one of readiness to fight. The owner's son went to the private viewing chamber's arched window, where the sands shimmered and glowed with heat. Sitting on a nearby bench, Blacktooth leaned in and slapped Sorban's knee. Today's games were the first for Blacktooth to attend since having his ankle smashed by Brontus of the House of Ustda. He'd come to see Sorban fight and made his way to the lower chamber on a pair of crutches.

The older fighter offered a comforting smile, revealing a single incisor sunk deep into an otherwise barren gum line. *"You do what you do,"* the Sunjan's expression said.

At that one look, Sorban felt immensely more focused. He took to wrapping his hands, pulling the ribbons tight around his fingers and his palms, remembering his departed friend Baylus. Memories of laughter, conversations, and mugs of beer filled his head. Baylus had won the championship the same season Sorban started his fighting career, and because they were both Balgothan, they immediately got along, speaking freely in their own language and complaining about the Sunjan way of doing things. Baylus was a quiet mentor back then, enjoying his celebrity status after his earning his gladiatorial crown and even inviting Sorban to stay at his residence during the off season, to sharpen his existing skill set with some informal training. Sorban learned from the Butcher, and during those months, he saw firsthand how Baylus still loved the Pit. Though he had no need to return to the arena, the sport was clearly still in his blood. Many a story of violence and valor Baylus told over drinks, and somewhere during those days and evenings, Sorban knew, just *knew* the champion would one day return to the games to try his luck again upon the arena floor.

True enough, that day arrived.

Sorban had cheered for his countryman during the battle against Goll and seen him easily controlling the fight, winning it . . . until the upstart Kree killed his friend and mentor.

The shock hammered Sorban like a fat nail through the heart. Baylus was gone . . . just like that, claimed by the very games he so loved.

After seeing to and completing the burial of Baylus the Butcher, Sorban stalked the morass known as general quarters, seeking the man called Goll. He searched until Salwark lured him away with promises of revenge. The opportunity never arose, however, as the battered Kree had disappeared from general quarters, hiding from Sorban's wrath. His focus settled upon defeating all those placed before him, hoping to win the games in honor of his fallen countryman, hoping beyond hope that one day . . . he'd face Baylus's killer.

That didn't happen, though.

Unknown to Salwark however, Sorban had already talked to the Madea about Goll and found the arena official rather receptive to a possible—unofficial—blood match with the Kree. Sorban wondered if the Madea had been an admirer of Baylus. Perhaps he didn't like the idea of a Free Trained killing a champion, or maybe he simply didn't like Goll and his dogs calling themselves a house.

"Fight your match, and emerge victorious," the Madea had said. "And we'll see."

That alone sent Sorban's hope spiking.

If Salwark did talk with the Madea, the Balgothan hoped the owner would pick his teeth beforehand.

Blacktooth leaned back, pulled his crutches closer to his arms, and eyed the Balgothan with approval.

Sorban gathered a pair of metal gauntlets, the knuckles bristling with needles, and pulled them on with rising aggression.

The day had been dismal.

When Qualtus the Orator wove colorful spells of grandeur around the opening fights but then the dogs failed to perform, that reflected badly upon him. The wasted effort left him with a rancid rumbling in his guts. However, after another afternoon of uninspiring hacking by the games' criminal element, relief once again surged through the Orator. The house fighters were about to take the stage, and the ever-exciting Balgothan was slated to pull steel in the arena confines. The very notion set Qualtus's mind afire in anticipation. Sorban was a right and proper hellion, just the thing to start the day anew when the dungeon gurry had failed miserably.

"Men and women of the Pit," Qualtus began, lifting his skinny arms to the heavens, beckoning thousands to listen, "once again we will be treated to a display of weapons and of heart."

Qualtus stressed the heart part, to clear the air of the offal that had failed to entertain. No Jackals had been scheduled that day either even though the last few showings had the Nordish prisoners of war practically mauling their dungeon mates.

In any case, the Orator hoped the next match would satisfy everyone.

"With great pleasure, I introduce a warrior with one goal upon his mind, to return the champion's crown to Balgothan hands. His name is whispered within the loathsome bowels of the Free Trained and spoken in respectful tones among the great schools and houses of Sunja, Pericia, and Vathia. He is a forge whose fires only get hotter with time. A mountain about to shake forth an avalanche. A *beast* in search of a bloody good meal."

The words rumbled out of Qualtus, and he complimented himself at the sudden inspiration. *Good theater*, he thought, *and very well done.*

"He is here to once again prove he is a force to contend with, to ensure his name will be remembered within these walls. I give to you . . . Sorban! Of Balgotha!"

Rousing applause greeted the gladiator emerging from the portcullis.

Qualtus motioned for quiet and got it, loving his sway over the audience. He adored that effect.

"Facing this hellion is a warrior seeking to return to his winning ways . . ."

The Orator's words caused Wocello to frown behind his caged visor. *Seddon above*, he grumbled internally, pausing upon the stairs to the rising portcullis. Lose a few matches, and they're ready to toss you aside like a crack's scrub brush. He listened to the Orator go on about his woes within the Pit, wondering if he should seek out the man some evening and tell him, over a good rattling, that his words weren't appreciated. As house master Burco Ustda had once reminded him, the Orator might very well state the obvious without meaning to offend, but Wocello should draw strength from those words and prove the old bastard wrong.

That idea greatly pleased Wocello.

The season had plagued him with three losses to his four victories. The worst defeat came two fights before, when an overhand blow from a mace grazed his shoulder and blackened the skin underneath, despite his armor. The joint still ached when he lifted his arm higher than his collarbone. As a result, heavy cloth padded the area underneath his regular leather, and he pulled a chain-mail shirt over everything. The added weight of the chain mail didn't bother Wocello. He was a big man, strong, with muscle coated in a layer of fat and with a chunk of his right nostril missing from one crack of a flail.

Wocello looked intimidating at the most casual of times, with a low brow, cold blue eyes, and a mouth of yellow teeth appearing strong enough to grind though wooden planks. When he put his mind to it, however, when he truly felt the need to menace foes and ordinary passersby alike, he could contort his face into something shocking.

Listening to the Orator's introduction, he summoned that killer's face and resumed walking toward the arena opening.

The day had come for Wocello to record a victory, and a glorious one at that.

As far as he was concerned, the season was going to be a long one—plenty of time to return to winning ways.

Sunlight enveloped the black shirt of mail. Wocello's visor was a display of harsh pageantry, with a wide bib over the eyes to block the sun and three fins sprouting from the helmet. Ornaments of small solemn figures, perhaps gods, adorned the sides. His mighty arms, scarred and bound with cloth bandages, wielded a great two-handed sword the length of a man's leg.

As they closed, Wocello eyed the bright plumes adorning Sorban's helmet, on the sides and over the crown. Holes punctured the visor, the mouth area protruding like an iron bubble. Wocello wasn't one for arena greetings. He didn't feel the need to say hello to whoever he was trying to butcher.

As far as he could tell, Sorban was of the same mind.

When he got within range, Wocello lifted his blade high over his head, daring the Balgothan to come closer. Sorban didn't engage, however, and peered over the edge of his round shield. A sword's tip appeared just below the barrier, like a thick and shiny thorn. Wocello had expected a quarterstaff, but Sorban had changed his weapons.

No matter.

The sun beat down upon the two combatants as the Sunjan feinted here and there, causing the crouched Balgothan to flinch. The crowd didn't care for such tactics. Nor did they enjoy waiting for their violence and so voiced their annoyance.

Perhaps the heat was bothering Wocello. Perhaps it was the audience. Maybe he'd just had enough of holding a heavy hunk of metal over his head.

The sword came down in a broad scything arc, with power enough to split a world.

Sorban dodged the cut, spun, and backhanded, raking his short sword across the side of Wocello's head. The sword clanged into Wocello's visor, stunning him just enough to send him staggering. Sorban punched his shield's edge into his opponent's wrist, and the great sword fell. Wocello cringed, his grunt of pain swallowed by the audience's approval.

The Balgothan struck Wocello's helm a second time, driving him to his knees. A sheet of blood erupted from underneath the man's face cage, and when he looked up to see where Sorban was, the Balgothan smashed his shield into the Sunjan's face.

It was short, ugly, and to the brutal point.

Unconscious before he hit the ground, Wocello fell backward, one leg bending awkwardly enough to evoke winces and hisses from the crowd.

Sorban kicked the great sword away. He stomped on Wocello's midsection, buckling the defenseless man. He raised his sword, relented, and dismissed Wocello by walking away from the finished pit fighter.

The Balgothan halted, dropped his shield, and pulled the helmet from his head in a sparkling arc of sweat.

"I want Goll!" Sorban shouted at the audience. "I want the Kree who killed Baylus the Butcher! I want his head!"

He slowly turned around, addressing the Orator. "I want Goll's head! Give him to me!"

The crowds took up the chant of "Goll's head! Goll's head!" filling the brilliant bowl that was the arena.

44

The man knows what he wants, Curge thought, observing the decisive victory and wondering if the Balgothan was up to the task of challenging the Kree. Curge intended to keep a close watch on that one, just in case Sorban swayed the Madea into awarding him the desired fight. The victory over Wocello had certainly convinced the crowds.

The harsh roars of the spectators hurt his ears. Curge glanced around. The viewing box had been empty when he arrived, and even though he knew Gastillo was dead and gone, he still expected to see the gold-faced owner when he opened the door. Instead, he'd discovered the entire area vacant except for the manservant waiting to fill his goblet with wine.

Curge sighed and finished off that very drink. He growled for more and got it right away. A man could get used to such luxury. He imagined royalty lived as such, which led to him thinking he *was* a king, of the games at least, or at least nobility. Either one suited him. He wasn't picky.

The chanting died away as Sorban exited the arena floor. Attendants rushed to Wocello's aid and attempted to revive the unmoving pit fighter. A door slammed behind Curge, startling him just a little, but he didn't let it show.

Nexus.

"No interest in the day's opening match?" Curge asked after the wine merchant settled down one seat over, holding his own shiny goblet.

"Bah." Nexus spat and took in an unhurried mouthful. "I've other interests beside this. Butchery on a scale you could only dream. Bloody business all round. I might tell you just to see you sicken."

That made Curge curious. "You've heard of Gastillo's passing?"

Nexus rolled his eyes and sipped before answering. "Of course I heard. What of it? Can't say I'll miss his shiny face around here. My people say it was one of his men. His best man, in fact. The one called Prajus."

"I've heard the same."

"Gastillo," Nexus fumed, his sallow complexion studying the stands teeming with spectators. "What was that man thinking? To let a dog like that turn on him?"

"I've thought about that myself," Curge admitted. "In fact, my spies inform me he was last seen talking to you."

Nexus cleared his throat and looked Curge straight in the eye. "Now listen here, *Dark* Curge . . . If I wanted the man dead, it wouldn't be a tragic scene cut from a Perician stage."

"What did you talk about, then?"

"No business of yours." Nexus chuckled with salty exasperation. "You going to avenge him? If so, seek out that Prajus pisser out there, in the arena. I imagine there'll be plenty of Gastillo's men seeking his death in the Pit. But I'm generous today. Perhaps sympathetic to what happened to that golden-assed punce. Gastillo wasn't happy with the games. He sought my advice in matters of business. Seems he wished to leave all this wonder behind. I made it clear to him yesterday I had neither the gurry time nor patience to advise him."

Looking back at the audience, Nexus drank again. "Lords above. The day I wish to introduce a once gladiator to civilized business is the day I perish. Perhaps by having sea crabs dig their way into my hole and snap away at my spine until it severs."

Curge studied the man's profile, seeking signs of lie-telling. He couldn't discern anything of the sort.

"Stop looking at me with love in your eyes," Nexus warned without turning.

Curge did, but he wasn't satisfied with the merchant's admission.

"Have you drunk to Gastillo's memory?" Nexus asked.

"Ah yes, we were great friends," Curge said sardonically before a scowl crossed his face. "Really, Nexus. I despised every moment in the man's presence. Much like you, in fact."

"Tread lightly, Curge."

"The only thing that upsets me is something you've already touched upon. Prajus. He'll pay for that killing."

That quieted the wine merchant. "How do you mean?" he asked guardedly.

"Prajus. The man's season is finished. No one will take him in, not after what he's done. And if he does fight as a Free Trained, every gladiator will be hunting for his head. A trophy head, I might add. Especially Gastillo's pack. I might not have liked his company, but his men were loyal."

That made Nexus chuckle. "Loyal enough to kill him."

"You know what I mean."

"Perhaps the Chamber will do something about him."

"Prajus?" Curge shook his head. "They've no reason to. The killing happened outside of the Pit. Truth be known, the other houses will absorb those fighters wishing to continue. The ones they want, anyway. In a very short time, Gastillo's name will be forgotten. If he's smart, Prajus should leave the city for the lesser games. That is, if word of him killing his house master doesn't reach the houses in those parts."

Nexus studied his goblet. "A pity. Prajus was a fine warrior. Very capable."

"Still is," Curge allowed. "But he's all alone now."

Nexus didn't respond.

That aroused Curge's suspicions. "Something troubling you, Nexus?"

"Gastillo's death," the wine merchant answered easily enough. "That's all . . ."

Halfway through the last fight, Nexus stood and left Curge's company without a word. He thought about Gastillo's death, had been thinking about it ever since his agent informed him of the killing and the man responsible. What he hadn't divulged to Curge was that Prajus himself and a small pack of loyal followers had graced his audience chamber that very morning, just after Nexus enjoyed a breakfast of boiled eggs and fresh grapes.

The four brutes had all resembled worried children. Nexus smiled at the memory.

He granted them permission to stay upon his property until he returned from the day's events. In truth, he was curious about the arena's mind on such matters. It secretly pleased Nexus that Curge hadn't known about the gladiators' place of hiding. Gastillo was an idiot, a gullible topper hiding behind a mask of gold. Whatever had driven the man to attempt killing a beast like Prajus was a mystery in itself. Nexus wondered if Gastillo's lapse of reason had been a result of their negotiations. If so, the man was weaker than he'd suspected.

Still, Nexus supposed formal thanks were in order to his human weasel Bojen, for locating Prajus and his outlaw gang before they fled the games entirely.

The man's season is finished. No one will take him in, not after what he's done. And if he does fight as a Free Trained, every house fighter will be hunting for his head.

He should have thanked Curge for saying that. That kind of information would make the approaching discussion much more interesting.

His koch awaited him, surrounded by a dozen personal guards. A manservant opened the transport's door and closed it behind the wine merchant. There, in the warm shadows of the interior, secret delight spread through Nexus's person. It remained with him all the way back to his private properties, situated near the well-guarded and patrolled estates belonging to the nobility.

ABOUT THE BLOOD

Upon arriving home, he gave instructions to a waiting Bojen. He then marched directly to a chamber brightly lit by a wagon wheel of burning candles hanging overhead. Rosemary scented the air, though not too heavily. A large square table, pitted in places from the slamming down of mugs or goblets, dominated the main floor. Rich Sunjan and Marrnite tapestries adorned the walls, covering the otherwise bare timbers. The hanging cloth depicted various scenes of nature, except for one in which a heavy hammer fell upon a waiting anvil. It seemed odd, especially when one considered the surrounding silver-threaded stags charging through forests.

That was how Nexus liked it, though.

He sat at the table's head, settling into a striking chair of polished wood.

In short time, his white-bearded agent entered, leading four of the most sullen and dejected faces Nexus had ever seen in a long time. The way they walked in, wary and hollow-eyed as if about to receive judgement, made him even more pleased.

"Stand," he commanded them, the word echoing in the room. "There. The end of the table. Let's have a look at you."

Prajus held his head higher than the others, not yet ready to submit to the merchant. Nexus smiled inwardly. He'd break him soon enough.

His trainers, Bernd and Rezzo, entered, and Nexus indicated they wait close by. The trainers eyed the foursome reproachfully. Word traveled fast amongst the houses and the schools.

"Well," Nexus began and sat up in his seat. "Dead men can apparently walk after all."

Silence answered that.

"I've just come back from the games, where I conversed with Dark Curge. You know who Dark Curge is, correct?"

The four men nodded, though Prajus just barely. Nexus noted a faint slip of the brave face. The man was worried after all.

"You know what he had to say of Gastillo's death? He said—which one of you dogs is Prajus, by the way?"

The three indicated Prajus as he lifted a hand.

"Ah. Well, according to Curge, your season is over. There's not a house or school or stable within Sunja that will take you in after what you've done. Did you hear me? No one. You three? By association alone, you are probably equally finished. In fact, I'm not even sure my training staff would want anything to do with you. Any of you. And yet, because of my generous nature, I've granted refuge to you all, especially *you*, Prajus."

"Thank you for that," the gladiator replied quietly.

Nexus leveled his icy gaze at the handsome Sunjan with the short white hair. "You address me as *Master*, you white coil of maggot shite," he warned with iron in his voice. "You address me as befitting my status, and you don't forget it, else my guards spread your rosy cheeks and prod you with their spears. Repeatedly."

Prajus's face tightened around the jawline, and his eyes narrowed. In the end, however, he lowered his stare.

Not so bad at all, Nexus thought. "As I was saying, according to the Dark One, you're finished. My man Bojen has said as much. Said no one will even look at you for what you've done. No one will allow you to fight under their name in Sunja. Not you. If you continue to fight as a professional gladiator, the best you might be able to do are the games in Vathia. And that's only until they discover who you are. What . . . you've done. Do you agree?"

Appearing like worms feeling the hook, Prajus and his pack nodded.

"You actually killed your last owner," Nexus continued with forced wonder. "The very man who fed you; provided you with shelter, weapons, and armor; and trained you. You killed a man who, by all accounts, invested a large sum of coin into your miserable hide, and you *killed* him. I don't know what brought that about. I don't care who brought it about. He challenged, and you killed him. Gastillo's dead, and you are as unwanted as . . ." Nexus's eyed the ceiling, searching for a suitable simile. "As blood ticks suckling a dog's blossom. Am I right?"

"Yes, Master Nexus," they muttered, aware of their situation.

"Well . . ." The wine merchant leaned forward, placing his elbows upon the table. "What should I do with you? How will you profit me? Your very presence here will cause a considerable amount of ill will from the other owners. It's wiser if I simply turned you away. But I saw an opportunity in you. Truth be known, and fortunate for you, I don't care what the other owners think of me. I'm searching for talent. My own gladiators are enjoying a degree of success within the Pit, but . . ."

He allowed that to hang.

"You, Prajus. I've seen you fight. I actually have reason to kill you now, simply from the monetary loss invested in the men—*my* men—that you killed. But I'm a merchant. I've a sense for worth and opportunity. Perhaps we can come to an understanding of sorts, make it so you'll have a room this night. By the way . . . how is it you got away from Gastillo's gladiators and guardsmen?"

No one answered, but eyes flickered to Prajus, who said, "A passing Street Watch heard the commotion. Thought it strange. They demanded entry into the grounds and, after a round of questioning, decided I was innocent and let me go. These men followed."

"Innocent?" Nexus barked and hid his smile behind a hand. "You're far from innocent, Prajus. Not guilty of murder, I suppose, but far from innocent."

Despite the rebuke, Prajus straightened, sensing a change of fortune upon the air.

"You other three," Nexus said in a dead tone. "Get out. Now. Never come back."

The dogs behind Prajus stiffened and looked at their leader. To Nexus's secret glee, the indifferent bastard didn't even so much as glance at them—a true snake if Nexus had ever seen one.

"Don't make me repeat myself," Nexus warned, scalding them with his eyes. "Bojen."

Upon hearing his name, the agent, who had quietly made his way to the rear, rapped upon the main doors. The doors swung open, and the household guard, in full fearsome battle armor, presented themselves, swords and shields at the ready.

The four men had nothing but the scant clothing on their backs. Three of them tensed, poised to run or fight to the death.

"Prajus?" one of them asked, his tanned face becoming angrier with every passing beat.

Six armed guards marched into the room. At least that many were waiting outside.

"Prajus?" the tanned pit fighter asked a second time.

"Be quiet," Nexus said with disdain. "Guards, if these three speak anywhere between here and the main gates, you have my permission to gut them."

That stunned the three pit fighters into silence.

"See to it they leave without damaging anything in a fit of despair or anger," Nexus continued. "If they do . . ."

He chopped the air with an open hand.

"As you wish, Master Nexus," one of the household guards said. He stepped aside, as did the others behind him, creating a lane.

On cue, Bojen gestured for the expelled gladiators to leave. Their expressions amused Nexus. He was even more impressed with Prajus's indifference.

The three rejected men followed the guards outside, glancing back in hopes Nexus might change his mind.

He did not.

Once the room cleared, Nexus studied Prajus. "I've wanted you dead for some time now. But as I've said, I recognize opportunities when they present themselves. If you were to fight for me, under the School of Nexus, what would you give me?"

Prajus didn't hesitate. "I'd give you the honor of housing a champion these very games."

Nexus took his time considering the offer, even flicking his eyes to the trainers present.

"Would you oversee him?" Nexus asked, knowing the answer.

"We would," the trainer called Bernd replied at once.

"Would our lads accept him?"

"They would if it was your wish."

Nexus allowed time for that statement to reach full flavor.

"The riches would be considerable," Prajus said, brow lowered and watching his potential house master.

The wine merchant scoffed. "I know that, you treacherous cord of gurry. Coin is the only reason I'd take you in. Have no doubt there."

"I can give you that," the gladiator said.

Nexus grimaced, making a scene of being tortured with the decision. In his mind, he'd already won. "Doesn't it give you fear," he asked, genuinely curious, "knowing that no one will stand behind you after what you've done? And that once you do fight, every house will be after your head?"

Prajus didn't hesitate. "Let them. It won't be my head rolling in the sands. And no, I'm not fearful. Perhaps worried that my season might be done, but not fearful. I know what I'm worth. At the very least, I'll find employment elsewhere. A war, maybe."

"Then perhaps I'll leave you to it."

"If you'll have me," Prajus offered, "I'll fight for the School of Nexus. I'll bring you victories and the heads to prove them. Truth be known, I'd kill Gastillo a second time if I could. And if the Street Watch hadn't happened by when they did, I would've killed whoever challenged me afterward."

Nexus gripped his almost nonexistent chin. "I believe I'll take that chance," he finally decided. "I'll back you. You are now under my banner, Prajus of Sunja. Sunja, correct? Good. Just making certain. Some of these shaggers from far-off lands speak the language as naturally as any. Twists my guts. But heed my warning, Prajus, you insolent, rebellious maggot. You do as I say. You do as *they* say."

He stabbed a finger in the trainers' direction.

Nexus's gaze settled upon his newest gladiator. "I'll say this once. I'll warn you of this once. I'm *not* Gastillo. My fortunes aren't resting upon your shoulders. I'm in these games because it pleases me to win. I think you might do that. But understand: if you displease me, if you show the slightest hesitation for one of my commands, one of *their* commands, I'll have my lads hold you down while I personally screw my thumbs into your screaming head . . . by way of your eyes. You serve me, now. And I am a harsh master. Do you understand me, you brazen ring of a dog blossom?"

A somber-looking Prajus didn't flinch. "I understand."

"Your companions"—Nexus pointed toward the door—"I cast them out. What do you think of that?"

"They weren't my companions."

Cold, Nexus thought in admiration while struggling to keep his face impassive. The pit fighter was cold, ruthless, even. He'd be a success in any business venture. Nexus could tell.

"Bernd. Rezzo," Nexus said.

The trainers came to attention.

"Take this hellpup away, and show him his quarters. Inform Tino. Make it known he's one of us now. Anyone who takes offense to that may leave immediately. Place guards about the barracks in case of any words. Give them permission to discipline if necessary. Prajus."

The gladiator and wine merchant regarded one another.

"Welcome," Nexus said. "To my school. Such as it is."

The man dipped his head, not taking his eyes off his new employer. "Thank you, Master Nexus."

He said it with genuine respect, which was a good sign, but Nexus wondered if Prajus knew he was serious with his threat of blinding. Truth be known, Nexus would yank the man's tongue from his head if he detected the slightest insolence.

When the trainers and newly acquired killer departed the audience chamber, Nexus desired to indulge in some very expensive wine from his private stock. He offered a silent thanks to Gastillo. *To think I'd been prepared to pay good coin for the services of Prajus.*

How the world surprised him at times.

45

After spending the night at Shan's house and offending his wife yet again with the crowd, Goll recruited Clades to accompany him back to the arena. The Kree wanted to see if the Madea had kept his word about delivering scrolls to their private chambers. He had discussed his intentions with Clavellus, who, with the rest of the Ten, would later meet the house master before the Gladiatorial Chamber.

People cluttered the street, making walking tiresome and allowing the morning sun to bake them just a little longer. Goll stopped for children darting before him, paused for clusters of old Sunjan men and women, and threaded a slow, dangerous path amongst farmers leading cows, sheep, and horses.

"How did you ever do it?" Goll asked Clades upon barely dodging a stream from a voiding cow.

"What?" the soldier asked.

"Live here."

"I grew up here," he answered simply. "It's home."

"And you married here?"

"Fortunate enough, yes."

"Brave man."

"You're not married?"

Goll shook his head. "Not to a woman. Not yet. To the profession, yes. Time enough for women after."

"You hope."

"Not really. If it happens, I'll pursue it. If it doesn't, I'll probably be dead."

"Master Goll, thank you again. For allowing me to serve the house. Even Pratos and Valka are pleased with their positions."

"Thank you," Goll said, directing the gratitude back while avoiding an open cart filled with fragrant chickens. The farmer sitting high in his wagon's perch and steering a team of two horses studied the Kree with a puzzled frown.

"We appreciate having you," Goll said.

"I fought in the Pit once, did you know?"

A pair of short elderly ladies armed with walking sticks and pointed elbows cut across Goll's path, halting him.

"You did?" he asked. "Is that how you met Shan?"

"No. He's the regular healer of my wife and me."

Ah, Goll mouthed before his attention was occupied with how to best maneuver around a line of brown-robed Salish priests. "Never knew that. Wish to return to the Pit?"

"What?" Clades asked, half a smile on his face.

"Do you wish to return to fighting?" Goll asked. "Under the house's name?"

That struck Clades as an interesting thought, and it showed.

"No," he finally answered. "Perhaps not."

"Because of your wife?"

"Because of my wife. She'd never forgive me if I perished."

"Suppose not," Goll said and picked up speed, knowing the arena was drawing closer. "Think about it, anyway. Discuss it with her if you like. With the season as long as it is, I don't think there would be an issue with you returning. What was your record?"

Clades smiled. "One loss."

"You didn't win?"

"No."

That didn't impress Goll. "But you survived."

"I did. In one piece, as well."

"Perhaps it's best you remain a guard, then."

"Perhaps, Master Goll."

Past the wagons, the livestock herds, and over the heads of the surrounding people, the towering walls of Sunja's Pit loomed. The street opened onto the stone-tiled expanse surrounding the impressive structure. A crow glided overhead. Goll concentrated upon moving through the tides of fragrant flesh. He and Clades emerged from the masses and approached the arena's Gate of the Sun. The smells of fresh roasting meats wafted from nearby food stands. The Pit's imposing heights shielded them from the sun's glare, and the two men soon entered the tunnel system. They made their way beneath ground level, stopping upon arriving at the Ten's assigned chamber.

The door was open just a sliver.

Goll yanked it open.

Naulis whirled, overbite and sunken chin a-quivering.

"Lords above," the messenger gasped, visibly shaken. "I might've just pissed myself."

Goll ignored him. "Any news?" he asked, moving inside with Clades at his back.

The small man struggled to compose his skinny self. "None, Master Goll. I just wandered back from the Madea, who told me to stick my head inside here."

"He sent you here?"

"He did. There are no new matches upon the board yet. But the Madea told me to stay close by. Not that I want to. The stink about this place thickens by the day."

That put a smirk upon Goll's face. The Madea was finally doing his job. "We'll be leaving the city this morning," he said. "after we visit the Gladiatorial Chamber. If you learn anything, meet us there. Spare you a trip to the villa. Where's Borchus?"

The man paused. "I don't know."

"But he sent you here?"

"Well, yes."

"When did you speak with him last?"

"Last night."

"And?"

"And he told me to come here this morning. To general quarters. I hate general quarters, Master Goll. It smells. And that's not the worst—"

Goll raised his hand. "You saw Borchus last night?"

Naulis swallowed. "I did."

"Where?"

"At my home."

"Where is he now?"

"I don't know. I don't know where he lives or sleeps. He's become very cautious these days. I didn't expect him last night, but he informed me to let you know all is well."

That did nothing to reassure Goll in the least.

"Lords above," the Kree muttered and remembered the Salish brotherhood wandering the streets. He couldn't remember if they worshipped Seddon or the Lords, but he felt the need to call upon one of the heavenly deities.

"You have a message for him?" Naulis asked, thumbing a strand of greasy hair from his eyes.

"Yes, I'm not pleased with his service."

Downcast, Naulis nodded. *Oh*, he mouthed.

"Tell him that when you meet again," Goll said.

"I don't know when that will happen. He usually finds me. Believes it safer that way."

Frustrated with the spy and absent agent, Goll left the room with Clades following him. The house master prepared himself for the confrontation with the Gladiatorial Chamber.

The games' ruling body hadn't pleased Goll either.

The wagons halted before the five-story building housing the Gladiatorial Chamber. The tall structure nestled against the northern wall of the arena itself, its lofty heights allowing Chamber members to view the fights from high above if they desired. Gray-and-white rock composed the outer shell of the building while a row of six white marble columns rose from street level to a broad overhang, offering protection from the elements if needed. The bases of the pillars were chiseled into scenes depicting small battling figures and ferocious animals. A pair of great oak doors, fashioned to fit an archway, lay just beyond the marble giants. A dozen Skarrs stood at attention on either side of the entrance, their visors dull but watchful.

Clavellus stood before the majestic sight and committed it to memory, drawing fresh ink over the old pictures of his mind. He studied every crook and crevice, every angle and weather-born scratch, fearing he might never see it again in his lifetime.

Machlann stood beside him, studying the establishment with a scornful eye as if, after all these years, nothing had really changed. "Did you ever think," the trainer asked in an uncharacteristically low voice, "that we'd ever see this beast again?"

Clavellus shook his head. "No. Never."

"But here we are."

"Here we are."

"We should've accompanied the lads inside."

That made the taskmaster frown. "That would only rouse a commotion. Besides... the place is probably infested with spies. It's bold to be standing here, truth be known."

"They already know about us," Machlann growled but glanced around nevertheless.

Koba's intimidating bulk stood a few paces back, near the corner of the first wagon. The house guards lingered nearby, as well as Junger, who hung about the rear of the second wagon, where Brozz rested.

"Not that I'm worried." the old trainer resumed. "Nothing will happen with this pack standing about."

"No, I suppose not."

"Still think it's an idea to go inside?"

Clavellus shook his head. "Go on, then. You don't need me."

"You talk better than I do," the trainer admitted. "You're all silk. I'm all scrub brush."

"You talk fine when you're not training hellpups."

"You're right. I do. But you'll have their attention all the same. Perhaps even more." Machlann studied the building's heights. "Never truly liked this place."

"I did hear Odant still holds power over the rest."

"Still? A wonder."

Clavellus nodded that it was.

"Unfortunate we can't stay for the day's fights," Machlann said.

"Unfortunate, indeed," Clavellus said, thinking of Dark Curge's warning weeks before. "Goll wishes to return."

Looking sour, Machlann didn't comment.

"Fear not," Clavellus said. "The season's a long one now. We'll be seeing plenty of action before it's all done."

The old trainer eyed his companion. "Do I looked fearful to you?"

Clavellus frowned.

Around the edges of the square, where the sun whitened flat fitted stones, children skipped and ran while people walked and lingered. Not many food stalls or merchants were to be seen, fewer than Clavellus remembered. He supposed administrative duties held no attraction for most people. He watched the people meandering the fringes of the square and wondered if any of them were spies of Dark Curge.

Not that he was worried by that.

46

"You waited a long time before?" Muluk whispered in Kree, feeling more secure in his own tongue. The chamber's shadows lent his battered but healing features an even more menacing appearance.

"A long time," Goll answered in kind, minding the dim interior and appreciating the coolness.

"With Halm?"

"Aye that."

"What he's doing now, I wonder?"

Goll's brow shrugged. "Doing whatever he likes, I suppose. That's his way."

"I wonder if he met the woman again."

"Ah, her."

"What do you think?"

"About the woman?"

"Miji, I think her name is."

"She'll either be flattered, or she won't," Goll said, the Chamber's inner doors holding his attention. "He hasn't returned to us yet, so maybe he's charmed her. The Zhiberian is a friendly sort."

The description placed a smile upon Muluk's face. "He is that. I remember when I first met him. In the Pit. We could've stood there and talked the whole time. And after, when he won, we went looking for drinks. Can you believe that? Not many would do such a thing."

"Not many," Goll agreed.

"Goll," Muluk said, suddenly serious, "I've been thinking. None of this would have happened if it weren't for you. None of it. I certainly wouldn't be here. I'd still be out there, begging for a bit of work. Perhaps even scraps. But because of you, I have more now than I ever did. Than I ever thought I would. A bed at night. Food on the table, usually *hot*, and prepared by someone else, even."

"Thank Clavellus for that," Goll pointed out. "It's his servants doing the cooking. And it's his property."

"His beer too."

They both smiled at that.

"Well, just so you understand... the way I see it, I wouldn't be here if it wasn't for you. *He* wouldn't be out there if it wasn't for you. So, if I haven't said it already, thank you. For all of this." Muluk gestured with his nearly fingerless paw of a hand.

At a rare loss for words, Goll nodded somberly and kept his silence. That butchered hand bothered him. Muluk's wounds, sustained while protecting the Ten's coin, were because of him, in his mind. If he turned his head, he'd see that unsightly knot of pink scar tissue where Muluk's left ear was no more.

Goll didn't turn his head, though. He focused on the arena messengers flittering about.

"And I don't think you should return to fighting," Muluk said.

That fishhooked Goll's attention. "What?"

"You heard me. I think you should stay away from the sands entirely. I knew you would win yesterday, but there's always a chance..." Muluk gently chopped at the air, making his meaning clear. "One error on your part. One surprising move from your opponent, and you might not come back. None of this would have ever happened without you. None of it. And for that reason, you should stop. Because if you *die* out there, I feel this house, this very fragile house, will fall apart."

"You'd manage."

"Me?" Muluk said in complete surprise and chuckled. "I'm a *punce*, man. I'm not a leader. Look at me." He held up his mutilated hand again and wiggled the stumps of the missing digits.

"Muluk," Goll explained quietly from one corner of his mouth. "If there's anything *I've* learned since meeting you, it's that you're every bit as important to the house as any other. I might have led you here, but a head is nothing without a body. Without a *heart*. You think about that. You think you do little, but in truth, you do that which . . . I cannot. You're a friend to all. Much like Halm, in that sense. I saw you sitting next to Pig Knot when he was in sour moods. I saw you go searching for him when he'd gone for long periods. I see you talking to the guards, talking to the servants. In fact"—Goll smiled—"all you *do* is talk. I'm still wondering how you'll fare with Ajik, but you'll find a way to talk with him as well. And Ajik aside, people listen to you because they want to. They don't always do that for me."

Muluk's hairy features creased in thought.

"And if someone crosses you?" Goll smiled faintly. "Well, just ask those six dead men who tried to steal our coin. And you without a stitch on."

"All right, how about this, then? I don't *want* to lead. There. I said it. Which is why I prefer having you alive."

"You might not want to lead, but there are those who would argue that's the reason why you *should*. If I should perish, I'm saying."

"You're not going to perish."

"You weren't so confident a moment ago," Goll countered.

The inner doors opened, and a robed man motioned for both of them to enter.

"We'll talk about this another time, if you wish," Goll said, rising.

Both house masters followed the Chamber man inside.

The red wood of the semicircle dais appeared all the more polished because of the surrounding drab walls. Raised above a creamy marble floor, the seats of the Chamber members were empty. Despite the heat outside, the inner chamber was cool. Goll stopped at a waist-high table designated for visitors, and Muluk flanked him. There they stood and inspected the dismal grayness of the stone.

"Where are they?" Muluk whispered.

Goll didn't know and turned. The attendant stood near the closed doors, along with a handful of armed Skarrs on either side of the entrance.

Then, as if the question had been overheard, three Chamber members filed into the room. Their robes of gold and white appeared all the more regal against the gray stonework and polished wood. All three appeared well fed and were in various stages of balding. As they found their seats, Goll recognized the one-eared man, his hair and beard neatly cut short, and recalled the other wizened faces.

"Master Goll, is it?" asked the one-eared man, whose scars served warning not to waste his time.

"It is," he answered, knowing full well they knew his name.

The one-eared individual regarded Muluk. "And you are?"

"Muluk. Same house."

"The Free Trained one," smirked a long-bearded man with a ruddy face. His belly forced him to lean back from the panel before him, and he appeared to hitch his hand upon a hip as he inspected the men.

No apology was offered for the slight, which bothered Goll.

"So, young Master," Odant rumbled and finished with a disturbing swallow. "What is it you wish to discuss?"

Silence ensued.

"Where are the other members?" Goll asked, still managing to sound civil.

"I'm Odant," the one-eared man announced, as if he hadn't heard the question. "That one is Soranthus. And this is Pallus."

Pallus continued to smile as if addressing naughty children.

Soranthus, to his credit, appeared to be the youngest of the three, while Odant, with his ashen features and missing ear, looked the oldest. Pallus seemed a few years younger but in better health.

"The others could not be present," Odant finished with a rattle and puffed out both his cheeks.

Goll allowed the silence to deepen then asked, "And why not? Isn't that the function of the Chamber? To hear the concerns of the house masters?"

The expressions of Odant and Soranthus didn't change, but Pallus's smile widened, exposing amber teeth spaced far apart.

Color crept into Goll's cheeks. "Is something the matter, Master Pallus?"

The Chamber member's amusement didn't fade, but his brow crinkled ever so slightly, as if puzzled. "Say whatever it is you've come to say, Free Trained." He chuckled. "And be off. More important matters await us this day."

Goll didn't immediately respond, yet much later, in other selected company, Muluk would report he actually felt heat radiating from his friend's person.

"Master Pallus," Goll began, speaking slowly, with a nearly perfect inflection of the Sunjan accent. He focused on the member with an unwavering stare. "I've been taught from an early age that men in positions such as yours are to be respected. I'll let that jab go unanswered and hope there won't be another."

Pallus's brow arched, yet his smile remained.

Odant's red eyes shifted from Goll to Pallus and back to Goll, rolling in their sockets as if badly in need of tears. "Say your piece, Master Goll," he rasped wearily.

Soranthus watched the two house masters, his thoughts expertly hidden.

Goll kept his chin high. "I wish to discuss a lack of recognition within these chamber walls."

More silence.

Pallus squinted as if growing less interested with each passing moment. A stoic Soranthus didn't blink, content to wait for more.

"A lack of recognition?" Odant repeated sleepily and rested his chin upon a hand.

"Aye that, a lack of recognition."

"We heard you the first time," Pallus said, shrugging his shoulders.

"Well then, listen," Goll said right back. "We paid a generous sum of coin to be formally recognized by the Chamber. To be rightfully considered a part of this season's games and any that follow. We believed that included being addressed and treated with respect equal to the other, more venerable houses, regardless of history. My issue with the games and the Chamber this day is to ask why we *aren't* receiving that courtesy and respect?"

Odant absorbed the little speech, rubbed his nose, and looked at the other members. Pallus seemed right and proper entertained, as if he'd discovered an abandoned dog performing tricks for attention. Soranthus, however, leaned back with a troubled but thoughtful expression.

Odant cleared his throat again, a nasty, volcanic sputtering on the cusp of becoming ugly. "You are given," he said after the rumble had passed, "every courtesy as any other house, school, or stable." The Chamber member sighed then, as if hoping the explanation would soothe any ill feelings.

"We are not," Goll retorted.

The one-eared member didn't blink. "You are."

"We are not."

Pallus chuckled and gazed at the ceiling.

Odant glared and smacked his lips. "Master Goll, we're very busy this day and don't have the time or patience for such . . . bantering."

"There have been two slights against the House of Ten," Goll explained. "The first is how we're being notified of scheduled fights. We haven't been receiving them."

"Are you not outside the city?" Odant asked.

"We are. Roughly half a day's travel."

"Is that walking or wagon or horse?"

"Wagon."

"Then distance is a problem."

"We should have schedules left in our private chambers, then," Goll said. "In a timely fashion so that our messengers can easily retrieve and deliver them to us."

"Noted," Odant allowed.

"We recently received word that the season has been extended by the king. We were never officially informed of this even though, by my estimations, we were in the city when you were addressing concerns of all other house owners and masters."

Pallus scratched his belly and looked at the ceiling.

"A messenger was sent," Odant explained. "You must have already left your quarters. One was not sent to your villa. Our messengers do not venture beyond the city's walls. To do so would . . . thin out our resources. I suggest if you wish to receive such notices, you should designate a closer address."

"Our private chambers are fine," Goll said. "Just leave any scrolls inside, in plain sight, where they can be easily found."

"Then that will be done," Odant said, believing the hearing concluded. "Anything else, Master Goll?"

The house master remained behind the table. "One final item."

Pallus slapped the wood before him.

Odant and Soranthus waited with neutral expressions.

"Respect," Goll began. "As the member on your left has so boldly let slip, Master Odant, there seems to be a lingering belief that the House of Ten are Free Trained. We are Free Trained no longer. I believe we've lifted ourselves above that distinction. We have paid your fee and formally registered for these games within this very room, before yourselves and six others like you. Some people might think we're mocking the integrity of the games. That is not true. Truth be known, we're making history. We're motivated. And determined. To prove all doubters wrong. We intend to surprise those people."

"Do you, now?" Pallus quietly sneered.

"We do. Surprise a few. Startle a few more. And genuinely frighten the remainder. I wonder what group you'll belong to, Master Pallus."

House master and Chamber member locked gazes then.

"I wonder," Pallus stated with evil sweetness.

Muluk fidgeted uneasily.

"Ah, yesss," Pallus said, his eyes narrowed. "I think I remember you now. Didn't you fight a Free Trained dog just yesterday, Goll?"

Goll bristled. "I'd remind you to use titles within the Chamber."

"You ... speak very well, Goll," Pallus observed. "Well enough for a Kree visiting our fair city. I could almost respect you ... if I didn't know where you came from, that is. You see, I'm one member of this council who wanted your house bid to be thrown out of that door behind you. Just like the gurry it is. Truth be known, I still do, but I understand the Chamber's financial needs to take your coin. Now? I'll wait for the other houses to drive you from the games. To slaughter every last one of you dogs as you appear upon the sands. Before you stain it any further."

"I'll be pleased to disappoint you, Master Pallus," Goll said after a moment, controling his voice.

"Disappoint me?" Pallus snorted. "It's already *begun*, lad. How many hellpups do you have left in the games? Four? Three? It's a much longer season, now. How long do you think they'll last out there? Against true, battle-tested gladiators? Against trained killers hunting for their heads?"

"As long as they have to," Goll answered.

The elder member snickered with undisguised dislike. "I'll tell you one thing, Odant," Pallus said and pointed at Goll. "I *like* this one's mindset. I do appreciate an iron will. It'll be exquisite watching him break. If he wasn't such an affront to the whole business—"

"Master Pallus," Odant rumbled, not bothering to look in the other's direction.

Pallus studied the older man's profile for the length of a heartbeat, then he relaxed and quieted, but a little smile remained.

Odant allowed a moment of silence. "I won't speak honeyed words and attempt to hide Master Pallus's disdain for your house, Master Goll," he explained slowly. "I believe you to be an intelligent man. You know this would be the way. That there would be more than a few individuals who are . . . skeptical, critical even, of your ambitions. Like Master Pallus, here. I don't think that should be a surprise to you. Am I correct?"

Goll simmered. "You are."

"So, we will strive to do better to include you in our future meetings. I will ask you for something in return, Master Goll. Your task, as it always has been, will be to prove you're a legitimate force in this year's event. Do that—have your pit fighters do that—and I think you will sway some opinions. Not all, but enough. Do that, and I think you won't be so . . . sensitive about your Free Trained beginnings."

Pallus remained quiet, but he leered at the pair of Kree men.

"Wise counsel, Master Odant," Goll coolly admitted.

"Is there anything else?"

"No, Master Odant."

"Anything from you?" the Chamber member asked Muluk.

For a moment, the once gladiator couldn't find his voice. "Ah . . . no. No, Master Odant."

"Then we're done," Odant declared.

47

With the sun already nearly unbearable, Junger shifted and fidgeted outside the wagon, no longer comfortable. Sweat ran down his back and soaked the shirt he was wearing. It would need a washing upon returning home. On impulse, he glanced into the back of the second wagon. The canvas flap was hitched back to allow light inside. The interior was shaded, so he would avoid burning his skin, but he would still bake. The heat was merciless.

Sore and battered from his most recent match, Brozz attempted to relax near the rear gate, his forked moustache raised in a little smile. His hands rested near the place the awful spike had pierced him. A thick wad of clean cloth was bound across his midsection while blood flies of some unknown species buzzed around him.

"The sun . . . is too much for you, Perician?" he asked in a pained voice.

"It is," Junger answered. "It's a terrible heat."

"Midsummer," Shan observed, sitting a little farther inside the same wagon. "It'll be this way for another month before it cools, and it'll be a slow cooling at that. Must be hellish upon the arena floor."

"I don't look forward to it," Junger admitted.

The Sarlander's face scrunched in blunt puzzlement. "You fight near naked, anyway. What difference is it to you?"

"I don't like the heat," Junger explained simply. "All that armor. Sweat sliding into your eyes and cracks. Cloth clinging to your frame. Not for me."

A blood fly pitched on Brozz's forehead. He shooed the thing away. "Doesn't like the heat," he whispered and quietly chuckled. "He ends fights . . . in a heartbeat. Never pulls steel on his opponents. And . . . and won't wear armor because . . ."

"It's too hot," Shan finished with a smile.

An amused Brozz exhaled mightily, grateful for the diversion.

Junger squinted a question at the pair. Brozz smiled, which ended with a grimace. He looked at his stomach wound.

"Easy there," Shan advised, leaning forward. "Just allow the salve to do its work. Try not to tighten your muscles too much."

Concerned, Junger stepped closer and peered in on the wounded Sarlander. "There's a good thing to keep in mind, good Brozz. If you can't fight, there's plenty of drinking to be done. You can join Muluk and Clavellus. If you drink, that is. Do you?"

"At times."

"You'll be in good company then, with those two," Junger noted. "Especially now, with Halm and Pig Knot gone. Muluk in particular will need someone to drink with."

"Junger," Brozz said quietly and twirled a finger, indicating the man turn around.

The Perician did and saw two young women eyeing him from across the square.

"Admirers of yours?" Shan asked.

"No idea."

"They know you. Your reputation is spreading."

"A few more victories and . . ." Brozz grimaced. "The children will know you."

Junger waved to the young ladies, attractive in their simple summer robes tied off at the waist. The gesture pleased them, and they walked off, whispering to each other.

"You might be a force in the arena, Junger of Pericia," Shan observed, "but you're terrible with the ladies. If you had asked nicely, they might've offered to clean you up after a fight. Wipe down all that sweat."

That lit up Brozz's bruised features.

A few passing Sunjans witnessed the female attention Junger had just enjoyed. They slowed and puzzled over who he was. The Perician turned his back to them.

"Why not wave?" Brozz asked, feigning puzzlement.

Junger frowned.

"Why not?" Brozz persisted. "They recognize you."

Junger wasn't interested.

"A true swordsmaster would wave to *all* of his admirers, I would think, not just the pretty ones."

The healer smiled and glanced away.

"I think I liked you better when you had very little to say," Junger noted, glancing from one to the other. "Both of you."

Muluk and Goll exited the Gladiatorial Chamber.

"We're leaving," Goll announced.

"All settled?" Clavellus asked from the first wagon.

"As much as I suspect it will be."

"That's the Chamber for you."

Just then, Naulis emerged from the crowds, drawing the Ten's attention. Without a word, the spy quickly approached Goll and handed over a bound scroll. Goll cracked the wax seal and unraveled the document. The Madea didn't have the steadiest hand for writing, but Goll finished the message and handed it to Clavellus.

"Sorban," the taskmaster said after reading.

"Sorban," Goll repeated.

The house members boarded the wagons, and the drivers got the transports moving. Wheels rattled over the nearly level roads but dipped in places with jarring thumps, hard enough for Muluk to reach for balance.

"So what happened in there?" Clavellus demanded of the two house masters. The canvas covering colored the taskmaster's face in shadows.

Machlann sat nearby, waiting.

Goll told them everything as Muluk, sitting next to the rear, grabbed the canvas covering the back and flapped air into the interior.

"Nothing surprising there," Clavellus said once Goll finished. "Nothing at all."

"Their . . . amused arrogance . . . irritated me," Goll said.

"That one called Pallus was the worst," Muluk added, holding the canvas back.

"Use that," Clavellus said. "And make them choke on their words."

Goll relaxed and endured the near insufferable heat. He looked out the back of the wagon, seeing Sunja's streets pass by. *Make them choke on their words.*

That wasn't a bad idea at all.

48

After Hadree had passed away, every day since then threatened to pull Sindra deeper into a bog of misery and despair. Her heart felt as if it had been cleft in two. She knew the old man wouldn't have wanted her to act so, but for the life of her, she didn't have the fight to continue. Several times, she'd caught herself looking toward the end of the bar, expecting to see him there with his woolly face cupped in those ogre's mittens that resembled hands, gray eyes staring off into space, and ruminating upon some odd splinter that had caught in the netting of his mind: inconsequential nuggets of thought like "Why do people dislike creatures with many legs?" or "Does the sun ever sleep? Is the moon its cousin?" When Borchus was around, he'd challenge those thoughts or expand upon them. Their talks weren't always productive and were even more confusing at times, but they were never boring.

Those were silly thoughts and lengthy talks, and Hadree would reflect upon them . . . often . . . deeply.

However, Hadree wasn't standing at the end of the bar anymore.

Hadree was gone.

She absolutely did not want to call him *dead*, not just yet. *Gone* was far easier to accept, and since he was gone, he'd be returning someday, or she'd go to him, her adopted father, wherever he was, and hope to find him in good health and spirits, perhaps even pondering those little things that held no interest to her but which fascinated Hadree to no end. She dearly missed her adopted father. She missed his spotty yellow smile, hard to the mischievous and the devious but sweet to her. Also, oddly enough, she missed his scent—an odd mixture of mild sweat, smoke, and cooking spices that clung to his person. Hadree hadn't been much of a carpenter or a worker of metal. He disliked farming and stayed away from cutting wood and digging for water. Life in a Klaw didn't appeal to him at all.

Strangely enough, however, he liked *feeding* people. He enjoyed cooking something good and feeding them first, himself second. Watching people eat his food, be it bread, sweet pastry, or spiced roasts, put him in very fine spirits. In fact, that was how he'd come along to find Sindra, or so he told her. He'd been peeling potatoes when he heard a knock at his kitchen door, and a little girl, barefoot, dressed in a filthy sack, and smelling as foul as a shite trough had the iron to ask if he had anything to eat as she couldn't wait until later to search the garbage.

Hadree had taken her in, cleaned her up, and made certain she'd never have to pick and claw her way through a refuse pile ever again.

Gone now.

They'd had talks in the past about how the alehouse would be hers when he died. Sindra hated those conversations . . . despised them. However, Hadree would bring the subject up every now and again, always while talking about the alehouse and never when she was in a foul mood. He was good like that.

His will had been iron, and he made his wishes known. The alehouse was hers and hers alone. Hadree told her she was the daughter he'd always hoped for and that though the alehouse wasn't much, not much at all when one considered how big Sunja was or how big the world was, those timbers overhead and everything underneath were hers. Thus, a little girl who couldn't remember eating garbage and couldn't remember who her parents were but had been fortunate enough to find someone who cared, had come into ownership of an alehouse.

The cost had been terrible, though.

Sindra tried to keep the alehouse working and even kept on Hadree's guards, who gradually spent more time watching her than keeping the peace. The alehouse threatened to become a nest of debauchery and wickedness. Sindra wasn't about to let Hadree's home, *her* home, sink to a place from which there would be no redemption. An alehouse could be a warm fire or a raging tempest, and Sindra realized losing control was a real concern.

That was around the time Tilo had approached her.

He walked into her life with a beard resembling a wild, slovenly bush in need of watering. A pair of black eyes resembling unlit coals dipped in pitch peered out from the depths of that weathered face. He wasn't a tall man but was thick in the chest and stomach, the years having transformed muscle into fat. He sauntered along, unhurriedly, with a cane. A group of four warriors followed him into the alehouse, carrying weapons, sporting scars, and projecting an aura of menace the likes of which she'd very rarely encountered. One of the four was the biggest man Sindra had ever seen. Two of the guards hung back at the main door, holding onto sword hilts at their waists. The other two, including the mountain, stayed upon the fat man's heels.

Tilo wandered into the alehouse and saw it was empty of people. He noticed Sindra's hired guards all sitting around a table, drinking and talking. He eyed them critically but, once he'd passed them, ignored the four. Then he looked at her, his cane tapping as he walked over to where she stood behind the bar, cleaning mugs.

"You Sindra?" he asked in a puff of rancid breath and a flash of ill-kept teeth.

"I am," she said, removing her hands from the counter and thankful for the barrier between them.

The old man studied her for a bit, neither hard nor friendly. "My name's Tilo. I own a house of pit fighters."

Sindra nodded, having overheard the name from Borchus and Hadree.

"These your enforcers?" Tilo asked, not bothering to spare them another glance.

Sindra nodded.

"Not much of it, are they?"

The guard called Mori, who fashioned himself as dangerous, stood and eyed the back of Tilo's head from underneath a lowered brow. That was Mori's way of showing he wasn't pleased about something.

Sindra thought it pitiful. "Not really, no."

"I've heard you've had trouble keeping order here," Tilo said, "since Hadree's passing."

Thank Seddon he didn't say death. Sindra wasn't sure she could have kept her composure. "Aye that."

"You need enforcers. *Real* enforcers." His lips tightened into a sour ring. "Not them."

"I can hear you, old man," Mori said.

At that, the mountain and his companion made themselves known. They turned upon Mori and the three other seated guards, who'd become very quiet since Tilo started talking.

In the face of the mountain, Mori's hand went to his sword hilt and rested there.

"I knew Hadree," Tilo said calmly, ignoring what was happening behind his back. "He wouldn't want his guards sitting at a table like that, enjoying their time like an afternoon ripe for drinking."

"No," Sindra agreed wearily. "He wouldn't."

"Allow me to replace them. With a true enforcer."

Those black glistening rocks embedded deep in Tilo's head held Sindra's gaze and didn't waver, didn't flinch.

"All right," she said.

"Sindra!" Mori exclaimed.

"You're dismissed, Mori," she said quietly. "All of you. You were paid last night, so consider that meal and drink payment for your time today."

The words thundered in the room.

"This isn't right," Mori said eventually, lower lip trembling as his attention flickered between Sindra and the mountain.

"Nothing's been right recently," she admitted. "This might be the first right thing I've done."

"Hadree wouldn't have it!"

That angered her. "Go, Mori. And if you come back, you come back in peace."

Mori held his ground for a beat longer, undecided. He and his companions weren't the most physical of men, but somehow under Hadree, they'd been mustered into a capable enough force. Under Sindra, they'd become more of a burden, a nuisance, with sly looks and smiles. Worse of all, they'd displayed reluctance to take commands from anyone *not* Hadree... especially a woman.

"Go on, then," Sindra repeated.

As if proving a point, Mori didn't move.

Then Tilo half turned and looked at the mountain.

"Gurga," the house master said.

The mountain's face hardened, and the dull crackling of joints filled the alehouse.

Sindra realized in alarm that the sound was Gurga's knuckles.

His hands were tightening into fists.

A sheen of sweat covered Gurga's face even though it wasn't warm. The sweat soaked the man's black beard and hair. The mountain took one step forward, which counted as two for anyone else, and the three men sitting at the table scrambled to their feet. They left in a rustle of cloth and boot heels.

To the man's credit, Mori held his ground. "This isn't right, Sindra. It isn't right."

"Leave, Mori."

Gurga took another step, and Mori retreated toward the door, escaping the mountain's shadow. He didn't look back when he left the alehouse.

When all four of her guards were gone, Tilo returned his gaze to Sindra.

ABOUT THE BLOOD

"You're truly as lovely as a bell," he said, surprising her. Before she could reply, Tilo spoke again. "Hadree and I had an arrangement. Gladiators sometimes frequent this place. Not many, but enough. He would talk to them. Listen. And if he overheard something of interest, he'd get word to me. Since his passing, that hasn't happened. He mentioned you. Made it clear if . . . well . . . I knew he would leave the business to your hands. So I ask you to do the same for me as he did. Just listen. Talk. And tell me anything of interest. In return, I'll give you Gurga. If you wish it, he'll be your enforcer from this day forth."

Sindra studied Gurga then looked at Tilo. "What will this cost me?"

"Nothing," the gray-bearded owner said.

Sindra wondered if the man had even blinked since arriving.

"Give him a room up above, and feed him. He'll protect you and this place. He'll keep the peace. Peace is what I want. Gladiators are strange creatures. They train for hell yet avoid violence once free of it. If there's peace to be had here, they'll return. When they do, just listen. Talk a bit, even. But listen. Listen for injuries or any details concerning who they fight for. I'll have a man visit you every so often. That person might change at times, but they'll always identify themselves as working for me. Tell them anything you hear. Anything of interest. And that's all. Agreed?"

The question made her think of Borchus, who'd disappeared from her and Hadree's life months earlier. The short man had asked her to do exactly the same but didn't say to whom he was reporting. She had even done such favors for Borchus—mostly because it was Borchus—and because a part of her liked the idea of passing along morsels of information. Also, she'd been good at it, according to Borchus, anyway.

Sindra gazed up at Gurga. "Just one guard?"

Tilo's brow knotted in puzzlement. "Damnation, girl. How many do you need?"

*

All that had happened nine years before.

Even after nine years, the memory remained bright despite others fading with time, and in those years, Gurga's presence had maintained peace within the alehouse. A few scuffles occurred, but nothing he couldn't handle, not even when the drunks drew knives. Looking back, he was the best decision she'd made since assuming ownership of the alehouse. Mori and some of the other guards even returned, occasionally, after a few years, no longer sullen or angry at having been cut loose. That was good.

Over those years, Tilo had sent three different agents to visit her. The first was an older gentleman called Magsto. Sindra enjoyed talking with him as he took care in his appearance and smelled faintly of perfumed water, just enough to draw a woman in close, yet not overpowering. Magsto frequented the alehouse for about three years before a younger man called Slosa replaced him one evening without explanation. While Slosa wasn't a charmer like Magsto, Sindra came to like the agent's peculiar alertness. His eyes flittered about the room, watching everyone in every direction, almost birdlike in a way. Sindra would chuckle at the man's wary demeanor even though he made her nervous at times. Slosa lasted only about a year, however, and disappeared without a word of warning, much like Magsto . . . like Borchus. She never asked Slosa what happened to Magsto.

And she never asked Senturo about Slosa.

Senturo.

Where she had fond memories of the other agents, she didn't care at all for Senturo.

Senturo was a predator of women and anyone else perceived weaker than himself. He was also a manipulator of people and a liar. Sindra didn't like him because he stared and talked to her as a child at times. His smile wasn't truly a smile but rather a showing of teeth. Any evening when he didn't appear at her alehouse was enough to make her happy.

Her alehouse—she still felt strange calling it that even after all those years. Tonight, the place had filled quickly with the usual collection of drinkers, revelers, and rogues. At least, she thought of them as rogues. They ate, drank, and added coin to the strongboxes located underneath the bar's counter, which would be emptied out back into larger containers during the night. The atmosphere seemed relaxed enough, and Gurga presided over the entire scene from his post at the main entrance. Not a man alive would cross the enforcer, and the last drunken bastard who had woke up the next morning in the gutter *across* the street, where Gurga had flung him.

The alehouse. Never a boring evening. She oftentimes *wished* for a boring evening. Sindra offered the best value for her prices: a serving staff who worked hard, cooks who could actually cook—a huge advantage over her competitors—and a spacious, well-kept interior. Her rooms upstairs were cleaned daily and in high demand, not like some other lice-infested hovels. If a customer actually complained, she took action immediately. Sindra ran a good business, a smart business, and she'd learned it all from her long-deceased mentor and adopted father, Hadree.

Memories of him visited her more often since the appearance of Borchus. She welcomed them, but a few times, she had to steal away to the inner office for a moment to compose herself before the emotion revealed itself upon her face. His passing had deeply troubled her, leaving her the loneliest she'd ever been—a period of time she never wanted to visit again and had armored herself against.

All those thoughts cluttered her mind as she stood in the bar's background and stared off into space.

Then Senturo stopped before her, on the other side of the counter, displaying that unfriendly glare of teeth intended to be a smile. He sent a shiver through her as keen as a northern wind.

"Sindra," he said in his warm-as-honey voice.

She didn't answer him.

"No?" Senturo asked with a sad frown. "Something bothers you?"

Sindra didn't bite at that bait, either.

"It's a shame to see such an attractive face so sour," he carried on, focused entirely on her and heedless of the crowds. "But then again, there's something lovely about it as well."

"You have . . . a snake's tongue," Sindra said, pausing when one of her male workers passed before her.

"Some say," Senturo agreed, looking around. "Some say. Well then, shall we go around back?"

Without waiting, he walked over to the bar's end and wandered through the kitchen door. The gall of the man burned Sindra. He was becoming far too comfortable around the alehouse, far too comfortable with *her*. She thought to not go back there with him, but then a foul sensation overcame her resolve. The sooner she was done with him, the more quickly she could clear the air.

Reluctantly, she wandered into the kitchen. Tilda saw her, and Sindra's mood was reflected upon her friend's face. Tilda knew Sindra's thoughts about Senturo. The man was a hellion draped in handsome skin.

An open door to the back room beckoned. Sindra entered. A lit lamp rested upon the table, and Senturo, in wicked fashion, sat upon a chair with his knees spread wide. His pose and smile reminded her of lizards sunning themselves.

"Close the door, please," he requested.

Sindra hesitated. "No."

"Close the door." He smiled. "Please."

Closing the door uneased her. Still, she masked that feeling and complied. She placed her back against the door and watched him warily, making no move to encourage any unwanted attention.

"The only thing I've been hearing about is the death of the one called Gastillo," she reported.

Senturo tsked and scowled in good humor. "Please sit."

"I'd rather stand."

"Please. It would make me happy."

"I have no desire to make you happy, Senturo."

He chuckled and leaned back, running a finger under a chin shaven perhaps only a day before. His blue eyes, haunting in a way, held her gaze. "Harsh words from someone I think of as a friend."

"A friend?" Sindra exclaimed softly. "When have I ever called you a friend? I don't like you. I don't think I ever did. You disturb me."

"I do that to people."

"Let's just finish this, and you can be on your way, hm?" Sindra said. "As I was saying, the only talk has been about this one called Gastillo. And the one called Prajus. He killed the owner of a house."

"Yes, he did." Senturo nodded. "An act of impulse, I imagine. On both sides. Prajus is probably regretting what he did. So many terrible things happen because of impulse."

"Not that it bothers you," Sindra said.

"Nothing bothers me."

"So I see," she said, the door's latch at her back. "Well, that's it. Nothing since the other day you stopped by. And by the way, you didn't pay for your drink."

"You're an attractive woman, Sindra," Senturo said, the words turning her blood to ice.

Seddon above. That was *all* she needed.

"You owe me coin for that drink," she said, hoping to divert that unwanted direction of talk.

"And you're unmarried," he continued, refusing to change the subject. "Some would say it's unfit for a woman of your age and beauty to be unwed. Especially one who manages an alehouse. You really should do something about that."

"I've *been* doing something about that," Sindra countered.

"I've been thinking." Senturo stood like a crow about to take wing. He was a tall man, not the tallest, but almost a full head over her. Sindra didn't want him to stand. She didn't want him to come any closer.

She felt for the latch.

In a flash, Senturo charged her, pressing his chest to hers and seizing her hands in a powerful grip. His eyes narrowed as he studied her, his not-a-smile full yet sympathetic.

"Just a moment ago," he whispered, his breath warm on her forehead. "Of how we've come to know each other. Over the years. I've never really noticed you before."

Sindra didn't move. "I don't think Tilo would appreciate you doing what you're doing," she pointed out, maintaining her calm.

"Tilo," Senturo repeated, his face moving above hers, as if savoring her scent. "He's an old man now. Very old. Do you think I fear him?"

His hands tightened, but Sindra stared back just as hard. "I think . . . you'd best let me go. Let me go, and I'll forget this meeting."

"*You* might." He smiled again, his teeth wet in the scant light. "*I* won't. I don't understand why I haven't noticed you before. Your . . . womanly charms. You are—"

A knock at the door interrupted him, and his grip upon Sindra's hands relaxed. That was all she needed, and she swung the door outward, just missing Tilda's startled face.

"I'm very sorry, Lady Sindra," her friend said sadly, "but that roast is nearly ready, if you were going to watch it, that is."

"I am, and thank you," Sindra said, nodding and stepping well away from Senturo. She spared him only a glance. "I believe we're done here?"

The agent didn't answer right away. He looked at Tilda and then Sindra with a sly eye, as if well aware she'd escaped his clutches . . . that time.

Sindra didn't care what he thought. "I believe we're done?"

"We are," Senturo allowed. "This night. I'll return soon enough. You have a back door here?"

"You know I do."

"Then show me to it, please."

She pointed, unwilling to budge.

"Sindra," he chastised, actually pursing his lips.

Seddon above. She composed herself and led him to the door, knowing the man was studying her from behind. The thought repelled her.

"Here," Sindra declared and removed two barring planks before throwing open the door. A dark alley waited, tainted with the barest smell of stale garbage.

Senturo ignored the alley and placed his back against the doorframe. He faced her, cocked his head, and smiled again, attempting once more to charm her with his snakelike wiles. If the act wasn't so sickening, Sindra might have found it sadly amusing.

"You're a crafty one," he said softly, as a compliment. "Truly crafty."

"I have to be. Now go."

"I'll go when I please," he whispered, flashing a warning look at Tilda only a few strides away. "But I think you and I will have another talk. Just know that I've taken notice of you, Lady Sindra. You are a lady, you know that? Perhaps not nobility but . . . a lady all the same."

His hand rose.

Sindra braced herself.

He caressed her cheek with the back of a finger, causing her to flinch. "And I think you won't say a word to Tilo. It'll be wise if you didn't."

He snapped the finger into his fist. Tucking away his teeth, Senturo sidestepped out the door like the two-legged snake he was. He bounced off the low step and walked off into the alley's darker regions.

"A good evening to you, sweet Sindra," he called back. "I'll remember our time together. I'm already looking forward to our next meeting."

She closed the door, angry.

"Ohhh, he likes you," Tilda teased with a yellow smile. "And he's handsome. I'd take that one and keep him hidden away at home. On his back, perhaps. And tied to a bed."

"You can have him," Sindra said with dislike. "Thank you for knocking at the door when you did."

"Oh that?" She waved a hand. "That was nothing. I heard the timbers creaking and thought you two might be . . ."

Sindra didn't have the patience for Tilda's tormenting. "No, we were not doing any of that."

"Not even a little?"

"Not even a little. And certainly not with him. And while it's still fresh in my mind, if he ever traps me in the back room like he did just now, don't even wait to knock, just go and get Gurga and have him break the door down."

"Even if you two are—"

"Are you unfit? I'd sooner stab my eyes out with wooden skewers."

That put a frown on Tilda's plain features. "Bit harsh."

"Tilda?"

"Yes?"

"Where's that roast you were talking about?"

That brightened her. "Over here. What are you going to do with it, exactly? I have to see for next time . . ."

Outside the alehouse, Borchus detached himself from the shadows and watched Senturo disappear around the right corner. The agent held his wounded side while his heart ached with disappointment. He'd heard the man call out to Sindra as he walked away, and Borchus wondered whether he'd just heard something he didn't want to.

Did Sindra have a man in her life?

That thought didn't sit well with Borchus, so when the door to the alehouse closed, he waited a few heartbeats before leaving the shadows. Head down and hand pressed to his side, he walked as stealthily as he could manage in his current condition. When he reached the alley mouth, he peered one way then the other and went after the stranger. People filled the streets, looking for alehouses or going about other business. Street lamps lit up portions of the road and faces. The man was a tall one, and

Borchus watched for the back of his bouncing head. He wanted to know more about him, especially what he was to Sindra.

A good evening to you sweet Sindra. I'll remember our time together and look forward to the next meeting.

Sweet Seddon above, how those words twisted Borchus's guts into a burning coil. The discomfort rose to his mind, collected there with suspicion, and slowly distilled into pain. When the back door had opened, he hid in the shadows, pressing himself against a wall hard enough to become one with the bricks. Merriment and loud voices from deep within the alehouse ruined any chance to properly hear Sindra and her visitor's conversation, but Borchus caught the stranger's happy words as he pounded feet up the alley.

I'll remember our time together and look forward to the next meeting.

Our time together.

Borchus slowed and stopped in the street, abandoning the chase. He stared as the night's stars filled the heavens above. If she did have a man, what business of it was his? None. She was Sindra, after all, and she'd made it clear several times in the past she would take whomever she wanted when she wanted. She'd said so with a smile on her face.

That was one of the things Borchus liked about her.

Maybe she'd found someone after all. That thought smacked him between the eyes with the force of a spiked hammer, leaving him stunned, speechless, and worst of all, poisoned with regret.

People moved past him, groups of men and women, couples holding on to each other, stealing away to more private settings. Their laughter and conversations reached his ears, but he didn't listen to any of them, not having the mind to listen.

He took a short while to notice, but when he did realize he was too much in the open, he pressed his wounded side and entered the shadows once again.

As the darkness slipped over his frame, disappointment drowned him.

49

Rain crashed against closed shutters and roused Brozz from sleep. He opened his eyes and listened, hearing the storm outside. He looked at the closed curtain of his quarters. His stomach pained him terribly, bringing a grimace to his dark features. He lightly touched the bandages covering the wound and gasped at the contact. When the pain passed, he tried to relax, to avoid clenching his stomach muscles.

A knock at his door distracted him.

"Are you awake?" Junger whispered from beyond.

Brozz frowned. "I am."

A hand pulled the curtain across, and the Perician peered inside. His features lit up in feigned surprise. "Ah, still alive. Excellent. I thought you might've died during the night. You didn't make a sound."

"Sarlanders don't die during the night."

"Is that so? You hold off until the morning, do you?"

Brozz stared at his visitor. "It's difficult to talk right now."

"Shall I get the healer?"

"I don't think he'll help."

"No?"

"He's done all that he can."

"Perhaps he hasn't," Junger said, glancing one way then the other. "Maybe he doesn't like Sarlanders. Especially the ones who fashion necklaces from the heads of crows."

"Don't you have training...or...something?" Brozz asked, his voice rasping.

"Not this morning." Junger nodded toward the shuttered window. "You hear that? That's a right and proper storm out there this morning. The grounds are drenched. Practically a flood. Not that it's a bad thing. The land needs the rain. Been far too dry this season."

Brozz grunted agreement, and the sparkle of pain silenced him.

Junger studied the prone Sarlander. "You probably won't be eating anything for the next couple of days."

"I'll eat when I want."

"Have you used the pisspot there?"

"No."

"Best you drink something."

"When I'm thirsty."

Junger nodded understanding. Before he could make another comment about Sarlanders, a clack of wood on wood distracted him. He and Brozz looked toward the shuttered window.

With the sound of falling rain in the background, Nala opened her eyes and studied the shadows of the ceiling timbers. She moved ever so slightly under an old blanket of summer silk, feeling a gnawing ache in her arms and knuckles. That was always the way when rain came.

"It's raining," she whispered.

"Huh," Clavellus snorted, suddenly awake.

She turned herself onto her side and, with a fond smile, studied her husband's aging profile. "I didn't hear you come in."

No response.

"You slept well last night," she whispered.

"Mm," he grunted, smacked his lips, and settled back. The rain continued in the background.

"Were you successful at the games?" she asked softly, cuddling into his body.

"Mm, aye that." He kept his eyes closed.

"Any deaths?"

"No."

"Our lads won?"

Clavellus took his time answering. "Our lads won," he whispered with a note of contentment.

"Wonderful."

He opened an eye and studied her. "You approve?"

"Of the games? No. That our lads won, yes. No one was injured?"

In the sparse light, his face tightened. "The Sarlander. Brozz."

"I know the one."

"You do?"

"After all those days of Machlann bawling his name? Yes, I certainly do. The face, anyway."

Clavellus grunted neutrally. "He was wounded. His stomach. A spike pierced his armor. Not all the way through, mind you. Shan believes he'll recover in time, but his season might very well be done."

"He'll live though, without any problems?"

The rain intensified outside the bedchamber as Clavellus gathered his thoughts. "He should."

"Good."

A faint smile hitched up one side of Clavellus's beard. "Getting attached to them, are you?"

"Truth be known, I don't talk to them enough to get attached," Nala explained softly, her hand sliding into the nest of Clavellus's chest. "But I have grown used to them being here."

"I said you would," he said, his smile turning evil.

Nala grabbed hair, eliciting a grunt.

"Goll fought as well," he said.

She waited. "And?"

"He won. Decisively."

Nala would've been surprised if the young Kree had lost. "Is he all right?"

"Fine. To my eyes, anyway. He was quiet most of the way home, but . . . he was pleased with himself."

"Really?"

"Yes." He paused, sorting through the previous day's memories and pulling one from sleepy depths. "It was as if . . . as if he realized his worth again. He barely spoke, but he was pleased. Anyone could see it."

"Hard to imagine. Him being happy. He's such a serious one. I'm happy none of our boys lost their lives."

"Our boys?" Clavellus asked.

"Our boys. I'm getting used to seeing their faces. And I've always liked seeing the villa full."

"You do, do you?"

"Hm. What was that you and Machlann once talked about?"

"What was that?"

"Establishing a town?"

Clavellus frowned sleepily. "Oh, *that*. That was merely drunk talk."

"Then it was you doing the talking," she countered. "What about it, then?"

He didn't answer right away, knowing that conversation would go to uncomfortable places, places he and she had been before and discussed . . . when they'd failed to have children of their own. Thus, instead of ruining a sleepy morning, he placed a hand on hers and gave it a tender rub. "Just talk. How are your hands and shoulders this morning?"

"The same," she answered. "Why were you so late returning?"

"The roads. Leading to Sunja's gates. Thick with wagons and people leaving the city. One wagon broke its axle. Slowed everyone."

"Did you bring us back anything?"

"All that you asked for."

She leaned into him just a little more. "Good. You're a good boy. We'll need some fresh stores soon. Winter isn't that far away. We'll need vegetables. Perhaps I'll purchase some in the days to come."

"Or send word."

"Or that."

"I prefer that."

She knew he did.

That's when they heard the crack of wood.

The sound turned their heads toward the shutters. Gray light outlined the square. Clavellus stood, joints crackling, his bony spine and frame draped in shadows. He ambled to the window and peeked outside.

"Lords above," he muttered.

"What is it?" Nala asked from the bed.

"That fool Goll. It's pissing rain, and that punce's on the training grounds swinging a stick."

Though the summer rains were filling the training grounds with puddles and soaking him, Goll didn't care. He had to do something, and he had to do it that morning. He stepped back from the practice man and realized he'd struck the target without thinking. Going through a set of strikes had brought him close to one of the wooden frames, and he lashed out just because it was there. He stopped and wiped the rain from his spattered scalp.

Nothing moved within the villa. Nothing stirred. The shutters to Clavellus's window were open, but Goll couldn't see the old taskmaster, not through the sheets of rain pouring out of the storm clouds.

Vowing to be quiet, Goll walked to an area free of targets and reset himself. The rain didn't bother him—not him. Energy from the previous day's victory lit up his heart and limbs, demanding to be released. Lords above, he'd defeated his opponent soundly and wished for others, wanting to resume the path that Baylus the Butcher had knocked him from.

That was his true purpose at the games.

ABOUT THE BLOOD

Thick, infernal clouds coiled and churned overhead. The storm's dull roar would keep the villa sleeping for a while yet, and even then, no one would be training in such foul weather. Nor would any matches be fought that day, which suited him fine. The others had no need to rise so early. *Let them sleep.* He wanted the grounds for himself, didn't want to be watched or supervised. All he needed was to move, to reacquaint himself with forgotten skills, to sharpen those movements long blunted, and to prepare for the next opponent.

Under storm clouds flickering with lightning, Goll of Kree lunged at an imaginary foe.

In Sunja, behind the high walls of a once-respected villa, another man practiced under the same clouds. Sorban left his companions to their dry quarters and whirled a new quarterstaff he'd prepared the day before. He spun the weapon, the stout length of wood turning end over end to the slap and slide of calloused flesh. Rain coated his muscular torso and limbs. A skirt of hardened strips covered his legs. He wore no sandals and didn't feel the warm puddles collected in the sands.

A wooden practice man waited just out of the quarterstaff's reach.

Sorban stared at the target, seeing it yet lost in thought. He didn't tire, didn't waver. Playing through his mind were memories of the one called Goll and the battle in which the Kree killed Baylus the Butcher.

Sorban intended to punish the Kree. He meant to beat the man to death. He meant to avenge his friend in exceptionally bloody fashion.

Without warning, Sorban stepped into the wooden target, smashing his quarterstaff into the head, the arms, the legs, and the head again. With no pause, no hesitation, the wooden frame trembled. Splinters flew. Sorban smashed imaginary elbows and knees and repeatedly jabbed the face, throat, and crotch. He stepped away and hooked legs, punching the quarterstaff's end into the unseen throats of fallen foes.

Every blow was meant to kill.

Instead of slowing down, he sped up, his anger fueling a terrible energy. He hammered that wooden frame.

The impacts became louder. His breathing became hungry barks.

In the buildings surrounding the training grounds, people stirred. Shutters creaked open though the faces beyond stayed out of sight. Doors opened partway, and dark figures lingered inside the gloomy light. The commotion drew gladiators and servants alike to the startling display of weapon mastery and determination, and as they gazed upon the awesome show, Sorban refused to relent. The clatter of wood upon wood intensified. The practice man flinched and rattled as if seized by violent convulsions. Splinters exploded from limbs close to shattering. Particles spun off into the sand.

The rain fell even harder, but the man swinging the quarterstaff did not stop, nor did he slow.

Sorban meant to break the target as he meant to break Goll of Kree.

50

Deep within the bowels of the Pit, men woke on stone floors or pallets laced with dirty, prickly straw. No sun shone in the cells. No rain fell. Only blackness was there, with the pulsating light from the braziers. A foul smell of voiding filled the air, wrinkling Arrus's nose. The Nordish man sat on the floor, rump on dry stone and his back to the wall. The braziers' light mesmerized him. It was the only thing to watch in the ever-present darkness.

"Feel like talking for a bit?"

The sound of Nordish syllables roused him from his hypnosis. After a moment, he recognized Rullik's voice.

"Certainly," Arrus replied and rested his head against the dungeon wall.

Silence, then.

"Well?" Arrus asked.

The Norjos man chuckled. "Apologies. Just wondering what to talk about, is all."

"You're a fine one. Asking for conversation and nothing to talk about."

"Suppose I am. Let me think. Ah yes. The jailors. They've been talking about you."

That got Arrus's attention.

"Seems you'll be fighting this day," Rullik said.

"Today?"

"Aye that. Today."

"You heard that?"

"I did."

Ivus's grace. Fear and anticipation coursed through Arrus, waking him better than a slap to the face. No one had been taken into the Pit the day before, when Rullik had heard the jailors speak of heavy rain. Today, however, his time in the arena was going to happen.

He discovered himself longing to breathe fresh air, of all things.

"Don't get all quiet now," Rullik cautioned. "When you're up there, show the Sunjans the mistake they've made. You show them that they've captured a pack of Jackals. And now they have to deal with them. *Ha!* I wish I was amongst the crowd. Just to see their faces."

"Not sure I even remember how to hold a blade," Arrus whispered.

"Oh, you'll remember," Rullik assured him. "When the bastard you're fighting starts swinging for your head, you'll remember. It'll all come back in a rush."

"I suppose."

"Listen now." The Norjos man lowered his voice. "From what I overhead from Runson and Balazz and those other blossoms, none of the other Nordish men have lost or died. You hear me? That's *significant* to them. And if you think upon it, the Jackals are being returned to their cells, but their opponents aren't. They *aren't*. All the remaining prisoners are seeing this. They *see* them marched past their cells. You understand me? That will be on the mind of whoever you fight. I tell you now, whoever they put into the Pit to face you will be shivering to the core."

A little smile crept across Arrus's bearded face. "You're a good speaker, Rullik. You should have led men into battle."

"What? On a front somewhere? *Pah.* Foolishness. Waste of time and effort. Not to mention lives. No, not me."

"Were you always a thief?"

ABOUT THE BLOOD

The ensuing silence made Arrus wonder if he'd asked the wrong question.

"No, not always," the Norjos man eventually replied. "I was a farmer once. No wife. No children. My father was a farmer, so I did as he. Only thing was, the almighty Curlord didn't think farming was in my blood. Or so I figured. Early snows killed my crops. Starving wolves killed my animals. Four years of that. Four years. And some hard times I remember all too often. Then, one day, a grain merchant tried buying what crop I had for a fraction of the price. I found out when I talked to another farmer in an alehouse that night. Well. I tell you. When a person has been beaten down by forces beyond his control, when one can't seem to buy or pray for good fortune, it's disheartening . . . infuriating when you learn your fellow countryman is stealing the eyes from your head."

"You stole from him?"

"It's my story," Rullik warned. "Let me tell it."

"Apologies."

"Accepted. So, aye that. I tried stealing from him. That very night. While half drunk, in fact, which wasn't a good idea. I weaseled my way into his house and wrestled with that tankard of cow piss while his wife and children backed themselves into a corner. Never knew the man had a family. To this day, I wonder who he cheated to get his wife. In the end, I got away with nothing. Just a few scrapes and bruises. Never found his coin. Gave him and his family an evil fright, however. Also, I learned two things from the whole matter."

"What?"

"Never drink before thieving. There are better ways to calm one's nerves."

Arrus smiled. "And the other?"

"Wait for them to be asleep."

Arrus's smile widened.

His amusement vanished when the brooding mass of Balazz stopped before the cell door. The Sunjan jailor, with his shaved head, glowered at the imprisoned Nordish man, studying him with morbid interest, as if wondering how he'd missed such an oddity under his care. Firelight glimmered at the jailor's back, throwing shade over his imposing face. Balazz spoke, a stream of harsh notes that had no meaning for Arrus.

"He says you're going to fight this day," Rullik explained when the jailor stopped for breath. "He says you're going to fight a killer of a man. One who's, ah, fought twice already."

Arrus didn't flinch under the jailor's gaze, but he didn't feel particularly eager about the match.

Balazz spoke again, and when he finished, he looked to the right and waited for Rullik.

"He says to enjoy these final moments," the thief translated, "because you'll get no rest in Saimon's hell."

Message delivered, Balazz smirked. He then waved, summoning several Skarrs who appeared from the fringes.

The jailor produced a key.

"Good fortune to you, Arrus," Rullik offered.

"Just do what you do," Heelslik said from the shadows, "and you'll be back soon enough."

The words didn't inspire Arrus. He wasn't the most capable of Jackals. His dead brother Kra had even told him that once.

Balazz unlocked the cell door.

The short sword was heavy in his hand. The blade was nicked and in need of sharpening. Arrus believed that simply getting hit by such a weapon might cause death. The sun hurt his eyes, causing him to squint against its glare. His limbs thrummed with nervousness, and his mouth had long since dried up. He badly wanted a drink of water but knew he'd get none until the bloody business was all finished.

Across the way, a man strode toward him. A big man, well-built and exceptionally pale, looking as if he'd been powdered by a noblewoman's hand. Like Arrus, the prisoner—called Brill—wore only a loincloth . . . that and a fearsome scowl. He carried a short sword and swung it about as though it was a broken branch and Arrus was in need of a thorough whipping.

ABOUT THE BLOOD

The closer Brill got, the louder the cheering became. It unnerved Arrus, making his heart race and the sweat ooze. Brill showed no trace of any nerves, and his narrowed eyes locked onto the uneasy Jackal.

When he was a few strides away, Brill charged.

The first swing sliced for Arrus's head. The Jackal bobbed under it. The second cut whistled for the Nordish man's face, but Arrus managed to dodge that as well. Brill's third strike was a looping swipe, seeking the back of his opponent's neck.

Arrus ducked, backpedaled, and escaped harm yet again. The Sunjans cursed and jeered the Nordish man in that gibberish they used as a language. He didn't need to understand the words. He *felt* the meaning just fine.

Brill pursued his opponent. He held his blade at the shoulder, poised to chop. The Sunjan's eyes were wide, insane looking, caught by the rush of combat and the crowd's desire for blood . . . *Nordish* blood.

Brill hacked, seeking to split Arrus's melon right down the middle. The Nordish prisoner avoided the blow but didn't expect a backhand cut—a horizontal arc of solid light powered by arm and hips. The tip of Brill's short sword grazed the right corner of Arrus's skull, finely splitting flesh to the bone. The blow drove the Jackal back in a spray of color.

The crowd's cheering spiked.

Brill smiled broadly at the contact.

Arrus, however, pressed a hand against the wound and scowled with murderous intent.

Black rage bloomed within his gut. It enveloped his racing heart and lashed brain, limb, and fury into that deadly combination where all acted as one. The despair born from his brother Kra having died at the hands of a faceless Cavalier lent Arrus even more strength, and all the pent-up anger and misery from being locked away in a lightless dungeon added its own shot of power.

For that one blistering instant, Arrus forgot who he was, where he was, and what he was doing.

All he knew was that he was outside, under the hot sun, being cursed by his sworn enemy ... and a man had just cut him.

Brill saw the death-caul expression on Arrus's face just before the Jackal charged and half cleaved the top of his Sunjan skull from his head. The edged *clop* of steel to bone strangled the audience's collective breath at once. The bone cap cracked open unwillingly, the blade uncovering the cerebral delights within. The Nordish man had moved so quickly, so powerfully, that Brill seemed motionless when the killing blow fell.

He toppled, the Jackal's blade left in his head.

When his senses returned, Arrus studied the dead man at his feet. His head ached. He wiped his brow. Blood coated his fingers. The arena was much quieter, however, as a lull had fallen over the audience.

That pleased Arrus immensely and lessened his pain.

The pause didn't last long.

One voice let loose, cursing him. Then the entire arena exploded.

He didn't need to understand the language to read faces. For all their culture and history, Sunjans swore a *lot*.

Arrus lowered his head, his limbs trembling in the aftermath. The Skarrs arrived, and facing a wall of swords and shields, the Nordish man allowed himself to be herded back to his cell, back into the deep, deep darkness, where the air smelled of unwashed crevices and horrible fluids.

When Balazz closed the iron door, the jailor fixed Arrus with a hard look, one meant to kill. He tossed a handful of rags through the bars and glared at the prisoner once again.

His chin held high, Arrus stared back.

If the jailor wanted to kill him, he'd have to enter the cell, and the Jackal, still bleeding and not so uneasy anymore, would greet him.

As if sensing danger, Balazz moved away like a great sweaty monster draped in leather.

ABOUT THE BLOOD

Arrus waited before addressing the sting above his eye. He gathered up the rags. He separated several, paying no mind to their stale smell, and placed one against the cut on his head.

Heelslik's voice floated from beyond the burning braziers. "He's returned to us, Rullik."

"He has. He has," Rullik replied.

"Doubtless, he's lost that boyish quality I've known and despised."

Rullik chuckled, the sound eerie in the dungeon depths. "Lost forever, no doubt."

"So how was it, boy?" Heelslik joked.

"A boy no longer," Arrus groaned. "Not in the ways of this place."

"You walked in," Rullik noted. "I saw that. So you weren't badly hurt."

"A Sunjan—I think it was a Sunjan—tried to scalp me. He opened my head just above my right eye. And there's a ringing in my ear. Otherwise, no. Not hurt too badly at all."

"Almost got scalped," Rullik mused. "That reminds me of a time I was in Paw Savage territory—"

"What of Balazz?" Heelslik cut in. "He didn't seem too happy with you."

"He wasn't." Arrus smiled. "I've no idea why. I didn't do anything to catch his attention."

"You lived," Rullik said. "That's enough. I overhear things here and there. The jailors delight in tormenting prisoners, telling them stories of the pits and the gladiators and the . . . the blood. They tell them the bloodiest tales just to hear those poor dogs whimper. They would do the very same with you as well, but they know you can't speak the language."

"Unfortunate," Heelslik said.

"Aye that. Thought you might think that way. You know something? They also gather beyond these walls, the jailors. I hear things. They have meetings, you see. Whole packs of them who disappear outside the doorway for Curlord only knows what."

"Perhaps just a meal," Heelslik commented. "Arrus?"

"Yes?"

"Are you bleeding?"

"Yes."

"Those rags Balazz had . . . Did he give them to you?"

"Aye that."

"Inspect them before you use them. Give them a smell, just to make sure no one's been using them to scrub their cracks with."

"They do that here?"

"They probably do much worse. Give them a smell, anyway."

Arrus did as told. "Nothing. Only stale cloth. Musty."

"Then rest, my young hellpup," Rullik said. "Tend to that head wound. Pretty it up before another Sunjan gets the chance to crack it open again. And listen, while I entertain you both with my adventures in the vast wilds of the Paw Savages."

"Paw Savages." Heelslik scoffed, already bored. "I'll listen only if you have a few women in there."

"There *are* a few women in there . . ."

Their conversation faded into the background. Arrus slipped to the floor, his backside connecting with stone. There, he sat and grimaced. The ringing in his right ear didn't stop, thrumming all the way through his head. He was alive, however, and back in the relative safety of the cell.

Balazz's face haunted his memory. Arrus pushed that image away and remembered the freedom of the arena sands, the hot sun, and the air thick with humidity but so good to breathe. The roaring crowds entered his thoughts, and he found that if he concentrated just a little, they almost sounded as though they were cheering for him.

By the grace of Ivus, Arrus looked forward to his next fight.

51

After two days of rain, a blinding white as fine as gold marked the distant horizon. The people of Clavellus's villa rose and got dressed, glad the storm was finished but cringing at the fearsome humidity clinging to the air. Two of the Ten would fight later that day, and more than a few were eager to leave for the city. Brozz would stay behind, still recovering from his wounds, as would Torello, who was incapable of any travel. The training staff, along with their healer, their once-Sujin guards, and the pair of gladiators scheduled to fight that day, quietly readied themselves for the long road to Sunja.

Looking stern and walking with a swagger, Goll moved around the wagons, answering questions with nods or headshakes. Junger waited on the training grounds, watching the sky and appearing ready for a walk upon the plains. He faced the east and the villa's high walls.

"You'll see more once we're moving," Goll said.

Junger smiled faintly.

"That's my way of saying get aboard a wagon," the house master warned.

The Perician glanced around the villa one final time, taking in the buildings and their shadows.

Then he did as told.

*

The roads punished the travelers and wagons alike.

They rocked and tumbled toward the city, and though they didn't bog down like before, when Torello had injured his ankle, more than a few worried about repairs to the wheels or purchasing new wagons entirely. Despite an unpleasant journey, however, they arrived before afternoon and proceeded to the Pit. Once there, the House of Ten unloaded themselves and their equipment and made quick time to their private quarters below the arena.

An empty room greeted them.

"Back again," Clavellus announced to bare benches, feeling a drop in temperature. Sunlight shone through the open window, and dust tumbled along the beams.

"Master Goll." Machlann picked up a scroll. "You'll be pleased to learn the Madea kept his promise."

The news didn't impress the Kree. "I suspect he's keeping a lot of promises these days."

That got Clavellus's attention. "Why do you say that?"

Goll dropped his sack of armor near a bench. "I confronted him the other day. And now, I have to face a sword brother of Baylus the Butcher? Aren't arena officials supposed to be above such things?"

Machlann and Clavellus exchanged looks.

"The Madea is a man," the old trainer warned. "A right and proper punce of a man. So he can be swayed. Especially when he's pushed."

Goll stopped and chewed on the inside of a cheek. "I didn't push him. I only told him I wouldn't tolerate any more gurry."

The arched window beckoned Clavellus. He planted an elbow on its sill and peered outside, squinting against the harsh glow. The arena stands were empty, but that would change soon enough.

"Don't concern yourself with the Madea," he said, smiling into the sun. "Just prove him wrong. Do that instead. Now, come here."

ABOUT THE BLOOD

Goll held up a hand, asking for a moment. He faced Muluk. "You place the wagers. Clades and Valka will accompany you to the Domis."

"Anything else?" Muluk asked, his mouth working underneath that dense nest of facial hair.

"Just be careful."

Muluk nodded that he would indeed do that. He located a small sack of coin, nodded to his assigned guards, and departed. Once he was gone, Goll turned to the window.

"Plenty of time for wagers," Clavellus said and indicated the sands. "Clear and pristine for now. Empty seats. Come see and drink it down. Sheer majesty, isn't it?"

Goll wandered over and looked outside, taking in the stands.

The taskmaster wasn't wrong.

Sunshine on his face, Clavellus nodded. "Get yourself outfitted and return here. We'll watch some fights."

And watch the opening fights they did.

The first string of matches consisted of the lowly criminals forced to spill blood. What the matches lacked in skill, they more than made up for in violence. The men hacked and stabbed at each other until one died, and all five matches resulted in a death. By that time, Goll had donned his leather armor and set his sword and shield aside.

"Savages," Machlann said after the last brutal contest, visibly disgusted by the showing.

"What's the Chamber thinking?" Clavellus wondered aloud.

"I imagine they're wondering how to make that shite pretty," the trainer grumbled. "Listen to those people. They're screaming at that gurry—as they should. I'd sooner drink a pitcher of pig piss than witness something like that again."

"That Jackal showed skill, I thought."

"That Jackal's a right and proper soldier, I'll remind you," Machlann said. "And it took a cut to the head to wake him up."

The fights were terrible, Goll quietly agreed, lacking style and skill and, oddly enough, purpose. In perhaps the one place where purpose should be perfectly clear, some of the combatants didn't seem particularly motivated. The Jackal had been one of them, but in the end, he showed promise. Considering the man was a prisoner of war, Goll doubted he'd see the Nordish man alive again.

The door opened then, and Muluk returned with his escort.

"All done?" Goll asked.

"A word with you," Muluk said, making his way through the room until he faced Goll. "There's a problem. With the wagering."

"What?"

"Seems that very few people are betting on Junger's opponent."

"*What?*"

"It's true. When word reached the masses that Junger was fighting, most immediately placed their coin on the man."

Goll looked at Junger, who was sitting with his head lowered.

"Understandable," Clavellus said under his breath.

"He's the clear favorite this day," Muluk added. "The Perician, they call him. Or the Perician Weapon. Even heard Perician *Wonder*."

Goll glared Muluk into silence. "You still wagered though, correct?"

"Aye that, I did. But the odds are so poor, so heavily tilted towards him. If he does win, we'll only get a pittance."

"When he wins," Clavellus corrected, gazing out at the packed audience.

"When he wins," Muluk agreed. "But . . . well . . . truth be known, I overhead another bit of news. There seems to be a bit of, ah, side wagering happening."

"Side wagering?" Goll asked for them all, perplexed.

"Aye that," Muluk said. "On whether or not he'll actually draw his sword when he fights."

Curiosity twisted the faces of both Clavellus and Machlann. Goll was speechless.

"I didn't wager on that, however," Muluk quickly explained. "And don't worry. There was no issue with wagering on your match. Sorban appears to be the clear favorite there."

Goll questioned his countryman with a wry look.

"Ah," Muluk restarted. "Not that it matters. At all."

Goll turned away.

Muluk hobbled back a step, favoring his leg, and warily eyed Junger, sitting close to the door. After waiting until Goll wasn't looking, he walked over and stopped before Junger. The Perician appeared very much unconcerned—comfortable even—bare chested and bent over with elbows to knees. His scabbard rested across his thighs.

"Junger," Muluk muttered, scratching at his beard.

The Perician glanced up at him.

"Ah . . . think you'll pull that steel today?"

Junger thought about it. "There's always the chance . . . but not likely."

A little smile spread across Muluk's face. He nodded furtively at the once Sujin called Valka, who quietly removed himself from the chamber.

Within his stable's private chamber, Grisholt stood with his back against the arched window and basked in the afternoon light. He held his chin high, in a kingly manner. The air currents were subtle enough to keep his scent close to his person. The perfumed water he had splashed upon himself earlier in the day bothered his men, but he didn't care. He'd paid good coin for the fragrance. Grisholt enjoyed wearing perfumed waters and took pride in his collection. Since the stable's coffers were overflowing, he had been purchasing new and exotic scents once unaffordable but which he'd yearned to own. *Honey for the ladies*, he thought.

The ill-hidden looks of distaste from Brakuss and his men suggested otherwise.

Grisholt ignored them. The lads had to understand that while they worked in a bloody profession, one didn't need to smell like an unwashed butcher.

The owner leaned back and placed his elbows on the windowsill. He beheld the studded-leather figure of Barros standing in the room's center, surrounded by his companions. Grisholt's eyes lingered upon the gladiator while his thoughts wandered. He'd ignored the preliminary matches with the criminals but had watched the Jackal's match, just finished. That captured killer showed skill, but the fight had ended far too quickly. As deadly as the Jackals were, they were not gladiators. They made no attempt at show, having no notion of theater or entertainment—just a quick battlefield killing and making for the exit.

No wonder they were winning their war with Sunja.

Grisholt rubbed his hands together, raising them to his nose to better enjoy the scent applied to his wrists. Barros's hooded stare met his. Today, the brute would fight a Ten man. Given the Ten's history, Grisholt thought the name fitting. *Tin.* Worthless. Weak. Easily breakable.

The prudish owner had been looking forward to this fight. Regret smoldered in his chest, however, for Barros's opponent wasn't the fat Zhiberian. Grisholt would correct that soon enough.

But first, the one called Junger.

"Barros," Grisholt said, getting the pit fighter's attention. "I want you to make that one suffer," he explained in measured intervals. "Make him suffer so that he's squealing out there. Like a pig . . . with its legs smashed. Make him scream. Scream, I say. I want the House of Ten to be livid with us, enough to send word to that Zhiberian pig bastard hiding in the forested wilds, thinking himself done with the games. Do that, and I'll double your winnings. Understand me?"

Before Barros could answer, though, a hard rap landed upon the chamber door.

Grisholt nodded, and Brakuss went to the entrance. He paused before opening it, his hand resting on his sword's pommel in case it was Razi once again.

However, standing outside was Nexus himself with a handful of guards at his back. The sight of the wine merchant surprised Grisholt.

ABOUT THE BLOOD

"Is this the quarters belonging to Grisholt?" Nexus asked and glowered, as if he was standing before the precipice of an absolute shite trough.

"It is," Brakuss answered.

"Tell him that Nexus of the School of Nexus wishes to speak with him."

Grisholt lurched away from the window and waved as if clearing the air. "Enter. Please enter, good Nexus."

Nexus did not, though. He stood his ground and glared. "Enter?" the merchant scoffed and studied the interior. "Don't flatter yourself. This isn't a social visit. And I'm saving my patience for the bald pisser waiting for my arrival in my viewing box. Seddon above, Grisholt, most people use a scrub brush upon their cracks. Try that next time, and save yourself a few coins."

The pleasant expression upon Grisholt's face faded.

"Listen to me," Nexus resumed, "for I don't have time to repeat myself. Lords above, man. You bathed in that shite far too long. It's breath stealing. Made me forget my place. Ah yes, now then. Your dog fights the one called Junger of Pericia this day, correct?"

Straightening his spine, Grisholt folded his arms in defiance, unimpressed with the merchant's lack of respect. "My man Barros does. What of it?"

"Your *man* means to kill him?"

"He does," Grisholt said, seeing no harm in revealing his plans.

"Excellent." Nexus held his nose. "Excellent. Make sure he does just that. The Perician is one pit fighter that concerns me. He concerns me a great deal."

"Does he, now?" Grisholt sensed opportunity. "How badly do you want him dead, then?"

"What do you mean?"

"I can give the order right now to have the man spared or killed."

"You just said your man intends to kill him."

"I've changed my mind. And I smell coin."

That irritated Nexus. "An opportunity for *coin*, is it? Amazing you can smell anything with that rat's piss smeared over yourself. Perhaps it's made you pickled? Listen to me. I'm not going to pay you anything, you unfit bastard."

"Then Barros will just defeat the man. And let him live to fight another day."

"He can't simply *defeat* the man," Nexus stressed through clenched teeth. "The Perician will . . ." The words sputtered into angry dismay. The merchant gazed upon Grisholt as if the man were a hairy spider in his bathwater. "Name your price, then," he finally grumbled.

"Five hundred pieces of gold."

The sum amused Nexus.

"And another five hundred to keep my silence," Grisholt declared.

"Your silence?"

"The Chamber won't think kindly upon your visit here, offering to hire my man to do a killing in the arena. Nor will the House of Ten."

"The House of . . ." Nexus's pale complexion reddened. "It's the *arena*, you punce. People *die* every day."

"If you won't pay, then . . ."

Brakuss cocked his arm to slam the door in Nexus's face, but the merchant halted the action with a hand.

"Six hundred," Nexus countered. "Total. Not a sliver more."

"Seven."

"Done," Nexus snapped. "All payable upon his death."

"Your word, Nexus?" Grisholt asked, halting the man.

"My word?"

"Say it."

The merchant spared a tight smile. "You have my word. I'll pay the price. Upon Junger's death."

"Excellent. I'll send someone for it."

Anger colored Nexus's cheeks. "Oh, you—"

ABOUT THE BLOOD

On Grisholt's nod, Brakuss slammed the door in the merchant's face. A heated squawking erupted from beyond, a shocking barrage of oaths that diminished as Nexus walked away.

For long moments, Grisholt stared at the closed door, annoyed at the encounter. He tugged on his beard, threatening to pull it free. *Nexus.* His dislike took root, flowering into resentment. His agent Caro had already informed him of Nexus and his acceptance of Prajus, the killer of house masters. That little bit of information had practically flowered across all of Sunja in very short time. Not even Grisholt would dare such an unfit action, for fear of drawing the other owners' wrath. Such disrespect to the profession wouldn't be tolerated. Truth be known, the deed displeased Grisholt as well. He'd known Gastillo—not well, but enough to exchange words with the gold-faced man—and thought him pleasant enough. Amongst the current house owners, Gastillo was perhaps a right and proper nobleman.

Grisholt had done a very bad thing by aligning himself with the Sons of Cholla, a very bad thing, indeed.

Nexus, however, had done much, much worse.

The merchant might've made his fortune in peddling wine, might've even managed to rise to the top of his profession, but by accepting Prajus, Nexus had essentially pissed in the face of every house, stable, and school owner in the history of the games. No one in their right mind would associate themselves with Nexus—not this season, and not any other—except perhaps Grisholt, out of courtesy. Theirs was a bond between thieves, so to speak.

However, Nexus pissed on Grisholt's boots as well, thinking he could get away with it. A mere wine merchant was playing at a game meant for gods and thinking himself far above his superiors.

Heat rose to Grisholt's neck and face.

"Barros," he said and casually produced the leather pouch containing the iron flask, the same iron flask containing what the Sons of Cholla had called Victory. "Listen closely, now. I want you to stretch the hide of that Perician topper across the arena floor. Stretch him until he rips apart. I don't want you to make an example of him. I want you . . . to make *history*."

An evil light sparkled in the pit fighter's eyes

In his semiprivate viewing box, Curge fought to contain himself as he waited for Nexus to arrive.

Rain had delayed the games for two days straight, but they finally ceased, and the emerging sun split the hillsides with brilliant swaths of gold. The Dark One made it a point to arrive early. He'd learned about Nexus taking in the outcast gladiator, Prajus, two days earlier, and during that time, while storm clouds emptied themselves upon the city, Curge suppressed the urge to travel to Nexus's estate and throttle the man. The wine merchant was a worm, no doubt—a venomous, disagreeable maggot of a man—but to harbor a pit fighter who'd killed his house master?

Unthinkable. Unbelievable.

The act had angered Dark Curge like nothing else.

No gladiator could harm his house master, no matter how skilled or favored the fighter might be. Such an action demanded the offender's swift death from the other gladiators or their employed staff, and if they couldn't manage the deed for whatever reason, then the gladiators from other houses would.

However, Nexus chose to ignore that.

Until two days before, Curge had tolerated the not-so-playful jabs and chuckled at the merchant's brazen demeanor and smugness.

His actions tarnished the sport's very heart. The man was smart, Curge knew, but taking in Prajus's unworthy hide was an incredibly stupid thing to do. Nexus should have been quietly killing the gladiator rather than taking him into his school. Disposing of Prajus would have earned him considerable respect in the eyes of his fellow owners. That alone would have annoyed Curge to no end.

But no.

Instead, Nexus did the worst thing imaginable. He had spread his cheeks and let slip a cow kiss on the very fabric of the games. He'd taken an unspoken yet recognized, time-honored rule and scrubbed the crack of his ass with it.

The merchant didn't belong to the sport and had no future here. Curge had no doubt of that. The man didn't understand the history of the games, the *meaning* . . . or the consequences.

Stormy weather had confined Curge to his manor for two days. In that time, he eventually calmed down though the very thought of Nexus feeding that treacherous maggot scorched his gullet. He wondered if the pig spawn truly understood his actions. Believing that Nexus didn't would have been more bearable, but Curge suspected the wealthy asslicker knew full well what he'd done and didn't care in the least.

That thought bothered Curge.

The sands distracted the troubled owner as the sun transformed the few remaining puddles into silver platters. Barefoot attendants dressed in skirts combed parts of the arena, dragging wide brooms over the surface. Moisture clung to the air, as thick as smothering fabric wrapped around one's face. An overhead tarpaulin shielded Curge from the harsh heat, but not from the burning sensation within his chest.

He already had enough to occupy himself with this season.

Men, women, and children emerged from stony portals. They drifted along benches, gradually filling the arena while searching for the most favorable seats. Curge glared at them, his inner temperature rising to disastrous levels. He dared not drink. A sip of the wine on hand would only unlock his barely suppressed urges.

The arena continued to fill with people. Nexus did not appear during that time.

The Orator introduced the first of the day's matches, a pitiful pairing of dungeon scroff that Curge could have killed with a look alone.

The day's fights commenced.

Dark Curge watched the first performance, his thoughts boiling. The fight finished, and he didn't remember who'd won. He scarcely heard the crowd's reactions.

By the finish of the third match, Nexus still hadn't arrived.

The servant attending to the viewing box sometimes moved about behind Curge, causing him to twist around at times, expecting to see the unworthy merchant. Thus, the manservant endured more than a few withering scowls from the one-armed Curge. The large owner squirmed in the hot shade while hearing the noise of the watching crowd. By the fourth match, he finally motioned for a goblet.

Midway through that fight, Curge heard the door open and close behind him. He restrained himself from turning. Nexus spoke curtly to the manservant, his words overwhelmed by the audience's sudden cheering.

As the noise subsided, Nexus sat down one seat over from Curge, leaving the space Gastillo would have normally filled.

"Curge," Nexus said without concern.

Curge's grip tightened around the goblet, and he didn't reply. If Nexus noticed, he ignored the lack of courtesy. After several long heartbeats, Curge turned and studied the wine merchant's sickly profile. He imagined himself rising, his shadow falling over Nexus, just before he slapped the wine merchant senseless. The trouble was that if he started there, he knew—just *knew*—stopping would be very difficult even when things became messy.

Something moved at the back of the viewing box, near the entrance.

He craned his neck. His brow furrowed at the surprise behind him, but only for a moment.

The merchant was smarter than Curge had given him credit for.

Not one, not two, but six armed guards stood at attention along the rear wall. The group wore leather armor, carried sheathed weapons, and regarded the large once gladiator with indifferent eyes.

ABOUT THE BLOOD

Nervous, the manservant stood with his polished platter held to his chest. The dog appeared right and ready to let slip a cow kiss right there. He met Curge's death stare.

The Dark One studied the servant. He studied the assembled guards.

Displaying a coolness tempered by years of bloody combat, Curge turned back to the spectacle of the games.

Neither owner spoke for a long time. Noise from the crowd filled the silence between the two men, but that was only a temporary thing.

"I knew," Curge rumbled, keeping his tone civil even as his temperature rose to dangerous levels, "from the very beginning, from the instant you showed your face here, you'd sour these games. But what you've done goes against hundreds of years of tradition. And honor."

Unconcerned, Nexus licked at the rim of a goblet, feathering the silver like a dog lapping at its own furry pearls. He shrugged upon finishing. "Truth be known?"

"Truth be known, you dainty punce," Curge growled. "What you've done is an affront. To not only the profession but to the history of the games."

Nexus drank a mouthful before responding and later licked a finger. "Then it was time."

Well aware of the guards behind him, Curge fought down his first impulse—which was to fling the insolent little man out over the arena sands.

Nexus cleared his throat. "These games are no different than any other business, Curge. You ask any merchant you like—any of them—and they will tell you to take advantage of an opportunity when one appears. Prajus was an opportunity. Prajus *is* an opportunity. He'll go far at these games. Even a maggot like me can see that. I believe he'll *win* these games. And the resulting coin and prestige he'll shower upon my name is well worth the sour frowns from the likes of you. Or any other relic of a more honorable age. If that wintry scowl is the price of seizing an opportunity, then scowl, good Curge. Scowl."

"That man killed his owner," Curge whispered. "His *house master*."

Nexus met his stare and held it. "Might I remind you, Curge, Gastillo challenged *him* to a fight. In front of witnesses. Prajus was guiltless. Gastillo was sloppy. Stupid. And because of it, he lost his life. Prajus wasn't at fault. Not in the least and certainly not in my eyes. And he's more than ready to split the heads of any thinking otherwise."

"He'll perish on those sands. I'll make certain of it."

"You'll try," Nexus said, "and I've seen enough of your dogs to know Prajus is their equal and more. There's only a handful of men who'll continue on to the final eight, and *he's one of them*. And when he becomes champion, history will remember me as the only one having the bells to give Prajus the backing he needed. And the rest of you? You'll be remembered for letting him slip through your fingers."

Curge sputtered, unable to summon words, and glanced back at the watchful guards.

"You know something, Curge?" Nexus looked away with a dismissive frown. "I've heard the games called games of blood. I believe that's true. About the season. Most of you—the owners, I mean—let your fighters have at one another like unchained dogs. Trained, of course, but dogs, nevertheless. And you sulk like children if your animal is killed. Even swear vengeance. But after losing several of my own fighters, prized investments in my eyes, I've realized one thing. These . . . games are not about the sport of combat. Nor are they about physical perfection or skill of arms. They aren't about the honor or the history or creating history, even. They're about the *blood*. They're about entering a tunnel of mayhem and emerging from the other side, scarred and bleeding but alive. As a survivor. A champion, even. You house masters watch these events like old men reliving their youth, your fighters being the toys, and the lot of you being careful not to break any of them. Or at least not too many to offend. This is wrong. I now realize if a house master has no more toys, he'll stop playing and go home, leaving it easier for those remaining to win."

Nexus faced the audience and sighed. "I know what King Juhn wants," he stated calmly, "a long and drawn-out season. But it's not what Nexus wants, Dark Curge. I want a season of carnage. I wish to see a field stricken with broken toys and dreams put to flame. I wish to see the last gladiator standing atop a field of the recent dead and my banner flying high over his head. And with Prajus, I have the means to do just that in the most entertaining way possible. So damn whatever King Juhn wants. And damn you and any other like you."

That almost lifted Curge out of his seat, but he gripped the arms of his chair and held himself back.

If Nexus noticed, he didn't react. "Do your worst, Dark Curge, because I'll be doing mine. These games are about the blood, Curge. I mean to have my share. And I mean to have a championship title. By any means possible."

In that space of breath, the voice of the Orator shouted for the next fight to commence.

At a rare loss for words, Curge turned, red-faced, to watch the next battle.

52

Since the day the old man had seen the reincarnation of Arco—the one called Junger—fight in the Pit, he'd been filled with a curiosity that his old bones could barely withstand. Old Tolgo talked with a fervor that edged upon madness, drawing concerned looks from his sons. His oldest boy, Nalro, listened to the stories, happy that the pit fighter had rejuvenated his ailing father, but concerned as well. His father's tale edged upon lunacy, but because it restored life to the old man's rheumy eyes, Nalro gave him the audience he so craved. Nalro didn't question his father's story of a lone warrior saving his village from raiders set upon pillaging, raping, and killing, but the tale of one warrior fighting off dozens of determined marauders was difficult to believe.

One thing was certain. His father believed.

Nalro didn't see any harm in entertaining that powerful belief. A long time had passed since he'd seen his father speak with such excitement, such conviction. Whoever Junger might be, he'd restored Nalro's father to a younger version of himself, defying the age creeping into his once-powerful frame. For that, the son was grateful.

The morning when Nalro stopped outside the Pit's many gates and read the schedule for the day's fights, the name of Junger caught his attention. He hurried home and rushed past his puzzled wife. He found his father behind the little house, where he would sit on an old chair and watch clouds tumble across the sky.

"What is it?" Tolgo frowned at his oldest boy, wondering why he was hurrying so.

"Today's fights. The one you call Arco's twin is fighting."

The words chased away the dullness in the old man's eyes. He studied his son's face, wondering if his words were truth, and saw that they were.

Tolgo struggled to his feet so quickly that he nearly knocked over his chair.

They made an event of it, eating at a food stall outside the arena and watching the crowds file through the gates. They joined the masses in due time, and Nalro sat with his father, shielding him from any overexcited individuals, and gazed down into the shining platter that was the arena floor. The afternoon raged with a terrible heat, and several times Nalro wiped his brow before checking on his father's condition with furtive glances. They had missed the first few matches, but that was of no concern to Nalro. His purpose was to accompany his father. The Pit's contests held no interest to him.

When the Orator drew breath and introduced the man called Junger, Nalro watched his father's eyes nearly pop from his aged face.

53

"Women and men of the Pit," Qualtus started while motioning for silence. "Women and men of the Pit... together we have witnessed epic battles upon the arena sands. Wondrous feats of arms. And strength. Together, we've witnessed gestures most noble... and most despicable. Honor. Betrayal. And we will witness all of this again in the years to come. But in all my years of speaking to you, of coloring these stories of the Pit, this... *theater*... in the brightest hues, I'm at a loss to describe this next gladiator. He hails from the House of Ten. A swordsman. The likes we've never seen before. Perhaps we'll never see the likes of him again. In a very short time, he has gone from obscurity... to being perhaps the brightest flame upon this stage."

Without even hearing the name, the crowds responded in a rush of noise.

The sound frayed Dark Curge's nerves just a little more.

"Only just recently, this man fought three times in one day," the Orator reminded them all. "*Three.* One after the other, putting down gladiators as if they were no more than weeds trampled underfoot. He surprised us all with his victories, without even baring the very blade that he carried into the Pit. Men and women of the games, I believe we're witnessing something truly spectacular this season. He's already become a story. Witness now, as the gladiator from the battered House of Ten, the one called Junger..."

Upon the very mention of his name, the expanding bubble of excitement drowned out the Orator's words.

Qualtus refused to be silenced, however, and gathered all of his strength for one last blast. *"Junger . . .* The Perician *Wonder—"*

Nothing more was heard. The arena exploded with an energy that could have flattened the entire city. The frenzied boom caused people outside beyond the Pit to stop and stare in wonder. Birds roosting below the city battlements took to wing. Farmers in the fields below the city's cliffs paused in their work, casting their questioning eyes toward the high walls.

Nothing else was heard from the Orator. The voices of thousands prevented him from continuing, so he dropped his arms and stood back on his podium with a knowing smile, pleased in the knowledge that Seddon above was probably taking notice . . .

Then he waited for the portcullis to rise.

In his private chambers, Grisholt bunched his head into his shoulders at the unexpected eruption of cheers.

"Sweet Seddon above," he said aloud. At least, he tried to say it.

Before realizing he couldn't hear his own voice.

The shocking outburst startled Curge enough that he flinched. He quickly composed himself, for fear of Nexus noticing just a seat away. He glanced in the direction of the hated wine merchant and saw the white topper gripping the viewing box's wall, visibly stunned at the crowd's reaction.

If not for Curge's own natural size anchoring him, the audience's vocal discharge would have rolled him over.

When Junger emerged from the shadows of the entrance tunnel, the crowds roared again.

Without armor, without a shirt, Junger meandered into the sunlight. His sword remained in its scabbard, and he clutched the sheathed weapon in both hands, across his pelvis. People stood and applauded and waved at him, and he took a moment to absorb the size and scope of the cheering masses. The outpouring of applause surprised him, but then again, he supposed that was to be expected after his last showing.

He thought that without the slightest hint of arrogance or conceit.

Nodding at a selected few, Junger turned, the sand's heat penetrating his boot soles, and lifted his sword in salute. That single gesture prolonged the cheering for moments longer, long enough that no one noticed the opposing portcullis rising.

When Barros emerged from his entrance, he added his own rage-fueled voice to the overwhelming flood of sound blasting the arena. The audience took notice of the Grisholt warrior, and like a flame deprived of air, the cheering died away.

They knew the man, knew his reputation.

Barros bellowed beastman nonsense and brandished his war hammer like a raised hellion bestowing curses. Biceps flexed and bulged. He shook with unchecked fury, his voice made metallic by his bulky pot helmet. He slapped his studded leather vest with a force that left many wondering when the blood would fly.

Across the way, Junger watched.

Sensing his opponent, Barros stomped and faced the newly named Perician Wonder. Rage blasted from the armored head. Barros stomped again, as if testing the very ground. He whipped his war hammer back and forth and, having enough of that gurry, charged his opponent.

The audience held its collective breath.

The Grisholt warrior closed the distance, rushing the poised Junger like an irresistible storm front about to level a city. The warrior reared his hammer back and swung with force enough to sweep away the first few rows of spectators.

Junger ducked under the swing.

ABOUT THE BLOOD

Barros gushed hatred and swung for the head, an arm, and the head again.

Junger evaded every blow.

Not only did he avoid those killing strikes, he did so so quickly, so assuredly, that he made the Grisholt terror seem almost rooted to the spot at times.

Enraged, Barros screeched and lashed out at Junger's face.

He missed.

He backhanded and missed a shoulder. He grabbed for Junger's head of hair and clutched empty space. He whirled into a second backhanded bash, whipping his hammer around with godlike force and damn near tearing asunder the very fabric of reality ... yet missed again.

Backpedaling out of harm's way, Junger held his sword in both hands at low guard, nimbly avoiding the strikes that would have burst him apart upon contact. His features were tight with concentration, but at no point did anyone detect fear from the pit fighter.

Failing to strike his target yet again, Barros reset himself and squared his shoulders. He visibly flinched upon realizing his opponent still lived, and the knowledge made him bawl in pure loathing. After getting that out of his system, Barros cocked back his weapon arm and howled.

He was only getting started.

The livid gladiator charged, seeking to put down the man who'd eluded him with all the grace of a wisp of smoke.

"Dying Seddon," Muluk whispered, unable to even blink at what was transpiring within the Pit.

With every attack, Barros became faster, his fury deeper, and his war hammer even more fearsome. The combinations weren't flowing, but they were so fast, so frightening, that it didn't matter. The hammer became a streak of iron, hissing at his opponent, and the slightest contact would surely rip free meaty chunks.

But as awesome as the Grisholt man was, Junger was more so.

Nothing touched the swordsman.

Nothing even appeared to come close.

When Barros's arms became streaks of iron, Junger became a blur. For every killer display of power the Grisholt man exhibited, the Perician disarmed it with nearly magical speed. Every time Barros swung and failed to connect, the Perician refused to counterattack, allowing openings and opportunities to simply pass by, dazzling the whole of the arena audience, and causing more than one to wonder why.

Machlann leaned forward and gripped the stone sill of the arch. Like everyone throughout the arena, his eyes were wide and staring. Unlike the mesmerized audience, however, he recognized what was happening on the sands, and understood the strategy.

"He's slowing down," the trainer muttered.

When Barros charged the Ten man at the onset of the fight, a supremely confident Grisholt knew the match was over before it even began. He'd heard about Junger, of course. He doubted a person lived in the city, who hadn't heard of the Perician. That would all change that day, however, and Barros would be known as the gladiator to have killed the Weapon, the *Wonder*, called Junger.

However, Barros couldn't hit the Perician.

At all.

For all of the Sunjan's inflated might, Barros only fanned flesh when he should've been destroying it. He stomped on sand when it should've been the bones of a fallen foe. Junger, with his dazzling speed, on the other hand, *infuriated* Barros and made the pit killer look as clumsy as a sick cow.

"Hit him," Grisholt whispered, his eyes narrowing in concentration, his eagerness for blood quickly transforming into impatience. "Hit him. *Hit him*."

Try as he might however, Barros could not.

For long moments, Grisholt's pit fighter swung and missed, swung and missed, and swung and *missed*, attempting to squash the Perician as if the man were the size of a troublesome gnat. His godlike grunts split the air. Barros didn't relent and didn't give up, but it became painfully clear to Grisholt that his man wasn't about to touch the Perician with his *breath*, let alone a weapon.

"Dying Seddon," the perfumed owner whispered, and his eyes widened while his heart frosted over with fear. "Oh no."

Brakuss crowded in from the right, his one good eye bulging.

The unexpected was happening.

The *impossible* was happening.

Barros was tiring.

The Grisholt gladiator swung for Junger's head once again and missed badly, stumbling a few steps past the Ten man.

Junger didn't retreat a great distance, choosing to remain within arm's reach, daring his opponent to try for him again.

Barros obliged, chopping for a shoulder and fanning only air. He backed away, his entire frame shaking from exertion. His cries of rage petered into pained gasps, sounds one might hear from an old man rather than a gladiator in his prime. The pot helmet only made the breathing even more disturbing, but in a sickly, near-death way. Head wavering, chest heaving, Barros tracked his foe. The spiked hammer flailed before Junger's face as if warding him off, missing its mark entirely.

The Perician didn't bother with parrying.

Or attacking.

A pitched wheeze escaped Barros, and he stopped in his tracks. He pulled the helmet from his head and tossed it. Sweat poured from his head. He bent over, clutching one knee while attempting to fill his lungs, and regarded his foe with squinty-eyed, undisguised revulsion.

Junger circled to his opponent's right, and Barros leaped after him, swinging at a shoulder. He struck nothing and staggered to a stop, kicking up sand upon halting. The angry gladiator righted himself, wary of retaliation, but Junger did no such thing. The Ten man seemed more inclined to evade and observe, and throughout the arena, the cheering intensified as the spectators caught on to the strategy.

Barros swung at a shoulder.

Missed.

He whipped the hammer at Junger's face.

Split only air.

Barros lashed out at a knee. Junger jerked it out of harm's way.

The effort overextended the Grisholt gladiator, and he fell, crashing like a once-magnificent column finally crumbling to time.

He landed flat on his chest, sending sand flying.

The arena erupted with the victory, the fever pitch deafening. More than a few observers covered their ears at the blast. Nothing could be heard over the insane cheering, and for several streets over outside the Pit, people stopped and stared, looking in the direction of the arena.

Back in the Pit, even though the fight was clearly gone from Barros, Junger didn't pounce upon the fallen gladiator. He circled the exhausted man, watching him.

Barros attempted to rise. He pulled himself up as far as his knees and elbows as if in prayer, all the while groaning and grunting. Spittle sprayed from his lips. Sand caked his face, and when he exhaled, dust speckled the air. He tried to rise, but the effort overcame him, and he collapsed a second time, much to the audience's resounding glee.

Junger, however, remained cautious. He approached the unmoving man, examining him while holding his sword at the ready, wary of a ruse. He prodded Barros's hip with a boot. When the gladiator failed to react, Junger nudged him again.

Quivering, Barros slowly rolled onto his side and stared up at the Ten man. Junger kicked away the war hammer. He crouched at his opponent's side and reached for Barros's chin.

The Grisholt gladiator gripped the Perician's hand ... but no strength was behind it. Junger pushed the hand away and again reached for the defeated man's chin.

This time, Barros didn't resist.

The Perician Wonder—as he truly *was* a wonder—held the man's face ... held it for a long time.

When he released it, Barros's head thumped to the arena floor.

A heartbeat later, Junger rose and brought forth his sheathed blade.

The Pit's walls trembled from the crowds' approval.

The Perician held his sword to Barros's neck, kept the pose to prove the fight was finished, then walked away from his defeated opponent. The discarded helmet lay in his path. As an afterthought, Junger kicked the thing to one side.

Barros emptied his gullet into the sands, but the noise was lost among the screaming of the crowds.

The sight wasn't lost on Grisholt, however.

Anger replaced his initial fear. The gray-bearded owner seethed, contemplating the loss and the consequences with the Sons of Cholla, who had no doubt placed a sizeable amount of coin on the fight . . . on Barros.

Grisholt released a frustrated hiss, long and loud.

The Zhiberian was gone, but the Perician had given him yet another reason to despise the House of Ten.

"It's him," Nalro's father shouted into his ear, the only way to be heard over the insane cheering. "Seddon above, that's him! That's *him*! I wager my life on it."

Nalro looked into the incredulous face of his father before switching to Junger's retreating back.

He believed his father.

"Still concerned about me?" Nexus asked Curge after the noise abated.

The one-armed owner regarded the wine merchant with an air of disdain. "Don't talk to me, Nexus. Not ever again. To me, you're of no more significance than the shite trough I filled this morning."

Interestingly enough, the wine merchant kept his mouth shut, and he didn't summon his guards, poised and ready at the back wall.

Knowing one last match was left in the day but also knowing he didn't possess the stomach to breathe the same air as Nexus, Curge rose. He ambled toward the exit door. The manservant who was attending him flashed him a worried look, but Curge ignored him.

Two of Nexus's guards positioned themselves in front of the door.

The Dark One stopped and glared, sending the message that he wasn't easily intimidated.

"Nexus," Curge called out, "get your dogs from the door before they anger me."

The merchant took his time responding.

Curge focused on one set of eyes, then the other. Neither guard betrayed any emotion, but they watched him, and he sensed a readiness to crack heads if the need arose.

Still, nothing came from the wine merchant.

The audience's cheering seemed very far away, and Curge continued to study the men blocking his way. One of them blinked slowly, taking his time, but the owner knew the man was exceptionally alert inside, ready for a confrontation.

"Nexus, I won't repeat myself," Curge warned and meant it. If he had to fight his way out of that room, he was going to grab Nexus's twig of a neck and snap it before one of his armed dogs finally cut him down.

The cheering melded with the ringing in Curge's ear, yet still no command came forth. The one-armed owner knew right then that there would be blood.

But then, as if remembering something, Nexus lifted a hand without turning his head. "Take care, *Dark* Curge."

The hand fluttered.

The guards barring the exit moved out of Curge's way. The manservant, gutless daisy that he was, exhaled in relief. Curge glared at one guard then the other, committing their faces to memory.

Then he smiled frostily at each.

Curge left the box then, not bothering to close the door. He followed the passageways to ground level, to the main corridor, where he met up with the menacing Demasta, the head of his own private household guard. A thick X of leather crossed the man's muscular chest. Dark in complexion, with an equally black beard trimmed short, the guard looked positively fearsome. Though not as tall as his employer, Demasta possessed an exceptionally willing mindset toward violence, one that Curge very much appreciated.

"Demasta," he said as the equally large man fell into step beside him. "I've decided to retire early from the games."

The house guard nodded and pushed forward, clearing people from his path with murderous looks alone.

Retire early, Curge mused. If he'd had to endure Nexus for another moment, he would've throttled the man right there and tossed his scrawny carcass out over the stands. Nexus's guards would've killed him in the resulting melee, and no doubt the manservant would've screamed like a five-year-old boy all the while, but Curge would have died with a smile . . . and not before killing those two asslickers daring to block the way.

Even if Nexus hadn't been a concern, Curge would still have been very disturbed about the one called Junger of Pericia. The display l he'd just witnessed wasn't ruined in the least by Nexus's unfit presence. He searched his memory and, for the life of him, couldn't think of a single gladiator within his ranks capable of defeating Junger. In fact, he was hard-pressed to think of *any* house gladiator skilled enough to defeat the Ten man. That worried Curge very much. If no one could stop him, the Perician would single-handedly capture the games for himself . . . and the not-quite-finished House of Ten.

The thought left Curge's bald crown aching, and he sought diversion. "By the way," he asked Demasta's back. "How many men are in our employment these days?"

"You mean guards, Master Curge?"

"Aye that, guards."

"Ten, Lord."

"Ten," Curge mused as he followed. The number surprised him.

He would hire more.

54

Junger left the exhausted Barros upon the sand. He walked past the fearfully smiling gatekeeper and the Skarrs lining the tunnels, who acknowledged him with not-so-secretive looks. Turning a corner, Junger walked the white tunnel back to the Ten's private chamber.

They were waiting for him. Hands clapped his shoulders. Congratulations and praise were heaped upon his name.

Standing before the window's arch, a stern-looking Goll shook his head.

"You didn't kill him," the house master stated.

Junger paused. "There was no need, Master Goll."

"*Eeeee*." Machlann released with a smile. "*That* performance spoke louder than any killing, my missus. Lords *above*, Perician. Lords *above*. I've never seen the likes before and daresay I'll never again."

"That was truly spectacular, young man," Clavellus added.

All the while, Goll hung back, his face neutral.

When the excitement abated, Clavellus turned to the house master. He clasped Goll's shoulder and rattled it.

"You're next," he said.

*

Sunlight streamed into the lower chamber, marking the dusty stone of the floor with its brilliance. Salwark stood just to the right of the arched window, dabbing at his forehead with a folded cloth and occasionally his throat. Perspiration saturated his underclothing. He swallowed, feeling just a little sick because he hadn't been able to eat anything before coming to the arena. He wasn't sure eating anything right then would help. Truly, he was too nervous to eat. He was always that way before a blood match.

This wasn't a blood match, though.

Watching the Balgothan Sorban prepare for his fight with the Kree called Goll, however, Salwark sensed that clarifying that distinction would not be wise. That alone worried him greatly.

Farther back from the sunlight, gladiators stood at solemn ease, ready to aid their fellow pit fighter if he required it. Facing a wall and head bent, Sorban wrapped cloth around his hands with intensity. No one spoke as he worked. He wove the material around his fingers and pulled it tight. Once that was done, he slapped the hard leather protecting his right shoulder then his left. Then he punched his midsection, three hard blows that exploded in the room, causing Salwark to flinch.

Having checked his armor, Sorban turned to a nearby gladiator and held out a hand. The gladiator sheathed it with a spike-studded gauntlet. Once it was pulled into place, Sorban adjusted the metallic fist and offered his second hand.

Salwark licked his lips. The Balgothan's mindset scared him like no other. He hoped the man realized what he was doing, that killing the Kree would have consequences. Though Goll had been Free Trained a time ago, the man presently belonged to a house, the same house where that hellion Junger of Pericia resided and fought. Salwark had also seen Junger of Pericia fight Curn from the House of Vandu. Curn was no mindless lout, yet the Perician had devastated the pit fighter in very short time. The Perician had devastated *everyone* he'd fought in very short time. Salwark had heard the stories, and he did *not* want the

House of Ten sending such a man after Sorban. The last thing Salwark needed was Junger seeking revenge on not only Sorban but the stable's remaining gladiators. That would be disastrous. Though his spies had noted Junger didn't seem inclined to kill a fallen warrior, that didn't make Salwark feel any better.

There's always the first time, he thought. Unless of course, Sorban can kill Junger.

Salwark licked his lips and tried to focus on the positive.

Sorban pulled on his helm, that frightening ape-feathered face of metal. Once it was in place, the man paused as if in meditation. Time flowed, but not one of the surrounding gladiators dared to break the silence. The crowds droned on in the background.

Sorban lifted his head. Stoic, Aidas stepped in and tightened the helm's chin strap while the Marrnite Zillari handed the Balgothan his quarterstaff. Sorban took the weapon and didn't offer any thanks to either man. That intimidating figure of violence and carnage then turned to Salwark.

He couldn't see Sorban's eyes, only slits of darkness.

A knock came from the outer door, signaling the time to leave.

Sorban left for the door, his intention painfully clear, at least in Salwark's worried mind.

The Balgothan meant to beat Goll to death.

Cheering and shouting enveloped Goll. The steps to the rising portcullis fluttered with light. He paid no heed to the welcoming applause. After Junger's victory over a known killer of gladiators, a three-legged dog associated with the Ten would have gotten a warm reception. Goll didn't care about what the audience thought of him.

His thoughts centered on the man called Sorban.

The Balgothan was seeking revenge for the death of Baylus the Butcher, the one man who'd defeated Goll soundly in the arena—in *any* arena. Baylus had overwhelmed him and ultimately spared his life, but when the positions reversed themselves, Goll killed the once champion. It had been instinctive, reflexive, and if he had the time back, he would've done differently.

The Orator finished his introductions, and when Goll stepped into the arena, Sorban was waiting on the other side. Clouds had moved in, casting shade over the sands and audience, but a single shaft of light pierced though the overcast sky, enveloping the grim gladiator and basking him in steely splendor.

Goll didn't like that effect.

The bright plumage of Sorban's visor blazed. The visor, sprinkled with holes about the mouth, smiled cruelly.

Goll steadied his breathing, narrowed his eyes, and went to meet his next challenge.

Sorban rolled his shoulders and began walking himself. He hunched over, quarterstaff readied, the needles of his metal gauntlets long and evil looking. The sun transformed his leather vest into a toughened hide. Eyes lurked somewhere in the empty cavities of Sorban's helmet, but Goll didn't see them.

The Balgothan didn't bother with words.

That suited the Kree just fine.

They met in the middle of the groomed sands, and Sorban moved first. He swept his quarterstaff up and over his head, spinning the weapon in a mesmerizing blur of wood and metal, and lashed out at Goll's head.

Goll was no longer there, though.

The instant Sorban whipped his quarterstaff high over his head, Goll lunged low and stabbed a third of his short sword through the Balgothan's lead foot, nailing the man to the ground.

If he screamed, the sound was lost in the voices belonging to the crowds.

Goll left his sword in his foe's foot and rose, well inside his foe's crumbling guard. He cracked his shield's edge off Sorban's chin. The blow staggered the Balgothan and hurled him back. His falling weight ripped his impaled foot from sword and sand, and when he fell, half the onlookers winced.

ABOUT THE BLOOD

Goll rushed in, seeking to end the fight. He stomped on an elbow, shattering the joint. Sorban rolled over, and Goll stomped on the other arm, breaking a wrist. The Balgothan grunted in misery. He attempted to rise on his good elbow, turning his back to his opponent.

In that moment, the memory of Baylus, crippled, revisited Goll. Time slowed, and in that tempest of cheers and horrified screams, the Butcher's whisper of *"No one needs to perish"* revisited him.

The words caught Goll off guard, and he supposed the dead champion was right.

The audience screamed, bringing the Kree back to the task at hand.

He chopped the shield's edge into the back of Sorban's neck. Twice more for effect. Sorban went limp at the first connection and didn't move after that, so Goll bent at the knees to finish the work. Then he retrieved his sword, secured a double-handed grip, and punched its dulled tip through the fallen gladiator's leather-bound torso. The blade had been blunted somewhat by going through the thin mail covering Sorban's boot, so Goll had to force the weapon through.

When the sword would go no deeper, Goll released it, leaving the weapon in the dead man's chest. The blade cast a grim shadow upon the sands.

Breathing hard, Goll studied the corpse. *No one needed to perish this day*, he thought, but words had been said.

Baylus was in the past, and even though Goll believed the Balgothan's ghost would haunt him to his final days, showing mercy to Sorban had never been his intention. To do so would convey weakness to the enemies of the House of Ten, and with Junger and even Brozz having refused to slay their opponents, Goll had to send a message of his own, as house master.

This was Sunja's Pit. The dusty, scalding heart of the games.

These *wonderful* games.

And he intended to win it all.

55

Dawn outlined the closed shutters in gold and lit up Halm's personal darkness. He opened his eyes sleepily, not yet ready to rise, and quietly snarled at the light. The night had been warm, and the single thin blanket drawn over his considerable carcass had been kicked into a puddle at the foot of the bed. He knew it was down there. The damn thing had coiled about his toes.

A contented sigh became a yawn, so he covered his mouth, not wanting to wake Miji next to him. She slept on her side, bare back to him, her untied hair spilling over white skin. Two dark moles stuck out from the curve of her shoulder blade, dotting otherwise flawless flesh. Halm's eyes wandered over her form as a satisfied smile spread across his face.

The urge to void took him, so he got up, grimacing with the movement. His bulk was still mending its many hurts, but the country air was helping. Miji stirred, causing him to pause on the bed's edge. The timbers creaked, and he froze. He waited . . . waited until he heard her breathing deepen. In time, he relaxed.

He carefully drew a finger under his healing nose and studied the floor, looking past the bandages covering his huge belly. He spotted his clothing nearby, so he gathered them up and made his way to the door. It opened with a click and a groan, which froze him to the spot as he glanced back at his lover's form.

Seddon above. Everything he did seemed to summon an ass whistle.

When Miji didn't wake, he quietly let himself out.

When he'd arrived in Karashipa, Miji wanted him to stay with her after the second night, in the house that had belonged to her departed parents. The home was small and clean, with a lingering smell of wildflowers. The interior was just the right size for two . . . maybe even three.

Miji was everything he'd hoped her to be: receptive, kind, considerate. Halm was surprised by how good he felt in her company. She laughed at his jokes and listened to his stories, and he found himself doing the same, captivated by her charms. He slept on the floor that third night.

By the fourth night, he was sharing her bed.

A barren fireplace dominated the main room. A small table and chairs, handmade and smooth to the touch, rested against the north wall. The smell of woodland herbs and spices drifted through an archway leading to a small pantry colored by many years. The floorboards, always swept, creaked like tight strings here and there, but Halm already knew where the worst of them were and easily avoided them. He pulled on his breeches and sandals. Feeling a desire for a walk—and the pressing need to piss—he let himself out and breathed in the country air. Across the way and over rooftops, dawn flittered through a dense screen of forest. Half the sun lay above those green heights. Things buzzed by his face, ignoring him, and Halm, out of habit, looked at his feet. No unconscious drunks were there to step over, no swaying brutes pissing in the alleys, no one asking him for coin . . . and no scurrying rats.

Halm trod a dirt path and rounded the house's corner, making his way to the treeline. There, he emptied the bull. Once finished, he tucked himself away and strolled down to the flat glossy mirror that was the lake. Not a breeze stirred the morning, and the water's surface glowed like silver. Dry rocks framed the shore. Farther out, an early-morning mist haunted the surface.

Like one big pisspot, Muluk had once said about the lake.

The Zhiberian smiled at the memory.

Miji's house was the closest to the water's edge. A small footpath that led back to the main road lay to his left, and across that a short distance was her little alehouse. The still-standing palisade that surrounded recently dead Thaimondus's residence loomed beyond that. Houses lined the road all the way back into the forest, and Halm spared them a solemn, contemplative look.

Sleep.

The place soaked in it. Even when the village was at its height of activity, the place soaked in sleep, as if spinning, slowly, in the deepest current of a dream, and he meant that in the best of ways. There was no hurry, no rush, just honest day-to-day work and survival in one small, forgotten corner of a very big world.

That suited Halm just fine.

He turned back to the lake, admiring the scene. A small wharf jutted into the water, long and set low to the surface, with three shallow boats tied to its length. Clouds resembling gray banners drifted across the sun's face overhead, pleasantly dimming the land. If he wandered back along the main road, he knew he'd smell the smoke of small wood fires being worked to life.

The setting was lovely, peaceful. He considered himself fortunate to see it.

Even better, he had a roof over his head and food for the table... and he had a woman. He believed he might've found himself more than a woman—a wife. *A wife!* He smiled at the thought, baring those ill-colored, overlapping shards that passed for teeth. He'd never believed such a thing possible. *Not bad at all.* Everything he wanted, everything he *needed* was in this place.

So fortunate. So very, very fortunate.

Halm sighed deeply, contentedly. Somewhere beyond the nebulous depths of the morning mist, a bird spoke brightly.

ABOUT THE BLOOD

He listened for it again. Standing at the water's edge, Halm's reflection wavered for a heartbeat, as if hooked at the shoulder. Then, slowly, as if remembering an item lost, he turned his battered frame.

His broken nose rose as if catching a whiff of something . . . distant yet familiar.

He stood that way for a time, staring off to the north.

Toward Sunja.

About the Author

Keith C. Blackmore is the author of the Mountain Man, 131 Days, and Breeds series, among other horror, heroic fantasy, and crime novels. He lives on the island of Newfoundland in Canada. Visit his website at www.keithcblackmore.com.

www.ingramcontent.com/pod-product-compliance
Ingram Content Group UK Ltd.
Pitfield, Milton Keynes, MK11 3LW, UK
UKHW041301180426
11947UKWH00009B/593

9 781039 483538